WINDFLOWERS

Claire has left behind the harshness of life in the outback for college and a career in Sydney. Estranged from her family, she is about to take up a position at a prestigious veterinary practice when her Great Aunt Aurelia summons her home to Queensland. Claire's relationship with her parents and sister has never been easy, and her mother, Ellie accepts that a reconciliation with her eldest daughter is long overdue. But to do so will mean she must face her own ghosts and reveal some shameful secrets. She only hopes her family is strong enough to survive the storm...

WINDFLOWERS

WINDFLOWERS

by

Tamara McKinley

Magna Large Print Books
Long Preston, North Yorkshire,
BD23 4ND, England.

British Library Cataloguing in Publication Data.

McKinley, Tamara
    Windflowers.

    A catalogue record of this book is
    available from the British Library

    ISBN   0-7505-1922-3

First published in Great Britain in 2002 by
Judy Piatkus (Publishers) Ltd.

Copyright © 2002 by Tamara McKinley

Cover illustration © Ben Turner by arrangement with
P.W.A. International Ltd.

The moral right of the author has been asserted

Published in Large Print 2002 by arrangement with
Piatkus Books Ltd.

Magna Large Print is an imprint of Library Magna Books Ltd.

Printed and bound in Great Britain by
T.J. (International) Ltd., Cornwall, PL28 8RW

I dedicate this story to the people I met on my travels around Australia, without whom I could never capture the true colour and warmth of the outback. To Charlie and his wife at the Blue Gum Cafe, thanks for the great breakfasts. To the manager and clientele of the Charleville Hotel for providing me with many an anecdote and a real insight into life in the Never Never. To the owners of Gowrie Station for their hospitality, billy tea and damper. To the Jondaryan Woolshed Historical Museum and Park Association for the chance to return to the glory days of the past when wool was king. And last, but not least, to the little boy who inspired this story. I never knew your name, but your image lived on long after we'd parted.

I dreamed that as I wandered by the way,
Bare winter suddenly was changed to spring.
There grew pied wind-flowers and violets
Daisies, those pearled Arcuturi of the earth,
The constellated flower that never sets;
P.B. Shelley 1792-1822

Prologue 1936

The dirt and squalor of Sydney's Domain was almost a year behind them as Ellie rode north to Gregory Downs with her father. The dirt track meandered in a blood red ribbon across the empty plains to disappear in the heat haze, drawing them ever deeper into the unknown. Yet, with money in their pockets and horses to ride, progress was finally easier than the months they'd spent tramping the wallaby tracks.

They were on the long stretch to Cloncurry when Ellie noticed the build up of cloud on the horizon behind them. 'Looks like a big storm brewing,' she warned. 'Better dig in quick before it reaches us.'

Her father John turned to look over his shoulder at the broiling clouds that seethed in the strangely yellow sky. 'Should be able to get to the Curry before it breaks.'

Ellie frowned. 'We won't make it,' she said firmly. 'The Curry's at least another two days' ride and the storm's not gunna wait that long.'

'Gotta give it a go,' he said as he gathered up the reins and smiled back at her with false brightness. 'If it looks like we can't make it, then we'll just have to find shelter and let it ride over us.'

Ellie looked into his handsome face, the despair at his lack of common sense weighing heavy. She was only a few weeks short of her fourteenth birthday and yet he seemed determined to treat her like a kid. She'd heard about the terrible storms they got out here in the middle of nowhere, and knew he was as scared as she was. If only he'd admit it, she thought crossly. If only he'd listen to me for once we might just get out of this alive.

'Where exactly?' Ellie replied with sharp impatience. 'There's not a hill or valley or outcrop of stone out here, and we might not have time to dig through that.' Her gaze swept their desolate surroundings. The boulder strewn track was concrete hard beneath its layer of sifting dust and the few blasted trees that wilted in the heat offered little shelter beneath their blackened branches. The nearest mountains were thumbprint bruises far into the distance.

'We'll find somewhere,' he said with his customary doggedness.

Ellie's brown eyes regarded him solemnly from beneath the raggedy fringe of tow coloured hair. 'Reckon we ought'a start digging now if we're to stand any kind of chance. Dust storms are killers, and we shouldn't mess with 'em.'

John's dark eyes became coldly determined. 'You've listened to too many outback horror stories during the drove to Longreach,' he snapped. 'You might be thirteen going on forty-five, but you don't know everything.'

Ellie shifted in the saddle as he glanced back at the darkening horizon. The wind was changing direction, but that didn't make her feel easier. The Aborigine stockman, Snowy White, had

14

warned her how treacherous the elements could be. Had described all too clearly how they lured unsuspecting travellers into a false sense of security before they unleashed their terrible forces.

John Freeman tugged his hat brim down over his dark eyes. 'We'll carry on,' he said with a firmness that brooked no further argument. 'The storm's miles away and by the look of it, is changing course.' He turned the grey's head towards the wide dirt track that disappeared into the far northern horizon and dug in his heels. 'Let's go.'

'Well I don't like the look of it,' she said stubbornly as she urged Clipper into a trot. 'Wang Lee told me about a mate of his got caught. Died too quick for anyone to save him – lungs full of dust. Wang Lee said death out here can come in a second.' She snapped her fingers. 'Just like that.'

'Shut up about the Chinaman and ride.' John slapped his horse into a shambling trot, and with a final glance over her shoulder at the broiling horizon Ellie reluctantly followed him.

'It's time you stopped listening to Chinese cooks and Aboriginal stockmen and began to have faith in me for a change,' he growled. 'I might be a bloke from the city, but I've seen us this far without advice from others – I'll get us to your Aunt Aurelia's.'

Ellie remained silent for she knew that her father's pride had been damaged enough and there was no point in arguing when he was like this. Their long trek from Sydney had been

15

daunting for both of them, but it had to be especially hard for a man who knew nothing of the outback and had the responsibility of his daughter to think about. They had survived – just – on hand-outs and dole tickets, but work had been hard to find and she knew her father was close to breaking point when they'd finally been taken on at Gowrie Station for the annual drove to Longreach. Ellie tipped her hat brim over her eyes to counter the glare and for the next two hours they rode in awkward silence.

The sky was darkening, but the wind had lessened and now there was an eerie stillness surrounding them. An ominous silence in which there was no birdsong, not even the sawing of crickets or the hum of flies. Ellie couldn't keep her fears to herself any longer. 'Storm's getting nearer, Dad,' she said with a calmness that belied her inner turmoil. 'Better find shelter in there.' She pointed off to the west to the stony outcrops and canyons that had soared out of the plains in some long ago volcanic eruption. The blue and red hills were ancient monoliths almost bereft of vegetation, the earth around them laced with deep crevasses and razor sharp obstacles of stone and scree. Ellie shivered despite the cloying heat of the windless plains for she knew it would take a great deal of courage to go into those deeply shadowed, sinister canyons.

John shook his head. 'Too dangerous,' he said shortly. 'Horses will break their legs. We'll go on a bit further and see if it flattens out. Perhaps there's shelter on the other side?'

Ellie was restless as she watched the approaching storm. 'We don't have time,' she fired at him. 'Better to find somewhere now.'

'You'll do what I flamin' well tell you,' he shot back. 'You're making a drama out of this just like your mother. Get a move on,' he ordered.

Ellie bit the inside of her lip to cut off the angry retort. She was nothing like Alicia and it was unfair of Dad to make the comparison. But if they didn't find shelter here they'd be caught in the open when the storm hit. 'I'm not a bloody kid any more, Dad,' she shouted. 'Why won't you listen to me for once?'

John's back was ramrod straight as he rode away, his gaze fixed on the empty horizon. There was no reply. No acknowledgement he'd even heard her.

The heat was oppressive, the silence profound as they left the volcanic hills far behind them and headed further into the vast plains. Ellie shot worried glances across to John as the fear grew. How to tell her father his judgement was flawed – that he should have listened to her – should have found shelter two hours back in those canyons? For there was nothing out here. Not even a shadow. Yet his stubborn determination to take charge had become too familiar over the past months and Ellie knew his pride wouldn't allow him to back down. He'd be damned if he was going to let something silly like a bit of a dust storm stop him – even if it killed the pair of them.

The morning wore on and Ellie had to hold tightly to her hat as the wind increased. With her chin tucked into her collar her eyes were slits against the dust that had begun to swirl around them – the wind driving into their backs – pushing them ever onward towards an empty horizon. She finally reined in her terrified pony and faced the terror that had stalked them. The sky was ochre, bruised by thunderous clouds that rolled ever nearer. The wind howled like a dingo as it swept across the plains flattening everything in its path. Trees were being uprooted and tossed skywards like matchsticks. Spinifex bowled across the plains and the dust rose like a great curtain in the south, blocking out everything behind it. They were in deep trouble and there was no escape.

She was struggling now to keep Clipper calm, holding on to the reins she rammed her hat deep into her dungaree pocket and lay flat against his neck as the wind tried to tear her from the saddle.

'Get off the road,' John shouted above the shriek of the wind. 'Dig in.' He grabbed her reins and tugged the reluctant pony to the shallow dip at the side of the rough track. It was just a trench forged over the years by the run-off water during the wet, but it was all the shelter available. They slid from their saddles and struggled to calm their propping, rearing horses as the veil of wind-spun dust tore across the plains and descended upon them in a banshee wail.

Ellie's scream was lost in the fury as she was plucked from her feet, ripped from the anchor of Clipper's reins and tossed like a rag-doll into the maelstrom. She felt John's grip on the hem of her dungarees, his desperate clutch at her waist as the wind tore at their backs. Then she was in his arms, held tightly to his chest as he was forced into a stumbling run. Slammed to the ground in a bone-numbing thud that took her breath away they were dragged along the scree. The howling fury rang in her ears and dulled her senses. Dust blinded her, threatened to choke her, filling her nose and eyes, gritting her tongue. Ellie clung to her father in terror as he fought for some tenuous hold on an earth that seemed determined to reject them.

All sense of time and direction was lost as she lay pinned to the ground beneath him. Eyes tightly shut she buried her face in his coat and fought to breathe as the vibration of his voice ran through him. But his words were whipped away as the world closed in, darkened and became full of stinging, smothering dust. Boulders lumbered and rolled, thudding into them before they bowled away. Stones were hurled as fast and lethal as bullets. Scrub vegetation entangled itself momentarily then was torn into the swirling darkness. Branches and twigs whipped past, spiny claws tearing at clothes and flesh like wild beasts. The howling demon of the wind seemed determined to claim them, yanking at their hair and clothes, shifting them further along the rough ground. For the first time in her life Ellie began to pray.

Joe and Charlie had said their goodbyes to the men at Wila Wila Station and now they were heading east to Richmond. They'd heard a cattle-man there needed help mustering his mob over to the coast and the chance to catch their first

19

glimpse of the ocean was an exciting prospect for the seventeen-year-old twins. The long months of tramping the tracks, of sleeping rough and collecting their dole tickets were over. The thrilling brumby muster at Wila Wila had provided them with horses, clean clothes and money in their pockets. No wonder they were on an adrenaline rush.

Joe ran a hand over his stubble. Being dark, his beard grew faster than Charlie's, and he hated the way it itched. He grinned across at his twin, noting the fair bristles on his chin and the blond hair curling over his collar. 'Reckon it's time we had a shave and haircut,' he said. 'Look like a couple of swaggies.'

Charlie laughed. 'Those days are over, mate. Reckon we'll have the girls crawlin' over us when we reach Richmond.' His blue eyes danced, the infectious grin showing strong, even teeth and the trace of newly weathered creases at the corners of his eyes and mouth. 'This is the life, ain't it?'

Joe grinned back. 'Too right, mate.' They'd come a long way from the broken down shanty back in Lorraine. A long way from the dreary years of poverty and heartache that had seen their parents buried and the farm re-possessed.

His attention was brought back to Satan and he grappled with the reins as the chestnut took it into his head to fight the bit. He'd broken the stallion back at Wila Wila, but the chestnut was still wild enough to cause trouble amongst the other horses in his string which was why he'd elected to ride him. The long journey to Richmond would be a chance to get to know each

20

other and find a compromise. Satan still champed at the bit and tried to pull Joe's arms from his sockets, but he realised the horse knew he was beaten and it was merely a token show of resentment.

'Reckon you oughta let me have him,' said Charlie as his speculative blue gaze roamed over the rich chestnut coat and proud head. 'I'd soon show him who's boss.'

Joe's wrists ached from keeping the reins taut and his patience was wearing thin. Charlie had had his eye on Satan from the start, and obviously hadn't forgiven Joe's luck at being rewarded for breaking him. 'Satan's mine,' he said firmly. 'He'll calm down soon enough.'

Charlie pulled his hat brim low and gathered up the reins. 'Let's ride. We gotta long ways to go.' He dug in his spurs, setting the black gelding into a fast gallop across the plains, his other horses stringing out behind him.

Satan shook his head, nostrils flaring, ears pricked as he fought the bit and tried to give chase. Joe hung on, sawing at his mouth in an attempt to keep the pace even. Richmond was at least a week's ride away and there was no point in letting Satan blow himself out. He frowned as a hot wind swept across the plains and tugged his shirt before dropping away with an ominous suddenness. Looking around him he realised the sky was sepia, heavy with purple thunderheads, the sun almost obliterated by a curtain of darkness that was sweeping up from the south. Solitary trees were stark monuments against the strange yellow light and the distant mountains brooded before the onslaught. 'Bloody hell,' he murmured. 'We're in for a beaut.'

Charlie was far off into the distance now, his string of horses kicking up dust in a great red cloud, but Joe realised he would slow down soon enough when he realised what loomed on the horizon. He set his string of horses into a canter, Satan easing his pull on the bit as he was given his head, the others picking up the scent of the approaching storm and lengthening their strides. Joe watched as his brother eased off and looked around him.

'Over there,' yelled Joe as he pointed to an outcrop of rocks. 'Dig in!' His voice carried across the deserted plains and echoed in the strange stillness that heralded the approaching storm as they raced for cover.

The outcrop reared from the plains in a soaring, jagged jumble of stark red and black. Trees clung to its sides and tufts of grass poked through here and there, but on the whole it was as barren as the plains, with slippery shale underfoot and glowering overhangs of rock that cast long shadows.

'Through there,' said Joe as he took the lead and pointed to a deeply shadowed canyon between overhanging rocks. There was an eerie silence as the glowering sky encompassed the earth and the world took on the hue of half-light.

The boys dismounted and the horses picked their way through the rocky outcrops and slippery shale, their hooves echoing in the stillness. Joe led them through the narrow gully and coaxed his horses up the slope to the cave. They had been lucky, he realised, for the cave's entrance was side-on to the approaching storm and it appeared to be the only shelter for miles.

The mouth of the cave was enormous and they led their horses further into the darkness. The scuttle of tiny feet told them animals were sheltering there already, and the stink of guano and the overhead rustle and squeak revealed a colony of bats. Joe and Charlie quickly hobbled the horses and lashed the reins to a thick pillar of rock that stood in the centre of the cave.

Charlie lit a match and peered into the dancing shadows. 'Looks like the black fellers were here first,' he murmured as the frail light picked out the ancient paintings on the cave wall. 'How big d'you reckon this is?'

Joe shrugged and carried on rubbing Satan down. The big horse was trembling, the sweat breaking out as the storm's approach resounded through the cave. 'Big enough to give us shelter, but we'd better keep an eye on the animals. They could bring this whole place down if they pull too hard on that pillar.'

Charlie rolled a smoke. 'They'll be right,' he murmured in his matter-of-fact way. 'Brumbies are used to storms.'

'Out in the open, maybe,' retorted Joe. 'Reckon they won't like it much cooped up in here.' He pulled the saddle blankets over their eyes, gave them a pat of reassurance, checked the hobbles and joined Charlie at the mouth of the cave.

They sat and shared a cigarette as they watched the forks of lightning jag to earth. 'Some poor bastard's getting it over there,' said Joe as he

23

followed the curtain of dust that whirled across the plains to the south. 'Whole bloody trees are being torn up and thrown about. Wouldn't like to be caught out in that.'

Charlie smoked the last of the cigarette. 'Reckon we was lucky to find this place.' He grinned as he flicked the butt and watched it being swept away. 'But I wouldn't have minded getting caught – can you imagine the rush you'd get? Must be the nearest thing to flying.'

Joe lifted a dark brow. 'Yeah, right,' he drawled with heavy sarcasm. 'You do come up with some bloody silly ideas, Charlie. Must be crazy to think getting caught in that lot could be fun.' He eyed his brother's profile and noted the shining eyes and rapt expression. There was no getting away from it, Charlie had always pushed his luck. He seemed to have no fear, no sense of danger at all. In fact, he thought with a grin, no bloody sense whatsoever.

The wind howled like a banshee through the tunnels and caves, making the horses prop and dance in their hobbles. Satan's eyes rolled white, his ears flattened to his head, nostrils distended and blowing as he pawed at the cave floor. Joe went to soothe him and the others, his hand gently running down their quivering withers. Brumbies or not, the animals were terrified, and he knew that given half a chance they would be long gone.

The wind picked up, shrieking through the canyons, tossing stones and trees and grass before it as its dervish whirls tore at the earth. Dust descended in a pall of stinging, blinding red to block out the meagre light and fill every crevice in its path. Joe caught Charlie's excitement and together they stood at the entrance to the cave, arms outstretched to the broiling sky – almost daring the storm to come and get them.

'See?' shouted Charlie as his hat blew back and his fair hair whipped his face. 'Told you it was a blast!'

Joe was about to agree when the wind swiftly changed direction and he was almost knocked off his feet and sent plummeting to the canyon floor. He grabbed Charlie's shirt and pulled him into the cave. 'Strewth, that was close. Better stay back before it blows you away.'

Charlie's blue eyes were bright with excitement. 'So what if it does?' he yelled as he tore free and headed back to the mouth of the cave. 'I've never ridden the wind.'

Joe grabbed his arm and yanked him back from the edge. 'Don't be such a bloody fool,' he shouted as he pushed him into the lee of a boulder and scrambled in beside him.

Charlie elbowed away. 'You ain't no fun no more,' he grumbled. 'It's only a storm.'

Joe didn't bother to reply. Charlie wouldn't have listened to reason anyway – not when he was like this.

The wind buffeted the outside walls of their hiding place, howling its fury as it bore down on them and shook the earth to its very core. Within moments it was no longer possible to speak or see, for the wind changed direction once more and spun dust and darkness into their shelter as if determined to seek them out. The brothers sat with their knees to their chins, arms tightly around their heads, noses buried, eyes shut as false night closed in. The screams of the wind echoed those of the horses as the dust storm battered the mouth of the cavern. Its howls rebounded off the walls and funnelled deep into the hillside tunnels with a bass moan that seemed to run shock waves right through them.

They huddled together for warmth. Shared the same mixture of fear and excitement as the storm raged around them. The terrible thrill of it all made Joe shiver. He wasn't proud of the fear that laced his excitement, but understood it came from an awareness of how precious life was and how much he wanted to survive to see the future he'd planned. Yet he knew that given the chance Charlie would have tempted fate, taken the mixture of fear and euphoria they shared now and used them as a defiance in the face of danger. They might have been twins, but they were very different, and sometimes his brother's almost careless attitude to life scared him far more than any storm. For Charlie would always want to live on the edge – live for the moment and not really care about the consequences.

Perhaps Charlie's right, he thought. Maybe I'm not so much fun any more. But we're not kids. We're seventeen going on eighteen. Surely with age came maturity? A time when we become responsible for our actions? He buried his head in his arms and turned his thoughts to the property he would have one day. To the horses and cattle he'd muster on green pastures, and the homestead he'd return to each night. It didn't

26

have to be grand, this place he dreamed of – just somewhere he could call home.

Charlie shivered as the cold wind tore through the mouth of the cave. This was life. This was living. This was part of the excitement he'd craved for so long in the dreary endless days of his youth when all there seemed to be was poverty and hard work. He grinned and instantly regretted it as dust filled his mouth and gritted his teeth. Spitting it out he buried his head deeper and imagined the future. A future of riding the plains with the wild horses. Of travelling vast distances to new adventures, new people, new places. This country was made for men like him. Men who called no place home, who forged new paths for others to follow and were of the stuff that made them legends.

Impatience rode his back as the wind tugged at his clothes and he longed to feel the wild freedom of that wind and to join it in its mad dash across the plains. Yet he knew the time wasn't yet right. He had a lot of living to do first, and for now he would have to be content to follow his brother's more measured steps.

They had no idea how long they remained huddled against that dank boulder in the darkness, but as the wind's shriek lessened and the sandblast ebbed they lifted their heads and listened. The storm was heading north, still blowing hard, still wailing and moaning as it tore a path of destruction across the empty plains – but for them the danger was past. They crawled from their hiding place, spitting dust, rubbing it from their eyes. They'd had a lucky escape.

The horses reared and propped as they took the blankets from their heads and checked them over. One of the bays had a cut on her leg where she must have knocked against the stone wall, but it didn't look too deep and Joe knew it would soon heal. Satan rolled his eyes, the whites gleaming in the darkness. He curled his top lip and snapped at Joe's hand as he adjusted the bridle.

Charlie laughed, the adrenaline still coursing through him. 'You'll never tame that bastard,' he said. 'Wanna give him to me. I'll soon show him.'

Joe stroked the long chestnut nose and traced the white flash on the proud forehead. 'Can't beat a horse into good manners,' he drawled. 'He lashed out 'cos he's scared. He'll learn when he's good and ready. Don't want to kill his spirit completely.'

Charlie snorted and took a long drink from his water-pouch. 'Bet ya a quid I could get him sorted in a day. How about it?' His blue eyes gleamed and the broad, enticing grin seemed forced.

Joe recognised Charlie's need to prove he was the better man – the stronger and more adventurous of the two who had the right of acquisition purely because he was an hour older and an inch taller. It was a familiar scene, one that had been played out ever since he could remember. Only this time the stakes were too high and he wasn't going to give in. He shook his head. 'Satan's mine, and he'll stay that way. No bets on this one,

Charlie,' he said firmly.

Charlie untied the reins from the stone pillar and led his horses to the mouth of the cave. 'We'll see,' he said under his breath.

Ellie opened her eyes. She was almost buried in her father's topcoat, the weight of him bearing down on her making it difficult to breathe. 'Dad?' She pushed against him in an attempt to wriggle away, but found she was stuck fast. Struggling to breathe, she began to panic at the lack of her father's response. 'Dad,' she said more firmly, giving him a hard jab in the stomach. 'Get off. You're squashing me.'

John lay still and heavy across her, his coat-tails flapping in the remains of the wind as it chased across the empty plains. Ellie squirmed and shoved, the onslaught of dread making her heart bang against her ribs as she realised she couldn't hear him breathing. 'Dad?' she yelled. 'Dad, wake up.' Terror brought the strength to push him harder.

John rolled away and lay still in the dirt. His face was ashen, streaked with dry, dust encrusted blood. His mouth fell open in a silent scream and his eyes stared sightlessly at the sky through the caking of dust.

'Dad?' she whispered, her trembling fingers covering her mouth. She was unaware of the tears splashing darkly on the veil of dirt that covered her hands as she knelt beside him and touched his cold face. His head rolled to one side and she flinched at the sight of the gaping hole where his temple had been. 'No!' she screamed.

'You can't leave me here. I won't let you. Wake up. Wake up!' She shook him, jabbed him, slapped his face, crying all the while for she knew it would serve no purpose.

John lay there as still and silent as their surroundings. One hand rested by his side, open to the sky, the fingers curled as if beckoning her to clasp them. Ellie threw herself across his chest, the tears coursing tiny tracks through the dirt on his clothes. 'You can't die,' she sobbed. 'I won't let you.' She rested her cheek on the still chest, pummelling him with her fists in a last ditch effort to beat him back to life.

But there was no answering movement, no rise or fall of that thin chest, no breath emanating from the open mouth. Bereft of strength she slumped against him and gave in to despair. He was all she had. Now he was gone.

The sun was almost at its zenith when she finally raised her head and faced reality. She looked at her father, so naked of all character and colour in death – so still and distant – like a stranger. She softly kissed his cheek. 'I love you,' she whispered. 'I know you didn't mean to leave me.' Ellie knuckled back the tears. 'But I'm scared, Dad. I don't know what to do.'

She knelt beside him and looked out at the vast emptiness. The storm had removed all trace of the track they'd been following and the few trees that had survived the onslaught were bare of foliage. The horses were gone. There was no sound, no welcome cloud of dust heralding another traveller. Even the birds seemed to have deserted her.

Ellie shivered despite the warm breeze that sifted through the dust. She had never felt so alone – or so small and insignificant. She crept closer to her father's side. Her gaze trawled the seemingly endless horizon for some familiar landmark as the sun beat down on her bare head, and finally, far in the distance, she saw the purple thumbprint of what she guessed were Cloncurry's guardian hills.

She finally steeled herself to look at her father, then shuddered. Flies were already swarming around his head, blackening the wound, crawling around his eyes and mouth. She knew then she had to find the courage to bury him. For death brought scavengers, she'd seen it on the roads they'd tramped despite her father's attempt to shield her from the horror. She thought of those bundles of rags that had once been men whose search for something better had come to an ignominious end. Picked clean by the crows and the dingoes they had become the forgotten and unmourned. Dad deserved better than that.

Ellie closed her eyes. 'Goodbye, Dad,' she whispered. Getting to her feet she retrieved her hat from where she had tucked it in her dungaree pocket and took a deep breath. Self-pity wouldn't help. She had to keep her wits about her if she was to survive.

Shadows drifted across the earth and she looked up. A flock of crows circled, dark against the midday sky. 'Go away,' she yelled, waving her hat at them. 'Clear off you bludgers. You aren't having him.'

She looked around, panic and frustration setting in. The horses were gone, and with them the packs that carried their supplies. She had nothing to dig with, nothing to frighten the birds away. In a flash of temper she dredged up all the swear words she could think of as she grabbed a sharp stone and began to scoop the earth out around her father's body. It was hard going and she cursed everything around her as the sun beat down and the crows gathered and the hole seemed to remain stubbornly small.

The heat was remorseless, the sweat evaporating on her skin as her thirst grew and work on her father's final resting place continued. Remembering the aboriginal stockman's advice, she picked up a small, smooth pebble and put it under her tongue. She didn't know whether it would lessen the terrible need for a drink, but it was her only option until she could find a billabong or stream. Dad had to be buried before nightfall. The sun was further west now, preparing for its final burst of glory before it dropped out of sight. She only had a couple of hours before dark.

Ellie finally took a breather. The hole was deep enough but her nails were torn and there was a throbbing pain behind her eyes. She knelt beside her father for the last time and folded his hands across his chest. With a sigh of regret she went through his pockets. There wasn't much there, he'd sold his watch and his snake-skin wallet some months back so they could eat. But there was the last of their wages and a couple of photographs.

She sat back on her heels and looked at the

creased and rather faded snapshots of her mother, Alicia, surprised he'd bothered to keep them after she'd shot through with her Texan oil man and left them to fend for themselves. It was then she realised Dad had never stopped loving Alicia – had always believed she loved them enough to return.

'Oh, Dad,' she sighed. 'She was never coming back.' She tucked the snapshot and money into the pocket of her dungarees and sniffed back the tears. Dad never had been able to see Mum for the selfish bitch she was, but it wasn't her place to judge – for despite streetwise maturity she'd gained in the Domain she still found the adult world far too complex to fully understand what went on between men and women.

She began to push the dirt back into the hole, covering first his feet and then – the hardest part – his face. As the mound of cinnamon earth finally covered him completely, she realised the shallow grave could be too easily scavenged by dingoes. The storm had littered the ground with rubble and shale and soon she had enough rocks to pile them thickly over the makeshift grave. There could be no headstone, not even a crude cross to mark this place she thought sadly. For there was nothing at hand.

'What now?' she muttered as she knelt there. She had never been to a funeral before, but she wanted to do the best she could for this lovely man who'd cared for her so much and had seen her through some of the worst times in her short life. Hesitantly, she began to recite the Lord's prayer. It was the only prayer she knew, but the words seemed to fit the occasion and she was sure God wouldn't mind if she didn't do things exactly right.

Ellie finally got to her feet. 'Amen,' she whispered. The grave looked so small, so isolated in the great emptiness of the outback she wondered if she would ever find it again. She looked to where the Cloncurry hills brooded in the orange glow of sunset and took a step towards them.

A soft growl stilled her.

Eyes wide with terror she looked over her shoulder.

The dingo was thin, her coat as ochre as the earth, the white flash at the tip of her tail twitching in anticipation. She was not alone. She stood, alert and still, her pups close by.

Ellie looked into the cold, unblinking eyes and knew what she wanted. She saw the teeth as the animal curled back her lip, and the drool of saliva glisten on her muzzle. She gathered small rocks and began to thrown them, screaming as loudly as she could in the hope she could frighten it away.

The dingo retreated a little way off and sat down. It would soon be dark. She could wait.

The horses were obviously still unnerved by the storm and Satan was proving difficult to handle as the twins left the rock canyons and headed back to the plains. 'Gotta speed it up, Joe,' said Charlie as he came alongside. 'We lost nearly half a bloody day because of the storm, and that job ain't gunna wait for us.'

Satan wasn't the only one affected by the storm,

thought Joe. Charlie was obviously still on a rush. 'Let the horses calm down first. If I give Satan his head he'll take off like a rocket and the others won't be able to keep up.' He kept the pace at an even trot, the reins held tightly, his knees clamped against Satan's flanks.

Charlie tipped his hat over his blue eyes as he surveyed the miles in front of them. 'Keep this up,' he drawled, 'and we'll lose that flaming job.'

'Stop your bloody whinging,' Joe retorted. 'Ride too hard and they'll get blown. Then we won't be getting anywhere. This is fast enough.'

Charlie remained silent, but Joe could tell his impatience was rising. It was in the set of his shoulders, the whites of his knuckles as he gripped the reins and the small pulse that beat above the lightly stubbled jaw. Tough, Joe thought. No job was worth breaking your bloody neck for, and if Satan unleashed the nervous energy he'd been storing up, then that was a real possibility.

The sun was high in the sky as Joe finally let Satan lengthen his stride into a gallop. The big horse was sweating, but giving him his head in short bursts meant he no longer pulled and fretted and the other horses didn't seem to mind too much and were keeping up.

'Did you hear that?' said Charlie as they reined in some time later.

Joe nodded, his gaze trawling the landscape. 'Yeah,' he murmured. 'Probably just a dingo.'

Charlie shook his head as the sound drifted across the plains again. 'Never heard no dingo make that kinda racket before. Sounds more like

35

a woman.'

Joe laughed. 'Got women on the bloody brain, mate. Ain't seen one so long you're beginning to imagine things.' Yet as the ethereal sound came again and was swallowed up by the silence he frowned. 'Reckon we ought to go see anyhow. If it is a woman then she's in trouble.'

Charlie ran his fingers through his hair and adjusted his hat. 'Wish I'd had time for a shave and a wash,' he said with a rueful grimace. 'Must stink like a dingo.'

'Don't reckon she'll mind too much,' retorted Joe. 'It's not as if you're taking her to a bloody dance.'

They grinned at one another and headed south towards where they thought the sound had come from. The job at Richmond would still be there tomorrow.

Ellie's initial terror had been replaced by a cold determination to survive. Throwing rocks and screaming was having little effect on the dingo, and her own energy was sorely depleted, the raging thirst making it difficult to think clearly. She was panting as she stood there and faced her silent, waiting enemy.

The dingo bitch lay with her muzzle resting on her paws. Her ears were pricked, her yellow eyes watchful as her pups gambolled around her.

Ellie was all too aware of the sun's path westward – of the lengthening shadow she cast across the ground. She would have to do something before it was too late. For the dingo hunted at night. She had eyes that could see in the darkness and a sense of smell that would seek out her prey. There would be no hiding place.

The dingo snapped at her over-exuberant pups before lying on her side for them to suckle. She had no fear of the darkness. There was time enough to feed her young before the night's hunt – and her quarry was an easy one.

Ellie took a step back. Then another, and another. Her pulse was racing and she muttered to herself as she tamped down on her fear and forced herself not to break into a run. 'If I run she'll chase me. If I run she'll chase me,' she muttered through chattering teeth. It was a mantra. It kept her going. One more step back followed by another and then another and two more.

The dingo sat up, ears pricked up, pups scrambling beneath her. She watched Ellie, her yellow eyes never leaving her retreating figure.

Ellie shuffled further and further away, her attention fixed to those eyes. If there was only some way of distracting her, she thought desperately. If only something else would appear for her to hunt. Where the hell were all the bloody rabbits when you needed them? Dust rose from beneath her boots as she backed away. The heat of the afternoon sun beat on her back and still the dingo bitch remained watchful.

Sliding her foot back she rolled her instep over a large stone and lost her balance. Fighting for purchase, she felt her ankle twist painfully then she was down in the dirt. Her breath exhaled in a grunt as she fell hard on to something in her jacket pocket. Ignoring the pain she scrambled to her feet, her attention returning immediately to the dingo.

The yellow eyes were fixed on her as she shook herself free from her pups and got to her feet. The tail was down, shoulders hunched. She was poised for flight.

Ellie scrabbled in her pocket and pulled out Wang Lee's parting gift. This was her only chance, one she'd forgotten – until her fall. Discarding the box and tissue paper she breathed a sigh of relief when she saw it wasn't broken. She held the tiny, ornate mirror up to the sun and aimed the flash of dazzling light directly into the dingo bitch's eyes.

The animal shook her head and sidestepped the blinding glare.

Ellie moved the mirror, praying the sun would last longer than the dingo's determination. She twisted the glowing glass until the sun's glare was magnified and directed fully into those yellow eyes.

The dingo backed off, her ears down, tail between her legs. Shoulders low she turned and slunk away.

Ellie was trembling so badly she could barely stand. Yet she remained there as the dingo and her pups loped across the plain and it was only when they had become mere specks in the vast landscape that she allowed herself to think she might be safe.

Joe had caught the momentary flash of something in the distance, but it was hard to tell where it had come from, and now the screaming had stopped they had no point of reference. He reined Satan in. The stallion was blowing hard, the sweat foaming on his neck and flanks from the hectic ride across the plains. Joe took off his hat and wiped away the sweat from his face with his sleeve. 'Can you see anything?' he panted.

Charlie screwed up his eyes and trawled the horizon. 'Not a flaming thing,' he muttered. 'And there was me all set on rescuing a damsel in distress.'

Joe eyed their surroundings thoughtfully as he eased his shirt collar and tried to garner a breath of coolness from the breeze that had come with the approaching sunset. Someone was out there, but they could ride all day and still miss them by a mile. The outback plains were just too vast and with the coming night, a lone traveller could simply disappear.

They climbed down from their exhausted horses and led them in an easy walk. 'It was probably only some swaggie letting off steam,' muttered Charlie. 'The glint you saw more than likely came off his bottle of grog and now he's sleeping it off.'

'Not long ago since we was on the wallaby tracks, mate. We might not have had the pennies to buy the grog, but can you remember how lonely it was? How vast all this emptiness was? Reckon we ought to try and find him. Just to make sure he's not crook.'

Green eyes met blue as they remembered the nights huddled beneath a canvas shelter that never seemed to keep the rain out. Of the miles they'd walked in the sweltering heat to get to the next police station and collect their measly dole ticket. There had been no such thing as brotherhood amongst the swagmen they'd come across. Their determination to find work and their youthfulness had set them apart. There had been nights spent in a police cell after being caught riding the rails without a ticket. A beating that had left Charlie almost senseless for twenty-four hours and long, endless days when there was no food, no shelter and no work.

'We had some good times though, didn't we?' Joe stared off into the distance as a scuff of dust drifted up into the sky. 'Like the muster up to the Curry and the brumby run. Made some good mates.' He came to a standstill, his focus intense upon the horizon. 'Over there,' he said pointing. 'Something's stirring up the dust.'

Ellie's boots scuffed the dirt as she trudged towards what she hoped was Cloncurry. She had little idea of how far away it was, but that held no fear for she'd walked for many miles during the past year and was used to it. Yet the isolation seemed to close in as darkness beckoned, and for the first time in her life she felt truly alone. There had always been Dad to talk to – to walk with – to share the aches and pains and the hardships of tramping the tracks. Now there was no one.

Thirst was her biggest enemy. She had gone almost a full day without a drink, now her tongue felt swollen and she couldn't summon up enough saliva to spit out the lingering grit. Running her tongue over dry lips she searched for some sign of an underground stream, a borehole or watering trough. Her spirits sank. There was nothing but a few scrubby trees, an occasional glimpse of the dusty road and the dying glare of the red sun.

Heat still shimmered on the distant horizon as papery grass rustled and gum trees wilted. The tramp of her feet was a lonely sound in that endless wilderness, accompanied only by the irritating buzz of flies and the occasional caw of a rook. Then the all-encompassing silence was broken by another sound and she came to an abrupt halt. Shielding her eyes from the glare she watched the emerging black silhouettes of two riders as they rode out of the sunset.

Elation at being discovered was tempered by caution. She'd spent too many months in the Domain to trust anyone at face value – especially strangers. She bent and picked up a heavy rock. There was nowhere to run and nowhere to hide, and if they meant to harm her then she'd go down fighting.

She watched as they dismounted and realised they weren't much older than she was. One was dark, the other fair. Good looking boys, all whipcord and wire and obviously used to life in the outback. Yet it was better not to let them know she was a girl. It wouldn't be the first time she'd had to play the charade, and after the muster up to Longreach she'd had plenty of practice. She rammed her hat low over her raggedy hair, squared her shoulders and faced them. 'The name's Ed. Who are you?'

Two pairs of eyes widened in astonishment. One pair of blue that reminded her of the sea, and the other as green as winter grass. 'Strewth,'

41

breathed the fairer of the two. 'What's a little bloke like you doin' out here on yer own?'

'Mindin' me own business,' she fired back as she drew herself up to her full five foot and half an inch. 'And I ain't little. I'm nearly fourteen.' She caught the look of disbelief that went between them and wished for the hundredth time she was taller – it was embarrassing being a squirt – nobody took her seriously. She lifted her chin. 'Who are you?' she repeated.

'I'm Joe and this is me brother Charlie. Reckoned you might need some help – but seeing as how you're so grown up perhaps we'd better be on our way?'

Ellie noticed the teasing glint in those emerald eyes and found she couldn't help but return the beguiling smile. Yet she couldn't quite dismiss the sudden portent that this meeting would some-how change the course of all their lives – a portent of distant shadows they had yet to see.

Chapter One

Thirty-Four Years Later

Claire struggled with the spare tyre and once she'd finally got the damned thing in place she eased her back and glared out at the deserted highway. The endless miles of Queensland's outback lay before her, the heat dancing in waves along the horizon. She hadn't seen another car for hours, and although she was perfectly capable of changing a wheel it would have been nice to have had help. That was why she disliked the outback – it was too empty – too lonely; after her five years in Sydney, she had become used to people and noise and the bustle of city life.

Her mood was dark as she smeared the perspiration from her face. Her long fair hair clung to her neck and the cotton minidress that had been crisp this morning was now crumpled and limp. This was no way to celebrate her graduation from Veterinary College, and if she'd had her way, she'd have been on the beach with her friends instead of stuck out here in the middle of nowhere. But the summons home to Warratah could not be ignored. Aunt Aurelia had made it clear it was time to clear the air and put an end to her estrangement from her family. And no one argued with Aurelia. Not if they valued a quiet life.

She twisted her hair into a rough knot and

tethered it with a clip then took a long drink. The bottle had been on the passenger seat and the water was unpleasantly warm. But it did the trick, and she was soon tightening the last bolt and lowering the jack. Throwing the tools into the back of the van, she climbed in and switched on the engine.

The van was an old green Holden her dad had picked up at an auction in Burketown. It looked a wreck, but the Warratah mechanic had stripped the engine and it purred as good as new despite the rust showing through the chipped paintwork and the rear doors needing to be tied at the handles to keep them from bursting open. She'd had plenty of offers to decorate it with flower power daisies and Ban the Bomb insignia, but had resisted. It was bad enough driving the thing through Sydney's traffic without looking as if she was part of a circus.

Claire let the engine idle as she lit a cigarette. Thoughts of home and family had come to the fore again, and now she was only a few days from Warratah, she was experiencing a mixture of emotions. It would be good to see the old place again. To breathe the scent of the citrus yellow wattle trees and the profusion of roses that clambered over the old homestead. Her mother, Ellie, had a passion for roses and in the soft outback nights the musk of them filled the house. Yet she remembered the tense atmosphere between them all on the last day five years ago, and knew this summons home was Aunt Aurelia's attempt to put things right. And that made her uneasy. For the questions that haunted her were

44

finally to be answered – and she didn't know if she was ready. Her life was settled in Sydney. She had friends there and after Christmas would take up the job offer in a prestigious veterinary practice. The shadows that had once haunted her were almost banished, and she didn't relish the thought of their returning.

Stubbing out her smoke, Claire put the van in gear and headed back on to the highway. She was not the same naive country girl who'd left Warratah all those years ago, and despite the olive branch being offered by her aunt, she knew this was not going to be an easy home-coming. Yet she was wise enough to realise she couldn't run for ever. It was time to face the truth, no matter how harsh.

Ellie had had a restless night. She didn't like sleeping alone, but her husband was away on the annual muster and the house seemed to echo now both Leanne and Claire had left home. She'd lain there in the darkness listening to the old timbers creak and sigh, wondering where the years had gone. It felt as if it had only been such a short while since she'd arrived at Warratah – a skinny kid with no possessions but a few ragged clothes and an old pony – yet here she was rapidly approaching her forty-eighth birthday and mistress of one of the biggest cattle stations in Northern Queensland.

The ghosts of the past crowded in and she gave up on sleep. Tossing back the sheet she clambered out of the big brass bed and padded barefoot into the kitchen. It was the centre of the house, the place where the children had played and homework had been done while the men discussed the stock, the weather and the price of beef. It looked so tidy now she realised, as she waited for the water to boil, so ordered where there had once been a jumble of riding boots in the corner, dirty laundry piled in a basket next to the boiler, toys and discarded books left lying where they fell. Happy days, she thought wistfully.

'Sign you're getting old when you complain how tidy everything is,' she muttered crossly as she poured the water over the tea and added two spoonfuls of sugar. She took a sip and grimaced. Talking to herself was another sign of age but she'd found herself doing it more often lately. The truth was she missed her girls. Missed their bright chatter and their energy – even their flaming rows. It was just too damn quiet.

She looked around the kitchen, seeing it properly for the first time despite the hours she spent in here. The timber walls and ceiling were dark with smoke from the ancient range they'd replaced five years ago and the linoleum was cracked and faded from primrose yellow to a pale cream. The solid kitchen table and chairs had been made in the carpentry shop and were scarred by years of abuse from children and drovers and the cupboards were mismatched and needed a coat of paint. The sink was old, the gas fridge unreliable, the curtains faded at the window, and although she'd been tempted by the magazine advertisements to have one of the new, streamlined kitchens, she preferred things as they were. This was home, she was at ease here.

Without really knowing why, she drifted from the kitchen into the square hall at the front of the house and opened the bedroom doors on either side. There were four in all, added as the years went by and the children came along. Her own room looked out to the gum trees and the billabong, the muslin curtains drifting in front of the flyscreens, diffusing the bright light that came in the afternoon. The brass bed almost filled the room, the lace mosquito canopy adding a touch of exotica. Photographs lined the battered dresser, paintings of horses lined the wooden walls and the polished floor gleamed beneath the scattered sheepskin rugs.

Ellie smiled as she softly closed the door. It was their refuge, the one place in all the madness that went with running a place like this that they could escape to and find one another again.

The girls' rooms had been almost stripped of any sign they had once lived here. Apart from a few outgrown toys and books there was nothing much to show for their twenty-odd years of habitation. Ellie tweaked the patchwork quilts, plumped pillows and fingered through the books and riding trophies. Leanne was married now, with a home of her own, and Claire ... Claire was newly qualified, with a bright future in the city and a lifestyle that Ellie could only guess at. There had been little communication between them over the past five years and she realised sadly her eldest daughter had become a stranger.

Impatient with her gloomy thoughts she shut the doors behind her, grabbed a sweater from the hook by the screen door and went out on to the verandah. It was still dark, the moon high in the sky, the stars so clear and bright it was almost as if you could reach out and touch them. Ellie breathed in the scent of wattle and roses that mingled with the more earthy smell of horses and cattle and good rich soil. Life at Warratah was all she needed, the seasons following one another almost effortlessly as cattle were born, branded and put out to pasture before they were rounded up, selected for breeding or the stock yards.

She sighed as she looked out into the darkness to the pastures she knew stretched further than any eye could see. She would never leave this place, this beloved corner of Queensland, for it had been mother and father to her for most of her life. The land had been nourished by her sweat and the blood of those closest to her. Had demanded her strength and courage as no human had ever done.

The rocking-chair was old, the runners creaking beneath her slight weight as she sat there on the verandah with her cooling tea and watched the dawn bring colour and warmth. Ghostly white mitchell grass turned silver, the dew glittering millions of diamonds in the new light. Gum trees cast deep shadows over the impacted red earth of the cattle pens and corrals, and the billabong was pewter bright between banks of weeping willows and spinifex. Her smile was one of pleasure and sadness as she realised how long ago it was since she'd first set eyes on Warratah, and as she sat there in the burgeoning light she felt the ghosts of the past return once more – and they could no longer be ignored.

The boys gave her water and set about making a camp-fire. 'What we got here then?' muttered Joe as he peered into the gloom.

Ellie turned and shrieked with joy. 'Clipper! You're safe.' She ran to the pony as it trotted towards her, the grey in his wake, and flung her arms around his neck. 'Oh, Clipper,' she breathed into the dusty coat. 'I thought I'd lost you as well.'

'Steady on, mate. It's only a scruffy old pony.'

Ellie turned on Charlie. 'Might be scruffy to you but he's all I got,' she yelled.

'Sorry I spoke.' Charlie backed off and returned to help his brother at the camp-fire.

Ellie heard them laughing and realised she'd overreacted and had probably blown her cover by blubbering over Clipper, but as she took the saddles off and brushed them down she relaxed. They would have said something if they'd been suspicious.

After a supper of smoky billy tea and damper drenched in golden syrup Ellie began to enjoy their company. The twins seemed honest enough – just ordinary country boys. They were handsome and strangely similar despite their different colouring, and she liked the way their eyes creased at the corners when they laughed. And they did a lot of laughing. 'Where you from?' she asked in a quiet moment.

'Small town south-east of Brisbane called Lorraine. Probably never heard of it,' said Joe as he blew on his tea. 'Just finished mustering brum-

49

bies over in the Territory.'

'Sounds exciting,' said Ellie. She glanced across at the magnificent chestnut hobbled under the trees. 'That where he came from?'

Joe nodded. 'Broke him meself. Satan's a devil of a horse, but there ain't none better.'

Ellie smiled but kept silent. She felt the same way about Clipper, even though he was past his prime and most people probably saw him as just an ordinary old stock pony. She emerged from her thoughts aware Joe was watching her. His scrutiny made her uneasy, for it was as if he suspected she wasn't all she seemed. 'Something bothering you, mate?' she asked.

'I was wondering what you're doing out here on yer own,' Joe said, his dark hair flopping into his eyes. 'What happened to yer mum and dad?'

It was obvious he wasn't going to let it drop, so Ellie decided to tell him the truth – or at least part of it. 'Me and Dad were signed off from the drove up to Longreach and was on our way to the Curry when the storm hit.' She swallowed hard. 'Dad died,' she said curtly. Tears blinded her and she angrily dashed them away. 'I buried him back there somewhere,' she said, waving her arm towards the darkness.

Charlie gently squeezed her shoulder. 'Good on yer mate,' he said softly. 'Must have been real tough.'

Joe swept the dark hair from his forehead and scratched his chin, his green eyes gleaming with humour as he looked at her more closely. 'You sure you're tellin' us the truth, kid? You ain't running away from somewhere are you?'

Ellie rammed her hands in her pockets and stood over him. 'I ain't a liar,' she snapped. 'Dad's dead. Mum shot through years ago and I'm on me way to Gregory Downs. So stick that up yer arse.'

Joe leaned back, his hands up in submission as he roared with laughter. 'Whoa there mate, I didn't mean to get yer back up.' He looked at his brother who was also laughing. 'Jeez. He's fiery for a little bludger. Worse than you Charlie.' He finally stopped laughing and his expression grew serious. 'How you planning on getting to Gregory Downs?' he asked. 'It's a fair cow of a way. What's there for you?'

'I got an aunt at Warratah Station,' she said stoutly. 'And it ain't that far. I've walked further.'

She saw the interest flare in their eyes. 'Walked?' said Charlie. Joe whistled. 'Looks like we've met the youngest swaggie in town,' he murmured. 'Where you from originally, kid?'

Ellie sank on to her bedroll as memories flooded back. 'Sydney,' she said quietly. 'Dad lost his job and the house a coupla years after the stock market crashed in twenty-nine. We lived in the Domain for two years and been on the road for nearly nine months.'

The boys nodded as if they understood what this meant – had experienced something similar. Encouraged, Ellie carried on. 'Dad was an accountant. Had no idea what it was like out here in the Great Wide, but he learned pretty quick. We both did.' She stared into the camp-fire flames as she thought of their long trek north. 'Work wasn't easy to come by, especially not with

51

a kid in tow,' she said bitterly before falling silent.

'So what happened?' prompted Joe softly.

Ellie stared into the fire. She'd realised by the time they'd reached Charleville that she would have to do something to help. If she'd been a boy, then it was possible they'd have been more welcome on the cattle and sheep stations. Once her hair had been cropped and she'd adopted the stance and swagger of the boys she'd known back in the Domain all she'd had to do was persuade Dad to accept her as Ed. It was the start of better times. 'Me and Dad got a job at Gowrie Station. I worked with the cook, Wang Lee, and Dad helped the horse tailer.'

'We know the place,' said Charlie eagerly. 'Head stockman's a mate. Snowy White. Good bloke for an Aborigine. Tells bonzer stories.'

Ellie grinned. 'The best,' she agreed. 'Wang Lee was all right once you got past his bad temper. He was a good bloke too.' She fished in her pocket and pulled out the ornate mirror. 'Gave me this at the end of the drove. Saved me life.'

'Funny thing to give a bloke,' muttered Charlie as he eyed the gilding and brightly coloured stones embedded in the frame.

Ellie shoved the mirror back into her pocket. It had been a mistake to show them such a feminine present. She hurried on to explain how the mirror had saved her from certain death – embellishing the tale, drawing it out, making it more daring and exciting, just like the men used to do around the camp-fire each night. 'Wang Lee was always giving me presents,' she added. 'Had a bit of a fall and hurt me foot on the drove,

52

and he made me this stick so's I could walk easier.' She pulled the gift from the saddle-bag and the intricate carving of bison and coolies on the walking-stick was duly admired.

'Reckon it's time we had some sleep, mate. Early start in the morning.' Charlie unrolled his blanket, placed his saddle more comfortably and settled down. Within moments he was snoring.

Ellie looked at Joe and grinned. There was something still within him that she recognised in herself – an ease with his surroundings and the life he led. 'Reckon I wore him out,' she said quietly. 'The blokes on the drove were always telling me to shut up, but I can't help it if I want to learn everything.'

Joe smiled, his dark eyes emerald in the dying flames. *'Everything's* a lot to learn in a few months,' he drawled. 'Reckon you'll get there soon enough.'

It was dawn when they woke. The ashes were cold, the chill of outback winter still glittering frost on the red earth. Joe rolled over beneath the blanket, gleaning the last of the warmth before he had to face the day. He watched as Ed got the fire going again, set the billy and prepared his horse and pony. The kid certainly knew his way around a camp, but the niggle of doubt made him frown. He was smart as a whip, that was obvious by the way he'd survived, but he wasn't telling them the truth – he was sure of it. Yet there was something else. Something less tangible that made him uneasy. For he was being drawn to this kid, and it had suddenly become important to protect him.

Impatient with his thoughts he shucked off the blanket and went to sort out his horses. He was probably comparing Ed's experiences with his own childhood. Of the loss of his parents and the heartache of seeing the only home he'd known taken from him. He moved around his string of horses, rubbing them down, releasing the hobbles, tacking up – yet his thoughts were miles away.

Dad had built the house when he and Mum had first moved to Lorraine as newly-weds. The verandah was shady, if a little off true, the roof was corrugated iron that had been much mended over the years, and termites had done their best to bring down the timber walls and frame. On leaving, he'd made the mistake of looking back. The three-roomed shack already looked abandoned. The walls sagging just that bit more where weeds pushed through the wooden slats, the roof settling lower on the rotten rafters making the verandah more askew than ever.

Joe sighed as he scratched his chin and headed back to the makeshift camp. It never did any good to look back, for the past couldn't be changed. It was a harsh lesson – one that Ed would have to learn on his own.

Breakfast was cold damper with a hunk of corned beef and a mug of steaming tea. They ate quickly and almost in silence. They needed to be on their way before the sun rose too high and the heat and flies became unbearable.

Charlie threw the last of his tea over the fire, then kicked dirt over it to quench the remaining embers. 'Better be off then.' He gathered up his saddle and blanket and looked across at Joe. 'We'll take the kid to the homestead when we get there. They'll know what to do with him.'

'What homestead?' Ellie's brown eyes regarded them solemnly beneath the ragged fringe.

'Wilga Station at Richmond,' said Charlie as he saddled up. 'Got a job there if we get to it in time.' He gave a telling look at the sun. 'They'll see you right.'

'I ain't goin' in that direction,' came the firm retort. 'Warratah Station's north-west.'

'That's flamin' miles away,' said Charlie impatiently as he buckled straps and sorted out the stirrups. 'You'll have to stay with us until Wilga, then work something out from there.'

Joe grinned when he saw the stubborn tilt of the chin and the fiery gleam in the kid's eyes. He had a feeling Charlie had met his match and was interested to see how far the kid would get before there were fireworks.

'I ain't going to no station in Richmond. I'm going north.' Hands in dungaree pockets, chin up, shoulders squared, the kid glared back at Charlie.

'Well, we ain't takin' you. So quit yer whinging.' Charlie looked to Joe for support. Realised he wasn't going to get it and with a sigh returned to eye the kid standing so defiantly in front of him. 'You'll have to come with us, mate.'

'No, I don't.' Ellie hoisted herself into the saddle and gathered up the reins. 'I'll make my own way to Warratah.'

Charlie rammed his hat on. 'Flamin' kids,' he sighed. 'Never flamin' do as they're flamin' told.'

He strode over to the pony, startling it by making a grab for the reins. 'You'll bloody do as you're told, or I'll take me belt to you.'

'Try that and I'll knock yer flamin' block off,' came the retort as the heavy walking-stick was drawn from the saddle bag and lifted high.

Joe had seen enough. 'That's it,' he said sharply. 'Quit it, both of you.' He stood between his brother and the kid. 'We'll take you to the Gregory. If your aunt's grateful enough, perhaps she'd give us a job to make up for the one we're losing.'

The grin was broad in the urchin face, the freckles dancing across the snub nose. 'Too right she will.' The reins were gathered once more. 'Better get going then.'

'Are you gunna let this ankle-biter tell us what to flamin' do?' gasped Charlie in amazement. 'How do we know this aunt's going to give us work? It's as dry as a snake's arse in the Gregory, and from what I hear, most of the stock up that way's long gone.'

'We can't let him go alone,' retorted Joe. 'He's just a kid, and he's too little to fend for himself.' He leaned closer to his brother. 'Drop it, Charlie,' he warned softly.

Charlie glowered, turned away and climbed into the saddle. Yanking his hat over his eyes he glared at both of them. 'There'd better be a job at the end of this, mate,' he warned Ellie. 'Or there'll be trouble.'

They had travelled for days, following the devastating trail of the storm as it wound itself

56

down across the plains. The Curry had been badly hit, with roofs torn away and stock tossed for many miles before being dumped and left for dead. The long track beyond the Curry had been obliterated and as they turned off at Threeways and made their way towards Gregory Downs they saw trees uprooted and fences sagging in dunes of red sand.

Ellie looked around her as she rode alongside the two brothers. It was a desolate place, this land where her aunt lived, and she wondered how anyone could exist out here. It was dusty, the grass silver and sparse, with mile upon mile of emptiness. The great river was a mere trickle as it ran towards the northern coast, the billabongs turned to clay pans beneath the weeping paper barks and she-oaks.

Yet, as they headed further west she began to understand why her aunt had chosen to live out here and could imagine how it must look when the rains came. For as they rode through the gorge that would take them on to the far south-western edges of Warratah they entered another world. A world of incredible green after the scorching plains, with tall pine trees and fig and cabbage palms. The creek was deep and mysterious where tortoises played and freshwater crocs lurked, and the bush surrounding it was alive with the sounds of jabirus, and black and sulphur crested cockatoos. Flashes of bright reds and blues and citrus yellow darted between the trees as a myriad of birds were startled from their perches, and the gentle grey wallabies sat up, tensed for flight as they watched the intruders make camp.

Joe had caught a yellowbelly one day and dug out some yabbies which were like tiny cray-fish, and they'd cooked them over a fire, the delicate white meat so delicious she'd still been licking her fingers long after the meal was over. On another day Charlie had taken the rifle and shot a couple of ducks, which she helped to pluck before they were spit-roasted on twigs over the camp fire.

As the days wore on Ellie found herself drawn to these boys. They were easy to talk to, easy to confide in; their shared experiences of life on the wallaby tracks brought them closer, and as each day passed she realised what a wrench it would be when it was time for them to part.

Yet this new found friendship was marred by her deceit. She bit her lip as they approached the first of the fences that surrounded the vast acreage of her aunt's property. With the drought in full force there was no guarantee she'd even be able to keep her promise of work, and after the lies she'd told them, her conscience bothered her. As Ed she was accepted as one of them – a mate they were helping on the way, with a promise of work at journey's end. Yet she'd maintained her silence on her true identity, for although they were both fun to be with, Charlie had shown signs of an erratic temperament. He'd been angry enough at having to bring her all the way out here – goodness only knew what he'd do if he discovered she'd been lying and there wasn't any work at the end of it all.

They rode on for most of that day and half the next. There was still no sight of the homestead and she was beginning to wonder if they would ever find it amongst the low hills that were dotted with stunted snappy gum. Yet she was taking pleasure in the timbered country with its gidyea, eucalypt, turpentine and wattle trees, and found she was enjoying her journey over the spinifex grass to the more open red soil country and pleasant waterholes that lay in the shadows of limestone caves and flowering bloodwoods.

Ellie relaxed on Clipper's back. The skewbald had filled out now he'd had a few days of good grass and fresh water, and his coat gleamed. Even the grey looked healthier, but she could see the animal was tired and she hoped he would last out long enough to take a well-earned rest at the cattle station. For the grey was all she had left to remind her of her father.

They finally came over the low rise of a hill and there, in the valley, was Warratah. Washed in golden sunlight the homestead sprawled at the centre of a blood red yard, its rusting corrugated roof almost smothered in the snowy blossom of a jarrah tree. Purple bougainvillaea and red roses clambered up the water tower and a lime green pepper tree offered shade by the cattle pens and corrals. A stand of citrus yellow wattle trees dappled the horse paddock and the sun glinted on the pool of water still standing in the billa-bong. To the north of the homestead yard was a dirt runway, the twin prop plane a mere speck of white against the red.

Joe let out a soft whistle. 'Strewth. That's some place your aunt's got.'

Ellie felt her spirits lift. Warratah was more

59

beautiful than she could ever have imagined, and as she gazed down at the sprawl of outbuildings and stables and the sleek cattle in the pastures, she knew that given the chance she would never leave. With growing anticipation, she nudged Clipper into a canter down the gentle slope.

As they crossed the pasture she caught the sound of a hammer ringing against metal and noticed the forge. Men bustled in the yard, carrying bags of feed and saddles, calling to one another above the low of the cattle. There were numerous wooden shacks dotted around the homestead yard and cattle corrals and she could only guess at what they might be, but it was the fine looking horses in the paddock that drew her attention, and the cacophony of barking blue heelers in the enormous kennel yard that made her smile.

The scent of the roses and the wattle was heady, their heavy fragrance filling the torpid air even from this distance, and Ellie felt the first tremor of doubt. Dad had never really told her much about this place, and he'd certainly never said her aunt was rich. Yet as they approached the final gate that would lead them into home yard, she noticed how the verandah sagged off to one side, the screens needed mending and the roof had been inexpertly patched beneath the tumble of white blossom. The paint was peeling, the steps up to the wooden verandah were termite chewed and the white trellis lacing the edge of the verandah had definitely seen better days.

'Looks like we got a welcoming committee,' muttered Joe as all work stopped and fifty or more pairs of eyes suspiciously watched their approach. 'You sure this is the right place?'

Ellie nodded as the sulphur crested cockatoo screamed abuse from his perch on the verandah. Her mouth had gone dry and her heart hammered for she'd recognised the elegant blonde who'd come to stand at the railings and knew it could only mean trouble.

'Crikey,' gasped Charlie. 'Is that old dragon yer aunt? Wouldn't want to bump into her on a dark night.'

'Bugger off,' yelled the cockatoo. 'Repel boarders.'

Ellie stifled the nervous giggle as she looked at the extraordinary woman waiting for them on the top step. Dressed in a man's jacket and with baggy trousers stuffed into thick woollen socks, she stood squarely on the verandah in sturdy brogues. The monocle glinted in the glare, the pipe smoke drifting, leaving its mark in a wave of ginger across the front of the thick silver hair. Aunt Aurelia was certainly nothing like she'd expected. In fact she looked incongruous against the female wisp of white that was draped against the verandah railings.

'Dad said Aunt Aurelia was fair dinkum,' she said with more optimism than she felt as they approached the homestead. 'She might look fearsome, but Dad said she's a bonzer lady with a good heart.' She took a deep breath in an effort to still her racing pulse. 'It's not *her* you've got to watch out for,' she added bitterly.

'Who's the bloke standing next to your aunt?' muttered Joe as they walked the horses shoulder to shoulder towards the verandah.

Ellie shrugged. 'Dunno. She's a widow.' She saw her aunt screw her monocle more firmly in place as she tried to make out who the visitors were, and realised she was eyeing Joe's horse with deep suspicion. Ellie became suddenly aware of how they must appear to the three people on the verandah. The tough little stock ponies were poor relations to the prancing chestnut, their own appearance dirty and ragged after their experiences in the outback. But there was nothing she could do about it, and once she'd told them who she was it wouldn't matter anyway.

'Don't fancy yours much, Joe. But the other one looks ripper to me, mate. Who is she?' asked Charlie admiringly as the vision in white raised one elegant hand to shield her eyes from the glare. He slicked back his fair hair and re-positioned his hat. 'Looks like the ride was worth it after all.'

Ellie's retort was stillborn as the woman's voice drifted all too clearly across the yard.

'I'd send them on their way, if I were you,' she said firmly in her plummy English accent. 'Rough looking bunch, even if they are young.'

'Don't look any different from a thousand other outback kids. And no one's going to be sent packing,' drawled the man from the shadows. 'It's an unwritten law out here to give food and shelter to strangers, no matter what they look like.'

Ellie wondered who he was in relation to the women, yet he seemed sensible and matter-of-fact, and she liked him for that.

The woman sniffed. 'Well don't let them in the

house, Aurelia. They probably stink to high heaven and will end up robbing you blind.'

All the old anger rose in Ellie as they came to a standstill in front of the verandah. She slid from the saddle ready to do battle when she was halted by the deep contralto of her aunt's voice.

'Stay there,' she ordered. 'If it's work you're after then I'm sorry.' She put up a hand to staunch Ellie's protest. 'But I'll gladly give you tucker and a bed for the night.'

'I told you we shouldn't have come all this flamin' way,' hissed Charlie before Ellie could get a word in. He turned back to Aurelia. 'We come 'cos of him,' he said crossly as he pointed to Ellie. 'Now we've lost a good job in Richmond and got nothing to show for it.'

Aurelia frowned as she adjusted her monocle and looked down at Ellie. 'Do I know you, son?' she asked kindly.

Ellie was about to speak when an impatient voice interrupted. 'For heaven's sake, Aurelia, of course you don't.' The heavily made-up eyes flashed over Ellie with disdain. 'He's just a filthy urchin hoping to get something out of you.' She turned to face Ellie and the boys, her tone imperious. 'Clear off and get some food from the cookhouse, then be on your way. There's nothing for you here.'

Ellie had had enough and all the years of hurt and resentment burst from her in a torrent of rage. 'Selfish bitch,' she spat. 'You haven't changed a bit, have you? Still ordering people around, thinking you're so much better than everyone else when all the time you're just a

63

mean-minded, spiteful cow.' She was red in the face and panting as an awestruck silence fell.

'Fair go, Ed. Bit strong, mate,' warned Joe as he put a placatory hand on her shoulder.

'Repel boarders,' shrieked the cockatoo who was now getting thoroughly over-excited. 'Rollocks.'

Ellie shook Joe's hand away. 'You weren't dumped in the Domain 'cos she wanted a good time with her latest boyfriend,' she snapped. 'You weren't left at five years old wondering what you'd done that was so bad your mother hated you enough to leave you behind.'

Aurelia gasped, and Ellie could see she was torn between horror and mirth as she stepped down from the verandah and crossed the yard. 'Elspeth?' she boomed. 'Is that you under all that grime?'

Ellie's chin was resilient, her gaze defiant as she pulled off her battered bush hat to reveal the shaggy crop of fair hair. At last someone had recognised her, but the wait had been agonising. 'You must be Aunt Aurelia,' she said simply. 'This is Joe, and Charlie.'

She flinched as her mother's screech tore through the silence. 'Elspeth? Elspeth, what's happened to your hair? And why are you dressed like that?'

'Shut up Alicia,' murmured Aurelia. 'The poor child's obviously been through enough without you banging on about things that don't matter.' She clasped Ellie's hands. 'I'm glad you're safe my dear,' she said softly. 'We've been so terribly worried.'

Ellie looked up into the calm grey eyes and realised she had an ally. But before she could say anything, she was swept in to a generous embrace that almost smothered her in an ample bosom. Ellie clung to the soft, welcoming anchor. Aunt Aurelia might look fierce, but she obviously had a good heart and, unlike her mother, had really cared what happened to her. Tears pricked as the weariness of her long journey and loss of her father swept over her, and it was only the explosion of Joe's laughter that drew her from the embrace.

'Bloody hell! You mean we've been dragged halfway to the north pole by a bloody sheila?' he spluttered. 'Well if that don't take the flamin' biscuit, I don't know.'

'Flamin' biscuit,' yelled the bird as he danced along the perch.

'Fair go, Joe,' said Charlie through his own laughter. 'She never let on either way, and sure had us both fooled. What a coupla gallahs we turned out to be.' He got down from his horse and shook Aurelia's hand. 'Glad to meet you at last, missus,' he said as the smile tugged the corners of his mouth. 'You'll have to excuse me brother. Didn't mean no disrespect.'

He was almost knocked down by the whirlwind that was Alicia as she shoved him out of the way and tore Elspeth from Aurelia's arms. 'My baby,' she wept as she carefully avoided contact with the filthy dungarees and jacket. 'Thank God you're all right. We thought you were dead. What on earth was your father thinking of to bring you all the way out here?'

65

Ellie felt the bile rise at the hypocrisy of it all and pushed her away. The last thing she needed was one of Mum's dramatic turns.

But Alicia didn't seem to notice as she looked out over the paddocks. 'Where is he by the way? It's time I gave him a piece of my mind.'

Ellie wiped her nose on her sleeve. She had a handkerchief, but knew this would annoy her mother far more than anything else and got some satisfaction from the look of disgust on Alicia's face. 'He's dead,' she said flatly.

'Dead?' gasped Alicia. 'He has no business being dead. How dare he do that and leave my precious baby all alone in the middle of the desert?' She lunged towards Ellie in an attempt to embrace her again.

Ellie sidestepped the clutching fingers and stood in the lee of Aurelia's bulk. 'He didn't do it on purpose,' she snapped. 'In fact he was trying to protect me from the storm. Reckon he saved my life.'

Aurelia glared through her monocle. 'For goodness sake pull yourself together Alicia and stop making that awful racket. You're upsetting Elspeth and poor old Kelly's beside himself.' She put a firm arm around Ellie's shoulders and led her up the steps. 'Come on,' she said bossily. 'Time you met Kelly. You two as well,' she added over her shoulder to Charlie and Joe. 'I have a surprise for you both.'

'Reckon we've had enough surprises for one day, missus,' chuckled Joe.

'You'll like this one,' said Aurelia firmly.

'You're not going to...?' Alicia began to protest.

'I'll do what I want when I want,' said Aurelia. 'This has nothing to do with you, Alicia.' She introduced them to Kelly. 'My late husband won him at cards down in Sydney,' she explained. 'Unfortunately he was owned by a sailor with a questionable line in vocabulary. I've tried to teach him some manners, but I get the feeling he enjoys shocking people.'

Ellie put out a tentative finger and stroked the snowy feathers. She'd never been this close to a cocky before and was wary it might bite.

'Urrgh?' said Kelly as he cocked his head and fanned out his yellow crest.

'He wants a biscuit,' said Aurelia. 'It's time for tea, but first let me introduce you to Jack Withers. He delivers the mail.'

Ellie noticed the way her aunt blushed, but as her fingers were engulfed in a large hand she looked up at Jack Withers and grinned into friendly eyes and a sun-baked face. If only her mother wasn't here, she might have really enjoyed this home-coming.

Aurelia ordered a fresh pot of tea from Sally, the house lubra, and once they were all introduced and sitting comfortably, she coaxed Ellie into telling her about the long trek. After the long silence that greeted Ellie's tale of horror Aurelia folded her arms beneath the headland of her bosom and smiled at the two boys. 'I arranged for a reward for Ellie's safe return,' she began.

'Don't do this, Aurelia,' warned Alicia. 'Can't you see it's a put up job?'

Joe put his cup down on the table. 'I don't like what you're suggesting, missus,' he said, the mildness of his tone belying the anger in his green eyes. 'See, me and my brother don't like being called dishonest, and what we done for Ed – I mean Elspeth – well we'd've done it for anyone. So I reckon you should keep your opinions to yourself.'

'Too right,' muttered Charlie and Ellie in unison.

Alicia went pale, the long red nails clutching at the rope of pearls around her neck. 'Well, really,' she gasped.

Aurelia ignored her. 'As I was saying,' she said firmly. 'There is a reward of a hundred pounds and I would like you two boys to share it.' She looked across at Ellie and smiled. 'You've brought our girl safely through, and I only wish I could have thanked her father as well.' Her monocle plopped onto her chest and she sighed. 'It seems we've all misjudged him terribly, and I'm sorry for that.'

'A hundred quid?' breathed Joe. 'Bloody hell.' He reddened under the stern gaze of the older woman. 'Sorry missus.' His broad grin creased the early lines at the corners of his eyes, making him very handsome. 'It's just we never had that kind of money before.'

'Just so,' she said stoutly. 'I hope you use it wisely.'

Ellie came back from the past and shivered despite the warmth of the early morning sun. For the dark shadows of those times were still long enough to touch the next generation.

Chapter Two

Leanne hoisted the saddle and tack on to her hip and crossed the yard to the stables. Angel, her husband of eight months, was out East checking stock in his capacity as Government vet, and Jarrah was quiet for a change with most of the men out on the joint annual muster with Warratah. She would have gone with them, but she had a favourite mare in foal and couldn't risk leaving her.

She dumped the saddle in the tack room, grabbed a carrot from the feed store and headed for the stalls. Bonny had been brought in from the paddock and was in solitary splendour in the biggest stall, eating her head off and getting fatter every day. 'How's my girl, today?' she murmured as she took off her gloves and stroked the dusty neck.

Bonny curled her top lip and blew a raspberry before she dipped her head and searched for the treat she knew Leanne always had in her pocket.

Leanne shook back her dark curls and laughed as she held out the carrot. 'I know what you mean. Life's a bitch, isn't it? Never mind, girl. You'll soon get your figure back.' She pushed her out of the way and checked her water bucket and feed bag then left her to it. There wasn't much to be done until the foal arrived and she wanted to finish the accounts before Dad and the others got back.

The sun was high and the gallahs were squabbling in the gum trees as she walked across the yard and up the steps to the verandah. It was quiet with the men gone, but she could still hear the ring of an axe and the clang of someone hammering metal in the forge. The cookhouse was deserted, as was the bunkhouse, but the aborigines' humpies on the western edge of the pasture still hummed with life. The kids were playing football, the dogs were barking and smoke from their fire drifted skywards as usual. She shooed away the few chooks that had strayed on to the verandah and slammed through the screen door.

Jarrah homestead was grander than the one Dad had built at Warratah. No expense had been spared when the original owners had carted blue stone all the way from Sydney to build it. The tiled roof and screened verandah meant it was cool in the summer and waterproof in the wet, and in the cold winter nights it was cosy to snuggle up with Angel in front of the fire that roared up the vast stone chimney in the lounge.

Leanne eased her sweaty shirt from her jeans waistband as she entered the cool dimness of the lounge and breathed a sigh of pleasure. She loved this room with its shelves of books and trophies. The beams were dark from the smoke of the fire, the floor polished, the chairs saggy and baggy and just right for flopping into after a hard day's work. The windows looked out over the yard to the front and the miles of green pastures and pine clad hills to the back, and although they had a generator for electricity she preferred to light the oil lamps at night – it was softer and more romantic than the bright overhead light.

She ran her fingers through her short dark curls and thought of the plans she had for Jarrah. For she would own it one day, she was certain of that – why else had Mum and Dad let her manage the place under supervision these past two years? She smiled as she kicked off her dusty boots and threw them in a corner. She might not be as academic as Claire, or as attractive, but she was ambitious enough for both of them and the plans she had would prove once and for all that you didn't need to pass lofty exams to make your mark.

The old jealousy rose bitter in her throat. Tall and slim, with a model's figure, Claire had the ability to look good in anything and could float through maths and science exams as if they were easy – and although she suspected Claire was Mum and Dad's favourite despite the recent estrangement, she'd come to terms with it and knew her future lay here on the red earth plains with Angel.

Leanne padded into the kitchen and after washing her face and hands thoroughly, made herself a mutton sandwich and a cup of tea which she took to their bedroom. As in Warratah, the house was laid out with a square hall, the other rooms leading from it. Their room faced north so it was cool in the heat of summer, and the muslin curtains billowed delicately from the breeze that drifted down from the hills that lay only a few miles away.

She'd stuck pictures of her favourite horses and

71

the certificates she'd won at the stock shows and gymkhanas on the wall alongside Angel's posters of the Argentine pampas. There was a postcard Claire had sent from Sydney, and the usual clutter of family snapshots, old letters and discarded books on the dresser.

Biting into her sandwich she dumped it and the tea on the dressing-table and changed her shirt. She eyed her reflection in the mirror as she brushed her short dark hair. If only she had her sister's cheekbones, she thought longingly as she puckered her lips and sucked in her cheeks. She realised how ridiculous she was being and giggled. There was no doubt about it, she would never make the cover of Vogue even if Angel did think she was gorgeous.

Her gaze fell on the photograph Aunt Aurelia had taken four years ago. It was a good family photograph, and because there were so few of them around, Leanne had kept it. It had been taken the day Claire left for Sydney and her first semester at university. Claire looked cool and sophisticated in her cheesecloth mini dress and buckled shoes – exotic against the drab uniform of jeans and shirts the rest of the family were wearing. Mum was smiling, her light brown hair falling in her eyes as usual, and Dad was handsome and obviously ill at ease in front of a camera.

Leanne grew thoughtful as she picked up the snapshot and studied it more carefully. Perhaps it hadn't been such a good photo after all. Mum's smile seemed forced, Dad actually looked shifty and Claire... Claire looked as if she'd been crying. At the time, Leanne had put it down to the fact she was leaving home – but with the benefit of hindsight she now wondered if there was something more.

She replaced the photograph on the dressing-table and finished her sandwich. Claire had been in a strange mood that day she remembered. It had started the night before when she'd come back from Jarrah and asked about the gravestone. Mum had given some vague explanation, Dad had been unusually sharp with her and after a heated exchange the subject was dropped. Yet there had been a tension in the house and it hadn't been dispelled the next day. In fact the estrangement had begun that day and had lasted for five years. Now Claire was coming home again, and she had a nasty feeling things were about to change.

Leanne stared out of the window, but she didn't see the waving grass or hear the chortling kookaburras – she saw only the gravestone that had been set apart from the others. Its very isolation was a mystery, but the fact it bore the family name and was on Jarrah was something that had never been fully explained, and she too was curious to know why. Yet the estrangement it had caused between her sister and her parents was a warning not to broach the subject. Curiosity was all very well, but it wasn't worth falling out over and she had too much to lose.

Snapping from her thoughts she realised she'd already wasted enough time on Claire, and her sister was perfectly capable of standing up for herself. This enforced homecoming might clear the air a little, but Leanne had become used to having her parents' undivided attention and hoped Claire would keep her visit short.

Leanne opened the bottom drawer of her dresser and pulled out the roll of drawings which she carried back into the kitchen. With them spread over the table and held down by saucepans, she leaned on her elbows and looked at the future – a future she didn't dare reveal to her parents or Angel until Jarrah was truly her own. A dream she'd nurtured ever since she'd come to realise she and Jarrah were made for each other.

The jarring ring of the telephone broke her concentration and she snatched it up. 'Jarrah Downs,' she said sharply.

'This is Angel.' He pronounced it the Spanish way with a soft 'g' despite the fact he was second generation Argentine-Australian.

Leanne felt her knees go as the warm, honeyed voice poured into her ear. Angel Carrera was the best looking man alive and she still couldn't believe he was her husband. She sat down and nestled the receiver to her ear. 'G'day, Angel.' Her voice was husky with desire. 'What can I do for you?'

'There are many things,' he purred down the line. 'Getting you into bed for one. But unfortunately for now I have to be practical.' His tone became business-like. 'Have they finished the muster yet, Leanne? I need to check the stock before they're trucked to Brisbane and my schedule's getting very full.'

'Lucky stock,' she said dreamily. Leanne closed her eyes and wished he had the time to put her

74

on his schedule. He'd been gone for almost two weeks and she was in need of being checked over herself. 'They're not back yet but I expect them any day. Mum's already arranged for our company trucks to be on stand-by at the end of next week.'

'I'll pencil you in for next Wednesday then.'

His voice was mesmerising, the hidden agenda behind the words all too clear and Leanne gave a tremulous sigh. 'Can't you make it any sooner?' she murmured.

His soft groan came down the line. 'I would my love, but you know how it is at this time of year. Everyone wants to get their stock to market.'

'How's it going over there in Cloncurry?' She didn't really care, she just wanted to keep him talking so she could hear his voice. It had been lonely without him.

'Good,' he said, distracted somewhat by the interruption of a colleague. 'Must go. Got a thousand things to do. Catch you later.'

The line went dead and Leanne slowly replaced the receiver. Angel Carrera had olive skin and black, black eyes that seemed to smoulder right through her. He was thirty – but what did a seven year age gap matter when he was her perfect man? From the moment they had met the fireworks began. Passionate and opinionated, their personalities clashed at every turn, but their fiery relationship sparked so hotly they couldn't bear to be parted.

Leanne sighed as she rolled up the plans and returned them to their hiding place. Perfect he might be, but his work meant he was away from her at long stretches of time, and although she trusted him, she wondered how many other women found him irresistible. Wondered if he'd ever been tempted by women prettier than her.

Her thoughts in turmoil, she decided to leave the accounts until tonight. What she needed to do now was go for a long ride and use up some of her excess energy. It was Sunday. She had two days and three nights to prepare for his home-coming. For like Jarrah Downs, Angel Carrera belonged to her and she had no intentions of losing him.

Ellie was sick of her own company. It had been almost two weeks since the men had left for the annual muster and she was going stir crazy. The house was cleaner than ever, the windows polished, screens re-meshed, even the verandah railings repaired. She'd been meaning to do that particular job for ages and had finally decided it was no good waiting any longer. After her usual chores of mucking out stables, feeding chooks and pigs and checking over the new litter of puppies in the kennels, she'd spent the previous day oiling the saddles and harness in the tack room and cleaning the horse-brasses they used for the dray when they went to shows. Yet she remained uneasy, her thoughts always returning to Claire's imminent arrival and the effect it would have on them all.

With the morning chores over, she climbed the steps and slammed through the screen door. The last of Claire's infrequent letters was on the kitchen table. She knew what it said for she'd read it a dozen times – but it was the things Claire hadn't said that bothered her the most. The letter was polite and distant, with a maturity and forthright approach to her enforced home-coming that heralded trouble for all of them.

Ellie sat down in the battered chair and stared at the blackened beam above the new oven. 'What the hell am I going to do?' she murmured. She didn't know how long she'd sat there, but as the mellow chime of the grandfather clock in the hall brought her back to the present, she realised she couldn't face this alone. She would have to go to the main homestead and speak to Aurelia.

Having showered and changed into a cotton dress, Ellie brushed her thick brown hair and left it loose to swing above her shoulders. She'd soon have to start colouring it, she thought as she spotted yet another lurking grey hair. But what the hell? There were far more important things to think about than grey hair and another birthday. She added a dash of defiant red lipstick, a spray of perfume, picked up her bag and slipped her feet into sandals. With sunglasses perched on her nose and a floppy hat rammed on her head she ran down the steps into the yard.

Having told the mechanic where she was going, she drove the utility out from behind the tool shed, checked it had enough petrol and headed towards the first of the five gates that separated the two Warratah homesteads. Aurelia had instigated this home-coming, it was only fair she should share the burden. And this wouldn't be the first time she'd helped Ellie out of a tight situation.

The young Ellie felt at odds with life on War-ratah, for despite the warm reception from Aurelia and the burgeoning friendship with the two boys, she remained uneasy in her mother's company. Aurelia had been kindness itself, despite her gruff manner and overbearing heartiness and had quickly cleared her younger sister out of the only spare room and made it more welcoming for Ellie. Yet there were only two ways of avoiding her mother: hiding in this bedroom, or spending hours with Charlie and Joe out on the plains as they repaired fences and cleared carcasses from the billabongs. She usually chose the latter, but the drought had killed a great many of Aurelia's cattle, and the sight of crows pecking and flapping over the bodies made her feel ill. The nightmares were all too frequent, the reminder of the crows circling above her dead father still too raw.

She had returned from her latest trip with the boys the night before, now she sat on the patchwork quilt and leaned against the iron bed-head as she studied the brass fittings. There was just too much to contend with, she thought wearily. She'd answered all the questions Alicia had fired at her, born the brunt of her histrionics and stood up for Dad when the sniping got too much. With the nightmares plaguing her after the long days in the saddle and the endless arguments she was exhausted.

There had been little time to mourn Dad. Even less to take in everything that had happened since they had first been abandoned by Alicia in

Sydney. It was as if time had lost all meaning. The last few years merely moments she'd dreamed about, lost in the void of grinding poverty and the weary miles they'd traipsed to get here.

She turned towards the window and climbed on the wide ledge Aurelia had covered in thick, squashy cushions. It gave her a perfect view of the yard and she could see the boys emerge from the bunkhouse, chatting to the other men as they crossed to the cookhouse. Smoke rose from the chimney and she knew the high rafters would soon be ringing with the sound of boot heels, clashing crockery and men's voices. The earthy smell of horses and cattle would intertwine with the heady scent of frying steak and eggs and the heat would have the windows running with condensation.

Her gaze trawled home yard, across the cattle pens to the carpenter's shed, past the tack room and forge to the tool shed and grain store. A flock of pink breasted gallahs swooped from their perch in the pepper trees and soared in a glorious cloud above the paddock where the stock horses cropped beneath wilting gums. Kookaburras chortled and the rolling pipe of the magpies down by the creek was the sweetest sound she'd ever heard.

Ellie turned from the window and sighed. This home was in such contrast to the ones she'd had over the past five years that she felt out of place – adrift amongst unfamiliar surroundings despite her aunt's kindness and the splendour of it all.

The Domain had come as a shock after the

79

pleasant house in Surrey Hills with its small back garden and neat facade. The makeshift tents and humpies were rife with rats, the lack of food and decent clothing something she'd had to take in her stride along with the stench and grime of poverty. Dad had tried his best, but she'd known he was out of his depth and giving in to despair. Ellie had quickly become streetwise. She learned to steal from unwary shopkeepers and rummage in the bins behind the fancy restaurants that were still open in the city centre. They had survived on hand-outs and soup kitchens, sharing liceridden blankets in the Salvation Army hostels, garnering warmth from the hundreds of bodies pressed tightly together on bare floorboards when the winter took hold.

Life on the road after that had been far more pleasant despite the constant hunger. And even though they'd often slept in ditches and in the hollow boles of trees, they had finally felt in charge of their destiny as they'd headed for Warratah. Life might have been tough, their surroundings harsh, but it had brought them closer than ever – their reliance on one another forging a tight bond.

Ellie smeared back the tears as she rested her cheek against the cool window pane. Dad had found a pride in himself again as he learned to ride and to work alongside the tough men who lived out here. He'd come to terms with losing everything and was starting to look forward to coming here and beginning again. Fate was cruel.

She sniffed and looked out of the window

again. Clipper was growing fat and sleek and the old grey seemed to have taken on a new lease of life now he didn't have to work any more. If only she could feel as settled, she thought sadly. If only I didn't feel trapped between Mum and Aunt Aurelia – if only I didn't miss Dad so much.

A sharp rap on the door was followed swiftly by Alicia. 'So this is where you're hiding,' she said brightly. 'I thought it was time you got out of those disgraceful old dungarees and tried being Mummy's little girl again.' She deposited a pile of frothy dresses on the bed. 'I wasn't sure what size you were, so I brought a selection with me from New York.'

Ellie eyed the frills and ribbons, the white collars and daisy prints with disinterest. 'I'm nearly fourteen,' she said coldly. 'They're meant for kids.'

Alicia made the bed dip as she perched on the counterpane and lit a cigarette. 'You can't dress like that for ever,' she said firmly. 'It's time you forgot your life on the road and looked to the future.' She blew a stream of smoke to the ceiling as she patted her peroxided hair. 'A future where you'll wear dresses and go to parties, not muck about in the stables with ignorant natives and sleep out in fields with itinerant drovers.'

Ellie looked at the chiselled features and marvelled that she felt nothing for this woman. There had been a time when she'd cried herself to sleep wanting her mother, needing her there in the long, lonely nights following her abrupt departure. Yet Alicia had never materialised, and as the months turned into years, the memory of

81

her had faded and now she was a stranger. 'Not much chance of parties out here,' she said finally. 'This lot would only go to waste.'

'That's what I've come to talk to you about,' said Alicia who appeared unfazed at Ellie's abrupt manner. 'We aren't staying. I've made arrangements for Jack Withers to fly us up to Darwin on his mail plane.'

'Darwin?' Ellie's heart hammered as fear swept through her. 'What's in Darwin?'

'A way out of this godforsaken place,' said Alicia with feeling. 'I've booked us on a ship to England.'

Ellie slid off the window-seat and stood before her. 'I don't want to go to England,' she said firmly. 'I belong here.'

It was as if Alicia hadn't heard. 'We'll stay with your grandparents for a while; there's a very good school down in Sussex where they can knock that ghastly colonial whine from your accent.' She finished her cigarette and with blatant disregard for the geraniums, stubbed it out in a flower pot. 'You'll soon forget all this nonsense, and wonder why you ever wanted to stay here. And if you're a good girl, I'll even buy you a pony.'

Ellie balled her fists. The temptation to slap that cold, over made-up face so great she was almost vibrating. 'I'm not going to England. I'm not going to some fancy school. And I'm *not* changing the way I talk,' she said through gritted teeth. 'As for bribing me, you can save your money. I got a pony already.'

Alicia gave one of her tinkling laughs that made Ellie shudder. 'I'd hardly call that bag of bones a pony, darling,' she drawled. 'More suitable for the glue factory. Wait until you see the Arabians my father has at stud – you'll soon change your mind.'

Ellie's rage was electric, freezing her to the floor, making it impossible to find the right words to express her loathing and her fear. And she was fearful, for her mother seemed determined and although she was soon to be fourteen – in the eyes of the law she was still only a kid. A kid with no voice. A kid whose future was held in an adult's hand. 'I won't go,' she said with icy determination. 'You can't make me.'

Alicia stood and smoothed her skirt. 'I can and will,' she said calmly. 'It's time you had a decent education and learned some manners. Your father meant well, but he had no idea of how to raise a daughter and it's my duty to put things right.'

'Don't you dare blame Dad,' Ellie snarled. 'He done what he thought best, and I bet he never thought of it as a *duty*.' She took a trembling breath. 'You can stick your fancy school and your bloody horses. I ain't going.'

'That's enough,' Alicia said coldly. 'I will not have this rudeness.'

Ellie put her hands on her hips. 'I'll speak to you any way I like,' she retorted. 'You shot through and left me and Dad so you could marry your Texan. You never cared what happened to either of us – so why should I do what you want just because you're divorced and on the lookout for another sucker? I'm not leaving here. I don't want to. I don't love you. And you're the last person on earth to tell me what to bloody do.'

She was trembling as she gathered up the dresses and flung them to the floor. 'And you can take those and give them to someone else,' she stormed.

'You ungrateful guttersnipe,' spat Alicia. 'How dare you.' The slap came from nowhere, cracking against Ellie's cheek, stunning her to silence. 'You're coming to England and that's final. A dose of boarding school will hopefully teach you some manners, and if that doesn't work a touch of the strap might not come amiss.' Alicia's tone was as cold as her blue eyes.

'I can hear you in the yard,' said the calm voice from the doorway. 'Are you bullying that child again, Alicia?'

'Get out, Aurelia. This has nothing to do with you,' snapped Alicia.

Aurelia moved into the room and eyed the situation. 'I think it does,' she said calmly. 'You've upset my niece, and I don't agree with hitting her just because she doesn't see things as you do. This is a peaceful place, and I aim to keep it that way, so I suggest you clear off and cool down.'

Ellie was trembling with rage. She could still feel the sting of Alicia's slap, but it only confirmed her dislike for the woman who insisted upon calling herself 'mother'.

'Mind your own damn business, Aurelia.' Alicia scooped up the discarded clothes. 'She's my child and I'll deal with her in any way I want.'

'Not in my house,' Aurelia fired back.

The demeanour was calm again, the face a mask beneath the make-up. 'We won't be bothering you for much longer,' she said coldly. 'Jack's flying us up to Darwin the day after tomorrow. The boat leaves for England next week.'

'You're more of a fool than I thought,' snapped Aurelia. 'Haven't you read the papers or taken in any of the Home Service broadcasts? There's civil war in Europe.'

'Rubbish,' said Alicia as she folded the dresses. 'It's Spain in uproar, not Berkshire.'

'Spain won't be the last of it,' warned Aurelia. 'Mark my words Alicia. If you insist upon disregarding Ellie's wishes I'll get a court order to stop you.'

'I'd like to see you try,' she sneered. 'Where are you going to get a lawyer out here?'

'At the end of a telephone line.' Aurelia folded her arms and returned glare for glare.

'No lawyer worth his salt would give you custody over me. I'm her mother.'

'You lost the right to call yourself that a long time ago,' said Aurelia firmly. 'Have you stopped to think what Ellie wants? Or is your ego so vast it hasn't occurred to you she might be happier without you?'

Ellie was mesmerised as they towered over her, deep in their own conflict. She felt her spirits lighten as Aurelia fought her corner – at last she had a voice.

Ellie's thoughts returned to the present as she brought the utility to a halt and climbed out to shut the final gate. The old homestead that had stood on Warratah for almost a century was now in sight, and as she stood there in the sibilant heat she gazed at the sway-backed roof and the cascade of white jarrah blossom that threatened to smother it. She was almost the same age as Aurelia was when they'd first met. Yet those long ago days were suddenly not so far away, and it was as if she was replaying those childhood scenes – scenes that were to change her life for ever.

She hadn't been at the homestead the day of the planned flight to Darwin, but had made her escape very early in the morning to accompany Joe and Charlie out to Six Mile Creek. Aurelia had told her later what had happened.

The sisters were squared up. Alicia's blue eyes were furious, her expression grim. 'Tell me where she is,' she demanded.

'I can't do that,' Aurelia said flatly. 'Elspeth had no wish to go with you, and after what I've seen, I can't blame her.'

Alicia lit a cigarette and snapped the gold lighter. 'Elspeth's my daughter, and if I want to take her to England you can't stop me.'

'I can,' retorted Alicia. 'I phoned my solicitor the night we had this same argument and Jack's bringing the papers with him. The courts have given me full custodial rights to Elspeth until she's twenty-one.'

Alicia paled beneath the powder, making her lipstick garish, the rouge an angry streak against the icy cheek. 'You did what?' she breathed. Then she shook her head. 'You're bluffing. The courts take months to decide anything.'

'Not when a child is at risk,' said Aurelia firmly.

'Elspeth's an Australian. The courts have no wish to see her forced to go to England with a mother who has already abandoned her once. Your history of divorce and erratic behaviour has only enforced their opinion that you aren't a fit mother.' Aurelia sighed. 'I see their point, Alicia, and if you'd stop to think you'd realise I'm right.'

'Never.' Alicia smoked her cigarette with fierce intensity.

'Be honest for once. You don't really want Elspeth. You just like the idea of being the glamorous mother of a tragic waif.'

'That remark's unfair. I demand you take it back.'

Aurelia carried on as if she hadn't spoken. 'Ellie's not a puppet you can dress in frills and lace who'll let you pull the strings. She won't allow you to ignore or sideline her when you've run out of patience. She's too strong a character, and there have been too many years of growing up without you for you to influence her now.'

'I think I know my own daughter,' began Alicia.

'No you don't,' her sister fired back. 'You'll find she'll be an encumbrance – a nuisance during school holidays when you'd rather be socialising. You're not offering her a proper home where she can blossom and become the woman she was meant to be, but life in a dreary boarding school with holidays spent in the company of elderly grandparents.'

Alicia turned to face her, the glimmer of understanding softening her expression.

Aurelia pressed her point. 'Do you remember how much we hated boarding school? How do

87

you think Elspeth will fare in such an alien world? She's Australian, with an Australian pride that will make her stand out far more than her accent. She'll have no connections, no friends, no one to turn to when homesickness becomes overwhelming. She's used to freedom, to a life on the move – putting her in that place will kill her spirit.'

'It might make a lady of her,' retorted Alicia.

'It might,' Aurelia conceded. 'But she'd be happier finding her way here where she belongs.' She waved a hand to encompass the land that stretched beyond the eye in every direction. 'She's a part of all this, Alicia – the long trek from Sydney has merely endorsed that – made the tie to the land stronger than perhaps even she suspects.'

'But she needs me,' insisted Alicia as she stubbed out the half smoked cigarette.

Aurelia shook her head, sorry for this spoiled, selfish woman who would never see beyond her own needs. 'You've been away too long, Alicia,' she said softly. 'She's grown up without you.' She put her sturdy arm around the slender shoulders and felt her tremble. Alicia did care what happened to Elspeth, she realised. Yet she wasn't able to sacrifice her way of life for her. 'Before you go I'd like you to grant Elspeth one thing,' she said with a gentleness that belied her steely determination.

'What's that?' The face was still pale beneath the makeup, the smile tremulous.

'The freedom to choose. It's a rare gift, Alicia. And only you can give it to her.'

The eyes were bright between the false eye-lashes, the scarlet lip caught between pearly teeth as Alicia fought to maintain control. She turned away, her fists bunched on the verandah railings as she watched the small aircraft land on the dirt runway.

Aurelia felt the familiar warmth run through her as Jack Withers loped from the plane and across the yard. He was a good looking man she noted not for the first time. Not classically handsome, in fact some might even have said he was ugly with those irregular features. Yet there was a vitality in that lean frame and intelligent face. Something dangerously attractive in the humorous eyes and sensuous mouth. And as she watched his approach his gaze held her, the glint of laughter drawing them further into conspiracy.

She pulled her thoughts together and took the papers he'd brought. There could never be anything between them and she had no intentions of adding to the gossip that flowed unceasingly over the two-way radio. At fifty she was far too old and set in her ways to have her head turned by a rogue with laughing eyes.

Having swiftly read the papers, she handed them to her sister. Alicia scanned the closely typed print with myopic intensity – she was too vain to admit she needed glasses. 'Do I have to sign anything?' she asked with a distinct lack of her usual verve.

Aurelia silently pointed to the appropriate place and Alicia signed it with a flourish. 'There,' she sighed as a single teardrop glistened on her lashes. 'Elspeth's in your hands now. Take care of her, and tell her I'll always be thinking of her.'

Aurelia nodded. It had been quite a performance. Judged so finely she wasn't sure if it was play-acting or real. But to give her sister her due she genuinely seemed to believe she'd always think of her daughter. 'She's got a home here for as long as she wants it,' she said through a constricted throat.

She watched the propellers begin to turn and as the little plane trundled down the rough landing strip Aurelia knew that for Ellie's sake it was right for Alicia to leave. Perhaps one day Alicia would realise what she'd lost.

Despite the flat tyre, Claire had made good time since leaving Sydney five days before. The van rattled and complained as it sped north and her thoughts drifted over the past five years and the man whom she'd thought she'd loved. He'd got what he wanted, then he'd dumped her for someone else. In a way, she admitted, he'd done her a favour. For once dumped, Claire had focused more intensely on her work and the results were better than even she could have envisaged.

She grinned as she thought of Aunt Aurelia's gruff wisdom. 'Men are all right in their place, dear,' she'd said. 'Just as long as you show them where that place is. You get one life – live it for yourself, not through a man.' Aurelia was a woman with ideas way before her time, and although Claire didn't know if she agreed wholeheartedly with her, she admired the old girl and wouldn't have dreamed of arguing. Yet despite her yearning for equality and a career, Claire knew that deep down she wanted a husband and children one day, and a marriage as strong and loving as that of her parents.

The dusty stretch of bitumen wound endlessly through the heart of outback Queensland, the view in the wing mirror the same as through the windscreen. Yellow grass rippled in the hot wind beneath an endless blue sky, slashes of dark red appeared at the roadside where the earth met the tarmac and lone trees stood sentinel on deserted plains. The heat shimmered on the horizon and wedge-tailed eagles hovered on the thermals above giant termite mounds and clumps of silver spinifex. Compared to the Blue Mountains it was stark and arid – yet Claire had to admit it had its own majesty, its own timeless beauty.

Claire's thoughts turned to her mother. She'd heard the story many times, but it was only now as she was driving effortlessly along the same road that she realised the full extent of her mother's brave achievement. She tried to imagine how it must have felt to be a child, alone and afraid – with her father's isolated grave far behind her and endless miles still to travel. She could almost see her now in the heat haze. A little girl in oversized dungarees that drooped to the toes of her boots, the battered bush hat low over her ragged hair as she squinted into the sun and wondered if she would ever reach her destination.

Claire lit a cigarette and leaned an elbow out of the window as the radio blasted out the Beach Boys between the static. Not much chance of surf

91

out here she thought wryly. Even the wind was hot, the sun scorching her skin, the sweat making her shirt stick to the leather seat. She finally pulled over to the side of the road. It was time to have a drink and stretch her legs.

With the engine off, the silence closed in. The sibilant chatter of a myriad number of insects enhanced that silence and, as Claire stepped from the van, she felt the full force of the outback's grandeur. There were no houses, no barns, not even a fence post or telegraph pole to be seen. The sound of her sandals on the grit seemed loud, the ticking of the cooling engine almost like a clock on countdown.

Claire shivered despite the furnace blast of the breeze. In a few hours she would see the first of Warratah's ninety-five thousand acres. In less than a day she would begin the quest for truth – and in a sudden flash of insight she realised that quest could ultimately destroy everything she had ever known.

Aurelia adjusted her monocle and with a snort of impatience tried to stir life into the old range. The damn thing was playing up again and the kitchen was chilled. That was the problem with old age, she thought crossly as she threw the poker into a corner and snatched up a disreputable old jacket. Cold and damp got into eighty-year-old bones more easily and things like recalcitrant ranges were just another reminder of the passing years and her rapid progress into decrepitude.

With a jaundiced eye she glared around the

kitchen. Like Ellie's newer homestead it ran along the back of the house, facing north so it remained cool in the summer. Nothing much had been done in here for years, and the shelving sagged beneath the weight of numerous tins and jars. Pots and pans hung from hooks on the blackened beam over the range, fly papers dangled darkly from the ceiling and the chairs and tables were littered with old newspapers, farming catalogues and the leftovers from her last meal.

She removed a boot from a chair and sat down. To anyone else it might have looked a mess, but she knew where everything was and always refused to allow the house lubra to tidy up. It was the one room in the house that felt better when it was cluttered, for it somehow muted the voices of the past and left a veneer of life as it had once been. 'Jessie,' she shouted. 'Where are you?'

The soft rasp of bare feet crossing the hall was followed by a dark face peering around the kitchen door. 'You alonga me, missus?'

Aurelia eyed Jacky Jack's granddaughter and smiled. The girl was about sixteen and hadn't yet turned to fat like her mother. There was an elegance about the way she moved silently around the house, a pride in the tilt of her chin, yet when it came to work, Jessie was like the rest of her tribe. 'I thought I asked you to stoke the range this morning?'

'Me alonga feed chooks, missus. Do later,' she mumbled.

'You'll do it now,' she said firmly. 'And when you've finished you can make a start on the washing.' Aurelia noted the downcast eyes and the strands of straw that were caught in the tangle of ochre curls. Jessie had been messing about with that young jackaroo again – she knew the signs and just hoped she hadn't got herself pregnant. There were too many kids in the aboriginal humpies as it was – some of them questionably light skinned despite her rule against fraternising with the drovers and stock-men. But men would be men and some girls would always be willing.

She watched Jessie grapple with the range then left her to it and wandered into the hall. It was long and narrow, cutting through the centre of the house from the kitchen to the front door and verandah. Two doors on the right led to bed-rooms and the one on the left to a sitting room that ran from the front to the back of the house. The homestead was smaller than Ellie's for there had been no children until she'd come along.

Aurelia walked into the sitting room. It was a good room – always welcoming with the sun's glare diffused by the foliage of the pepper trees outside the windows, and the warmth of antique silver glinting against the richly burnished dark oak furniture. There were valuable oil paintings on the wooden walls, exquisite figurines dis-played in a Victorian cabinet and crystal vases and decanters glittering rainbows across the white painted ceiling. On the solid beam above the red brick fireplace there was an antique ormolu clock which solemnly ticked away the time in the embrace of two rather smug cherubs, and amongst the clutter of bills, postcards and letters was a brace of gold candlesticks that held the remains of ancient candles which had gathered dust and cobwebs.

She clucked with impatience and dusted them with her handkerchief. As much as she loved this glorious country, the Australians were the most infuriating people she'd ever dealt with. Their over-familiarity and lackadaisical manner was enough to try the patience of a saint, and although she willingly acknowledged sainthood wasn't her forte, she did wish the Australians would pull themselves together. A dose of boarding school and English winters in a draughty manor house would have knocked them into shape – just as it had for her.

Aurelia shook out her handkerchief and stuffed it in her pocket as she eyed the snapshot of Claire. Never one to shirk a responsibility, she wondered if perhaps she'd been mistaken in forcing the girl to come home. Yet there were things that needed sorting out before it was too late, and someone had to make the first move. Not that there was much anyone could do about any of it, she thought as she sank into a chair and reached for her pipe. The seeds of the coming disaster had been sown many years before and it was the next generation that had to reap that particularly bitter harvest.

Her pipe helped her put things into perspective and despite the doctor's advice she'd refused to give it up. Packing it with her favourite brand of tobacco she took time to light it and savour the rich fragrance which even after all these years still reminded her of the Scottish Highlands and the grouse moors where her father had taken her and Alicia shooting as young girls. In her mind's eye she could still see the verdant hills and soft heathers and the mellow stone walls of the crofters' cottages.

With the pipe smoke drifting to the ceiling, Aurelia leaned back and closed her eyes. It had come as a surprise to her when, years ago, she'd realised how much she loved it here – how much she would miss Warratah if it was ever taken from her. For there had been a time when she'd railed against the fate of being left widowed and childless to fight the elements and strange customs of a colonial outpost. Then Ellie had come along and she'd been given a second chance to reaffirm her commitment to Warratah – a commitment she'd never regretted – a commitment Ellie had taken on gladly.

'You'll set yourself alight one day,' came the voice from the doorway.

Aurelia's eyes snapped open and she hastily brushed smouldering tobacco from her jacket lapel. 'Ellie,' she said. 'I was just thinking about you.'

They kissed and Ellie plumped down in the other chair. 'Contemplating the insides of your eyelids, more like,' she teased.

Aurelia tapped the dottle into the fireplace and put the pipe in her jacket pocket. 'I wasn't asleep,' she denied vigorously. 'Just resting my eyes. I'll get Jessie to make us a cuppa.'

'You'll be lucky,' Ellie said with a laugh. 'She's over by the barn making eyes at that new boy you took on.'

Aurelia grunted with disgust, hauled herself out of the chair and stood by the fireplace. There was no point in beating about the bush, she knew Ellie's reason for coming. 'I'm surprised you've left it so long. I expected you at least two days ago,' she said baldly.

'So you've had a letter too,' murmured Ellie as she tucked her hair behind her ears. 'What did it say?'

Aurelia looked at the expressive brown eyes and the freckles that dusted Ellie's snub nose. She'd grown into a becoming woman, but Aurelia was still reminded of the ragged urchin she had once been. It was there in the narrow chin and slender frame, and in the experience behind the eyes. Poor Ellie, she thought sadly. She's been through so much – it wasn't fair she should have to go through it all again. But she had to. They both had to if things were ever to be right in this family again. 'She wants answers,' she replied finally.

Ellie's eyes were dark with pain. 'I should have told the truth from the beginning,' she murmured. 'But I thought I was doing the right thing by remaining silent and never dreamed it would turn out like this.'

'Truth has a nasty habit of forcing its way to the surface,' said Aurelia gruffly. 'Claire's an intelligent girl. She was bound to question things sooner or later.'

'So will Leanne once she realises why Claire's come home,' sighed Ellie.

Aurelia watched as Ellie pulled a pack of cigarettes from her pocket. The younger woman's hands shook as she made several attempts to

97

light one, and when she'd drawn the smoke deep into her lungs she got out of her chair and began to pace.

'Perhaps you should have a word with Leanne?' muttered Aurelia. 'I must be frank with you dear, I never liked the idea of all this secrecy, and with Christmas coming up...' She tailed off. Ellie didn't need reminding of what would happen then.

'I was trying to protect both my girls,' she replied as she stood with her back to Aurelia and stared out of the window. 'But all I've done is make things worse,' she added as she folded her arms around her waist and burst into tears.

Aurelia put her arm around her. She couldn't begin to understand the pain Ellie must be going through and there was nothing she could do but offer comfort. For Claire's imminent return had already opened a Pandora's box of memories – memories that had lain dormant for years – powerful memories that could tear this family apart.

Chapter Three

Claire's pulse raced as she turned off the highway and began the long approach to Gregory Downs that would take her on to Warratah. The road was still good, but several miles on it would become stony, with potholes and water run-offs to slow her down. The van was beginning to complain and the temperature gauge was permanently on hot. Her own fear of what was to come had given her a headache. They both needed a breather.

The broad sweep of gravel in front of the Gregory Downs Hotel was enticing and, as it was the last place to get food and petrol before she began the last leg of her journey, Claire drove in and parked next to a battered utility. She switched off the engine and leaned back. Her reluctance had grown over the last few hundred miles, now her mouth was dry and the headache pounding. She dug in her bag for an aspirin and swallowed it with a mouthful of lukewarm lemonade.

With a grimace she eyed her sweat-stained shirt and grubby shorts. They'd been clean on this morning, but with the heat and dust coming through the open window they hadn't stood a chance. Rummaging through the bags behind her seat she pulled out a long Indian cotton skirt that had been tie-dyed in purple and lavender and looked better when it was creased. It had an elasticated waist so it was easy to pull on and dispose of the shorts without showing her knickers. The shirt would have to do she thought as she looked over at the long, low building and caught a glimpse of someone peering through a window. She wasn't about to flash her assets to all and sundry even if they were meagre.

The Gregory Downs Hotel was squat and straddled the red earth beneath a canopy of shady trees. The roof was rust red, the timbers dark from age and the elements. A verandah ran the width of the front, sheltered by the usual sloping addition to the roof. The building probably hadn't changed much since the eighteen hundreds when it had been a staging post for Cobb & Co. They'd be used to people looking bedraggled, she decided. This wasn't a smart city hotel where you had to dress up to the nines to be allowed in.

Grabbing her bag she climbed out of the van and slammed the door. The heat was intense even beneath the dappled shade of the flowering red gums and the gallahs' chatter was muted as if they too were wilting. The sun glared on a utility's wing mirror and she noticed the thick red clay that clung to the tyres and the bags of tools in the flat-bed. Obviously a local, she thought fleetingly.

She slung her bag over her shoulder and swiftly plaited her hair so it fell in a single swathe to her waist. It was cooler once the weight was off her neck, and having tied it with a scrap of ribbon, she felt marginally presentable. Crossing the gravel car park she stepped onto the shaded verandah and pushed through the screen doors.

The smell of fresh coffee assailed her as she entered the general store that took up most of the reception area. She'd by-passed breakfast this morning at the hotel in Cloncurry and suddenly realised she was very hungry.

The woman behind the counter was fat and cheerful and well into middle age. Her generous curves were imprisoned in a sprigged cotton dress, the buttons down the front almost losing the battle to keep her decent. 'G'day luv,' she said, the brown eyes sweeping over her with friendly curiosity. 'Come far?'

'Sydney,' Claire replied without thinking.

'Strewth, that's a long ways,' she replied as her gaze took in the long skirt, the plait and the gold hoops in Claire's ears. 'One of them hippies, are yer? Bit off the track for Nimbin, luv.' The gaze was friendly, but openly curious, the chubby arms folded beneath the pendulous bosom as she settled in for a long gossip.

Claire knew she'd made a mistake blurting it out like that, but she'd been away too long and had forgotten the way of things out here. Now she'd be stuck in an endless round of questions, for visitors had to be few and there was nothing an outlander liked better than a good gossip. 'That coffee smells good,' she said hurriedly. 'Any chance of some breakfast?'

The expression changed suddenly to one of delighted surprise. 'I know who you are,' the woman said as she snapped her fingers. 'You're Ellie's girl – the one that went to university.' She put more strain on the buttons as she squeezed through the gap in the counter. 'Name's Lila, by

101

the way. Pleased to meet yer.'

Claire gave up all ideas of getting breakfast for at least half an hour. It was bound to happen so close to home, but right now all she really wanted to do was get some food inside her and try to prepare herself for the home-coming. Yet she had to learn to adjust to the way of things again. Had to remember the pace was slower than in Sydney and people expected to take their time over inconsequential chatter. 'Claire,' she replied and smiled. 'University's finished.'

'Your mum and dad must be very proud of you,' Lila beamed. 'Just fancy. Another vet in the family.' She gave a hearty laugh. 'Reckon that'll save a bob or two – not that it'll make much difference with all the pies your dad and mum have got their fingers into.'

'Breakfast?' asked Claire hopefully. She hated discussing the family wealth and tried to avoid it whenever possible. Tall poppies were frowned upon both here and in the city – it was a way of Australian life. You could be as successful as you liked, but you never talked about it.

'Too right. And I've got a surprise for you. Come on through.'

The plump fingers clutched her arm and Claire was almost dragged into the dining room. It was dimly cool and green from the diffused light coming through the stand of pines at the back of the hotel. There were several tables, each covered in a checked cloth that matched the curtains. Vases of plastic flowers stood beside the condiments and bottles of red sauce in the middle of each table and the walls were lined with bright

102

posters of tropical beaches. Only one table had a diner.

'Matt,' the woman called. 'There's someone here you should meet.'

Claire hitched up her shoulder bag – she had hoped to eat in peace so she could prepare herself for her arrival at Warratah, but Lila was obviously having none of it.

'Matt Derwent. Claire Pearson.' Lila stood back once the introductions were over, her hands clasped at her waist, eyes bright with some hidden agenda.

Matt Derwent was tall. All whipcord and wire, as her father might have said. He seemed to have taken on the colours of the outback and become at one with it. From the straw coloured hair and ruddy face to the ochre stained boots and moleskins, he was obviously a man at home in the outdoors. Her hand was enveloped in his large paw and she found she had to look up into his hazel eyes. It was an unusual occurrence and Claire found she rather liked the feeling of being small for once.

'G'day,' he drawled. 'Heard you were coming back.' He grinned, showing even white teeth and a cobweb of lines at the corners of his eyes.

'Matt's a vet too,' said Lila conspiratorially.

Claire struggled to contain the giggles as she and Matt exchanged looks. 'You must be new around here,' she said unsteadily. 'I don't remember meeting you out on Warratah.'

'Started last year,' he replied before turning back to their audience of one. 'Reckon we could both do with some coffee, Lila.'

'I'm on to it,' she said cheerfully as she cleared Matt's dirty plates and laid another place. 'Now you two young things must have plenty to talk about, so I'll leave you to it. Breakfast won't be long, Claire.' She bustled away and slammed through the swing doors to the kitchen.

Matt lifted a brown eyebrow. 'Young things?' he murmured with a glint of humour.

Claire giggled and sat down. 'Reckon Lila's into matchmaking,' she whispered as she pulled her cigarettes from her bag and offered him one. 'I shouldn't let it bother you.'

He blew smoke and laughed. 'Doesn't worry me,' he said. 'Quite made my day.'

She eyed him through the smoke and grinned back. 'I suppose this is where I say you don't look a day over twenty-five?'

He sipped his coffee. 'You could, but you'd be lying,' he drawled. 'I'm thirty-eight next birthday and beginning to feel it every time I get called out in the night.' With a rueful grin he stretched a long leg into the aisle. 'Knees are shot from playing Aussie rules at university, and when it's cold they creak like rusty hinges.'

Lila appeared through the swing doors and happily poured coffee as they chatted about their work. 'I knew you'd have a lot in common,' she said cheerfully. 'So nice to see you getting along.'

Claire bit the inside of her lip to stop herself from laughing, and when she caught the glint of mischief in Matt's eyes she had to look away. Matt Derwent was having a strange effect on her and she found herself being drawn to him despite having only just met him.

Breakfast duly arrived and Claire tucked into the egg and bacon with gusto as Matt drank his coffee and told her about his widely spread practice. The bacon was crisp and the eggs fried just the way she liked them, all soft in the middle so she could dip her toast. Not the healthiest of breakfasts she admitted as she finally put her knife and fork together, but it certainly filled a gap and chased away the headache.

She caught him watching her and blushed. 'I don't usually eat so quickly,' she said. 'But I was hungry.'

He shrugged. 'I don't know where you put it all,' he drawled as his hazel eyes drifted over her. 'There isn't much of you.'

'Hollow legs,' she said firmly. He smiled a slow smile and she felt her insides flip. She really shouldn't have had that second fried egg. 'So,' she said before the silence became prolonged. 'What's your speciality?'

He looked at her, the humour tugging the corners of his mouth. 'You mean apart from being called young and having breakfast with a stunning blonde?' he teased.

Claire reddened and was furious with herself. Matt was flirting and she was suddenly awkward and almost shy. This was no college boy or callow youth – this was a man who was obviously more sophisticated than she was and who'd probably got a wife tucked away somewhere. 'I meant professionally,' she said rather more sharply than she'd intended.

'Oh, that,' he said airily as he drained the last of his coffee. 'Farm animals mostly, but my main interest is horses. In fact I'm due up at Jarrah soon. Bonny's about to drop her foal.'

Claire saw this as a chance to turn the conversation. 'How's Lee getting on?' she asked, reverting to the family's habit of shortening her sister's name. There had been few letters between them during the past five years and she was curious. Perhaps now they were mature they'd get on better.

'Good. She's getting the hang of things fast. Leanne is born to it, she won't have many problems unless she tries to do too much at once.' He paused for a moment. 'Your dad did the right thing letting her learn like that. It's given her the freedom to grow up and prove she's capable of running a big station like Jarrah.'

Claire picked up her cigarettes and hitched her bag over her shoulder. The talk of Leanne had helped make up her mind on how to approach the dreaded home-coming. Now, having been thoroughly unsettled by Matt, she was eager to be on her way. 'I must be going,' she said lightly. 'They're expecting me home today and I don't want to get caught on the road after dark. A mob of roos nearly wrote the van off before and the last thing I need at the moment is more garage bills.' She was babbling and knew it. So did Matt if the look in his eyes was anything to go by.

They stood and shook hands. 'Catch you later then,' he said softly.

Claire felt the warm strength in his fingers as he held her hand for a fraction longer than necessary and knew they would meet again. Matt was the sort of man who would seek her out, and she wasn't quite sure how she felt about that. For he was a danger – a complication she just didn't need right now.

It was going to be a long night. Bonny had waxed up two weeks ago, now the milk was dripping from her udders. Her eleven month gestation was up. She had scraped her bed and started sweating this afternoon and after a quick examination Leanne realised the muscles either side of her tail had already relaxed in preparation for the birth. There was no way of knowing how long the mare would be in labour, but Leanne suspected it would happen some time during the night and had called the vet. She was quite capable of delivering the foal, but had learned from bitter experience it was better to have professional help close by in case of emergencies – for the distance the vet had to travel was too far for him to get here quickly.

She left the restless mare with one of the native jackaroos who was a natural wizard with horses, and after chatting to a couple of men who were sitting in the warm evening smoking their cigarettes and yarning over beers she went into the homestead and turned on the lights. She had a couple of hours before she had to check on Bonny again and it was the perfect time to sort out her clothes and decide what to wear for Angel's return next week.

Her wardrobe was sparse, filled with working clothes and only one or two dresses. Boots lined the floor and the single pair of strappy, high-heeled sandals looked impossibly delicate beside them. Having tried everything on, she decided she looked best in moleskins with the emerald green shirt that enhanced the colour of her eyes. A dress was too much, the old jeans too casual and unflattering.

She washed her hair and brushed it until it shone blue-black in the electric light, and then added a touch of make-up to her eyes and mouth. Tiny gold studs glinted in her ears and a thin gold chain glittered at her tanned throat. There was nothing she could do about her hands she thought ruefully as she looked at the short square nails that were, as usual, ingrained with grime from the stables. The skin was darkly tanned and the palms were rough from riding without gloves and grubbing about in the vegetable plot. She regarded the result in the mirror with a critical eye. Apart from her hands, she scrubbed up pretty well. 'Angel Carrera you'd better watch out,' she murmured. 'You won't stand a chance of sleeping for at least a week.'

'Sounds ominous.'

Leanne spun round. She'd been so wrapped up in her dreams she hadn't heard anyone come in. 'Claire,' she gasped. 'What are you doing here?'

They stood in awkward silence for a long moment before they tentatively embraced.

Claire's smile was uncertain as they stepped away from each other. 'I thought I was expected?'

'You are. You were,' Leanne stuttered as she tried to put her thoughts in order. Damn Claire for turning up like this. 'But we thought you'd be going to Warratah.'

'Couldn't face it,' said Claire as she sank on to the bed and lay back on the pillows with one slender arm shielding her eyes from the glare of the light bulb. 'It's been one hell of a drive and I'm too knackered to get into the family thing tonight.' She eyed her sister. 'You don't mind do you, Lee? I'm not interrupting anything am I?'

'Of course not,' replied Leanne as she hurriedly changed back into her old jeans and a sweatshirt. 'Angel's away on government business, but I might be out most of the night sitting with Bonny. Reckon she's due to drop her foal any minute.'

'I didn't realise earrings and make-up were necessary for foaling,' her sister teased.

Leanne shrugged. She was embarrassed to be caught on the hop and put out by the elegant beauty who lay on her bed as if she owned it. 'I just wanted to see how I'd look in something other than this lot,' she said vaguely as she ran her capable hands down the denim.

Claire laughed, climbed off the bed and began to sift through the clutter on Leanne's dressing-table. She picked up a lipstick, tried it, grimaced and wiped it off. 'You don't fool me, little sister,' she said fondly as she tested a perfume on her wrist. 'Angel's obviously due home, either that or you've got a secret lover.'

Leanne blushed furiously. 'We've only been married a few months,' she snapped. 'We might be country hicks, but we do have morals out here.' She snatched the expensive perfume away and hid it in a drawer. She hated it when Claire went through her things.

109

Claire raised an eyebrow. 'Touchy,' she said. 'I see things haven't changed much.'

It was not an auspicious beginning. Leanne decided to change tack. 'Have you eaten? I've got some mutton stew. It's not brilliant, but it doesn't taste too bad.'

Claire eyed her younger sister. 'Did you make it?'

'Yes,' she replied defensively. 'My cooking's a lot better since you were last home.' She led the way into the kitchen, ladled out some of the stew and sliced into the freshly made bread. 'I even do bread now,' she added with asperity.

Claire swung her long plait back over her shoulder and sat at the kitchen table. 'Good on you,' she replied as she tasted the stew and added salt and pepper. 'This isn't bad,' she murmured in surprise.

Leanne felt the heat rise in her face as she dipped her head and concentrated on her meal. 'Don't patronise me, Claire,' she warned evenly.

Claire put down her knife and fork. 'Fair go, Lee. What's biting you? You haven't had a decent word to say to me since I arrived.'

Leanne folded her arms, the meal forgotten. 'Why have you come back?' she demanded. 'There's nothing here for you.'

There was a protracted silence as the two sisters eyed one another. 'Aurelia gave me no choice,' Claire said finally. 'Don't worry, Lee. I'm not about to encroach on your life any more than I have to.'

Leanne felt a twinge of unease. Perhaps she had been a little harsh, but Leanne disliked being on

110

the defensive and saw no reason why she should explain herself or her almost manic fear that Claire's return would in some way endanger everything she held dear. 'Sorry.' Her tone was grudging. 'It's been a long day, and with Bonny about to drop her foal it's going to be a long night. You caught me on the hop.'

Claire smiled and seemed to accept her apology. 'Is Matt Derwent coming over tonight to see to Bonny?' she asked cheerfully.

Leanne nodded. 'How do you know Matt?'

Claire stacked the plates and put them to one side. 'I met him this morning,' she said casually. 'I rather liked him.'

'He's a good ten years older than you, I reckon,' retorted Leanne. 'I'll grant you he's good with horses, but he's not your type.'

Claire's blue eyes were steady, but her mouth twitched with a smile. 'And what is my type, exactly?'

'City slicker,' she replied. 'Wealthy and flash with his own practice and a big house over-looking the harbour where he keeps his speed boat.'

Claire's laugh held a note of bitterness. 'We've been apart too long if you think that,' she retorted. 'Money isn't everything, Lee, and we've both been around men for too many years not to know that the packaging doesn't always live up to the contents.' She smiled. 'I don't know how we got into this. I only met the man this morning. It isn't as if I'm about to marry him!'

Leanne finished her cigarette and began to chew thoughtfully on the last piece of crusty

111

bread as she studied her sister properly for the first time. Claire looked tired, but then who wouldn't after driving several thousand miles in less than a week? Yet her usually fair skin was lightly tanned and she looked wonderfully chic in the bright coloured minidress that showed off her endless bloody legs. She was glad Angel wasn't due home yet. His hot-blooded Latin machismo meant he fully appreciated beautiful women and she didn't fancy being once again in Claire's shadow. She'd suffered that ignominy all through her teenage years.

It was only when Claire lifted her bright blue gaze from the table that Leanne realised with a jolt of unease that her sister was more than tired. The shadows in her eyes were almost haunted.

Matt Derwent flew through the darkness towards Jarrah Downs. He didn't mind night flying, in fact he enjoyed it. There was a sense of peace up here amongst the stars, a tranquillity he'd rarely found on *terra firma* except in rare moments when he went bush walking or for long rides. His life was hectic, but he didn't mind that either, for it had helped him get over Laura's death and gave him something to cling to when the memories refused to leave him alone.

He adjusted the controls. The little plane almost flew itself, such was the wonder of modern mechanics, and all he had to do was aim it in the right direction and look for the flares that marked the runway down below. Staring out at the galaxy of stars he thought of the Aboriginal belief that each dead soul had to make their way through the jaws of Bigaroo, the giant snake, to the Land of Perfection. From there they were given a glimpse of the world as it once was and how it would be before they ascended to a wondrous kingdom in the sky. Each soul became a star, glittering in the great swathe that white man called the Milky Way.

His smile was tinged with sadness. It was a good story, told to him by an old tribesman shortly before the cancer killed Laura. It had brought some comfort to him in those early days when he'd been alone in their rambling house, haunted by her memory and thoughts of their short time together. For to believe she watched over him and that he could look up and see her shining brightly in the firmament had made her seem less distant.

Matt rubbed his hands through his hair and scrubbed his face. It was only a fairy story told to children to still their fears at night – a gentle and rather sweet way of explaining what happened when a loved one was sung back to the earth. Yet there was a great deal of wisdom in those old legends, and he for one liked to think that maybe the Aboriginals had got it right and Laura was one of those twinkling stars. She'd always loved diamonds.

The distant glow of twin rows of oil pots brought his thoughts sharply back to the matter in hand. Jarrah was up ahead and he had a plane to land.

As the little plane touched down and bounced along the dirt runway, he wondered idly what Claire was doing and whether he would see her tonight. Then he remembered she'd said she was going to Warratah and was surprised at how much this disappointed him. Claire was an unpretentious girl despite her wealthy upbringing. She also had a great sense of fun and he'd enjoyed their breakfast together. Yet he wondered if she even realised how beautiful she'd looked this morning, with her hippy clothes and her gypsy plait and earrings.

His smile was tinged with sadness as he taxied along the runway and drew to a halt by the railings that enclosed home yard and the stables. Finally, he must be over mourning Laura, for until now he'd not looked at another woman or even contemplated starting again.

'Trust me to fancy the one woman that's way out of my league,' he muttered as he collected his bag of equipment. 'She's too young, too gorgeous and far too rich for you, you old bludger. So you'd better forget it and keep your mind on your bloody work.'

'Talking to yourself?' Leanne appeared out of the darkness, hands thrust into the pockets of her jeans, a thick sweater drooping almost to her knees.

'It's something we old blokes do now and again,' he retorted. He noticed she'd put lipstick on and that her hair was freshly washed and gleaming in the light of the stable yard. Leanne was beautiful, but she wasn't a patch on her sister. He became impatient with his thoughts. Whatever was the matter with him? Both sisters were almost young enough to be his daughters, he reminded himself sharply. 'How's Bonny?' His tone was gruff.

114

'Working at it. The amnion sac is already showing and she'll go down any minute. I've left Claire with her.'

Matt felt his pulse quicken and the colour rise up his neck and into his face. Luckily for him, Leanne was busy and hadn't noticed. 'Let's get on then,' he said briskly.

The stable was lit by kerosine lamps, the shadows deep in the corners beneath the heavy beams. Inquisitive heads appeared over the adjoining doors and he stroked the velvet noses as he passed by. The scent of manure and straw mixed with the softer tang of the leather bridles that hung from a nail on the wall was familiar and welcoming. The warmth a boon after the sharp wind that blew down from the hills.

Matt glanced around. There was no sign of Claire, but he could hear her soft voice as she talked to the mare in the strange silence that always accompanied a foaling. Unlike human labour the mare was stoic throughout and rarely made a fuss. Stripping off his jacket he rolled up his sleeves and washed his hands and arms in the bucket of hot soapy water Leanne had prepared for him.

It was only when he stepped into the stall that he saw her. The mare was down, her legs tucked beneath her and Claire was gently easing her hand into the birth canal to check the foal's nose was lying along the delicate, soft hoofs. Then, as he watched, the mare rolled on her side and stretched out her legs and began to strain.

'G'day,' Claire said as she glanced over her shoulder. 'You want to take over now?'

Matt shook his head and folded his arms. 'You seem to know what you're doing,' he replied.

With calm authority Claire grasped the hoofs and began to gently pull down. It was important to get the foal's chest over the pelvic rim because it was compressing the umbilicus. The foal took his first breath and moved his front legs, but his hind quarters were still in the birth canal and this kept the mare on her side. One kick from those tiny hoofs and he could detach the cord and start to bleed. Claire pinched the cord and swabbed it with antiseptic as the foal finally slithered into the fresh straw. 'You've got a colt,' she said.

Matt felt like a spare wheel in a tyre factory, but he didn't mind. It was interesting to see Claire at work, and he was fascinated by the different aspects of her character – one minute the giggling conspirator, the next the capable vet.

The mare began licking her foal, cleaning him up, stimulating him into getting on to his feet. Then she stood up, the amnion sac still attached. She nuzzled the foal then decided she wanted some breakfast after all her hard work and began to crop at the fresh straw Leanne had put down earlier.

Claire stood back and washed her hands. Matt tied the sac up with string so the mare wouldn't trample it – the weight of it would draw it down and out eventually. But if it took more than twenty minutes it could mean trouble, and he'd be dealing with septicaemia. He then turned to the foal who was struggling to make sense of his long legs and injected him with penicillin. The cord was still open to infection.

Matt stood back and let nature take its course. He glanced across at Claire and saw her enchantment. He understood how she felt, for the birth of a new life was a wonderful moment, one which always stirred his emotions.

The three of them watched as the tiny creature propped himself up on his two front legs, but couldn't figure out how to lift his bottom from the straw and fell on his side. Then he tried lifting his hindquarters first, but his front legs wouldn't obey him and he nosedived into the wooden wall that divided up the stalls. At the third attempt he got all four legs entangled and ended up in a heap, only to be encouraged once more by his mother. Then, finally he found his feet and tottered stiffly to where he could smell her milk and began to suckle hungrily.

Matt smiled and turned to Claire, wanting to share this magic moment with her. It was as if the world had faded and there was just the two of them in that pool of light. Everything slowed and came into sharper focus as Claire gave a soft cry of pleasure. He could see the single teardrop suspended from her lashes – watched it glitter and tremble before it fell. He blinked and looked away. He was getting to like this girl more and more; if he didn't watch out he'd make a complete idiot of himself.

Chapter Four

'I don't know why you needed him here last night,' said Claire as she poured another cup of tea. 'I am a qualified vet and perfectly capable of dealing with a mare in foal.'

'How was I to know you'd be here?' Leanne buttered toast and chewed it as she cleared up the remains of their supper from the night before and prepared for the day. 'You never told me you were coming, and I'm not a mind-reader.'

Claire started on the washing up. 'You could have rung him,' she said stubbornly. 'Could have stopped him coming all this way once I was here.'

'I didn't think,' said Leanne sharply. She crashed the pots down on the marble worktop and stood with her hands on her hips glaring at her sister. 'What's it to you anyway?' she demanded. 'He's the local vet, we're on his rounds. Why are you getting so stirred up?'

Claire realised she was making a big deal out of nothing, and trying to say anything to Lee at this time of the morning was always hazardous – especially after their lack of a good night's sleep. 'I'm not,' she replied. 'He just unsettles me, that's all.'

Leanne's green eyes widened. 'Matt Derwent?' she scoffed. She rammed her hands in her pockets and eyed her sister thoughtfully. 'Is there something you forgot to tell me about your meeting yesterday? I noticed how he looked at you last night, and wondered then if there was something going on.'

Claire shook her head. 'Fair go, Lee,' she exclaimed. 'We met by chance, we talked, I found I liked him. End of story,' she said firmly.

Leanne frowned as she reached for her hat and boots. 'He's obviously smitten,' she muttered. 'And you're all fired up. Reckon it isn't as clear cut as you make out.'

Claire decided this conversation was getting out of hand and changed the subject. Drying her hands she turned to face Leanne. 'The van's all right out front isn't it?'

Leanne rammed her feet into her boots and squashed her hat over her hair. 'Makes the place look as if the gypsies have moved in, but it's not in the way. I've got the mare and foal to see to and I need to talk to the men about preparing for the arrival of the stock. Some of those corrals need repairs and the termites have made a meal out of the corner of one of the barns. Will you be here when I get back?'

'Probably not. It's time I went home – I can't put it off any longer.'

Leanne took a deep breath and folded her arms. Her green eyes were steady as she regarded her sister. 'You've never told me what it is that's been needling you all these years, Claire. Why won't you talk to me?'

'And have my head bitten off?' Claire sighed. 'We've never had the closest relationship, Lee,' she said quietly. 'And going by the way things are between us at the moment nothing's changed.'

119

'Try me,' Leanne demanded.

Claire glanced out of the kitchen window towards Jarrah's graveyard. 'You don't have the answers,' she muttered. 'There would be no point.'

'How do you know if you won't discuss it with me?'

Claire looked away. 'Because if you did know anything you'd have told me,' she said flatly. 'In spades.'

Leanne had the grace to redden. 'I'm not that much of a bitch,' she muttered. 'I've not been invited to this family pow-wow,' she said bitterly. 'Don't you think I have a right to know what's going on?'

'Probably.' Claire put her hand on her sister's shoulder.

'But I'm not keeping secrets from you, Lee. Just trying to make sense of suspicions and doubts.' She gave a tremulous smile. 'There's nothing really tangible I can put my finger on. Perhaps this family conference will make things clearer. Give me some slack, Leanne. Please?'

Leanne nodded before she turned away. 'I reckon you're just making a drama out of nothing. Whatever it is, it can't be that bad.'

Claire watched her leave and heard the slap of the screen door as her sister hurried out. 'I hope so, Lee,' she murmured. 'But what if you're wrong?'

Ellie had lain awake in the darkness, her mind going endlessly over the things she had to say to her daughter when she came home. She knew

Claire was with Lee over at Jarrah, she'd telephoned the night before and one of the men had told her. And although she understood the girl's reluctance to put off her return she wished she'd come straight here. The sooner the waiting was over the better. This was like playing Russian roulette.

The sun was barely touching the horizon when she saddled up her favourite horse and released the blue heelers from the kennels. They set out across the pastures into the sunrise as the dew sparkled in the grass and the birds began their morning squabbles. The dogs, delighted to be free, streamed ahead of her, tails aloft, ears pricked, their coats gleaming blue in the dawn light as they sniffed out rabbits and small vermin.

Ellie made an effort to relax, but her thoughts and memories refused to allow it, and after a couple of hours she returned home. She was in the paddock rubbing her horse down when the ancient utility roared into the yard and came to a screeching halt in a cloud of dust. She grinned and went to meet her visitor. There was only one person who drove like that.

'You can tell an old woman to mind her own business,' grunted Aurelia as she struggled out of the utility and planted her sturdy brogues in the dust. 'But I thought you might need some support.' She straightened the ancient jacket, adjusted her monocle and glared through it defiantly.

'Always,' said Ellie. 'But...'

Aurelia rummaged in the utility for her bag which she stuffed under her arm. 'No buts, Ellie,' she said firmly. 'I instigated this. We must stand together.'

Ellie took her arm to help her up the steps and was brushed away with an impatient grunt. Aurelia might be eighty, but she was a tough old bird, and just her presence gave her strength for what lay ahead.

Claire pushed through the gate. The picket fence had been painted recently and the grass cut so it formed a pathway through the little cemetery that stood beyond home yard on the edge of Jarrah's home pasture. Bright red bottle brush vied with the delicate cream of native laurel, white warratah and yellow banksia in the hedge around the outside. The red and green flowers of the delicate kangaroo paw danced amongst the longer grass where pink headed parakeelya and yellow daisies glowed in the sun. A jacaranda tree dripped purple blossom from fern-like foliage, and the golden rain of a delicate acacia offered scented shade to the weathered wooden seat in one corner.

Claire stood there for the moment, drinking in the atmosphere. She could hear the muted sounds of life as it went on at Jarrah, and the soulful cry of a crow as it flapped from the top of a tree and flew away. The haunting single note of a bellbird rose above the sibilant insect chatter and a kookaburra chortled as if he had a secret and was keeping it to himself.

She slowly walked amongst the graves. There were one or two Victorian table tombs that were surrounded by rusting iron railings – a posthumous sign of wealth for the Irish pioneers that had cleared this land nearly two centuries ago and given it a name – some so badly eroded by the elements and their covering of lichen it was impossible to read the epitaphs. Tiny granite crosses were the only reminder of stillborn babies and children who'd died from fever or snake bite and Claire felt saddened as she thought of the mothers who'd buried them here. It must be the deepest sorrow to bury a child. It didn't fit the proper order of things.

Moving on, she finally came to the more recently interred. The headstones were marble and finely carved by masons, the epitaphs clearly visible. The last member of the Maughan family was buried here in 1946 – the year she'd been born. She stood there for a moment then reluctantly stepped from the path and made her way through the long grass to the far corner.

The headstone was leaning and almost buried in the undergrowth, but as she pulled the trailing fronds of wild bougainvillea away from the marble, she was able to read the enigmatic epitaph. Kneeling in the torpid heat of that tiny outback graveyard she sensed the spirit that still lingered here and recognised the same restlessness that had been with her for years. It was time to go home. Time for some answers.

The van creaked and groaned and the temperature gauge rose as Claire drove the two hundred miles between the two stations. The sun was high as she crested the final hill and looked down on Warratah and she pulled up the handbrake

123

and switched off the engine. Climbing out, she shielded her eyes from the glare and surveyed the only home she'd ever really known.

The old homestead stood beneath the flowering jarrah, almost dwarfed by the water towers that were covered in clambering roses and purple bougainvillea. The original outbuildings were tumbledown in the shade of the ghost gums but still served their purpose, and the corrals and paddocks were neatly fenced. Horses cropped the verdant grass down by the bore and the glint of pewter traced the creek from the billabong as it wound through the property and disappeared into the distant hills. She could make out the roofs and chimneys of the newer homestead on the horizon, and the series of gates she would have to drive through to get there. The sense of belonging pervaded her. This was home, and she'd been away for too long.

As she drove on and through the final gate before home, she ran her tongue over her parched lips. Her hands were moist as she gripped the steering wheel and her pulse was racing – there was no turning back.

Ellie was on the verandah when she first saw the cloud of dust in the distance. She drained the gin and tonic and put the glass on the table before running nerveless fingers through her hair. She would find a way to get through this, she told herself firmly.

The van ground to a halt in a cloud of red dust, the door swung open and there she was. Ellie forgot the years of silence between them, the hurt at not being invited to the graduation and the row before she'd left for Sydney. This was her beloved daughter and she had finally come home. She ran down the steps to hug her. Holding her tightly, she breathed in the scent of her, relishing the feel of her arms around her once again. 'I swear you've grown,' she said with a tremulous smile as she looked into Claire's face.

'Fair go, Mum,' Claire teased. 'I did all my growing when I was thirteen.'

Ellie beamed up at her, taking in the beautiful eyes, the sensuous mouth and the slender figure. Her little girl had become a woman over the five years they'd spent apart. A woman with a life of her own and a bright future – if they could get through these next few days unscathed. 'It's good to have you home,' she breathed. 'I've missed you. We've all missed you.'

'Let the dog see the rabbit,' said Aurelia bossily as she clambered down the steps and almost pushed Ellie aside. 'How's my girl?' she boomed as she put her arm around the slender waist and planted a whiskery kiss on the proffered cheek.

'Good,' said Claire as she gave her aunt an affectionate squeeze.

Ellie noticed how, despite her facade of cheerfulness, there was tension in Claire's shoulders and a brittle quality to her laughter. Her daughter's obvious pleasure at coming back to Warratah was tempered by the shadows in her eyes – shadows of fear and mistrust.

'Let's get out of the sun and have tea,' she said with forced brightness. 'You can unload that thing afterwards.'

Claire reached into the van and dragged out her cumbersome overnight bag which she dumped on the verandah. 'I've brought presents for everyone,' she said as she flopped into a chair and fanned herself with her hat. 'But they're buried somewhere in the back of the van.'

Ellie, who preferred not to have a maid in the house, rushed into the kitchen and made a pot of tea. The kettle was always on the hob, so it didn't take long. She added the pot to the tray she'd laid out earlier and with a sudden calmness she never knew she possessed, carried it all back out to the verandah.

Aurelia was firing rapid questions at Claire about her degree, her graduation and her love-life. Pipe smoke was billowing, grey eyes were bright with a resumed energy for life and the deep frown that had creased her brow in recent days was almost gone.

'Let the poor girl catch her breath and drink her tea,' Ellie said quietly as she set down the tray. 'We'll hear it all soon enough.' She passed cups around and offered sandwiches and cake. 'I hear you've already met Matt Derwent,' she said between sips of hot, sweet tea.

Claire grinned. 'It never ceases to amaze me how fast news travels out here. The bush telegraph is obviously still alive and well and doing good business.'

'Nothing much escapes,' murmured Ellie. 'You have to remember that despite the distances out here, we're really only a village. The population is less than one of Sydney's suburbs and growing smaller every year. The youngsters are leaving – they don't have the same feel for the land as our generation.'

'And what does this village gossip have to say about me and Matt Derwent?' Claire asked with wry humour.

Ellie smiled over the rim of her teacup. 'Nothing much, but Lila Smith down at the Gregory Hotel reckons you're made for each other.' She put down her cup and reached for her cigarettes. 'Poor Lila. Reads too many romantic novels.'

Inconsequential chatter went back and forth as they finished their tea – then dwindled into an awkward silence. The tension was growing. Even Aurelia was feeling it, Ellie noticed, as the old lady fiddled with her pipe and dropped her matches.

'So why the summons?'

Claire appeared relaxed as she sat back in the chair, but Ellie could see the alert stillness in her. She dragged on the last of her cigarette before stubbing it out. Her pulse was racing. The moment had come. Yet the strange calmness remained with her and she was able to think clearly. She circumvented her daughter's question with one of her own. 'I hear you've been visiting graveyards again,' she said quietly into the brittle silence. 'Now, why would you do that, I wonder?' She lifted her gaze to her daughter's face, almost afraid of what she would see there.

Claire returned her look, the gaze steady, the face perhaps a little paler than before. 'I want to know why it's there considering its obvious family connection. And why no one will give me

127

a proper explanation. I was hoping this summons home would give me the answer.'

Ellie was aware of Aurelia's concerned expression. Aware of the past closing in – surrounding her – taking her back. 'If you want to know the history of that grave and the reason for its isolation, then the best place to start is the beginning,' she said softly. 'You know the story of how I first met Charlie and Joe on the matilda, but I suppose the history of why that gravestone is at Jarrah really began several weeks later.'

She stared out across the yard to the distant horizon, aware of the expectant silence from her daughter. Taking a deep breath she began to speak. 'As the weeks went by Charlie grew more restless. The drought had a stranglehold on Warratah and there wasn't enough work. I think he was sick of me traipsing around after him and his brother – sick of being told what to do by an old battleaxe with a voice that splintered the eardrums.'

Ellie glanced across at Aurelia. They both knew how she'd been perceived all those years ago and Ellie realised the old girl was rather proud of the fact. 'The crux came when a passing drover told him about a horse muster over in the Territory.'

'I gotta go,' he said excitedly. 'The muster starts in two weeks and it'll take all of that to get there.'

'There's work here if you look for it,' Joe replied as he lifted bales of feed from the storehouse and loaded them into the back of the ute. 'What you wanna go haring off for when we already got tucker and shelter? The old girl might be fierce, but she's dinkum all right.'

'Old battleaxe more like,' Charlie retorted. 'Getting her bloody money's worth making us work for bed and board.'

'Fair go, mate,' Joe said with a sigh as he leaned on the pitchfork. 'She gave us a hundred quid for bringing Ellie back. What more do you want?'

'Work. Excitement. I dunno,' said an exasperated Charlie waving his arms in the air. 'But I gotta get out of here. This place's closing in on me.'

'And what about me? Do I figure in these plans of yours?' Joe said calmly.

Charlie shrugged. 'You can come if you want,' he replied with enough grudging nonchalance to hide his hope Joe would do just that. For despite his yearning to roam free again, the thought of setting out on his own had suddenly become daunting.

Joe went back to loading the feed, his expression enigmatic, his silence making Charlie edgy. 'Well?' he said finally. 'Are you coming with me or not?'

'Don't reckon I will, mate,' Joe replied eventually. 'It's time to settle in one place for a bit, see if I like life out here. I got money in me pocket now, and until it rains I can't see no point in moving on and scratching for a living.'

Charlie sighed. 'You got no sense of adventure, Joe. Why get stuck here working for your tucker when you could be out riding with the brumbies?' He warmed to his theme, his blue eyes gleaming with the thrill of it all. 'Think of how it felt, Joe. Remember the rush we got from

129

it.' He put his hand on his brother's shoulder, willing him to change his mind. 'Come on, mate. Come with me.'

'Not this time, Charlie,' replied Joe. 'I've seen enough of the matilda to satisfy any adventure I might have been looking for.' He slung the pitchfork into the flat-bed of the utility, and stood squarely in front of his brother, his hands deep in his pockets. 'I need time,' he said firmly. 'Time to catch me breath and make up me mind about what I really want to do. Aurelia's money has given me that chance, and I don't want to make the wrong decisions just because you're all fired up.'

'But there ain't nothing here but a bunch of bloody women telling you what to do,' Charlie said in exasperation. He was suddenly afraid. Afraid of losing the one person that meant anything to him.

'Fair go,' his brother said mildly. 'There's enough for me to do here, and when the rains come Aurelia will need help mustering the stock.'

Charlie's boyish grin faltered. 'And what if it doesn't rain? What then?'

Joe eyed him steadily. 'I'll take me chances. This place is the nearest thing to home and I ain't gunna walk away from it – not even for you, Charlie.'

Charlie hadn't meant for things to turn out this way – but on the other hand he needed to be free. He kicked at the dirt. 'So this is it then?' he muttered.

Joe touched his arm. 'We knew it would happen, mate,' he said. 'You and me want differ-

130

ent things. I've had it with living on the tracks –
don't need to wander no more.'

Charlie shrugged off his hand, the beguiling
smile no longer in evidence as Joe's calm determination forced him to realise he'd meant what
he'd said. He followed his brother's gaze as it
drifted to the paddock where Satan was cropping
the silver grass and knew this was the moment of
parting. Yet now it was here, he was reluctant to
take the next step. 'All this will still be here when
the muster's over,' he said quickly. 'Come with
me now, Joe, and if things don't work out you can
come back.'

Joe shook his dark head. 'I'm not leaving,
Charlie. Sorry.'

The twins stood for a long, silent moment, each
with their own thoughts. There was still time to
change their minds. Yet they recognised the
other's need to follow their own destiny and
neither of them could find the words to convey
how painful this was.

Charlie slicked back his hair. It had grown long
again and glinted in the sun. 'I'll be leaving
before sun-up tomorrow,' he said finally. 'If you
change your mind...' He looked hopefully at his
twin, willing him to see the apprehension in his
eyes.

Joe threw his arms around him, and the clamour
of conflicting emotions that raced through
Charlie made it difficult for him to speak. He
slapped the broad, muscular back and held him
close as he remembered their childhood together
and the long trek they'd taken to get this far.

'You take care of yourself out there,' Joe's voice

131

was gruff as they drew awkwardly apart. 'And keep in touch. You're still my brother and I don't want to lose you.'

Charlie turned and headed back to the bunkhouse. Their life together was over, and although the need for adventure gnawed deep, there was still a part of him that longed to be like his twin. Longed for the sense of contentment and inner stillness Joe seemed to carry with him. Yet he understood why they had to part, for if either of them were to make something of themselves, they could only do it alone.

Joe had meant to wake early the next morning to say goodbye to Charlie, but after a day of shifting feed bags and digging fence posts, he'd hit the pillow and had slept deeply for over nine hours. Now the sun was streaming through an empty bunkhouse and the clock on the wall showed it was well past seven. He leaped from bed, pulled on strides and boots and fought with shirt buttons. He'd wash later. Charlie's bed was empty, his bluey gone from the bedpost, but there still might be time to catch him – still the possibility he'd changed his mind.

Crashing through the bunkhouse door he stepped into the yard. Charlie's string of horses was gone from the holding paddock. He was too late. With his spirits low and the brightness of the morning sun taunting him, he crossed the yard to the cookhouse.

The Aborigines were sitting around their fire as usual, their dark skins deflecting the sun like negatives against the red backdrop of the yard as their gaze followed him. Some of the children were playing with the scraggy camp dogs in the dirt, their sharp cries and laughter drifting on the soft breeze. But Joe was hardly aware of their cheerful greetings, for it was as if his twin's departure had taken a part of himself – leaving a great void he was sure could never be filled.

The stock horses and utility were gone and Joe realised the skeleton crew of men still employed on Warratah were already out in the pastures finishing the posts and fencing they'd started the day before. Smoke curled lazily from the homestead chimney and a barefooted lubra was hanging out washing. Aurelia and Ellie were having breakfast on the verandah, the gleam of white feathers luminous in the shadows as Kelly preened. Yet the strong sense of something being wrong made his steps falter and he came to a standstill. Everything looked as it always did. And yet... He turned slowly, taking in the already familiar surroundings, marking it against his memory. Then his gaze fell on the far paddock and he understood.

'No,' he rasped. His feet pounded across the dusty yard as he raced for the paddock. 'No!' he raged as he climbed the railings and searched for his beloved Satan. 'Come back Charlie!' he yelled into the miles of empty silence. 'Come back you bastard!'

'What's happened?'

The light voice startled him and he turned towards it, stumbling down from the railings, almost overwhelmed by rage and frustration. It was as if he'd become a child again. A child whose favourite toys had been stolen – only to be returned broken when Charlie had grown tired of them. A child who'd finally been betrayed beyond endurance. 'Me bastard brother's nicked me 'orse,' he rasped. 'He's stolen Satan.' He blinked rapidly, unwilling to break down before an audience. He could have done without Ellie at this precise moment.

'Aunt Aurelia saw him real early this morning when he came for his fifty quid,' said Ellie softly. 'She did say she thought it odd you'd given him your horse.'

Joe clenched his fists, his rage cold and unremitting. 'I'd never give him Satan,' he said through gritted teeth. 'He knew bloody well I'd never give him Satan. That's why the bastard took him when I was asleep.' He stared off into the distance. 'I'll kill him,' he muttered. 'I'll bloody kill him if he dares come back after this.'

Ellie placed her hand in his and they stood there for a long time staring out over the lonely miles. The silence between them wasn't awkward for it was as if they were suddenly in tune with one another's thoughts. Joe looked down at the kid beside him and knew she understood that they were like the flowers that drifted with the wind across this great empty land. Hostages to fate – their life's patterns marked only by the footprints they left in the dust.

'It was just a horse,' breathed Claire.

Ellie shook her head. 'Satan was more than just an ordinary horse to Joe,' she said softly. 'You have to remember the world was still staggering

134

from the Wall Street Crash. The boys started out with nothing but their blueys on their backs and the clothes they stood up in. Satan had been caught and broken by Joe – the stallion was a symbol of how far he'd come – what he'd achieved. On the practical side, a horse back then represented a mode of transport and the means to work. Without it a man had nothing.'

Understanding shone through as Claire remembered how devastated she'd been when her first pony had broken his leg in a rabbit hole and had had to be put down. Claire was ten when it happened, but she still had a photograph of him in her wallet. She watched the shadows flit over her mother's face and knew this dredging up of the past was proving painful. Yet beyond that pain she sensed Ellie felt a release in the retelling of the story; for secrets had a way of souring life – of colouring it in different hues. 'So what happened?'

Her mother's eyes were as dark as molten chocolate, the freckles not quite hidden beneath the dusting of powder as she turned her face to the sun. 'Charlie's conscience began to bother him,' she replied. 'But that didn't hinder his pleasure in Satan's ability to run like the wind. He kept telling himself Joe would get over losing the horse – that he'd find another and forget all about Satan.'

Ellie smoothed the skirt of her cotton dress and leaned forward to rest her elbows on her knees, her chin cupped in her hands. 'But it was at night when he lay by the camp-fire and looked up at the stars that the reality of what he'd done made

135

him uneasy. They weren't children any more. The loss of the horse would mean far more to Joe than any of the toys Charlie had filched during those younger days. He knew that taking Satan was a mean thing to do to a brother who'd always stood by him.'

Claire saw the sadness in those dark eyes and almost wished she could turn back the clock and leave the past where it belonged. But the floodgates were opening and she was hungry to learn more. Hungry and yet afraid for the consequences.

Ellie was still speaking, her voice low as night descended and stillness crept over Warratah. 'The long, lonely hours in the saddle and on the wallaby tracks had enforced the bond between them, making Charlie realise just how much his twin meant to him; yet it was not in his nature to admit his mistakes – not in his nature to turn around and ask for forgiveness.' She bit her lip as she lowered her gaze. 'Life was tougher in those days and both boys learned early that only the strong survived. Charlie felt that he and Satan were two of a kind – freedom seekers – happiest when out in the vast emptiness with only the wind and the sun for company. If he and Satan had stayed on Warratah their spirits would have withered. He believed this land was made for men like him. Men who weren't afraid to take their chances. Men who could turn their backs on loved ones and forge a future amongst others of his kind.'

Ellie sighed as she stood up and crossed to the verandah railings. With her gaze fixed on the pale

136

yellow light drifting from the bunkhouse windows she leaned against the post. 'But fate has a way of tricking us,' she said eventually. 'Two years later Charlie was made to learn a very harsh lesson.'

Aurelia pulled her jacket more firmly over her bosom. It was getting cold – a sure sign they'd have rain some time tonight. Yet it would be a shame to spoil the mood by going indoors and this part of the story was almost over. She glanced across at Ellie and their eyes met in a silent acknowledgement that although this retelling of the history of Warratah was painful, it was better out in the open.

'It was a month before Christmas of 1938,' she began. 'Ellie was sixteen. The drought had already lasted six years. Ellie had had the usual ghastly frothy dress from her mother which went straight to the house lubra for one of her kids, and we were sitting in the kitchen discussing Australia's commitment to the Commonwealth and the part our men would have to play if war was declared.'

Aurelia glanced across at Ellie again and knew she was remembering certain elements of that conversation only too well. She felt the heat rise in her face and looked away. Claire didn't need to know about her and Jack – not yet. 'I had come to think of Ellie as my own child,' she said hastily. 'She was still short and far too thin, but she made up for that with a personality that could not be ignored. She also had a strong will and a short temper.' She and Ellie exchanged glances and

137

smiled at the memories of the tussles they'd had through those awkward growing years.

'Joe surprised me by staying on after that to-do with his brother, but he had a natural way with horses I admired. A shy, almost gentle nature, and a smile that warmed me to him. He was intelligent and amazingly well read for a country boy and I'd grown to like him very much. Seamus Maughan on the other hand was a rogue,' she said fondly. 'A dark haired, Irish boy with laughing blue eyes and a restless spirit that often led him into all sorts of pickles. I was much taken with him, and as he was Mickey's son and heir to Jarrah, I had high hopes for him and Ellie.'

Aurelia fell silent as she remembered how the three youngsters had taken to each other. She'd called them her Three Musketeers and when work allowed it, they were rarely apart. Seamus and Joe had forged a strong bond in the wake of Charlie's departure, and didn't seem to mind Ellie tagging along as they rode out across the plains. They were both several years older than Ellie, but she'd noticed how the girl's eyes shone when she worked alongside Joe in the stables, and how she seemed bewitched by Seamus' blarney. Mickey Maughan and his son were regular visitors to Warratah and Aurelia had tried not to comment on how Ellie would make a point of sitting next to Seamus at the dinner table. She'd known Ellie was in the throes of hero-worship, and hoped that one day this might turn into something more tangible.

She sighed. They had been happy days despite

the drought and the threat of war, for the world had still been innocent then. 'The drought broke that day. It started with a clap of thunder and the sky grew dark and before we knew it we were all dancing in the mud, drenched to the skin and as drunk as skunks from the sheer relief.' She paused. She remembered that day only too well – for it had been the day she'd broken down and cried for only the second time in her life. 'We were safe,' she whispered. 'Warratah would survive.'

'But what has this to do with Charlie?' asked Claire with a frown. 'I thought you said something happened to him?'

Aurelia smiled at her. Claire had the same inquisitive mind as her mother, the same persistent need to know it all. 'It might not seem as if it does just yet,' she murmured. 'But you have to understand how things were on Warratah in those days, how relationships were beginning to form that would have a bearing later on.'

Claire shivered and pulled a cardigan out of her bag. 'So what happened to Charlie and Satan?'

Aurelia looked across at Ellie. 'You know that part of it better than I,' she said. 'Perhaps you'd better tell her.'

Borroloola was a country town in the middle of nowhere that had dusted itself down to prepare for the annual excitement that would be crammed into this one weekend. Nothing much happened in this sleepy outback town in the Northern Territory except for the yearly weekend race meeting, and it almost looked startled in its

139

bunting and banners as Charlie led Satan down the main street that Friday morning.

The locals looked stiff and awkward in the unaccustomed catalogue dresses and suits and hats as they paraded their finery and renewed acquaintances with neighbours they rarely saw. Visitors from the city swaggered self-consciously down the main street, out of place in their polished boots and fashionable bush hats, making the kids on the boardwalks snigger. Yet there was an air of excitement that couldn't be denied, a warmth of feeling even for the townies – for Borroloola was momentarily alive again.

Charlie eyed the pubs that were already doing a roaring trade and thought of the cold beer he could kill after his long ride from the Alice. It would have to wait, he decided regretfully. Satan had to be entered into the race, and he didn't like the thought of leaving him outside a pub in case he was knobbled.

His stock horse danced away as three men were forcefully ejected from one particular hotel to carry on their fight in the middle of the street. They were blind drunk and Charlie, who was no stranger to what the drink could do, grinned and wondered if they even knew what day of the week it was. But seconds later they were all the best of mates and they staggered arm in arm back to the hotel for another drink.

Charlie continued on through the town and approached the racecourse which was a bright splash of colour in the midst of the ochre surroundings. It was already busy despite the early hour, and as Charlie led Satan towards the stalls behind the freshly painted stand, he took note of the sulkies and carts drawn up on the outside of the track where a dozen or so horses were already being worked. The Southern Cross fluttered lethargically above the single stand, and the narrow white fence surrounding the course looked stark against the backdrop of timbered hills on the far side. A brass band was tuning up and the bookies were oiling their throats in the beer tent before the day's onslaught.

He felt the first tremor of excitement as he watched the horses being worked on the fast, firm track. None of them had the class or speed of Satan he noticed happily. This should be an easy run.

This wasn't the first racetrack he'd been to since taking Satan from his brother, and it wouldn't be the last. The bloody horse was a marvel now he'd got the message and calmed down, and Charlie had made a fair bit of money on him. He led the chestnut into the stable yard, watered him and rubbed him down. The long journey hadn't affected him, he noticed. He looked as if he was raring to go.

'Nice lookin' horse,' drawled a familiar voice.

Charlie turned round sharply. 'Snowy White!' he exclaimed. 'What the blue blazes are you doin' here?' He looked in amazement at the rangy figure and strong, dark features of the Aboriginal stockman. It had been at least five years since he'd seen him back on Gowrie Station, and although there were strands of silver in the tousled redbrown hair, Snowy didn't really look any older.

'Having a bit of an 'oliday, ain't I?' Snowy said with his usual cheerfulness. They shook hands. 'Hear yer brother's still on Warratah. Shame you and him fell out.' He eyed the horse for a long moment then turned his accusing gaze back to Charlie. 'Ain't right, Charlie. Not another bloke's horse.'

Charlie was stunned to realise word of his theft had spread. 'Dunno what you 'eard mate, but me brother give me Satan. He's mine.' He squared his broad shoulders and defied Snowy to challenge him. If it came to a fight, Charlie thought heatedly, then he'd make mincemeat of Snowy even if he was bigger.

Snowy eyed him thoughtfully, seemingly unconvinced. 'Not what I heard, mate.' He must have seen the light of battle in Charlie's eyes, for he shrugged and chewed on a matchstick. 'Still, ain't none of my business,' he muttered.

There was a long silence as he stroked the chestnut's back. He seemed in no hurry to leave. 'What you reckon on his chances?'

Charlie was relieved to change the subject, but he'd learned early on in his intermittent racing career to be as cautious as an echidna, and he didn't know where Snowy's loyalties lay as regards to his brother or to his horse. 'You never know with these sort of meetings,' he replied warily. 'Could be a couple of good 'uns hidden away I don't know about. Local horses and the like.'

'Run 'im before?' asked Snowy with a little too much nonchalance for Charlie's liking.

'He's right. Got some toe, but can't hold it over

more'n a mile.' His expression was deliberately bland as he lied. Satan had proved himself several times over longer distances, but it would do Charlie's pocket no good to have the price backed down to odds-on if word got out.

Snowy ran an expert hand over Satan's gleaming coat. 'Looks better than that, mate,' he said quietly. 'I know a prime piece of horseflesh when I see it.' His expression was cold, his steady, amber gaze unnerving. 'Reckon you got a beaut there.'

'So what you been doing since we left Gowrie?' asked Charlie in a desperate attempt to get Snowy off the subject of Satan.

Snowy chewed on the matchstick, the shadow of his hat brim masking his broad features. 'This and that,' he drawled. 'Left Gowrie about a year back. Done some fence posting, mustering, horse-breaking. That's what I do now. Breaking for Vestey over at Wave Hill.'

Charlie reckoned Snowy had done all right for himself if he was working for Lord Vestey. The family owned at least seventeen cattle stations that ran in an almost unbroken line from Western Australia to the Overland Telegraph Line, totalling something in excess of over forty thousand square miles. 'Good on yer mate. But you're a long ways from Wave Hill. What's brought you to Borroloola?'

'I'm on me way to one of his other stations. They've got problems there and they want me to sort 'em out.'

Charlie realised Snowy was being as tight-lipped as he was, but let it pass. 'Don't happen to know if there's a job for me, do you?' he asked hopefully. 'I finished brumby mustering down the Alice and got nothing lined up.'

'We're always looking for ringers,' replied Snowy, his gaze still fixed on the magnificent stallion. 'Why don't you and me talk about it after the race?'

'Thanks mate. I owe you one.'

'Not if that beaut comes in for me, you won't,' Snowy said, his face lighting up with a smile. 'Reckon I'll put a couple of bob on him just to see what he can do. Catch yer later.'

Charlie watched as Snowy loped off into the milling crowd. Strange, he thought. I see the same faces and hear the same stories wherever I go. Distances might be endless, but everyone knew everyone else – and each other's business. It was as bad as living back in Lorraine. He stared off into the distance, seeing nothing as his thoughts whirled. It was worrying, though, how far the story had got about Satan. Perhaps he should change his name, pretend he was a different horse altogether?

Charlie chewed his lip as he pondered the problem. He couldn't afford to lose the chance of making money on Satan while he was running so well, yet he couldn't risk an enquiry into his ownership either. He patted the sleek neck and looked into the intelligent eyes. The only way to salve his conscience was to give Joe some of the prize money, but that would mean having to face his brother again having to admit he'd done wrong.

Impatient and uneasy, he blew out his cheeks

and stuffed his hands in his pockets. What was a bloke supposed to do, he wondered heatedly, when every option could only lead to trouble? If only he'd stop and think before he did things. If only he could resist the things that weren't his. But then life wouldn't be half as interesting, he admitted.

He forced the worry from his mind and changed into the white breeches and green shirt he'd bought to race in. Dressed and ready he pulled on the green and yellow cap and strolled out of the shadows of the stalls and pushed his way through the overexcited, beer fuelled crowd to register Satan for the fifth race and place his bet. After this race meeting, he decided, Satan would have a new name.

The Borroloola Stakes was a race of a mile and a half which would take the sixteen runners and riders twice past the stand before they reached the finishing line. The winner of the Stakes was expected to win the Borroloola Cup on Sunday and Charlie was already planning how he would spend his winnings as he and Satan trotted out on to the course.

He sat astride Satan as cocky as a rooster in a chook house as he waited for the starter to call them into line. He'd drawn number five, and the only competition looked like the rangy black horse with the good head and powerful lines that was second from the rails and the local favourite.

The starter called them into line and a hush fell. Satan was ready, ears pricked, nostrils distended, already lathering up as he danced on his toes.

Charlie became aware of the heat of the broiling sun that beat down from the raw sky. Aware of the smell of leather and sweating horseflesh – the rapid drum of his pulse. He heard only the sound of nervous hoofs in the dust and the curses of the jockeys around him as he shortened the reins and settled his feet more firmly in the stirrups. The track wound into the distance before him and he tugged down the peak of his cap as he squinted into the glare. He was planning his race.

'Go!' yelled the starter as he waved his flag.

Charlie got Satan away quickly to escape being trapped in that first mad dash, and once they had settled down he was on the rails, tucked in behind the black and another chestnut. They were all running easily as they led the mob around the first long bend, each jockey watchful of the other two.

The rest of the field began tailing off as they passed the stand for the first time. The spectators were already yelling and Charlie gave Satan a bit more leeway on the reins, but not enough to blow him too soon.

The leading chestnut was slowing now, his jockey urging him on with spurs and whip. Satan lengthened his stride, gaining on the outside of the black until they were racing side by side. Charlie kept his gaze focused on the other chestnut as they thundered around the last bend. The finishing line was already in sight.

The game little chestnut tried to make a race of it, but he just didn't have the wind, and as they passed the stand for the second time he fell behind with the others and Satan and the black were now neck and neck.

Charlie let Satan have his head. Standing in the stirrups he crouched over the arched neck and urged him on. The black was still beside him, matching him stride for stride. The winning post was less than twenty yards away.

The crack of the other jockey's whip lashed Charlie's cheek. He flinched, losing his balance and his concentration. The boot caught his leg, knocking his foot from the stirrups as the black began to draw away.

Satan's ears flattened at the unusual yank on the reins as Charlie desperately tried to maintain his seat. The black was a nose ahead now, lengthening his stride again, moving further on. Satan missed his footing, confused and frightened by what was happening to the man on his back. He stumbled, his front hoof digging into the hard, impacted earth, cruelly twisting the slender leg.

The black raced across the finishing line to the roar of the delighted crowd, the local jockey standing in the stirrups, his arms wide to receive their adulation.

Satan gave a whinny of fear and pain as he crashed to the ground. Charlie saw black spots dance before his eyes as his head hit the earth and the horse rolled on top of him. Winded, he lay there aware only of the silence that followed the other horses as they thundered past and the weight of Satan as he writhed in agony on top of him.

Rough hands pulled him to his feet as the vet

quickly examined Satan. Charlie was dazed and confused, but as his senses returned he became aware of the loud voices arguing around him and the satisfied smirk of the winning jockey looming out of the crowd.

'You no good mongrel,' he yelled, wrenching away from the restraining hands, trying to get through the crush to the weasel faced little runt. 'I'll knock yer bloody block off yer bastard.'

The smirking face disappeared in the crowd and Charlie suddenly became aware of one voice that stood out in the babel. It was a quiet voice, full of experience and sadness. 'This horse will have to be put down,' it said.

Charlie fought his way back to Satan, the copper taste of fear in his mouth, the sweat cold on his skin despite the heat.

Satan was lying on his side, the great chest rising and falling as he struggled to breathe. The beautiful sheen of his coat already looked dull, and the reproachful, pain filled eyes rolled up until only the whites were visible. His noble neck arched, the teeth bared to the sky.

'Satan?' Charlie whispered as he dropped to his knees beside the animal. 'Oh, Satan. What have I done?' At that moment he would have gladly taken the horse's agony on himself. Would have gladly sacrificed all the winnings he might ever earn if only Satan could be well again.

'Sorry, mate. Busted his leg good and proper. There's nothing I can do for him.'

Charlie looked up as he heard the click of the bullet in the gun chamber. 'Don't. Please don't,' he begged. 'There has to be some other way.'

The solemn face looked down at him, the eyes kind. 'There's no other way, son,' he said softly. 'Poor bastard's in agony. We can't let it go on.'

Charlie sniffed back the tears as he stroked the elegant neck and ran his fingers through the long mane. Satan seemed to become aware of him and gave a soft whicker that almost broke his heart. 'Do it quick then,' he said abruptly as he got to his feet and turned his back.

He was pushing through the milling throng, blind to where he was going, deaf to everything around him when the resounding crack of the gunshot froze him. He swayed, the echo of that shot ringing in his head, the white-hot rage building inside him until he could control it no longer. The crowd parted as he tore towards the weighing room. The other jockey was dead meat.

Charlie stormed into the room, slamming the screen door so hard it almost came off its hinges. 'Where are you, you bastard?' he yelled into the shocked silence. 'Come out and show yer face you yellow dingo.'

The skinny little man emerged from the back of the room, surrounded by six others who had the muscle to do his fighting for him. 'Looking for me?' he smirked.

'Too bloody right I am,' snarled Charlie as he lunged for the little man's throat.

Strong hands held him back and the other jockey's mates formed a tight cordon around him. 'Shouldn't play grown-up games if you don't like being beat,' the little man said.

'You're a dirty, stinking mongrel,' yelled Charlie as he struggled to be free of the restraining hands. 'You whipped me. Kicked the stirrups away. You're nothing but a bloody cheat.'

'I'd be careful with your choice of words, sonny,' said the little man coldly. 'Cheat ain't something *you* should be calling anyone.'

Charlie looked wildly around him. There wasn't a friendly face to be seen and the silence was electric. 'You *are* a cheat,' he shouted defiantly. 'If you hadn't done what you did, my bloody horse would have won.'

The men moved forward until Charlie could smell the beer and tobacco on their breath. Could see the contempt in their eyes and almost feel their blood lust. For the first time in his life he was afraid.

'Cheat's an ugly word, mate,' hissed the little man as he looked up at Charlie. 'An ugly word that suits bastards like you who steal another man's horse.' He looked around him as the others nodded their agreement, then back at Charlie. 'See we don't like bludgers in our town. Tall poppies what come in 'ere and try to steal what ain't theirs. So we got our own way of dealing with 'em.'

Charlie struggled to be free but the relentless grasp on his arms made it impossible. He was trapped. 'But it was you what cheated,' he yelled defiantly. 'You had me off.'

'I didn't see nothing,' said the course steward. He looked at the others. 'You blokes see anything like that happen?'

They shook their heads in unison.

The jockey stepped closer, the crown of his head not quite reaching Charlie's chest. 'My 'orse was always gunna win the minute we found out who you was and what you was up to,' he rasped. 'But I'm sorry about Joe's chestnut – he was a beaut – didn't deserve a yellow belly like you on 'is back.'

Charlie was sweating. The hard, swift punch in his gut made him gasp, his legs almost giving way beneath him. The hands let him go and he was shoved out of the door and into the dirt. He sprawled there fighting for breath, surrounded by gaping onlookers. His humiliation was complete.

'Get out,' shouted the chairman of the racing committee. 'And I'll see to it you'll never race again – not in this country anyway.'

The murmurs of disapproval followed him as the sea of jostling people curled away from him. Charlie rammed his hat on and, keeping his gaze fixed firmly on the ground, headed for the comparative safety of the holding paddock where he'd left his stock horses. If Snowy was amongst the silent crowd then he wasn't showing himself – and Charlie had a nasty feeling he knew who'd betrayed him.

Chapter Five

Ellie took the pipe and matches from the bedside table and switched off the main light. 'Smoking in bed's a dangerous habit,' she said gently as her aunt protested. 'You'll set the house on fire one of these days.'

Aurelia grimaced as she sat bolt upright against the pillows. 'Comes to something when a woman of my age and stature is bossed about in her own home.' She crossed her arms over the thick cotton nightdress and glared through her monocle.

Ellie smiled. 'This is my home,' she reminded her. 'Yours is almost an hour away.' She put the offending objects in her pocket. 'I'll give them back to you at breakfast. Now get some sleep and I'll see you in the morning.'

Aurelia slid down the pillows, her halo of white hair framing her face, the subdued light from the bedside lamp making her appear softer, younger. 'I thought that went quite well, didn't you?' she asked, changing the subject as she always did when she'd lost an argument.

Ellie nodded thoughtfully. 'I think so,' she said finally. 'But that was the easy bit. Things are going to get far more complex soon, and I'm not looking forward to it.'

'Know what you mean,' Aurelia said gruffly as she fought to keep her eyes open. 'Returning to the past is never easy – but I find I'm doing it more and more just lately.'

The monocle plopped on to her chest and Ellie smiled as the first soft snore escaped. Aurelia would sleep well tonight. She closed the door and padded across the hall to see if Claire needed anything. It was a nice feeling having the house busy again.

Claire was in bed reading a book with a lurid cover. Her hair sparkled like gossamer against the pillows and the cream satin nightdress gleamed against her tanned skin, and in that moment Ellie realised with a shock how much she reminded her of Alicia. Yet Claire had none of Alicia's traits, thank goodness. 'What's that you're reading?' she asked as she sat on the end of the bed.

Claire yawned and put the book aside. *'The Valley of the Dolls,'* she replied. 'I've been meaning to read it for ages, but until now I haven't had the time.' She grinned up at Ellie. 'It's a bit racy – not at all the sort of thing a carefully brought up young lady like me should be reading.'

'In that case you'd better give it to me when you've finished with it,' said Ellie with some alacrity. She bent forward and kissed her daughter's cheek. She smelled of soap and tooth-paste and her skin was soft and warm. 'It's lovely to have you home, darling,' she said for the second time that day. 'I just wish we'd cleared the air five years ago. I've missed you. It seems a shame to spoil your homecoming by reviving old history.'

Claire's eyes were very blue as they regarded her. 'You haven't said anything to spoil it so far, Mum,' she said. 'But I get the feeling there are

153

more serious things to come.'

Ellie looked away. She was afraid Claire would see her thoughts.

'Don't worry, Mum,' said Claire as she touched her arm. 'Whatever it is we'll get through it somehow. We're a tough bunch we Warratah women.'

Ellie smiled across at her, feeling her spirits lift. Claire was right. They were tough. They would get to the end of this – but she was dreading the road they would have to take to reach that final destination. She kissed Claire again and left the room.

Unable to face the empty double bed, Ellie pottered into the kitchen and made herself some tea. With the cup cradled in her hands she dragged a chair over to the new range and opened the door. It was definitely getting colder and she thought she heard the first splatters of rain on the corrugated roof. The Wet was early this year.

As she sat there in the glow from the fire her thoughts drifted back to her sixteenth birthday and the Wet that had finally ended the long drought. That was the problem with dredging up the past, for once it had been invoked, it refused to remain in the shadows. Yet not all the memories were bad and she smiled as she basked in the warmth from the range.

The breaking of the drought on her sixteenth birthday had brought life back to Warratah, and as they'd been preparing for the first muster since the rains she'd been forcibly reminded of her first drove with Dad and Snowy and Wang Lee. Joe and Seamus had noticed her unusual silence and tried to lift her spirits by teasing her, but as the men and horses gathered in the yard she couldn't help missing her father and wondering what had become of Wang Lee and Snowy.

The house creaked and settled as the wind picked up and rain splashed on the windows and dripped to the verandah, and in that cocoon of warmth she could almost hear Joe's voice again. 'Reckon you'll come across them some time,' he drawled. 'The outback's a small world, despite the distances between us all.'

She smiled as she remembered how Clipper had snorted in his ear – how Joe mussed the ageing pony's mane and made a fuss of him rather than look her in the eye. Poor Joe. He'd always found it easier to communicate with animals than with girls. Yet she'd noticed the way he watched her when he thought she wasn't looking. Noticed how he'd become tongue tied and awkward, the colour rising in his face as he stomped off and immersed himself in something physical rather than be alone with her.

Ellie leaned back in the chair and pulled her cardigan over her chest. Seamus on the other hand had never been shy, and never made a secret of his growing admiration. She knew his eyes followed her as she walked across the yard in her tight moleskins. Knew he hung around waiting for her to finish her chores so they could have supper together.

The rivalry between the boys was tacit, but she'd realised Joe knew Seamus had the edge. He was the son of a rich cattleman – the heir to

155

Jarrah. He was a guest on Warratah, not the hired hand.

She snuggled into her cardigan as she giggled. She'd been sixteen then – no longer the chatty little pest who followed the boys around and got in their way, but a woman-child who was beginning to understand the power she possessed and used it unashamedly by flirting. What a tease she'd been.

As the snores became progressively louder from the guest room, Ellie smiled. Not surprisingly, Aunt Aurelia hadn't been impressed by her behaviour back then. She'd come across Ellie leaning on the pommel of her saddle as she sat on Clipper and watched the boys preparing for the long drove to the stockyards. Both boys had turned to wave and she noticed how the colour rose furiously in Joe's tanned face as she grinned and waved back.

'You can take that silly look off your face,' Aurelia had said abruptly as she brought her horse to a standstill beside Ellie. 'I realise the hormones must be racing at the moment, but that's no excuse. Men have their place on this earth, but there's no profit in day-dreaming about them. There's work to be done.'

Ellie slammed the door shut on the range and switched off the light before padding back down the hall to her room. It had been a glorious morning that first day of the long drove to the stockyards, but things were about to change – for none of them realised it would be the last time they would ride together as the Three Mus-keteers.

156

Leanne emerged from the homestead on to the verandah. It was only just light, but the day promised well. She breathed in the scent of the flowers and golden wattle and revelled in the scent of damp earth and wet grass. Stepping down into the yard she crossed to the railings that surrounded home paddock.

Her senses sharpened and she experienced the same sense of awakening as the outback. The dry, dusty ochre plains had a different feel to them after the rain the night before. A fresh, clean, colourful ambience that lightened the spirits and made her wish she could hold a tune well enough to sing. The clear light sharpened the outlines of distant hills, making them almost three dimensional against the backdrop of the enormous sky. The creeks and waterholes were full to the brim with sweet, clear water, and the mitchell and flinders grass rippled in the light, warm wind like a great silver and green sea. Wild ducks gabbled as they swam and fished in the billabong. Bush turkeys stalked across the flower covered plains gorging themselves on the swarms of insects that had come with the rain, and the air was resonant with the call and colour of a thousand different birds.

Leanne drank in the scene before her as she leaned on the railing. Jarrah was at its most beautiful after the rain and she was privileged to be a part of it. She reluctantly pulled herself away and headed for the feed store. The rooster's call was strident as she loaded up the various buckets and headed for the coops and kennels.

With the smaller animals fed she dumped the buckets and went into the barn. Two of the farm cats were having a scrap. Growling like dogs, all teeth and claws they sparred and yowled and chased amongst the bales of hay before streaking through the door when they heard her approach. The cats were far removed from the fluffy, cute house pets in the city. These were skinny and feral and like everything else on Jarrah they were here for a purpose. Rats and mice had to be kept at bay and these two were particularly good at that. Leanne hefted a bale of hay and lugged it into the stables. She would let Bonny and her foal into the holding paddock as it was such a dry, warm day, then she could muck out the stable and fill Bonny's manger.

Bonny trotted happily into the paddock, the foal stumbling beside her with knock knees and unsteady legs. His pasterns were a little long for her to consider getting him trained up for racing, but they'd soon firm up and he'd make a good stock horse. She watched them for a while, noting how Bonny was foal proud and wouldn't allow the other horses near her baby. She smiled as the little fellow got the scent of his surroundings and tried to gambol. His balance left something to be desired, but he was only twenty-four hours old.

Foals were terrible time wasters, she thought as she left them to it and returned to the stables. She must have spent a good half hour mooning over him. One of the Aborigine boys was already making a start on mucking out and she rolled up her sleeves and pitched in.

She was sweating and filthy, her shirt sticking to her back, her face red, her hair falling into her eyes when she heard the unmistakable sound of a light aircraft touching down. 'Shit,' she breathed as she rubbed a dirty hand over her sweaty forehead. 'Shit, shit, shit and double shit.' She hastily scrubbed her hands and face under the cold water tap in the stable yard and wondered if she had time to rush indoors and change.

'G'day,' came the cheerful voice as Angel Carrera emerged around the corner. 'I see I'm expected.'

Leanne was furious she hadn't considered this might happen, and after all her careful plans he'd caught her on the hop. She knew she must look a fright, but it was too late now.

Angel Carrera wasn't too tall, or too slender, but just right. He had a slow, almost lazy manner of walking and he looked delicious in his white moleskins, polished boots and check shirt.

She smiled and looked up into smouldering black eyes that turned her knees to jelly. 'Bastard,' she said with a husky voice. 'You knew you'd catch me out.'

He swept her up in his arms and kissed her. Then without a word he carried her back to the homestead and through the screen door. Setting her on her feet his dark eyes took in the faded shirt, the mucky old jeans and scuffed boots. He smiled down at her. 'Come here, Mrs Carrera,' he growled.

They tore at each others clothes and fought their way out of hampering boots. Their skins touched and the electricity shot between them taking their breath away. The time apart had only served to kindle the flames and now they were free to gorge themselves.

Much later they were lying sated on the big double bed. 'I haven't caught you at a bad time, I hope?' Angel's hair shone raven black in the beam of sunlight pouring through the curtains as he ran his fingers over her naked body.

'Not at all,' she gasped as he played her as expertly as any violin virtuoso. 'Just earlier than I expected.' She was finding it hard to concentrate as the need for him began to well again. 'Didn't you get my message?'

'What message?' He leaned on one elbow, his dark brows came together in a frown.

'I phoned and told someone at your office that they'd been delayed because of the rain. One of the jackaroos rode in and told me they'd had trouble out on Ten Mile Creek.'

'Nothing serious, I hope?'

'They'll be here,' she said firmly. 'They've already mustered most of the country and have about a thousand head yarded up in each of the twenty holding paddocks. Dad's sending the first lot in later today so you can make a start.'

'I've only allowed a week,' he said thoughtfully. 'Think he'll get them through in time?'

She nodded. 'Dad knows he has to get them to the market.'

He smiled, his dark gaze dancing over her in a way that made her pulse race and her insides do cartwheels. 'Thought I'd get here early so everything's ready for their arrival,' he murmured. 'Can you think of anything we can do to pass the time?'

160

His wicked smile melted her and she ran her fingers over his flat stomach. His skin was cool, the line of hair beneath his belly button enticing. 'Oh, I think so,' she murmured.

Claire woke from her dream and lay there for a moment wondering what it could have meant. She turned on her side, drawing her knees to her chest, her eyes firmly closed. She wanted to hold on to that dream for it had brought a deep calm – a stillness she hadn't known for a long time. And as the sun began to drift through the window and warm her shoulders, she let her thoughts wander back over the dream that had seemed so real, so lucid and brightly coloured.

She had been surrounded by silence, swimming in a calm sea of almost impossible blue beneath a sky that seemed to stretch to infinity beneath a warm sun. Yet despite her usual fear of the ocean and the fact she could see no land in any direction, she was unafraid. Treading water, she'd looked down, and there hundreds of feet below her was an ancient, ruined city. The white colonnades were mostly still standing along the wide paved streets and the sunlight filtered through the water to make them gleam. As she floated there high above this wonderful place she wondered if it was the lost city of Atlantis, yet it didn't seem to matter – nothing seemed to matter.

Then, as she surveyed the silent streets and graceful columns she became aware of them rising towards her. Aware of the white lintel between two supporting columns coming

161

beneath her feet. Aware of it still rising and taking her with it. She stood firm on that cool marble as she was lifted high above the water, and there on the horizon was an island. An island that seemed to beckon. She began to swim, never tiring, never fearful she wouldn't reach it – for this was the place she'd sought for years.

Lacy ripples splashed softly on the crescent of white sand as she emerged from the water. She looked about her, seeing only a tangle of thorns and spiny bushes barring her way further on to the island. It was as she looked at that final frontier she realised she would have to find a way through that barrier. The prospect of the battle ahead held no fears – for once she'd gained the other side she knew she would find a peace that transcended all others.

Claire finally opened her eyes. The dream was still with her, the calm acceptance remaining even in the light of day. Perhaps it was an omen, she thought as she clambered out of bed and headed for the bathroom. An omen of a long battle ahead – one in which she had to fight with more courage than she'd ever known.

Chapter Six

Matt Derwent had a sleepless night and finally lost patience and clambered out of bed. The magpies were singing their purring warble and the parakeets were squabbling in the gum trees as he whistled up his three dogs and padded barefoot out on to the verandah. It was fresh after the rain, the earth still damp, the grass smelling sweet amidst the brash scent of wattle and pine. The dogs, an old blue heeler, a collie and a mongrel raced past him and soon disappeared around the back of the house. It was great to let them run free without fear of traffic coming along the dusty lane.

He breathed in the scents of a new day, relishing the coolness before the sun rose fully to scorch the earth again. He was glad he'd moved here, for there were no memories of Laura and their life together. No painful reminders of what had been and what might have been if she hadn't been taken from him so suddenly.

The little wooden house at Threeways was in sharp contrast to the rambling Queenslander he'd sold to come here, but the four rooms and tiny front garden suited him now he was on his own, and there were almost a thousand acres of good pasture out the back and thousands of miles of wilderness to explore beyond that. The Queenslander had been on the coast between

163

Brisbane and Coolangatta. The verandah looked out over crashing surf and miles of golden sand, the garden coming to an abrupt halt on the edge of the dunes. The town was similar in character to most remote Australian settlements, the inhabitants spread over several miles, mostly in isolated farms. There were shops, and an RSL club as well as a tiny cinema, a sailing and surfing club and a hotel. He and Laura had had a good social life. His small practice was busy with the local pets and the stable yards and small hobby farms that dotted the hills backing on to the coast, and the year before everything turned sour, he'd helped set up a rescue centre for injured and orphaned koalas.

It was different here. There were no clubs, no shops, just the hotel at Threeways which was almost fifty miles away and his closest neighbour. Yet the vast wilderness of Lawns National Park sprawled fifty miles to the west of him, and the Gregory River meandered peacefully through the verdant bush nearby. He'd spent many an hour fishing on its banks or canoeing to Crimson Finch Waterhole where wallabies and possums came to drink and a myriad number of birds flew in at sunset. It was a magical place.

Matt looked at his front garden and realised he needed to cut the grass. The cinder path was dotted with weeds and the mail box by the gate was in danger of falling off its post. The picket fence needed painting and the gate new hinges, yet he was in no mood to do anything about it today, for his thoughts were elsewhere.

He leaned against the verandah post and lit his

first cigarette of the day as he watched the sun come up. Kookaburras were already getting territorial in the bush behind him, and the mist was like candy floss in the tops of the tall trees. He tried to imagine Claire walking up that path, her smile one of pleasure at seeing him, her footsteps light. What would she think of this place after the grandeur of Warratah Station? What did she think of him?

Matt hitched up his trousers and, with a rueful grin, ran his hand over his naked torso. He still had a flat stomach and his arms and chest were fairly muscled because of the heavy work he had to do with the large animals he treated. Yet he knew he was far from the Aussie ideal of the blond surfer with a six pack stomach and bulging muscles. He was an old bloke pushing forty, with a crook knee and hair that refused to do what he wanted regardless of how much he spent getting it cut. A girl like Claire wouldn't look at him twice.

He became impatient with his thoughts and stubbed out his smoke. Ramming his feet into boots he grabbed an old shirt from the verandah chair and stepped into the yard. The cinders crunched beneath his feet as he made his way around the house to the stables. They were in good condition compared to the rest of the property and the concrete yard was scoured clean. The hay barn stood close by, the feed store off to one side, raised on bricks to ward off termites and vermin. His utility was parked under the lean-to at the side of the stables, his plane tethered at the end of the runway he'd had built on the far western side of the home paddock.

The dogs barked as they ran round him and he patted each silky head as he walked through the yard. His six horses peered out from their boxes and he opened the doors and led them out to the pasture. It was still too cold at night to leave them out, but the days were warm enough and there was plenty of shelter beneath the trees.

Leaning on the railings he watched them crop the long, green grass, their tails swishing, their coats gleaming. The dogs raced through the grass, noses down, tails up, ears pricked for the scent or sight of rabbits. He ran his fingers through his hair and grinned with the joy of a new day. A day in which sadness had been banished – where memories remained, but distantly and without pain. He was a lucky man, he realised. And while he was in such a good mood he should do something about Claire, for the thought of her wouldn't leave him and he knew he wouldn't be satisfied until he saw her again.

Claire had her usual cup of tea for breakfast and kept a stoic silence as Aurelia lectured her on the importance of eating a proper meal. They were in the kitchen, the scent of frying bacon mingling with the aroma of tobacco and despite her age, Aurelia had tucked into a large plate of eggs, bacon, sausage and fried bread before lighting her pipe. 'Do you have anything special to do today, Mum?' Claire asked as she helped with the washing up.

Ellie eyed her, her hands deep in soapy water.

'Not really. The chores were done while you were still snoring,' she teased. 'That's what city life does for you, Claire – teaches you bad habits.'

'Fair go, Mum,' she protested. 'I've been up for ages and it's only eight o'clock.'

'Precisely,' muttered Aurelia from her chair at the table. 'Day's half over.'

Claire grinned and decided it was wiser to say nothing. 'I thought we could go for a ride?' she said to her mother. 'It's been so long and I want to see Warratah again.'

'Good idea.' Ellie finished the last plate and dried her hands. 'Leave all this, it'll dry itself.' She turned to Aurelia. 'You don't mind being left alone for a while, do you?'

Aurelia grimaced. 'Don't have much choice these days. Can't ride any more and the sun's too hot for me now.' She pushed back her chair and stood up, her monocle glinting. 'Not much use for anything nowadays,' she grumbled. 'I remember when I could ride all day, sleep on the ground at night and do it all over again for days on end. I hate being old and bloody useless, but I suppose it comes to us all in the end.'

'The alternative isn't much more thrilling,' replied Claire with dry humour. 'I'm sure we could get the old trap from the barn and put Smoky in the traces again.'

Aurelia glared. 'Wouldn't be seen dead in that thing,' she retorted. 'I'd look like Queen Victoria.'

Claire and her mother exchanged looks.

'I saw that,' Aurelia snapped. 'Clear off and leave an old woman to her thoughts. All this stirring up of the past has made me remember things, and I want time and peace to give them my full attention.'

Claire could see the twinkle in her eye as they hugged and knew the old girl hadn't been too offended. It must be terrible to be old, she thought as she went to fetch her boots and hat, and very frustrating, especially for a woman who had once been so active and full of energy.

The yard was busy with men collecting their gear and loading up the utility. Doors slammed, spurs jingled and voices called. The atmosphere was light and filled with an energy she'd forgotten. Some of the faces she remembered, some were new, but they all greeted her with a smile and wished her 'G'day'.

'They're getting ready to go over to Jarrah to help with the mob,' explained Ellie as they tacked up their horses. 'They were going yesterday, but Lee said there'd been a hitch so we'll be starting later than expected.' She put her foot in the stirrup and swung into the saddle. 'Leanne's quite happy about the delay. Angel's unexpectedly home.'

Claire gathered up the reins. The gelding was a bit toey, but manageable. 'What's this husband of hers like?' she asked. She'd only seen the wedding photographs.

Ellie turned her mare's head towards the first of the gates that would lead them out into Gregory Downs. 'He's from Argentina – or at least his grandparents were – and he's the government vet and Inspector of Stock for this area.' She grinned and pulled down the brim of her bush hat. 'He's very handsome, and his manners are exquisite, but I wouldn't trust him as far as I could throw him. I think Leanne's got her work cut out there.'

Claire was intrigued. 'Why? You don't think he'll be unfaithful, do you?'

'Not yet,' replied Ellie as she leaned down and unfastened the gate. 'They're still at the honey-moon stage. But Angel's too handsome for his own good and with the amount of time he has to spend away from Jarrah, it's putting temptation in his way.'

Claire thought about her no-nonsense sister. 'Leanne might just be the one to pin him down,' she murmured as they began to trot through the long grass. 'Now she's got him, I can't see her letting him stray.'

Ellie squinted into the sun. 'Are we going to talk about your sister, or ride?'

'Race you to the waterhole.' Claire nudged the gelding into a longer stride and eased forward in the saddle. They left Ellie behind them in those few yards and Claire felt the exhilaration of riding with the warm wind on her face, her hair streaming behind her. The outback spread out in every direction, the green grass, the birds put to flight as they raced across the plains. This was freedom. This was life. She'd forgotten how claustrophobic a city could be. Forgotten how much she had once loved this magical part of the world.

Ellie raced up alongside, the mare lengthening her stride as she stretched her neck and pounded through the long, lush grass. Claire grinned as the gelding took the lead by a nose and hung on.

'You cheated,' gasped Ellie as she slithered

from the saddle and leaned against the mare's heaving sides.

'I know,' said Claire. She laughed as she dismounted and slapped the gelding's neck. 'It's the only way to beat you.'

They led the horses into the cool, green shadows of the trees. Water splashed nearby, birds called and the warm wind sighed in the tops of the pines. Threading their way through the bush they stopped by the side of the natural water-hole that formed an almost perfect circle beneath the sheer drop of a dark rock cliff. A waterfall trickled with a soothing splash into the clear, cold pool and tree ferns acted like umbrellas over the flat rocks and rough stones that formed a natural beach.

Ellie pulled out two tin mugs and they joined the horses at the waterside and took a drink. The water was icy, burning its way down Claire's throat. Yet nothing out of a tap had ever tasted as sweet. Once refreshed they sat on the flat rocks and leaned back on their elbows, enjoying each other's company after the years apart, re-tying the bonds, catching up on news of friends and the local gossip.

Claire finally lay back and gazed up through the palm fronds. The sky was blue with only a wisp of cloud. There would be no more rain today. Remembering her dream, she turned on her side and looked at Ellie. 'I'm ready to hear a bit more of the story, Mum,' she said quietly.

Ellie sighed and hugged her knees. She lifted her face to the dappled sunlight and closed her eyes. 'Are you sure?'

It was almost a whisper, and Claire felt the uneasiness begin to thread through her again. Yet the strange calm acceptance remained with her from that dream, and she knew that however bad things turned out, she would always have her parent's love. 'It's why I've come home. Better to have no more secrets,' she replied. 'As Aurelia said, I'm old enough to understand.'

Ellie's sharp glance was enigmatic. 'I hope so,' she murmured. There was a pause, then with a sigh, she began to speak. 'Charlie finally found work on one of the enormous stations on Halls Creek in Western Australia. Despite the vast distances out here, the story of Satan's theft and subsequent death had spread like a bush fire, and he'd found it the devil's own job to get work. Aurelia's fifty pounds was long gone by now, along with the prize money and two of his three remaining horses. He was almost back to square one.'

'Why didn't he come home?' Claire murmured. 'Surely he must have known he'd be forgiven?'

Ellie's smile was sad as she stared into the cool, clear depths of the waterhole. 'There were times when he longed to return. For he missed Joe more than he'd ever thought possible. Missed his quiet wisdom, his gentle approach to trouble and his loyalty. It was all very well riding across the red heart of the Northern Territory in his quest for adventure, but how much better it would have been if he could have turned the clock back and had his twin beside him.'

Claire watched the expressions flit over her mother's face and knew she was seeing things from the past, things that were already casting long shadows. She shivered despite the warmth of the sunlight filtering through the trees. Where was this all leading?

'Charlie wasn't brave enough to face his brother,' said Ellie coldly. 'Two years had passed. Satan was dead and his own reputation as a horse thief had set him apart from the men he worked with – how could he expect his brother to forgive him?'

'So, what did he do?' Claire prompted as Ellie fell into a protracted silence.

'The talk at that time was about war,' said Ellie eventually. 'You know what Australian men are like. They enjoy a good fight and like to think of themselves as tough and almost invincible. Mateship is the greatest honour one man can bestow on another, and when it looked as if we'd be dragged into the war in Europe they couldn't bloody wait to get their hands dirty.'

Claire was taken aback by the fierceness in her mother's voice. She'd never heard her speak like that before, never witnessed such coldness.

'Charlie was no exception,' she said with bitterness. 'He listened to the stories around the camp-fire during that branding drove and saw a way of redeeming himself. For the men who answered the call of war would be tomorrow's heroes. Heroes who would be welcomed home to stations like Warratah. Heroes who would be forgiven past sins and enfolded once more into the embrace of their families.'

Claire had many questions, but she remained silent as her mother stared into the past and

172

faced the things that bedevilled her.

'He wasn't the only one to enlist right at the start,' began Ellie again. 'Seamus decided he wanted to be a hero too.'

Claire noticed the glint of tears in her mother's eyes. 'Were you in love with Seamus?' she asked softly.

'I thought I was – but at sixteen everything you feel is intense. His leaving almost broke my heart.'

Claire stared at the waterfall and tried to imagine how it must have been for her mother all those years ago. There was little she could compare it to. The Vietnam war was big news at the moment, but it was too remote to have any real impact on her life. And although it had been the subject of some violent demonstrations back on the university campus, she hadn't known anyone who'd actually enlisted to fight alongside the Americans.

She shivered as she thought of some of the news reports – horrific images of children burning, people being executed, jet planes on bombing attacks and village huts blazing in the night skies. She realised she had been touched by war through the media, yet it hadn't reached out to her family or threatened all she knew, had never become personal as it had for her mother.

Seamus had kept his enlistment secret, turning up at Warratah with his father in his smart new uniform. He'd been so handsome, so young, so excited about taking his first real trip out of the outback and into adventure. He hadn't had to persuade Ellie very hard to take a walk with him, and they'd sneaked out of the homestead and hurried across the dry fields to the stand of trees at the far end of home pasture.

Ellie smiled as she remembered his kiss. It was her first and she would never forget it. His mouth was warm and after an initial wariness had become softly demanding. He'd held her tightly, his expression unusually solemn as he told her he'd return before she knew it. The war would be over soon and he wasn't going to chance missing out on it.

Innocent days, she thought sadly. Neither of them knew anything of the world or really understood the war that was being waged in Europe. Nor had they the experience or knowledge to express their feelings about his leaving except in a few fumbling kisses. She had been sad to think she wouldn't be seeing him for a long time. Excited that this handsome young man had kissed her and asked her to write to him.

Yet something in her had changed that day, and the hero-worship and adoration she'd once felt for him had disappeared, and in its place had come the warmth of friendship – a closeness that would remain with them for the rest of their lives – an unbearable sorrow at his leaving. But she was not in love with him, she realised. Could never promise to wait for him.

Seamus had sensed it too, for after those first few clumsy kisses they had drawn apart before standing hand in hand to look back on Warratah. They had seen the acknowledgement in one another's eyes that their lives were meant to follow separate paths, and although there was a tinge of sadness in that acceptance, there was also a certain release. For now they were free to follow their own destinies.

Seamus had left for Cloncurry the next day and Ellie had shed tears into her pillow as she prayed he'd return safely.

She emerged from her thoughts and eyed her daughter. 'I want you to imagine how it was back then,' she began. 'War was looming, the young men were leaving and everything we knew was changing. The "phoney war", as the Yanks called it, was only the start of real hostilities and although we were far from Europe, our lives were about to be changed for ever.'

She sighed. 'Seamus had already left, and we heard later he was in the same training camp as Charlie and that the two of them had become close friends. Aunt Aurelia and I were beginning to despair for the drought had returned and apart from Joe, we were left with old men, boys too young to enlist and our tribe of Aborigines to help run Warratah.' Her voice dropped to a murmur as she returned to the past. 'I was seventeen.'

Aurelia was now the proud owner of a radio, and each night she and Ellie sat in the kitchen and listened to the BBC news. 'What happens now?' asked Ellie as she switched the radio off. 'No one seems to be doing anything. Perhaps the Yanks are right about it being a phoney war and Seamus can come home?'

Aurelia concentrated on ramming tobacco into her pipe. 'Don't be naive, darling,' she muttered around the stem as she put a match to the tobacco. 'Hitler won't stop until he's got it all,' she said between puffs. 'With Russia on his side, he'll make a clean sweep right through Europe. I just hope the Brits have learned from the last war and are properly prepared – but I have a nasty feeling that isn't the case.'

Ellie thought about her elderly grandparents. She'd never met them, but felt she knew them through their letters and Aurelia's stories. They lived in a country mansion in England which had been the family home for three centuries, and if her aunt was right, they could be in danger. 'What about Mum, and Grandpa and Grandma?' she asked.

Aurelia chewed on her pipe stem. 'I very much hope it doesn't come to it, but I have no doubt Mother and Pa will defend their home to the last. They won't be pushed around by the likes of Hitler.' She dipped her chin and eyed Ellie from beneath her brows. 'Alicia is another matter. I suspect your mother is already on her way back to America.'

Ellie pursed her lips. 'There's nothing in the States for her any more,' she said thoughtfully. 'Chuck's houses and apartments have been sold off to pay his debts, and since the divorce, she's lost contact with all her friends over there.' She thought about it for a moment. 'She'll fall on her feet whatever she does,' she said finally. 'You know Mum.'

Aurelia nodded. 'It's not her I'm worried

about,' she said thoughtfully. 'The risk of invasion is high and I wish Mother and Pa would take my advice and get out while they can.' She sighed and tamped the tobacco down before relighting it. 'But they won't. Too English and far too stubborn.'

Ellie smiled. It was the pot calling the kettle black, only Aurelia would never understand.

Their conversation was interrupted by a rap on the screen door. 'Now what?' said Aurelia crossly. 'If that's another of the men coming to give me notice, I'll box his ears.' She hauled herself out of her chair and stomped out of the room.

Ellie smothered a giggle. Poor Aunt Aurelia – she'd always sound like a bossy schoolmistress. She listened to the mumble of low voices in the hall and looked round at the approach of tramping boots.

Joe was standing in the doorway, his hat screwed up in his hands, his green eyes seeking her out. 'G'day, Ellie,' he said quietly, following up his greeting with a grin that had a way of reaching right to her core.

Ellie smiled as she took in the broad shoulders, the muscled arms, square chin and wonderful eyes. She felt the flutter in her stomach, and the lurch of longing as she stood before him. 'G'day, Joe,' she said with unaccustomed shyness. 'Good to see you back.'

Joe, who'd been on the long spring drove, grinned again as Aurelia pushed past him and began to clatter glasses and beer bottles. 'I brought a visitor,' he drawled. 'Caught up with him when I went to see Seamus off in the Curry.'

He stepped aside, and Ellie finally became aware of the man standing beside him. She took in the rusty-brown halo of hair, the broad nose and amber eyes. 'Snowy,' she shrieked. 'How're ya goin?'

'Yeah,' he drawled. 'Good.' His face creased in a wide smile as he shook her hand. 'Don't need to ask about you,' he teased as he looked her up and down. 'You fair grown up since I last seen yer.'

'How's Wang Lee? Is Gowrie still as beautiful as ever? Have you seen any of the other blokes from the muster we went on?' Ellie finally ran out of breath.

'Reckon you ain't changed much, though,' he drawled as he rolled a smoke. 'Still full of bloody questions.' He grinned. 'But I ain't been Gowrie way in a while,' he said as he lit the cigarette. 'Been working for Vestey. But I heard Wang Lee's still there, and I met a couple of the other blokes in the Curry.'

'I suppose you're looking for work?' said Aurelia abruptly as she poured the beer into glasses. 'There's plenty of it now half Australia's men have rushed off like scalded cats looking for a scrap.'

Snowy shook his head. 'I'm off to boot camp in two weeks' time,' he said proudly. 'Joined up in the Curry. First black feller they took on. Reckon they didn't quite know what to do with me, but I heard there's more black fellers joining up from The Top End and Torries Straits, so I won't be alone.'

Ellie flinched as Aurelia slammed the beer on

178

the sidetable, spilling it on the polished wood. 'Of all the damn-fool things to do,' she stormed as she whipped round to face him. 'You Australians just love a fight, don't you? You're so macho and tough you can't see you're just being used as bloody cannon fodder.'

'Fair go, missus,' Snowy drawled as he shuffled his feet and backed off from the withering attack. 'Pig Iron Bob says we gotta help defend England – and I'm proud to do it.'

Aurelia gave an exasperated sigh. 'Prime Minster Menzies should think before he speaks,' she muttered. Then, as Ellie and the two men watched, she seemed to realise how unpatriotic and rude she'd been and made a tremendous effort to make amends. 'I apologise for my rudeness, Snowy,' she said finally. 'But with all the men leaving, how the hell am I supposed to run this place?'

'The same way you've always done,' said Joe firmly. 'You managed through the drought with only a handful of men and the stock-boys. You can do it again.'

Aurelia looked at him gratefully, and for the first time Ellie realised her aunt had grown fond of Joe despite her initial misgivings. 'Does that mean you'll be staying on, Joe?' Aurelia asked hopefully.

Ellie had to sit down. For in that moment she realised that if Joe left Warratah her world would collapse. She was in love with him. So deeply and passionately in love with him she suddenly couldn't imagine life without him. The realisation took her breath away – the force of it

179

hammering with her pulse as she awaited his answer.

'For now,' he said as he glanced across at Ellie. 'Pig Iron Bob also said we should consolidate our strength and our industries. The world's going to need meat and leather as well as wool, and we gotta see they get it.'

'Well thank goodness for some common sense in all this madness,' Aurelia breathed. She looked across at Ellie and smiled, seemingly unaware of her niece's inner turmoil. 'Seems we won't be losing all our young men,' she said brightly. 'We'll survive somehow.'

Ellie caught the glance exchanged between Snowy and Joe, and felt the chill of premonition. The light of battle shone in Joe's eyes just as brightly as in Snowy's. Joe wouldn't stay here in the middle of nowhere when his mates were at war. He wouldn't want to be called a cowardly dingo for not fighting. She could have wept. For she had only just found him. And now she was about to lose him.

The two week visit was almost over when Joe and Snowy left early one morning to ride out on to the plains and check the fences. There was no real need, but it was an excuse to spend time away from the homestead and the women to discuss how they really felt about the war and to catch up with news of old friends.

Heat shimmered across the horizon, and the gum trees wilted, their dappled shadows dancing over the grass that was already turning brown despite the rain they'd had in the past year or so.

The latest drought was beginning to bite, and Joe had helped Aurelia and Ellie move the stock several times to find better grazing. A kookaburra chortled in the distance, and the mournful three note caw of a crow seemed to be a portent of disaster as the two men rode easily in the saddle, in no hurry to get anywhere.

'How long you reckon you'll stay?' asked Snowy.

Joe looked out over the land and sighed. 'Not for long,' he said finally. 'I know Aurelia and Ellie are relying on me, but I gotta do my bit, Snowy. Can't let you blokes down by hiding away out here.'

'Times are gunna be hard for the women, I reckon,' said Snowy. 'Outback's no place to be left on their own.'

'Aurelia's tough,' said Joe firmly. 'She'll be right.'

They rode in silence, enjoying the sun on their backs, the warm breeze in their face. 'I gotta a girl down Longreach way,' said Snowy eventually. 'She was pretty crook about me joining up, but her old man's a tough old bludger, he'll see her and her ma through. They got a sheep station out in mulga country, but the drought ain't so bad over there.'

'Strewth, Snowy. You ain't got yourself hitched?'

Snowy grinned. 'No worries, mate. Me and Shirl ain't tied the knot. But it was a close thing I can tell you. When I said I was going up to the Curry to enlist she fair bit me 'ead off. And I reckon her old man woulda got his rifle out if I hadn't shot through when I did.'

'She ain't in the family way?' Joe's voice was sharp.

'Bloody hell, Joe. Give me some credit.' Snowy laughed and tilted back his head. 'I just ain't ready to be tied down yet, that's all. If she still wants me when the war's over, then I'll consider it. I'll have had me share of adventures by then and be ready to settle down.' He chewed on a matchstick for a moment. 'I'll still need to go walkabout now and then, mind. Can't lose sight of tradition, and a bloke needs space and time to think. But Shirl's mum's from the same tribe as me, so she'll understand and keep the old white fella off me back.'

The silence of the outback closed in around them as the horses plodded through the crisp grass. Joe's thoughts returned to Ellie as they always did when he was away from her, and he tried to imagine life without her and Warratah. His feelings had changed towards Ellie, for in the past few months she'd grown from a kid into a beautiful young woman. Gone was the easy way he'd once had with her, the camaraderie of an older brother diminished in this new and rather frightening depth of affection. Yet he was well aware that declaring himself now could destroy that delicate bond. Ellie was still only seventeen. She had carried a crush for Seamus right through the early years and now he was gone he wasn't sure if she was truly over him.

'Looking thoughtful there, mate,' said Snowy, breaking into his thoughts. 'Wouldn't have something to do with Ellie, would it? She's grown into a beaut little sheila.' He grinned, showing a broad gleam of very white teeth. 'Bit different to the larrikin she was on the drove. Fair wore me out with her endless questions and demands for Dreamtime stories.'

Joe shook his head. He had no wish to discuss Ellie – it was too personal. 'Have you heard anything more of Charlie since he joined up?' he said finally. It was a question he'd wanted to ask ever since he'd bumped into Snowy back in the Curry, but the time had never seemed right.

'Last I heard he was on his way to Europe.' Snowy fell silent, the shadow of his hat brim masking his expression.

'Good on him,' muttered Joe. 'Mighta known he'd be one of the first.' He blinked as he stared into the sun. 'But he coulda come and said goodbye first,' he added.

'Reckon he weren't too sure about his welcome here,' said Snowy thoughtfully.

Joe stared out at the miles of waving grass. The cattle were widespread, still sleek and fat despite the onset of drought. He loved this land. Loved it with all his heart. But he'd have given it all up for the chance to talk to his twin again. 'He knew I'd forgive him,' he said finally. 'A brother's more important than any horse.'

Snowy wiped the sweat from his forehead and hatband, his eyes screwed up in the glare from the sun. 'Charlie's not the kind of bloke to admit he was wrong,' he said slowly. 'After what happened to Satan, he slipped out of sight and no one knew where he was for months. I think he was genuinely sorry, but couldn't face the humiliation of seeing you again.'

'Just like Charlie,' said Joe sadly. 'Always going off half-cocked without a thought in his damn head for the consequences.'

'He had it rough, mate,' replied Snowy. 'Lost nearly everything before he got work over in Western Australia. Big Stan told me he turned up with holes in his boots and his arse hanging out of his strides.'

'And all because of a horse.' Joe looked across at Snowy as the question burned to be asked. 'Was it you told the racing committee about Satan?'

Snowy brought his horse to a standstill. 'Not me, mate. Wouldn't do it to a cobber, even though I thought what he'd done was dingo mean.'

Joe looked at him thoughtfully. Snowy had always been straight with him, but this time he wasn't too sure. 'So who was it then?' he demanded.

'One of the other jockeys,' said Snowy flatly. 'Bloke from Hells Gate who'd worked on this place over the few weeks Charlie was here. He recognised Satan immediately. Seems he had a lot of money on the local favourite and the jockey was a mate. They cooked it up together when they saw who they were up against.'

'I'm sorry, Snowy,' said Joe with a sigh. 'I thought it was you dobbed him in.'

'Nah, mate. Had a few quid on him meself. Reckon I was as cut up as Charlie when that beauty had to be put down.' He chewed on a matchstick as he rested his hands on the pommel and stared off into the distance. 'Didn't have the

184

heart to face Charlie after the race. I only heard what happened in the weighing-room through the bush telegraph. By then it was too late and Charlie had shot through.'

Joe gathered up the reins and adjusted his hat. It was a beautiful day and he wasn't prepared to let the storm clouds of war and family estrangement dull what was Snowy's last day of freedom before boot camp. Time would come when he too would have to leave this wonderful place, and he needed to embrace it so he could carry it with him into war. 'Let's put all this talk of war and Charlie behind us and ride. I don't know about you, but I've got the feeling things are going to change for all of us, and I want to make the most of this while I can.'

The rumble of war was the only dark cloud that hovered over the outback as drought once again took a stranglehold on the thousands of miles of grazing. Denmark and Norway surrendered in the spring of 1940, and this was swiftly followed by Holland in May. Belgium fell and the battle of Dunkerque began.

Ellie and Aurelia had long ago said their good-byes to Snowy, and promised to write. Now they stayed close to the wireless, making sure they were never too far from the homestead. They sat huddled with Joe over the ugly black box in the corner of the lounge as if by their nearness, they too could become part of the great battle. They listened in awe as the BBC described the thousands of little ships which sailed into the enemy bombardment and rescued hundreds of thousands of men from those bloodstained beaches. Cheered as the new English Prime Minister Churchill gave his rousing speeches, and cried as some of the rescued soldiers told their stories.

Yet the reality of their own battle was bringing them to despair. The outback was undermanned at the best of times, but since Dunkerque the steady stream of men signing up to be enlisted had grown into a flood. Warratah was at crisis point. They were gasping from lack of water, the price of feed was high and the grass – already brown and lacking any kind of goodness – was being hit by an explosion in the rabbit population.

'It's going to be a devil to survive this,' said Aurelia that evening as she switched off the wireless. Joe had left the homestead to return to his bed in the bunk-house. 'We're down to old men, boys and Aborigines. When Joe leaves we'll virtually be on our own.'

Ellie looked up from her knitting. 'He won't leave,' she said stoutly. 'He knows how desperately we need him.'

Aurelia's smile was sad. 'That sounds more like your heart talking, than your head, my dear,' she said softly. 'He's nearly twenty-two, Ellie. We both know he has to leave.' She put a work-roughened hand on Ellie's shoulder. 'If you love him as much as I think you do, then you have to let him go.'

Ellie rammed the needles into the ball of wool and stuffed it down the side of her chair. She didn't like the way this conversation was going. 'He's never said anything,' she said defiantly.

186

'And I'd have known if he was keeping a secret from me. I can always tell.'

Aurelia polished her monocle. 'Men like Joe don't share their thoughts and feelings,' she said evenly. 'They aren't the kind to make a fuss.' She fixed the monocle and folded her arms. 'These men of the outback are the strongest, bravest men I know, and you mustn't pin your hopes on Joe staying. He's an Australian, with an Australian pride in himself and his country that will never keep him tied to this place when his mates are doing their bit. You of all people should understand that.'

Ellie chewed her lip, her thoughts in turmoil. 'Has he said anything to you?' she asked finally. 'Is this your way of telling me he's leaving?'

Aurelia sighed deeply. 'He and I had a long talk this morning, and this is my rather heavy-handed attempt to forewarn you.' She reached for her pipe. 'Joe wanted to tell you himself when it was nearer the time, but I felt you should be prepared.'

Ellie stared back, betrayed. Why hadn't Joe had the guts to come right out with it and tell her instead of confiding in Aunt Aurelia? Did he think she was still too much of a kid to take it on the chin? She stood up and marched towards the door. 'I'm going out for some fresh air,' she snapped.

The screen door slammed behind her and she glared out from the verandah to the bunk-house with her hands rammed into her pockets. She wouldn't cause a scene. Wouldn't go rushing over there and beg him to stay regardless of how badly

187

she wanted to. She would show him she was grown up enough to deal with this in a mature and sensible manner and wait for him to come to her.

'Watch ya cock!' shouted Kelly.

'Shut up,' Ellie hissed as she tossed a magazine at him and threw herself into a chair. 'Just shut up and mind your own flaming business.'

Thanks to the endeavours of the men who'd once worked on Warratah, Kelly had learned a whole new vocabulary since the beginning of the war, and as the afternoon of the following day began to wane, he broke into a screech that made them jump. 'Bombs away,' he yelled. 'Up yer arse, Hitler.'

'Shut up, you dreadful old reprobate,' commanded Aurelia. 'How the devil am I supposed to do the accounts with you yelling in my ear?'

Kelly's coxcomb lifted as he strutted along his perch. 'Flak,' he yelled. 'Rollocks.'

Ellie giggled at the ridiculous contortions Kelly was going through. Her mood had lightened since the previous afternoon. A good night's sleep and a long, solitary ride over the plains had brought her to the conclusion that her aunt was right. Joe would go off to fight his war and she would have to let him. It was a fact of life, as indisputable as the rising of the sun. Just as her love for him should be all-embracing – generous enough to allow him to make his own decisions – it could not be selfish and restrictive, making him resent her. She would wait until he was ready to tell her he was leaving. And find the strength to smile and wish him well regardless of how painful their parting might be.

'Flak,' squawked Kelly as he marched up and down his perch.

Ellie burst out laughing despite her sadness. 'I swear Kelly's even got Hitler's swagger. All he needs is a moustache.'

Aurelia looked at him with a jaundiced eye. 'I knew it was a mistake to let Jack bring that newsreel out here. We should have shown it in the barn, not on the verandah where old smarty pants could get ideas.'

'Never surrender,' Kelly yelled in his best imitation Churchill. 'Flak, flak, flak.'

Aurelia lifted her eyebrow. 'Time to put his cover on,' she said firmly as she got up from her chair and approached the cage. 'Getting rather too pleased with himself.'

Kelly grumbled and bashed his water tray with his beak for a few minutes, then realised he wasn't going to be forgiven so gave up and went to sleep.

'Peace at last,' sighed Aurelia. 'I wish I could say the same about the state of the world.'

Ellie pulled off her boots and wriggled her toes. Then she untied the ribbon in her long hair and shook it free. If only Joe had the courage to talk to me, she thought. I know he wants to, because I can see it in his eyes. Damn this bloody war, she thought impatiently. It was so unfair.

'Ellie. Looks like you've got a visitor.'

Aurelia's soft voice brought her from her gloomy thoughts. She looked up at the sound of the clip-clop of hoofs on the impacted earth of the homestead yard and gasped. Joe was astride his horse, a manicured and polished Clipper on a leading rein.

Ellie was hardly aware of getting out of the chair and approaching the top verandah step. Yet she knew her face was radiant as she looked into Joe's eyes and finally acknowledged the feelings they shared. There was no need for words between them – their understanding came as naturally as breathing.

Joe brought the horse and pony to a halt beside the top step of the verandah. His gaze was fixed on Ellie's face, and after a long silence, he held out the leading rein. 'Come for a ride?'

Ellie took the rein and swung on to Clipper's back. Joe smiled down at her and in silent communion they rode slowly away from the homestead and into the sunset.

Chapter Seven

Aurelia was frustrated at having been left behind, but she was wise enough to know her limitations. Her riding days might be over, yet her refusal to be carted about in a trap like a dowager didn't mean she'd given up on life. She might be old and creaking, but it was far better than the alternative, and dying was not on her agenda.

She walked across home yard, poked her head into the stables, feed store and cookhouse and realised everyone had gone over to Jarrah for the mob's return. Feeling dejected and rather lonely, she went back to the verandah and settled into a deep chair. She'd have the devil's own job to get out of it again, but Ellie and Claire would be back soon.

She breathed in the scent of warming earth and the roses Ellie had planted many years ago so they trailed up the verandah railings and dripped jewelled colour over the roof. It was very peaceful, with only the hum of flies and the murmur of the women over in the native humpies to break the silence. Yet that silence made her realise how much she missed Kelly and his raucous yell. She grinned and she looked out over the paddocks and outbuildings, her gaze trawling the distance between the two homesteads. Kelly had literally fallen off his perch three years ago. He'd been overexcited about something and had died mid-squawk during a torrent of filthy language. Yet the memory of him was intertwined with so many other memories that his passing had come, not only as a shock, but with the sad acknowledgement that one more tie had been broken between present and past. Soon there would be none left.

She dropped her chin to her chest and let her monocle dangle from its ribbon. Jack had loved Kelly, and the two of them had forged a great friendship – but then what else could she have expected, for they were both beguiling. As the warmth of the day closed in and the mistral breeze wafted along the verandah, Aurelia's thoughts returned to the past and to the man who had taught her to love again – but who had ultimately broken her heart.

Jack Withers had been based up on the north coast before the war, and apart from co-ordinating news over the two-way and delivering the mail and supplies, was Warratah's only link to the outside world before the emergence of the miracle of radio. They'd had their run-ins over the two-way, and until Alicia's first visit to Warratah had never met.

She'd realised on that first encounter what a fascinating man he was; not particularly handsome, but with a twinkle in his eye and a great sense of fun. She was almost fifty-one as their friendship blossomed in the heat and dust of the outback – yet she was aware of how set in her ways she'd become and was wary of his intentions, uncertain of her own.

Things had come to a head on the night Joe took Ellie for that ride. She'd returned to the accounts after the youngsters left, but couldn't concentrate. The shadows of war were darkened by the onset of the second drought. The billabongs had dried up until they were just claypans, and the rivers were so low even the smallest birds couldn't wade. The red heart of Australia was gasping again and the stockmen and women had a different battle to the one being fought in Europe.

Thank goodness Jack's too old and sensible to rush off and get enlisted, Aurelia smiled to herself. Not that the army would take him. He was well past his prime as far as the forces were concerned, and she prayed it would stay that way. She left the account books open and stared off across home pasture. Jack had been a regular visitor over the past few years and their strange friendship had blossomed to the point where they spoke at least twice a week over the two-way radio. Aurelia had made it clear she was not about to become the target for gossip, and had maintained a stiffness during these conversations where they could be overheard by half the population. But when he came out to Warratah all that changed, and she was looking forward to seeing him again at the end of the week.

She forced herself to snap out of her daydream. She and Jack were in their fifties and just good friends she told herself sternly. There was nothing for people to gossip about. She pulled her thoughts in order. The accounts needed doing and she was wasting the last of the daylight. Yet she found she still couldn't concentrate and gave up.

With a smile of pleasure she remembered the early days of their friendship, when the battle of wills had become a game they'd both enjoyed playing. Yet there had been a subtle change between them during the past few years and she supposed it had all begun when he'd brought Alicia out here before the war. They had found common ground during Alicia's short, dramatic stay, an understanding that hadn't faded after her departure. There had been many visits to Warratah since then, and during that time she'd come to realise he admired her sparky spirit and warm generosity. For all her bossy ways, she knew she was a woman after his own heart. A woman who suffered no fools, and who was as straightforward as he and blunt in her opinions.

She giggled softly as she thought of the look in his eyes as he sparred with her. She suspected he thought of her as a cuddly armful if only he dared take liberties – the thought didn't displease her. The sound of his plane making an approach on to the dirt runway snapped her from her thoughts and she hurried down the steps to the utility. Something had to be wrong for him to come early, and her pulse began to race. With Joe's imminent departure the last thing she needed was bad news.

The wheels bounced on the hard dirt, the tail dipped and he was down in a cloud of dust. Switching off the engine, he climbed down in to the furnace blast that was Warratah Station.

'I wasn't expecting you until tomorrow,' she

194

said as she moved away from the utility. 'Nothing wrong, is there?'

'Just thought I'd bring the mail early,' he drawled with studied nonchalance. 'There's the supplies you wanted in the back as well.'

Aurelia smiled up at him. He didn't fool her a bit. 'Good to see you,' she said.

'I'll get the supplies,' he murmured. The colour rose in his face as he ducked his head and tipped his hat brim low.

Aurelia watched him lope back to the plane. He had a way of making her feel like a kid again – all hormones and awkwardness – which was ridiculous for a woman of her age and experience of life. They worked together in companionable silence, but she was suspicious of his sly glances and thoughtful expression. There was definitely a hidden agenda behind this unexpected delivery and she knew he would eventually get around to telling her the real purpose of his call – he always did.

With the supplies stacked in the flat-bed of the utility, he climbed in beside her and they roared back to the homestead. Aurelia knew her driving scared him witless and as he clung on to the seat she wondered how he'd feel if she asked him to teach her to fly. She grinned. By the look on his face he was probably praying she never would. 'You can open your eyes now,' she said with alacrity as she slammed on the brakes and killed the engine. 'We're here.'

Jack wisely kept his opinion of women drivers to himself and helped carry the supplies and the sacks of mail in to the homestead. Sally, the native housemaid, began to poke and prod through the supplies. 'Leave all that,' Aurelia ordered. 'A cuppa is what we want. And if I find you've been helping yourself to the sugar and syrup so you can give it to that no-good lazy Jacky Jack I'll take the whip to your bottom.'

Sally's eyes rounded, then she giggled for she knew Aurelia would never carry out the threat. Yet both women knew where they stood and Sally would get her rations just like everyone else. 'Me alonga you cuppa,' she said through her giggles. Her curly eyelashes dipped. 'G'day Boss,' she said shyly to Jack.

Jack nodded in acknowledgement and after asking about Sally's numerous kids followed Aurelia out to the verandah. 'Where's Ellie?' he asked as he realised they were alone for a change.

'Making plans for her future, I'd say,' she murmured.

Jack cocked his head. 'Sounds ominous,' he drawled. He took the tobacco pouch from his shirt pocket and began to roll a smoke. 'I see you've put Kelly to bed for the night. No wonder it's so quiet.'

Aurelia polished her monocle. He was playing for time, but she wouldn't let him get away with it any longer. Her gaze was unwavering as she faced him. 'So why are you really here, Jack?' she asked flatly.

She watched impatiently as he took his time to light his smoke before he sat back and stared out over the darkening landscape. 'I'm thinking of joining up,' he said finally.

Aurelia stared at him. She could feel the colour

rise and ebb in her cheeks as the shock sent her thoughts into overdrive. Then she laughed. 'Silly old fool,' she spluttered. 'Really, Jack. I wish you wouldn't tease.'

He took a deep breath. 'I might be fifty-six, but I've got a lot of flying experience behind me. I'm going to offer my services to the RAAF as a trainer.'

The colour drained from her face and the monocle dangled on its ribbon. 'You're serious, aren't you?' she said quietly. Her pulse was drumming and she was finding it difficult to breathe.

He nodded. 'I can't sit about doing nothing, Aurelia. I've got the experience to teach our young fliers and hopefully it might keep them alive a bit longer.'

'I thought all the air force volunteers were being sent to Canada to join the Empire Air Training Scheme?'

'Most of 'em,' he admitted. 'But there's a training base starting up here.'

Aurelia's thoughts raced. Yet she remained silent as Sally brought the tea and biscuits out on to the verandah, her bare feet making hardly a sound on the wooden floor. She put down the tin tray with a clatter, her wide, curious gaze darting from Aurelia to Jack before she reluctantly backed away and returned to the house where Aurelia knew she could comfortably eavesdrop from behind the door. 'So you won't actually be doing any fighting?' Aurelia demanded.

'Shouldn't think so,' he replied. 'Bit long in the tooth now unfortunately, and my reactions are too slow to be of much use in a dogfight.'

Aurelia expelled a long sigh of relief. 'Thank goodness for that.'

Jack stubbed out his smoke with the heel of his foot. He looked into her face, his expression serious. 'Does it matter that much to you if I don't fight, Aurelia?' he asked.

'It matters very much,' she replied, refusing to look at him. 'Very much indeed.' She saw him hesitate, then he took her hand and she felt his strong fingers trace the palm as he captured her gaze. Time had been suspended, and she couldn't have looked away if she'd tried.

'Do you care for me, Aurelia?' His tone was tentative, and she could feel the tremor in his fingers as he waited for her reply.

She looked back at him, her gaze steady on his rugged face. She had to be careful. This was getting too personal – too dangerous – and she didn't want to say the wrong thing. 'Of course I care,' she said firmly. 'I regard you as my closest, dearest friend.'

His thumb ran along her knuckles as she became mesmerised by his eyes. 'You're more than a friend to me, Aurelia,' he said finally. 'And I was hoping you felt the same.' He took a deep breath. 'Will you marry me, Aurelia?' He fell silent, as if afraid he'd said too much. Afraid she would reject him.

Then Aurelia did something she thought she would never do. She lifted his hand and kissed it. 'Oh, Jack,' she sighed. 'It's too late for us – much too late. The war's making fools of us all, and we must see this moment for what it really is.'

'And what is it, Aurelia?' he asked softly.

She let go of his hand and busied herself with pouring the tea. 'It's this bloody war,' she said sharply. 'People are falling in love and making promises and plans they would never have made in peace time. Look at Ellie and Joe. It's a prime example.'

Jack frowned, and Aurelia realised he had no idea what she was talking about.

'I've been in love with you since the first time I saw you,' he said forcefully. 'I want us to be married. And I think I'm old enough to know my own mind, Aurelia, so don't fob me off with excuses.' He glared out into the darkness. 'Now I've burned all my damn bridges,' he muttered.

Aurelia sat back in stunned silence.

His brown eyes sought her again. 'If you reject me now, Aurelia, then I'll just have to find another way to make you change your bloody mind.'

She was startled by the fierceness in him. This was a passionate side to Jack she'd never seen before and although she rather liked this forcefulness, she was unsure of how to react. Her emotions were in turmoil for she hadn't realised he felt so strongly.

Aurelia clattered china. She handed him the cup, but when he refused to take it, she placed it on the table between them. 'I had no idea,' she began. Then she stood up, squared her shoulders and looked him in the eye. 'My feelings for you are deeper than I'd thought possible,' she said in a rush. 'But this is not the time to let them get out of hand and run headlong into something we might both regret. There's a war on. We must remain sensible.'

Jack tried to break in, but she talked over his objections. 'I know you better than you think, Jack Withers,' she said sternly. 'Once you're in that damn uniform you'll be champing at the bit to get stuck into the real fighting. And I refuse to live my life waiting for the dreaded telegram. I've enough trouble trying to keep Warratah going without having to worry over you.' Her chest rose and fell and she angrily brushed the tears away. 'I've already lost one man,' she said flatly. 'I don't think I could face losing another.'

Jack seemed emboldened by her declaration and before she knew it he'd pushed away from the table and was embracing her. She struggled to shake him off, but found she needed him to hold her – needed to feel his warmth and his strength. 'This is very unbecoming,' she muttered, her face buried in his shirt. 'I don't know what's come over me.'

Aurelia slowly emerged from the memories to the brightness of a midday sun. Yet a part of her still remained in that soft night when there had just been the two of them and the scent of roses. It was strange how the memories should be so lucid and immediate, as if the hands on the clock had turned back and the intervening years were still to come.

She looked out over the pastures that shimmered in the heat and breathed in the scent of Ellie's roses. The same perfume had accompanied her during the hours following Jack's departure to the bunkhouse, she remembered. When she had needed the tranquillity of the night to think following his shattering news and her reaction to his declaration of love. Now, every time she smelled their perfume she was taken back.

She had sat in her old rocking chair staring over the darkened land as she thought about his proposal. Jack Withers was a man of hidden depths, she'd realised. A man of honour she would be proud to marry. Yet she'd been unsure of her own feelings, and despite Jack's obvious sincerity, had been unwilling to commit herself. For marriage would change things between them, take their friendship to another level that could ultimately destroy them – for there were no guarantees in this life, and living with someone was very different to the long-distance companionship they had then.

She'd been a widow too long. Had struggled to survive one of the harshest environments in the world for too many years to fall victim to something as ethereal and misunderstood as romantic love. As she had stared out at the silent pastures and the all-encompassing night sky all those years ago, she'd realised she was set in her ways and perhaps too independent – and Jack was not the sort of man to take a back seat. It was a recipe for disaster.

Aurelia's sigh echoed the one from the past. She'd learned that to love too deeply could be a weakness – a weakness that manifested itself only when that love was snatched away. As it had when Philip died. She'd mourned for months, the sadness turning to rage at the unfairness of it all until she'd been forced to accept the bitter truth that she was never meant to know the joy of children, or the peace of growing old with the man she loved. Yet she'd learned to live with loneliness, of being regarded as a queer fish among the other cattlemen, had survived drought and flood, pestilence and fire, and had finally been gifted with Ellie to love as her own. Perhaps her reluctance to accept Jack's proposal had more to do with tempting fate than her fear of commitment?

Aurelia's eyes closed and as sleep took her she saw again that slow smile. The smile that transformed Jack's rugged face and made his eyes dance with humour and love. Could feel his warmth and hear the beat of his heart. It was comforting to know he was near.

The passionate night had been followed by one of their heated arguments. Angel was attempting to put the boot in about the amount of work she was doing, and Leanne was having none of it. She was independent and perfectly capable of running Jarrah, and she didn't need her husband telling her what to do. Breakfast had been an awkward affair and Leanne sensed Angel was as relieved as she to hear the approaching thunder of hoofs. 'They're here,' she said unnecessarily as she reached for her hat. 'Better get on.'

He barred her way as she approached the screen door. 'I'm sorry about earlier,' he said firmly. 'But you are my wife and I don't think you should work so hard. I am the man of the house.

You should listen to me and know I only want what is best for you.' His dark eyes looked down at her, the humour touching the corners of his sensuous mouth. 'We can kiss and make up tonight.'

Leanne could have slapped him. But she didn't. It wouldn't solve anything. Angel was a macho Argentine with very fixed ideas when it came to women. She would just have to let him think he was in charge and go her own sweet way, and if he thought sex was the answer to everything, he had a nasty shock coming. She smiled sweetly, pretending to relent. 'No worries,' she said gruffly. 'I just hate mornings.' She rammed her hat over her curls. 'We'll talk later,' she muttered.

He smiled and held the door open for her. 'You are very fiery when you are cross,' he murmured. 'I like spirit in a woman.'

Leanne could feel her temper reach boiling point. 'Really?' she said with heavy irony. 'You ain't seen nothing yet, *hombre*, so watch out.' She pushed past him and stomped across the yard to the stables.

The cloud of dust swirled around the men and the cattle as they approached the distant dipping pens and stockyards. The crack of stock-whips split the air putting birds to flight, and the complaints of the bullocks was a rumble beneath the shouts of the drovers and the excited barking of the blue heelers. The country surrounding the two stations had been mustered in segments, and at the end of each day the bullocks were drafted off and penned in the holding paddocks, the rest of the mob left to wander back out on the plains again. It was the easiest method of handling vast herds, and the quickest way to get through them. At the end of the muster her father and the head stockman would have spent another two days drafting off anything doubtful so only the best were trucked to market.

'Good looking beasts,' said Angel as they approached the holding pens. 'Your dad certainly knows his cattle.'

So do I, she thought fiercely. 'He's had years of experience,' she replied as the bullocks poured into the holding yards. 'Used to drove the old stock-route to Longreach.'

'Where is he, by the way? I was hoping to have a word with him.'

Leanne eyed him suspiciously as she climbed out of the saddle and dropped the reins. No doubt he wanted to discuss her running of Jarrah. 'He's out with the others. You won't see him until the last mob comes in.'

Conversation came to a halt as they each set about their own tasks. Angel was soon lost amongst the cattle and Leanne was kept busy helping the stock boys. She grabbed a long pole and climbed the railings surrounding the concrete plunge. The bullocks complained and propped as they were forced up the race into the pit that was over six foot deep and fifty yards long. Leanne and the stock boys poked them with their long poles, making sure each beast was thoroughly immersed as it swam through the witches' brew of evil smelling arsenic that would kill their ticks. It was important they were tick free and in the best of health, otherwise they wouldn't be allowed to go to market.

With the first thousand head passed as fit, Leanne helped supervise their loading on to the fleet of Warratah's road trains. These enormous articulated trucks often pulled five or six trailers behind them and were the quickest way of transporting stock through the outback. They were an awesome sight as they hammered down the bitumen, usually shrouded in an impenetrable cloud of dust, but woebetide the hapless motorist who got trapped behind them or tried to pass – it was a growing hazard, one she'd experienced herself.

Leanne liked to hear her father's stories of the old days, and she knew he missed the romance that surrounded those great cattle droves. But time had moved on. Gone were the days when the stockmen had to drive the animals hundreds of miles from water-hole to water-hole. Gone was the insecurity of not knowing how many beasts would make the journey during the dry, for the losses through thirst, lameness, sickness and theft had been high. With the arrival of the road trains most of the old tracks like the Birdsville and Canning Stock Route were no longer maintained and many of the water-holes were polluted.

Angel came to stand beside her as the first road train left. His once pristine moleskins were red from the dirt and dust, his shirt sticking damply to his broad chest. He smeared a forearm over his brow as he took off his hat. 'It's a shame you can't slaughter the animals here and transport the carcasses,' he murmured. 'Must be hell cramped up in those trailers.'

'We'd end up with rotten meat,' she said firmly. 'Refrigeration's still too unreliable.' She looked at him and smiled. 'The drivers know they have to stop to feed and water them regularly. They'll be right.'

He grinned as he put on his hat. 'Reckon we've earned a tucker stop ourselves,' he said. 'I'm starving.'

Leanne thought of the casserole she'd left simmering in the slow oven and her mouth watered. They'd eaten nothing since breakfast and now it was almost the end of the day. Her imagination took flight as he drew her close and kissed her. Perhaps there would be time for a shower first, and a change into the green shirt and clean moleskins before they drank gin and tonics on the verandah and watched the sun go down. As she visualised the cosy meal they could share before making love in their big old bed, the ache eased in her back and weariness fled. Perhaps the day hadn't turned out so badly after all.

Chapter Eight

The stand of trees was over the brow of a low hill and down in the dip where the billabong watered the pastures. Joe brought his horse to a standstill and climbed down. His face was mostly in shadow, illuminated only by the fire of the last of the sunset as he reached for Ellie. Yet she could see his eyes and the love that shone there. Could feel the electricity between them as his strong hands lifted her from Clipper's back.

He held her close and she felt the beat of his heart. Closing her eyes she breathed in the scent of soap and leather and knew she would remember this moment for ever. They were so close – their lips a breath apart. She wanted him to kiss her. Was longing to taste the sweetness she knew was there. Yet she could see the questions in his eyes and could sense this was not the right moment and when he set her on her feet it was as if they were of one accord.

He took her hand and led her to the stand of trees, and there, beneath the branches of a coolibah tree lay a blanket, a basket and a fire waiting to be lit. 'I thought we could have a picnic,' he drawled.

Ellie sat on the blanket as he set the fire alight and hooked up the billy. She trembled with unfamiliar emotions as he unpacked the basket and laid out the chicken and ham and cold potatoes he'd persuaded the cook to give him. She knew him so well, and yet tonight he was different. Tonight it was as if he was trying to prepare her for something – something that in her innocence she only vaguely understood – something that would change them and the way they thought of one another for ever.

They sat closely together on the blanket as they ate morsels of chicken and ham and laughed as butter oozed down their chins from the coal-hot damper. Words were almost unnecessary, but as the meal progressed she could feel the tension between them.

'There are things I need to say, Ellie,' he began after the food was packed away. 'But first I want you to understand that I love you.'

His simple words made her want to cry. She ran her fingers over the strong chin and chiselled face. 'I love you too,' she whispered.

He took her hands and clasped them between his own, holding them against his chest so she could feel the drum of life course through him. 'I need you to be sure,' he whispered.

She nodded, unable to speak – the emotion of that moment was too great.

He smiled and pressed his cheek against her hands, turning the palms so he could plant a kiss in them. 'You're more precious to me than anything,' he murmured, his green eyes glimmering in the light of the quarter moon. 'And I will do nothing to hurt you – ever.'

The blood sang in her ears as his lips caressed her face. She melted into his embrace as his mouth sought hers and they kissed for the first time. It was a kiss far removed from the fumbling awkwardness she'd experienced with Seamus, for now the world and the moonlight floated around her. It was as if she was on a drifting cloud and nothing else existed but the scent and feel of the man she loved.

They eventually drew apart and, despite his hands resting lightly at her waist, she felt bereft like an island adrift in a great sea of dappled moonlight. She trembled from the sheer force of needing him. Longed for his kiss to last for ever, culminating in that final act that would make them one. For surely this was the reason he'd brought her here?

His lips brushed her cheek. His words echoing her thoughts as if he could read them. 'It wouldn't be right, Ellie,' he murmured. 'Not now.' His mouth touched her cheek with the delicacy of a butterfly, sending shivers of longing through her as he spoke against her skin. 'I want our first time to be when we're married,' he whispered. 'Not out here in secret as if we have something to be ashamed of.' He cupped her face in his hands and looked deeply into her eyes. 'Every part of me is crying out to make you mine, but this isn't the place – or the right time.'

Ellie drew away. Now, as she looked into those wonderful eyes, she understood the reason for his reluctance – the real reason he'd brought her here tonight. Dread made her reach for him and she touched his face as if by transmitting her fear he would change his mind about leaving. For she wanted to live this magic moment a while longer before he destroyed it.

He captured her hand and kissed the palm before holding it to his cheek. 'I have to be in Cloncurry tomorrow,' he said gruffly.

'Then love me,' she pleaded. 'Now, Joe. I want...'

He silenced her with a kiss. 'It wouldn't be right,' he said. 'Not with me leaving tomorrow.' He held her at arms' length. 'What if there was a baby? I wouldn't want you to go through the shame that would cause. What if I didn't come back?'

Her gasp of pain seared the night as she clung to him. 'Don't say that,' she demanded. 'Never even think it.'

'Promise you'll wait for me, Ellie?'

Ellie fell into his embrace. He was her anchor, her rock, and she clung to him with fierce determination. The ache for him had begun. The pain of having to let him go already sharp. Yet she knew she had to release him. Had to let him follow his destiny before he could return to her. And he would return – she was certain of that. Yet her youthfulness made it hard to express her feelings, and she had only the cliches of her favourite penny romances to help her. 'I'll wait for you,' she promised. 'I'll wait until hell freezes over and the moon falls into the sea.'

Ellie had stolen back to the homestead as the sky began to lighten and was surprised to see Aurelia waiting for her. Devastated by Joe's plans, yet soaring with the joy of knowing he loved her, nevertheless Ellie soon realised her aunt had her own concerns. In the few short hours before daybreak they grew closer than ever. No longer aunt and niece, but two women who shared the dread of an uncertain future.

The short flight to Cloncurry later that morning was over too soon, and as Ellie and Joe followed Aurelia and Jack out of the aerodrome, they knew their time together was almost over. A silence grew between them, words held back, thoughts kept tightly under control as they made their way hand in hand to the town centre.

Cloncurry looked as if it had been startled out of its usual somnolence and was dressed in bunting and flags, the brass band playing inexpertly on the town's racecourse. Utilities and cars and wagons and horses filled the streets as the locals mingled with the visitors for this special day, and the pubs were doing a roaring trade if the singing was anything to go by.

Ellie noticed the line of army trucks and the huddles of stalwart women as they watched their menfolk being taken away. It was a forceful reminder of why they were here. Determined not to give in to tears and histrionics, Ellie forced herself to remain calm as Joe tucked her hand in the crook of his arm. These were their last few moments together for what could be months – or even years. She was damned if she was going to spoil them.

She noticed the other girls eyeing him as they walked towards the tiny park on the edge of town and lifted her chin in pride. He was her man and he was handsome in the tan uniform, with the hat tilted at a rakish angle over his dark hair and the shadow already appearing on his square chin despite having shaved earlier. Yet he had eyes only for her. Wonderful eyes that were as green as winter grass between the thick black lashes.

'Let's sit down here,' he said as they reached a grassy patch beneath a giant red gum that was smothered in blossom.

Ellie glanced around. They weren't the only ones seeking these last few moments together, she realised. There were family men whose wives and children clung to them. Boys that looked impossibly young and surely not eligible for call-up whose mothers were doing their best not to fuss over them, and men whose faces looked familiar, but whose names she couldn't recall.

She sat on the grass, heedless of staining the cotton dress she'd worn especially, almost numb from the effort of having to keep her emotions under tight control. That's how things were these days, all buttoned up, tight and constricted – for a careless word or thought could strip away the veneer and leave a person vulnerable. 'There's so much I want to say,' she began. 'But I can't think – can't find the words.'

He traced a finger over her cheek and down to her chin. 'There's nothing to say,' he murmured. 'We know what's in our hearts and that's enough.' He caught a strand of her hair and tucked it behind her ear. 'Didn't you know that the Aborigines believe each of us has a spirit song? That this song can only be heard by the singer's soul mate?' He leaned close, resting his forehead on hers, his gaze reaching deep within her. 'Listen, Ellie,' he murmured. 'Listen beyond all this noise and hear the wind in the trees and the beautiful note of the bellbird. That's our song

212

and it will help keep us strong until we find one another again.'

Ellie thought it was a lovely idea, and although she only half believed it she was willing to accept it as fact if it made Joe's leaving easier for him. They kissed softly and with such sweet tenderness she thought her heart would break.

He finally drew away and reached into his pocket. 'Will you wear this while I'm gone?' he asked.

Ellie stared at the gold band with the single chip of diamond at its centre. She looked back at him, hardly daring to believe this was happening. 'Always,' she whispered.

Joe slipped the ring on her finger. 'When I come back I'll put the wedding band next to it,' he promised.

Ellie was determined not to cry. It would make it harder for them both if she did, and she wanted Joe to be proud of her – to remember her as strong and brave, not a snivelling wreck. She looked at the ring sparkling in the bright sunlight and vowed it would never leave her.

Joe unfolded the piece of paper that was tucked into the base of the jewellery box. 'This is a poem I wrote,' he said shyly. 'I wanted to express how I feel about leaving you and Warratah. I hope you like it. And when you read it, think of me and know I'll be coming home to you just as soon as I can.'

Ellie's fingers trembled as she took the neatly printed piece of paper. The words shimmered and blurred and she had to blink hard before she could read.

Come with me now to the billabong
Where the bellbirds sing in the trees,
And the dark, mysterious waters
Are moved by the sigh of the breeze.
And while the world is in chaos
With trouble rife near and far,
Here is peace to be shared with the windflowers
And the people who love Warratah.

'Oh, Joe,' she breathed. 'That is so beautiful.'

A commanding whistle tore through the babel of noise and into their private little world. The last convoy was about to leave.

'I'll come back, Ellie. I promise.' Joe pulled her to her feet and roughly drew her into his arms, holding her so tightly she could barely breathe.

Ellie clung to him, trembling from the effort to remain dry-eyed and in control. But it was the hardest thing she'd ever had to do, and when he kissed her for the last time, she was almost overwhelmed by despair.

As Joe gently pulled away Ellie saw how his hair glinted blue-black in the sunlight. Noticed how green his eyes were, how soft his mouth. 'I love you,' she said firmly. 'And I promise I'll wait if you promise you'll come back.' She leaned into him as the brass band marched past and the crowd around them shifted and sighed. She was aware of other women crying, of children's shrill calls and men's bluff voices, of the tears that threatened to choke her, and the way his arms enfolded her so fiercely.

When he pulled away from her again his face

was ashen, the green of his eyes clouded with pain. 'It's time, Ellie,' he murmured. 'I have to go.'

Ellie pulled the ribbon from her hair and thrust it into his hand. 'Keep safe,' she stammered as she fought down the tears and tried to smile. 'And don't be a bloody hero.'

'Ain't my style,' he drawled with studied bravado. He tucked the ribbon into his pocket and turned to Aurelia whose presence hadn't been noticed until now. 'Thanks for everything, missus. Take care of her for me,' he said gruffly as he gave her an awkward hug.

All too soon he was striding across the street to be met by a wall of khaki uniforms and a bellowing sergeant major. He turned and waved before climbing into the back of the army truck. Then, in a flurry of exhaust fumes and dust he was gone.

Ellie was aware of the tears that squeezed beneath her eyelashes and rolled down her face. Aware of her daughter's hand as it covered her fingers. Yet those few hours with Joe all those years ago seemed as if they had just happened, and she was still lost in the heat and heartache of that parting.

Claire's grip tightened, bringing her back to the present. 'You don't have to do this any more, Mum,' she said softly. 'I can see how this is hurting you, and I'm sorry. So very sorry I've caused you so much pain.' She paused for breath, her eyes bright with unshed tears. 'Let's forget the whole thing and start again. I don't need to know

215

anything more than I already do.'

Ellie sat up and smeared away her own tears. 'I'm afraid you do,' she said softly. 'This is the easy bit, there's far worse to come.' She took a deep breath. 'And it won't only affect you and me, but your sister, father and even Aunt Aurelia.'

'Then don't tell me any more. Leave it alone. Leave the past where it belongs if it's that painful.'

Ellie looked into her eyes and knew it was impossible. The reminders of what had happened would always be there. 'It's too late,' she murmured. 'I always knew the time would come, but I've put it off too long already – now it's out of my hands.' She could see the puzzlement in her daughter's eyes, the unshed tears of remorse for having brought things to a head. 'Don't blame yourself,' she said softly. 'Never blame yourself. None of this is your fault – or Leanne's.'

'What has Leanne got to do with all this?' Claire tossed her plait over her shoulder, dashed away the tears and lit a cigarette. 'I thought it was to do with you and me and that gravestone at Jarrah?'

'It has,' she said with a firmness that surprised her. 'But there are long shadows over that grave and ultimately they touch us all.'

'Then tell me now,' Claire demanded. 'Tell me what it is you're so frightened of.'

Ellie stared into the distance, her thoughts far away. 'They say the past can't hurt you. They say there aren't such things as ghosts,' she murmured finally. 'But I'm not so sure.' She turned to look at her daughter and cupped her chin in her hand. 'I'm not holding out on you darling,' she said with quiet firmness. 'You'll know it all eventually, but for now you must be satisfied with hearing how things were. How relationships had formed and promises were made. They do have a bearing on what happened later.'

'But you and Dad...'

Ellie put a finger against her lips to silence her. 'I know you have a lot of questions,' she said. 'But, please, Claire, let me tell this in my own way. It'll become clear soon enough.'

Claire had taken on the stubborn look that had become so familiar through those difficult teen years and Ellie smiled. 'Did I ever tell you how proud we all are of you?' she asked. 'Did I ever tell you how much we love you?'

'Not for a long time,' said Claire battling with tears. 'Dad was so angry when I left for Sydney, and I knew I'd upset you both by making a fuss.' She dipped her head, her voice low and cracked with emotion. 'I had this fear, Mum. This terrible fear I didn't belong. That's why I've stayed away. I thought you didn't want me.'

Ellie felt a stab of pain and reached for her beloved daughter. 'You're my girl,' she whispered. 'Always were and always will be. Why should you think you didn't belong here?' The fear was alive within her. The dread almost overwhelming.

Claire's eyes were swimming with tears, but her gaze was direct and penetrating. 'I've heard the rumours, Mum. I'm adopted, aren't I?'

Ellie felt the cold fingers of the past run over her and shivered. 'No,' she said with a firmness

217

that belied the anguish that was sweeping through her.

'And about time too.' Aurelia was sitting in the lounge, a whisky at her elbow, pipe smoke forming a cloud below the ceiling. 'Where on earth have you been all day? I had to get one of the boys to get me out of that damn verandah chair. Got stuck and had to yell for nearly twenty minutes before anyone heard me.'

Ellie flung her hat on a chair and rushed to her side. 'Are you all right? You haven't caught the sun have you?'

Aurelia gave a nonchalant shrug. 'I could have,' she stated, putting on a hurt expression. 'I'm far too old to be left for so long. At least at home I have Jessie to look after me. I might as well leave if you're going to go off every day.'

Ellie poured herself and Claire a whisky, lifted an eyebrow as Aurelia demanded a top up then sank into the couch with a sigh. 'I'm going over to Jarrah tomorrow for a couple of days to keep an eye on things. Claire will stay here with you and you can fill her in on the war years.'

'That's no consolation,' she grumbled. 'Claire won't be around much to keep me company.'

They looked at her sharply.

Aurelia lifted her chin, her eyes gleaming with mischief. 'Didn't I tell you? Must have slipped my mind after getting stuck in the chair and not having any lunch until after three.'

'What?' Ellie and Claire said in unison.

It had obviously been a fraught day, and Aurelia knew she'd teased them enough. 'Matt Derwent phoned. He's coming over the day after tomorrow to take Claire for a ride in his plane.' She gave a sly look across to Claire. 'Seems he wants to take you on his rounds for the day – show you off and let you see what life's like for a vet out here. Could be an interesting experience.'

Claire's colour was high, but Aurelia couldn't quite make out whether it was the effect of a day in the sun, or the thought of Matt Derwent. 'I'll go and see about supper,' she murmured as she carried her drink out to the kitchen.

Aurelia looked across at Ellie. 'Could do worse,' she muttered. 'I like Matt. Straightforward sort of chap. Good with horses too.'

'Careful, Aurelia,' warned Ellie with a soft laugh. 'You're beginning to sound like Lila down at Threeways.'

Leanne had laid out the table with candles and flowers in an effort to make the dinner romantic, and had showered and changed and dabbed perfume on her neck. They'd had the gin on the verandah at sunset, but the dinner burned as they made love on the lounge rug, and now they were both slightly drunk from too much wine.

'Early start in the morning,' she said as she smothered a yawn. 'Better finish up.'

'One more glass of wine?' He held the bottle above her glass, his gaze holding her.

Leanne was wrung out and desperate for sleep. 'I've had enough,' she said firmly. She pushed away from the table and carried their dirty plates to the sink. 'You know how I am in the morning if I don't get a good night's sleep,' she said as she poured hot water into the sink and added detergent. 'And my day starts long before yours.'

He came to lean against the cupboards, wineglass in hand as he watched her clear the dishes. 'Why do you work such long hours when you can afford to pay people to do it for you?' he asked softly.

'Because it's my station and I like to see things are done properly,' she retorted as she stacked the clean dishes. It was an argument they'd had before. 'Besides,' she added. 'It might look as if we're rich, but there's precious little of the folding stuff about.'

'But your father's business? The fleet of road trains? The two stations? There must be lots of money.'

Leanne threw the dishcloth into the sink and pulled out the plug. 'How much do you have in the bank, Angel?' she asked with deadly calm. 'What exactly do you earn a month and what are your assets?'

If Angel had not felt so secure in his opinions he would have backed off. Leanne was at her most lethal when she went calm. He frowned. 'Why are you asking me this? It is not a woman's place to know everything about her husband's finances.'

Leanne noticed how the Argentine accent came to the fore when he was sidestepped and felt a small sense of satisfaction. 'Think I'm being nosy? That it?' Her voice was still flat, but she could feel the anger begin to churn.

He shrugged. 'I think it is none of your business, yes.'

'Exactly. So don't assume anything about me, or my family, or how much we're worth, Angel Carrera. It's none of your bloody business.'

He held up his hands. 'Hey, Leanne. I'm sorry, all right? In Argentina the owners of the big cattle ranches never work. They pay an overseer to do that and spend their days riding across the pampas or doing deals in the city. I cannot see why it is not the same here.'

'This is Australia where the land is king and people work it and don't mind getting their hands dirty.'

His dark gaze swept over her, coming to rest on her hands that were gripping the back of a chair. 'The ladies are manicured and very beautiful in Argentina,' he said softly. 'They do not work. Their men provide.'

'Bully for them,' she snapped. She dug her hands in her pockets, ashamed of the dirty nails and rough skin.

He took her hands and held them. 'I want to provide for you, Leanne. To give you everything a beautiful wife should have.' He kissed her fingers one by one with deliberate, lingering passion. 'It is not good for a man to know his wife can do things without him. Let me take some of the burden from you. Let me be a partner in Jarrah.'

She snatched away from him. 'I don't own it yet,' she snapped. 'And when I do it'll be all mine. I've worked too long and too damn hard to hand over half. If that was your reason for marrying me, then you might as well leave now.'

Chapter Nine

Ellie was up early as always, the chores finished, the work schedule for the coming few days clearly laid out for the men left on Warratah. She was finishing her second cup of coffee as Claire walked past her bedroom door. 'Come in, darling,' she called as she packed the last few things she would need to take to Jarrah.

'Why can't I come too?' Claire asked with a sleepy yawn. 'I'd like to see Angel for myself.'

'I need you to keep an eye on Aurelia,' she said firmly. 'She's not as strong as she thinks she is. Besides, your young man's coming over tomorrow.'

Claire sat on the bed and leaned against the pillows. 'He's not my young man,' she said defensively. 'He's not even young. Leanne thinks he's as old as the hills.'

Ellie turned from her packing and eyed her daughter. She seemed more relaxed after their talk yesterday, but there was something in her eyes that warned her all was not well. 'And what do you think of him?' She watched as Claire began to fiddle with the mosquito net and was reminded how, as a little girl, she'd done the same thing when faced with a question she didn't want to answer.

'I've only met him twice. But he seems nice enough,' she finally replied with a casual air.

'Might be fun to go up in his plane though.'

Ellie perched on the corner of the bed. 'Are you still determined to take that job in the city? I was hoping you'd decide to stay on here.'

She sat up and plaited her long hair. 'It's a good job, Mum. I'd be stupid to turn it down.' Her eyes were bright with enthusiasm. 'I love it out here, Mum. It's got space and majesty and a kind of atmosphere you don't get anywhere in the world – except maybe America. But I've made a life for myself in Sydney. It's got a buzz all of its own, and if I'm to have a career, that's the place.'

'You won't have much time for a social life. The practice you're joining is large and widespread. Are you sure you won't feel stifled in the city?'

Claire shrugged. 'There's ten of us. If I go tropo, I'll just fly up here for the weekend.'

Ellie smiled as she got up from the bed and zipped her overnight bag. How things had changed since she was Claire's age. There had been few chances of going anywhere because of the war, and once Jack had joined up, there wasn't even the occasional trip to the Curry. Now Claire was blithely talking about flying up from Sydney for the weekend, and seemed to think nothing of it. She picked up the bag. 'Don't let Aurelia wear you out. She might be old, but she's still got all her marbles and can talk the hind leg off a horse.'

Claire laughed. 'I'm looking forward to it,' she said. 'Aurelia tells good stories and she does it so well it's as if I can see the scenes being played on a big screen.'

Ellie grinned. 'Comes from having a good

223

education back in England. She should have been a writer after all those books she's read and the life she's had.' She kissed Claire goodbye and ran down the steps, then turned and waved as she crossed the yard.

Leaving Warratah for Jarrah was really an excuse to escape. She was being cowardly, she admitted, but the past had closed in and the memories were smothering her. She needed to get away from the ghosts. Needed to catch her breath and renew her energy before she had to reveal the most harrowing part of the story.

Claire's secret fear had been banished. Yet there was a part of her that was unwilling to accept that was an end to it. She'd noticed the momentary hesitation before Ellie's denial. Had seen the flash of something dark in her eyes. Yet, surely Mum wouldn't have lied to her, not now, not when this homecoming was supposed to clean the slate? She watched the plume of dust fade into the distance as Ellie drove down the track. There was something her mother wasn't telling her and she was positive it was to do with Jarrah. For how else would Leanne be affected?

Aurelia was in the lounge, her post breakfast pipe already filling the room with smoke. Claire sat down, her thoughts uneasy. In an effort to clear her mind she looked at her aunt and put on a bright smile. 'Mum said you'd tell me what happened after you two were left alone on Warratah.'

Aurelia's monocle glinted in the light from the window. 'I'm not surprised Ellie left this part of

224

the story to me,' she said thoughtfully. 'She never liked the woman, and I can't say I blame her.'

Claire was intrigued. 'What woman?'

'Her mother,' said Aurelia flatly.

Claire sat forward in the chair. She'd met Alicia in London during her year out. They'd had an almost silent lunch at her club and had parted with as much enthusiasm for one another as two strangers meeting on a train. 'Alicia came back? Why? When?'

Aurelia packed her pipe and drew smoke before she shook out the match and flicked it into the fireplace. 'My sister has never been known for her selflessness,' she said coldly. 'She came out to avoid rationing and air raids in England. She had no thoughts for Mother and Pa who were far too old to cope with it all on their own.'

'How? I thought all flights and ships would have been cancelled.'

'Alicia always lands on her feet. She found a way.' Aurelia smoked her pipe, her gaze distant as if she could still see the colours of that bygone age.

Alicia was exhausted and bad tempered as she stood amongst the hundreds of screaming kids and their mothers and looked down from the high deck of the ship. They had crossed the world to be here, and now they'd arrived she wondered if it had all been worth it. Melbourne was as dreary as Liverpool, the drizzle casting a pewter dampness over everything, the leaden sky mirroring her mood.

'Is this Australia?' piped the voice beside her. 'I

thought it was sunny here?'

Alicia looked down at the little girl and tried to dredge up some enthusiasm. 'It is usually,' she said briskly. 'But this is Melbourne and they get a lot of rain, even in the summer.'

'Just like home,' said five-year-old Betty wistfully.

Alicia straightened the velvet collar of the child's camel coat and pulled up the white socks that had a habit of drifting southwards to the patent shoes. 'Let's see if we can catch sight of Mummy,' she said with forced brightness. 'She's probably down there somewhere in amongst all those people so we'll have to look very hard.'

Betty had been a good child throughout the journey despite her tender years, and although Alicia had found the whole enterprise wearing, she acknowledged that having Betty with her for twenty-four hours a day had made her realise just how much of Ellie's childhood she'd missed. Not that she wanted to prolong or repeat the experience. Six weeks of screaming kids, cramped quarters and seasickness was enough to banish any stray maternal feelings she might have once possessed.

She held Betty's hand as they looked over the railings to the quay. It was strange how things worked out, for if it hadn't been for Betty catching the measles, Alicia would never have had the chance of escaping England at all.

The first convoy had left Betty behind because of her contagious condition and Harriet, her mother, had been at her wits' end. Her husband was fighting in Europe and she had five children

226

to look after. With the real threat of invasion, the Commonwealth countries offered to give shelter to the women and children of Great Britain for the duration and she'd jumped at the chance. Then Betty had fallen ill and Harriet had begged her old school friend Alicia to look after her on one of the following convoys. It was a huge responsibility, but Alicia had seen it as a way of escaping the deprivations of war. She would have preferred to go to Canada, but she had readily agreed.

It hadn't been a cruise, that was for certain, she thought as she remembered the blood-curdling siren in the grim nights when they'd had to stumble from their beds in pitch blackness and pull on life-jackets. This had been followed by hours of sitting on a freezing deck that wallowed beneath them as the ship weaved in gigantic seas trying to shake off pursuing U-boats. Despite the flotilla of naval vessels that remained alongside throughout the journey, the tension was always high and tempers flared easily. Alicia had tried her best to remain cool and aloof, but there had been little privacy during the voyage, and she'd had to mix with people she wouldn't usually pass the time of day with.

Harriet pushed through the throng as Alicia and Betty finally emerged from the vast customs hall and swept the child into her arms. 'Thank goodness you're safe,' she said, the tears rolling down her powdered cheeks. 'I would never have forgiven myself if something had happened to you both.'

Alicia patted her hair and checked her

appearance in her compact mirror. The rain had made her hair go frizzy and her lipstick was smudged, but at least she didn't look as down-at-heel as her old school friend. Harriet had really let herself go. 'We were lucky we got here at all,' she said evenly. 'I thought I was going to die of *mal de mer* two days out of Liverpool.'

Harriet clung to Betty, the other four children tugging her coat. 'They weren't so lucky to just get seasickness on the following convoy,' she sniffed.

'What do you mean?' Alicia's tone was distracted as she put away the powder compact and began to search for a taxi. She was looking forward to a hot bath and some decent food, and she knew just the right hotel.

Harriet put Betty down, her eyes dark in her wan face. 'You haven't heard?'

Alicia was losing patience. 'Heard what? Do spit it out, Harriet, before we all drown in this damn rain.'

'The convoy that left a month after you was hit by a U-boat. One of the ships went down. Nobody survived.'

Alicia shuddered. It could so easily have been them. 'Nobody?' she breathed.

Harriet shook her head. 'When I think of all those children...' Fresh tears threatened and she hastily dabbed her face. 'Thank you for taking care of Betty. I don't know how I can repay you.'

'It was a pleasure,' she replied and tried to mean it. 'Now, can we get out of the rain?'

They managed to get a taxi eventually and bundled in with the cases and the children. It was a tight squeeze. 'Are you sure you don't want to muck in with us?' Harriet said as they drove through the city and came to a halt at the Imperial Hotel. 'I know the government housing they've allocated us isn't much, but at least it's a roof over our heads.'

Alicia had a fair idea what the housing would be like from the photographs of the barrack-like buildings Harriet had sent Betty, and she'd had enough of cramped quarters and screaming children. 'You'll be crowded enough without me,' she said diplomatically. 'I'm only staying in the city overnight, then I'm catching the train north.'

Alicia finally said her goodbyes and disentangled herself from Betty. 'I'll write to you,' she promised hastily as she fended off a snotty nose and sticky fingers. 'And if I'm ever back in Melbourne I'll come and visit.' The child seemed to be mollified by this and Alicia sighed with relief as she watched the taxi disappear into the traffic. She turned and headed up the steps of the Imperial Hotel. What she needed now was a bath and a long cold gin and tonic before a decent dinner.

'She hasn't changed much,' said Claire as Aurelia paused for breath and helped herself to a mid-morning whisky. 'I met her in London, and she was really only interested in her planned shopping trip and the cocktail party she was going to in the evening. She barely disguised her boredom when I told her the home news and what I'd been doing during my gap year.'

'My sister is one of this world's most selfish

women,' said Aurelia gruffly. 'But believe it or not, she does have a good side.'

Claire watched a parakeet wend its way along a branch of the tree outside the window. It was as deft as a tightrope walker, with eyes that reminded her somewhat of Alicia – for they were acquisitive and rather cold. 'She certainly takes care of herself,' she muttered as she remembered the expensively cut suit, the neat figure and perfect make-up. The hair was grey of course because she had to be in her mid seventies, but it was styled and glossy, the nails manicured, the rings on her fingers worth the price of a small hobby farm. 'But I can't see she has a good side, unless it's her ability to shop.'

'She can certainly spend money,' said Aurelia with a wry smile. 'But when she came out here during the war she showed us what she was made of and I have to say she did well. Surprised us all.'

Claire watched the old lady settle back with her whisky. 'Must have been a bit of a culture shock,' she said. 'I can't imagine Alicia getting to grips with cows.'

'She didn't at first,' said Aurelia with a snort of laughter. 'But things changed. They had to if we were all to survive.' She looked at Claire over the lip of her glass. 'You remind me so much of your mother,' she said. 'Proper little pest with all her questions. She'd follow me about the station and homestead never satisfied until she knew it all.' Aurelia grinned. 'Not that I find you a pest,' she added hurriedly. 'Just that you're as inquisitive as she was – and still is.'

Claire hid her smile behind her glass as she

230

sipped the whisky. She didn't usually drink during the day, especially in this heat, but it helped her to relax. For her sleep had been disturbed last night, with images her mother had invoked. Images that somehow didn't add up to what she'd been told so far.

In the days following Joe's departure Ellie immersed herself in the endless round of work. Yet the nights were filled with disturbing dreams that woke her drenched in sweat and calling for him. Her appetite had gone, but she knew she couldn't keep up the relentless workload if she didn't eat, and had had to force food down. Yet she'd also had to deal with the problem that was Aurelia – and that was most worrying.

Aurelia had grown strangely quiet following Jack's declaration and Joe's departure, and didn't seem to have the enormous energy and enthusiasm for life she'd once had. It was as she watched her aunt push away yet another plate of barely eaten dinner that things had come to a head.

'You need food to keep you strong,' Ellie said as she pushed back the plate. 'There's far too much work to be done now we're down to you and me and Jacky Jack to run the place. The stock boys are enthusiastic, but frankly they're more of a hindrance than a help when it comes to anything that looks remotely like hard work. If you fall ill I won't be able to manage,' she said with flat determination. 'You must snap out of this.'

Aurelia pushed from the table, the chair screeching along the floor. 'I'm not hungry,' she

231

said crossly. 'Don't bully me.'

Ellie took her aunt's arm, forcing her to turn and face her. 'We've got to carry on here, otherwise there'll be nothing for them to come home to,' she said in even tones.

Aurelia's defiant stare was fixed on a point beyond her niece, but Ellie knew she would respond sooner or later. Yet her manner frightened her. Where was the strong, seemingly invincible aunt who was afraid of nothing life could throw at her? Her aunt seemed to be a ghost of the woman she once was. 'Aurelia,' she said with authority. 'You must realise you can't go on like this. I need you. Warratah needs you. Jack wants you all in one piece when he comes back from the war.'

Aurelia drew herself up, the chin defiant, the bosom proud. 'I do more than my share,' she said defensively. 'I can't help it if I'm feeling my age and don't want to eat.'

Ellie put her arms around her. It was her turn to offer comfort – to console. 'I know,' she said. 'But Joe and Jack would hate to see you like this. Hate what you're doing to yourself. It's up to us to stay strong and do our best. Warratah must survive, Aurelia, and it can only do that if you take care of yourself.'

Aurelia pulled away, adjusted her disreputable old jacket and dredged up a smile. 'You're right.' Her tone was flat. 'Warratah seems to be the only constant in my life and I know I must do all I can to keep it going. But for now I need to keep occupied so I don't have time to think. My appetite will come back and so will my fortitude. We British don't give in easily.'

Ellie's reply was drowned by the roar of a plane circling overhead and they rushed to the verandah. 'Jacky Jack,' shouted Ellie into the darkness. 'Light the flares.'

'Yes, missus,' replied the Aboriginal stockman as he strolled past the verandah chewing on a hunk of bread and cheese.

'Today, Jacky. Move it,' Ellie ordered crossly. She watched him break into a loping trot. 'Damn man's been getting Sally to feed him again. No wonder half our supplies have disappeared.'

'I wonder why Jack's come back tonight?'

Ellie listened – glad to have this distraction. 'Doesn't sound like Jack's plane.' She tugged on her boots. 'Come on. We'll take the ute and find out.'

Ellie loved driving, and as Aurelia had been the one to teach her, she handled the ute in the same reckless manner. They raced out of the yard and headed for the airstrip that was now lit by the oil pots. The stock boys were dark shadows against the flames as they looked skyward and waited for the plane – they still thought it was a miracle from the sky gods.

She brought the ute to a skidding halt and they climbed out to watch the little aircraft make a neat landing and come to rest at the end of the dirt runway. As the twin propellers stopped turning and the noise of the engine faded, the door in the side of the plane opened and a man stepped out.

'I'll be blowed,' breathed Aurelia. 'It's Mickey Maughan.' She peered into the flickering light, her monocle glinting fire. 'And you'll never guess

233

who he's got with him,' she added in amazement.

'What the hell's she doing here?' Ellie's tone was sharp as she caught sight of the elegant figure at the top of the steps. She fingered the thin gold chain around her neck. Joe's ring was still hanging there, safe from everyday work, close to her heart – her talisman against everything unpleasant.

Aurelia shrugged. 'We'll soon find out.' She and Ellie looked at one another and although Ellie did her best to mask her feelings, she was unable to fool her aunt. 'Do try and be nice to her, dear. She is your mother.'

Ellie tucked the ring back and rammed her hands in her moleskin pockets. 'Only when it suits her,' she replied sourly.

'G'day, Aurelia, Ellie,' bellowed Mickey Maughan as he strode towards them. 'How y'goin'?'

'Good,' replied Ellie shaking his hand and wincing. Mickey never had known his own strength, and his bluff, hearty manner was a little overwhelming. 'How are things at Jarrah? How's Seamus? We've had several letters, but he never says very much.'

'Seamus is good. Somewhere in Europe. He doesn't say.' He took off his hat and scratched his head. 'Jarrah's about the same as everywhere. Dry, dusty, cows getting thin and out of condition. You know how it is.'

'Could someone help me with my luggage?' The plaintive cry came from Alicia who was standing in the doorway of the plane, her bags at her feet.

'Jacky Jack, take the luggage and put it in the back of the ute,' Aurelia ordered as Mickey rushed back to the plane and handed Alicia down as if she was the Queen of Sheba. 'Looks like your mother's struck again,' she murmured to Ellie. 'Poor Mickey's been on the lookout for years and by his expression I'd say he thinks he's in with a chance.'

'He'll find he's bitten off more than he can chew,' Ellie retorted as she watched her mother's stately progress across the landing strip. This was all she needed. What on earth did her mother think she was doing by turning up here in the middle of a crisis?

'Darling,' cried Alicia, throwing her arms around Ellie, seemingly unaware of her daughter's rigid lack of response. 'How grown up you are. And how pretty,' she enthused as she held Ellie at arm's length and regarded her delightedly.

Ellie maintained a polite facade as she was swamped in a cloud of perfume and face powder. She dutifully kissed the rouged cheek and endured the overenthusiastic welcome with icy reserve. Alicia's unexpected arrival was bad enough, but Ellie hated the thought of their quiet existence on Warratah being shattered. 'I thought you were staying in England to look after Grandpa and Grandma?' she said.

'I was, darling,' she replied as she hugged her sister. 'But I had a chance to come out on a convoy and here I am,' she said brightly. 'I just missed you in Cloncurry, but Mickey here,' her look dazzled the hapless man beside her. 'Mickey very kindly offered me a lift as his property's just

235

next door.' She smiled brightly. 'Wasn't that lucky?'

Ellie eyed Mickey who was gazing in adoration at her mother. Jarrah Downs was about two hundred miles away on the far eastern boundary line. Hardly next door. She let it pass. Mickey Maughan was old enough to take care of himself.

Sally was dragged reluctantly from her camp-fire to prepare another supper, and once their visitors had eaten their fill, Aurelia poured tea from the great iron pot that always hung over the range. Settled comfortably around the kitchen table, Ellie kept her thoughts to herself as the others began to talk.

'How are Mother and Pa?' asked Aurelia. 'I haven't had a letter from them in ages, and it's a bit worrying.'

'They're fine,' replied Alicia airily. 'Stubborn as always. Refuse to leave the house of course even though they rattle around in it. I had to get the builders in to erect the Anderson shelter in the back garden, but I'll be surprised if they use it.'

'Are things very bad over there?' Aurelia was prodding tobacco into her pipe and Ellie knew that the thought of her elderly parents alone and frightened made her angry, and if it had been at all possible, she'd have got someone to fly her to the nearest port so she could get to them.

'Everything's rationed of course,' said Alicia with a waspish snap. 'Can't get hold of a decent pair of stockings unless you've got friends in the black market, and the food they expect us to eat is disgusting. But apart from the odd bombing raid on seaports and airbases, things have been fairly quiet.'

'You obviously haven't heard the latest news,' said Aurelia around the stem of her pipe. 'The Germans started night bombing in September, and have hit London fairly thoroughly as well as some of the other major cities and ports. Churchill's calling it the Battle of Britain.'

Alicia lit a cigarette. 'At least Mother and Pa are well away from London,' she said. 'There's no airfield or port within fifty miles, so they should be safe.'

'I hope so,' said Aurelia with heartfelt vigour. 'I just wish you hadn't left them to struggle through on their own.'

Ellie couldn't remain silent any longer. 'How did you get on a convoy? I thought they were only for women with children?'

Alicia explained about Betty. 'It was either that or volunteer for something ghastly like the land army or the munitions factory. And I'd be absolutely useless at both. I'm not qualified to nurse or fire-fight, and the thought of driving ambulances around London in the blackout gives me the shivers.' She stubbed out her cigarette. 'Besides, I thought you'd need a hand here.'

Ellie dipped her chin to hide her smile as Aurelia nearly bit the stem of her pipe in two. At least Alicia's arrival had put a spark back into the old girl – maybe it would do the trick and get her back on an even keel.'

'The work's a lot tougher here than in a factory,' Aurelia said flatly as she eyed the long red finger nails. 'You'll have to learn to get your hands dirty.'

237

Alicia smiled brightly at Mickey. 'I'm sure I'll have to learn a great many things,' she said. 'But it won't be so bad if we have visits from our neighbours.'

Mickey reddened and looked into his mug of tea as if he depended upon finding an answer to Alicia's flirting in there. 'Reckon there won't be much time for visiting,' he muttered. 'I was in the Curry dropping off the last of me men. I'm down to me and the stock boys and a couple of old blokes who didn't pass the army medical.'

'Things are tough all round,' said Ellie as she finished the last of her tea. 'What with this drought, and the lack of station hands to keep the cattle from starving, we could all end up with nothing.'

'Some of the hardest hit stations are closing down until the war's over,' Mickey said solemnly. 'I can see their point, but Australia's gunna need beef and mutton to see her through and I reckon we gotta do our best.' He caught Alicia watching him and blushed. 'I'd volunteer to fight if I didn't have Jarrah to run,' he added hastily. 'Me son, Seamus, is already overseas, so I gotta stay.'

Ellie went to bed long before she heard Mickey's plane take off for Jarrah. Yet she lay awake, her thoughts troubling her. Warratah was bereft of labour, and now her mother had turned up it would put a further strain on the supplies. For she would undoubtedly prove to be worse than useless, and time spent trying to find something she could do would be time wasted.

She rolled over and buried her face in the pillow.

If only Joe was here, she thought as she held his engagement ring to her lips. If only she could see him again, listen to his voice and snuggle into his arms. The warmth spread through her and she hugged the pillow. She was determined to remain strong, to stem the overwhelming sadness that seemed to catch her unawares. Tears were wasted energy. She fell asleep and dreamed of green eyes and dappled moonlit shadows on the banks of a billabong.

It was not yet light when she awoke. She climbed out of bed and padded into the kitchen still half-asleep. Aurelia was busy stirring something in a pot and ordering a drowsy Sally about the kitchen. 'Wake your mother up,' she said briskly. 'We've a busy few days ahead and we're going to need all hands on deck.'

Ellie raised an eyebrow. 'What can she do, exactly?' she asked.

'She can ride,' said Aurelia shortly. 'And I need everyone to help round up the cattle and take them south to number twelve bore.'

Ellie felt her spirits rise as she went into the bedroom Aurelia and Alicia had to share now there were three of them in the two-bedroomed house. Aurelia had emerged from her gloom, her indomitable forbearance too strong to be quenched for long. Warratah would survive.

The big double bed was rumpled, the covers dragged over to one side. Alicia was fast asleep, one pale, delicate arm thrown over the eider-down, one slender leg peeking from beneath the sheet.

Ellie was about to rouse her when something made her still. She looked down at her mother, taking in the flawless skin, the blonde hair and painted nails. Alicia looked so fragile against the white sheets, so out of place in this little wooden house in the middle of nowhere, and for the first time in her life, Ellie realised how vulnerable Alicia was. She might be selfish and self-centred, a 'flibberty-gibbet' as Aunt Aurelia called her, but she'd come across the world in what could only have been a terrifying journey, so somewhere behind that delicate facade was a core of steel. Yet her vulnerability lay in her isolation – her failure to realise she alienated those who could have loved her without question.

Alicia opened her eyes. 'Good morning, darling,' she murmured.

Ellie pushed back her thoughts. Alicia needed her sympathy as much as a cow needed ticks. 'Time to get up,' she said briskly. 'Breakfast is ready.'

The elegant hand reached for the bedside clock, and the sleepy eyes widened. 'It's the middle of the night,' Alicia exclaimed. 'Go away, Elspeth. Let me sleep.'

'We always get up at four,' said Ellie as she pulled spare moleskins, shirt, jacket and boots from Aurelia's cupboard. 'Better hurry. We've got a lot to do.'

Alicia sat up, one silken nightdress strap drifting from her shoulder. She eyed the clothes Ellie dumped on the bed. 'You don't expect me to wear these, do you?' she said with a grimace. 'I shall look an absolute fright.'

240

'The cows won't mind,' said Ellie as she struggled to keep a straight face.

'Cows?' The blue eyes widened. 'What on earth have cows to do with anything?'

Ellie stood in the doorway, she could smell the bacon cooking in the kitchen and it was making her hungry. 'We're moving them today,' she said impatiently. 'So you'd better get a move on or you'll miss breakfast.' She closed the door and left her mother to it. She'd learn.

They had finished breakfast by the time Alicia emerged from the bedroom and were busy packing up the tucker and water-bags. The women turned and stared at the apparition before them, and Ellie had to bite hard on her lip to stop herself from laughing. Mum looked ridiculous.

Aurelia's moleskins sagged around the neat bottom and thighs and had been viciously gathered at the waist by a broad, sparkling belt Alicia must have brought with her. The shirt was unbuttoned at the neck, the collar turned up, the sleeves neatly folded back up the slender arms which jangled with bracelets. A brightly coloured chiffon scarf adorned her neck, and the tweed jacket was nonchalantly slung over narrow shoulders. The make-up was immaculate, the perfume exotic.

'You can take all that jewellery off for a start,' boomed Aurelia. 'You'll frighten the cattle.'

'Nonsense,' retorted Alicia as she pulled out a chair and sat at the table. 'One doesn't have to look like a rag-bag just because one has to work. I like to take pride in my appearance even if you don't.' She gave the house lubra a withering glare

241

which stifled her giggles immediately. 'I want bacon and eggs and toast,' she demanded. 'And don't overcook the eggs like you did last time I was here.'

'Too late for breakfast,' rasped Aurelia. 'Sally, get on with your chores.' She pulled a protesting Alicia from the chair and almost dragged her out to the verandah. 'Get those bracelets off and put your jacket on properly. There's work to do and I can't afford you going down with sunburn.'

Despite all intentions to the contrary, Ellie began to feel sorry for her mother as she took off the offending jewellery and shrugged into the oversized jacket. 'Come on,' she said kindly. 'Let's find you a hat and a horse.'

'Bombs away,' yelled Kelly from his perch. He eyed Alicia and lifted his yellow comb in recognition of an enemy. 'Sieg Heil!' he shrieked as he flapped his wings.

'What on earth...?' Alicia stood stock still on the verandah. She turned to Aurelia. 'I think that's disgusting,' she hissed. 'How dare you let...'

'Kelly has his own way of expressing himself,' said Aurelia nonchalantly as she caught Ellie's eye. 'I shouldn't let it bother you.' She smoothed his ruffled feathers, let him nibble her chin and made sure he had enough food and water for the next few days. Sally wasn't terribly reliable.

Alicia and Kelly glared at one another, but it was the bird who looked away first and concentrated on preening. 'At least I've won one argument this morning,' she said crossly. Grabbing the hat from Ellie, she glared down at her. 'And you can take that silly grin off your face,' she snapped. 'It isn't funny.'

Ellie ducked her head. Having Mum around certainly livened things up, but she knew that any prolonged visit from Alicia was bound to get on their nerves, and wondered just how long it would be before they had their first serious argument.

It was still chilly as they walked across the yard, the frost glittering in the trees where an ethereal mist entwined itself amongst the branches. The stock horses had already been gathered in the holding paddock for the muster and they milled around in expectation.

'I'll have that one,' said Alicia pointing a scarlet nail at a particularly handsome chestnut.

'He's a bit fresh,' warned Ellie. 'How long since you've ridden?'

'Just before I left England,' Alicia said evenly. 'I don't need you to tell me what I can and can't ride.' She opened the gate and moved quietly amongst the horses until she came to the chestnut gelding.

Ellie stood anxiously by as Alicia fussed him, saddled him up and checked the girths before swinging neatly into the saddle.

'Your mother was riding to hounds by the time she was six,' muttered Aurelia as she handed Ellie her stock saddle and prepared Boomerang for herself. 'Contrary to appearances, she can handle a horse – despite the length of her fingernails.'

Having coaxed Boomerang into letting her on his back, Aurelia let the horse prop and dance for a while, then firmly took control. 'Too fresh for his own good,' she muttered. 'Silly bugger thinks

243

I'm going to let him get away with showing off.'

Ellie watched her mother's hands on the reins, and the easy way she sat in the saddle and realised Aurelia knew her mother better than she did. She heaved a sigh of relief. At least that was one thing less to worry about, she thought as she headed for her own black gelding and began to saddle him. Clipper was getting too old for this kind of caper, and was spending a well earned retirement with Dad's elderly grey in the horse paddock where the grass was still lush from the underground bore that flowed in to the long, narrow billabong. She still rode him now and then, and since Joe's departure had spent quite a bit of time in his company.

The stock boys had rounded up the spare horses and these were in a string behind their mounts. They had loaded up the supply horses with the food and tools they might need over the next few days, and each rider carried their own sleeping roll and rifle. The horses had been spelled long enough for them to be on their toes and not all of them appreciated being disturbed from their grazing.

'As it's the nearest, we're mustering Gidgee Creek paddock first,' shouted Aurelia. 'We'll water them at number four bore before we take them on to the yard at Sand Hill. We'll change horses at lunch-time so our mounts are fresh for the yarding up.' She gave a series of loud whistles and as Sally and Jacky Jack's youngest daughter opened the gates, the dogs came racing from the kennel yard. They were a mixed bunch, but all with the distinctive markings of the blue heeler dog that led them. He was a good-looking dog, with intelligent eyes and a coat that shone blue in the early morning light, and he seemed to be delighted to be free.

Aurelia gave a sharp whistle and the dogs assembled obediently around her, tongues lolling, tails wagging, ears pricked. 'Let's get moving,' she shouted.

Ellie felt the sadness creep over her again as they moved out of homestead yard and into the paddock. Jacky Jack and his five stock boys were all that was left of the thirty or forty men who usually came to work during the droving season, for unlike Jarrah, they had no old-timers. She stared off into the distance, wondering where Joe was and if he thought of her at all. It felt strange not to have him beside her, almost as if a part of her was missing.

'Do stop day-dreaming, dear,' said Aurelia with asperity. 'You'll hear from him soon.'

Ellie's spirits rose as the nine of them rode on to the plains, the dogs keeping pace as the sun climbed higher and the horizon sweltered. The mob grew as they mustered the scrub, and the dogs and riders were fully occupied as they kept the three hundred or so head of cattle tightly bunched and pushed them along towards number four bore.

It was a mixed mob of breeders, yearlings, calves and bulls, and they'd had about three months of uninterrupted grazing since the last time they'd been handled and didn't like it much. Accompanied by the sharp crack of the stock whips and the constant drum of hoofs, the bulls

245

bellowed and the cows mooed for lost calves as red dust drifted skywards.

Aurelia and three of the stock boys flanked the mob near the front, and Ellie and Alicia had taken up position on either side further back, leaving the last two stock boys to keep the cattle bunched at the tail. The dogs were tireless, nipping legs and hides, rushing, bunching and gathering in the odd stray that tried to make a break for it.

Ellie kept an eye on her mother and realised she was holding up well despite the dust, the heat and the flies. Yet they were all relieved to see the bore on the horizon, for it had been a long morning and the sun's glare was relentless.

The mob picked up their pace as the stock boys began to throw water on the ground, and Ellie kicked her horse into a gallop as they thundered over the scrub plains towards the long galvanised trough.

'That's it,' yelled Aurelia as the mob reached the trough and drank thirstily. 'Lunch time.'

Two of the stock boys remained with the herd as the rest dismounted. The horse tailer swapped their horses for fresher ones while Jacky Jack and Ellie organised a meal of billy tea, corned beef and damper. There were dried apricots for pudding.

'I never realised how *ghastly* cows can be,' said Alicia as she fanned herself with her hat. 'Everywhere one turns there's the stink of hide and manure. And as for the flies.' She grimaced and fanned harder at the black swarm covering her lunch.

'You get used to it,' laughed Ellie. 'I don't even notice any more.'

They ate their meal quickly and got back into the saddle so the stock boys could leave the cattle and have their own tucker. Ellie could see Alicia was stiff from riding so long, but she grudgingly admired her for not complaining.

They pushed the mob ahead of them as the sun moved across the sky towards evening. The land was partially cleared, open country, with spinifex and mitchell grass already sadly depleted and offering little nourishment. As the sun began to dip they caught their first sight of the stockyard at Sand Hill. The boys rode ahead and opened the gate that led to a wide lane running parallel to the paddock fence. This lane was roughly four hundred yards wide, half a mile long and led directly into the stockyard.

'Keep 'em bunched,' warned Aurelia. 'Don't let 'em get away from you.'

The riders pushed the beasts forward at a fast pace with cracks of their whips and shrill whistles. The dogs barked and raced alongside, nipping and diving, twisting and turning, avoiding heavy hoofs and sharp horns, and the cruel lash of the stock whips that whistled past their ears. The bulls had become wary, sniffing the air, bellowing with rage as they realised what was about to happen. Aurelia shouted directions, and as the dust rose in great choking clouds the men and women of Warratah kept the mob tight, flanking every side, watching the bulls in case they broke loose. They urged their fresh horses on, pushing the mob into a trot. The calves

247

dropped back, exhausted from their journey as the cows mooed and some of the bulls tried to mount the heifers. They were now only three hundred yards from the stockyard gate.

One of the bulls spotted the gate and bellowed with rage. He stopped, wheeled around and broke into a fast gallop through the mob heading back down the lane for open country.

Ellie and Alicia were after him. Ellie's fresh horse lengthened his stride, shortening the distance between him and the bull. She rode full pelt alongside him, then drove the gelding into his side. The bull staggered and came to a shuddering halt.

Ellie swiftly looked back at Aurelia and the stock boys. They'd stayed with the restless mob. No help there. Then she saw a streak of blue shooting up the lane and watched in relief as the heeler dog raced towards them.

The heeler was on the bull in seconds, his teeth fastened on the poor beast's nose. With a bellow of rage the bull shook his head, but the heeler clung on, his teeth turning red from the blood as he was swung helplessly in the air.

The bull's eyes were tormented, his bloodied nose flaring. He raised his head, feet planted in the dirt, and shook the dog as if he was a rag. Then with one mighty thrust he freed himself and stood there bellowing.

The blue heeler hugged the dirt, hackles raised, sides heaving as the women cautiously moved their horses into position. He bared his teeth, growling deep in his throat, ears flattened, tense and waiting. The bull dipped his head and charged. The heeler sidestepped neatly and fixed his teeth in the bull's ear.

Alicia turned her horse to help the dog but was stopped by a shout from Ellie. 'Let the dog handle it. Keep away until we're ready to move the bull towards the pens again.'

Blood oozed from the bull's nose and ear, splashed on to the dog and the women who sat watching as he roared in frustration and rage. But the heeler ignored it, holding on with his teeth, determined not to be tossed again.

As suddenly as it had begun, it was over. The bull stopped roaring, his tongue hanging low as he gasped for breath. He appeared to be bewildered by the strangeness of events, but freedom was still on his mind as he turned and twisted and tried to escape the heeler. But the little dog was always there – always in confrontation – as stubborn as the bull.

Ellie settled her horse as she watched the bull turn and trot back down the lane towards the mob, the dog a short distance behind, heeling him all the way. She joined Alicia and they brought up the rear, their horses lathered in sweat from their mad dash.

'Get them in the yards quickly,' shouted Aurelia as she flicked the long stock whip and kept the bull moving.

Ellie and the boys forced the last of the cattle into the stockyards before the bull had time to make any further escape attempts. The game little dog kept behind, heeling the strays and watching closely as the gates were finally pulled shut.

Aurelia slid from the saddle and slapped her hat on her thigh. 'Well done, Alicia,' she boomed. 'Knew you had to be useful at something.'

Alicia almost fell from her horse in her weariness, but there was a certain glow of pride beneath the dusty, smeared make-up. 'That was more fun than hunting,' she declared as she dragged off her hat and brushed away the sweat from her forehead. 'But I'm exhausted.'

'Better get some food inside you then,' said Ellie with a smile. 'And get a good night's sleep. We've got to do this all over again tomorrow – and the next day – and probably the day after. This is only about a fifth of the herd. And they all need to be moved south.'

Alicia sank onto a log. 'Aren't we going back to the house tonight?' Her eyes were wide with horror.

'We'll be out here for at least five days,' said Ellie. 'Better make the best of things.'

'The best of things?' Alicia snapped. 'I'm filthy and need a bath. My face cleansers and creams are miles away, I've broken a fingernail and I haven't got a change of clothes,' she stormed. 'You should have warned me.'

Ellie was tired and her mother was beginning to irritate. 'There's water in the trough for a wash, and I've packed our toothbrushes and flannels. What more do you want?'

Alicia glared back, her fury obvious. 'You expect me to wash in that?' Her voice rose almost to a shriek as she pointed to the vile green bore water in the rusting trough. 'And to sleep out here where I could get attacked by snakes and

250

lizards and wild dogs?'

'You'll be quite safe as long as you stay by the fire,' said Ellie whose own temper was rising.

Alicia looked wildly around, but no one else seemed concerned. Then, as if realising she had no option but to remain in the bush she slumped against the log and drank deeply from her water-bag.

Ellie couldn't help grinning as she eyed the stained moleskins, the soaked shirt and scrap of bedraggled scarf. Mum certainly looked wrung out, but she had a suspicion she felt better after a day of real work than she would after lounging around in some smart hotel.

'May I ask what you find so funny?' Alicia asked mildly, her temper obviously cooled. 'Have you seen yourself lately – or is it just me that looks as if I've been dragged through a hedge backwards?'

Ellie grinned, not at all offended by the insult. 'Reckon if you keep this up,' she said through her laughter, 'we'll make a stockman of you yet.'

Chapter Ten

The drought took a firm hold and the women of Warratah battled for survival. Water was down to a trickle in the rivers and billabongs, the water-holes becoming clay-pans that could trap a beast and kill it as surely as a bullet. The earth became hard-packed, the miserable grass bereft of any goodness as the herd was moved from one pasture to another in search of better fodder. The only water available for the stock had to be pumped from the bores and even some of those were dry. The outback was dying – and with it had come disaster.

Dingoes and crows become bolder and more predatory. Trees wilted, their boughs dipping earthwards as if they too were exhausted from the heat, and as the rabbits devoured the poor grass, mobs of kangaroos and emus invaded the home pastures that still had bore water, and they had to be shot or scared away to preserve this precious commodity for the cattle.

The three women camped at night with the Aboriginal stockmen around a fire, the hard earth their bed, the sky their ceiling, saddle for pillow. They were armed with knives as well as rifles, for the poor beasts were dying, and there was nothing worse than the sight of a crow pecking out the eyes of a calf as it ran stumbling and screaming in blind terror. A swift slash to the throat was the most merciful way of putting the beast to rest, and it saved on bullets.

Ellie was surprised to find a growing admiration for Alicia. For after her initial horror at having to work from sunrise to dark, Alicia had grudgingly become accustomed to leaving her cosmetics behind. She'd filed her nails to a more manageable length, let the grey tendrils snake back into the blonde hair and no longer seemed to care if she had to face the day without lipstick.

There were certain tasks even Aurelia couldn't make her perform, such as helping with the spaying, or castrating, but Ellie realised she was doing her best. It had been strange to see Mum in the same clothes day after day and stranger still not hearing her complain. Perhaps there really was something to the British stiff upper lip, she thought wryly, for Alicia and Aurelia had proved they were as tough as any Aussie.

Yet there was something awe inspiring about the harsh splendour of this outback world despite the privations they were forced to accept, and as another Christmas and Ellie's nineteenth birthday approached, she realised her mother had actually come to look forward to patrolling the fields. She had even struck up a rapport with Jacky Jack and the stock boys and as the nine of them moulded into a team, past hurts and disappointments were put aside.

The radio was their most immediate link with the outside world, and every night one or other of the women would return if possible to the homestead to catch up on the news which was then relayed to the others.

253

'Pig Iron' Bob had narrowly survived a general election in October 1940, but two months later the government was defeated and Curtin became Prime Minister. Hitler's invasion of Russia in August 1941 radically changed the situation in Europe, and the whole pattern of the war was reshaped on 7 December, 1941 when the Japanese bombed Pearl Harbor.

On hearing this news, the women left the cattle to the stock boys and headed for the homestead. Surely, now they had been attacked, the Americans would enter the war and help the Allies instead of standing on the sidelines acting as bankers?

They huddled around the radio three days after the Japanese invaded South-East Asia, willing themselves to believe the assurances of Churchill that Singapore was impregnable. Their belief was shattered when the British battleships, the *Repulse* and the *Prince of Wales*, were sunk off Malaya. Bitter jungle fighting followed as the Australian Eighth Division and other Allied troops opposed the enemy's advance down the Malayan peninsula. The war was getting closer by the day and the threat to Australia was suddenly a very real possibility.

Ellie's birthday came and went and it was soon Christmas. Jack flew in from Darwin where he'd been training the flood of young volunteers who'd poured in from every corner of Australia, and Mickey Maughan, who'd become a regular visitor since Alicia's arrival, came laden with flowers, wine and a roasting lamb.

Yet despite the company and the unaccustomed luxuries, Ellie realised Aurelia was not her usual ebullient self, and suspected it had something to do with the pent-up excitement Jack Withers couldn't quite disguise.

They'd been listening to the war news that had come before the King's speech. Now the radio had been switched off and they each sat with their own thoughts, the cigarette and pipe smoke curling to the corrugated iron ceiling as they sipped the last of the brandy.

'I'm leaving Darwin,' Jack announced into the silence. 'Got an offer I couldn't refuse.'

Aurelia looked at him with a sharpness that showed her concern. 'I get the feeling it isn't in a nice safe office in the Alice.'

He shook his head, the silver threads in his hair gleaming in the light of the kerosine lamps. 'They want me to pilot a flying boat out of Broome,' he said with a calmness that belied the excitement in his eyes. 'There are civilians desperate to get out of Java and it's my chance to help them.'

'You've got a perfectly good job training young pilots,' she argued. 'Let some of them practise on the flying boats.'

He shook his head as he stubbed out his smoke. 'They'll be needed elsewhere,' he drawled. 'Besides, I've got experience of flying boats and don't need training. It'll save time.'

Ellie looked at him as Aurelia fell silent. She didn't know how they were going to see the war through without him. He'd always been there for them. At the end of the two-way radio, or in person on one of his short visits. He'd helped with the stock. Helped with carting the feed out to the animals and repairing the fences. Helped mend the old utility and keep the tractor going. Yet she knew it wasn't just his generous gift of time and mechanical knowledge she would miss, but the man himself. For Jack had become a trusted friend.

She watched as Aurelia touched his hand, and in that moment she realised how much her aunt loved him.

'You take care of yourself you silly old fool,' Aurelia said as she tried unsuccessfully to control her emotions. 'I'm going to need you when this is all over.'

'Is that a promise?' he asked, his gaze fixed on her face, the silent meaning so clear in his expression.

'Yes,' she breathed.

Ellie clapped her hands. 'If that means what I think it does,' she said. 'Then this calls for a celebration. Let's drink a toast.'

Mickey shot Alicia a hopeful look as he poured the wine. 'I don't suppose you and me...?' he began.

She shook her head. 'They say marrying twice is a sign of hope over experience,' she said lightly. 'To do it for the third time would be rather over-egging the pudding.' She smiled sweetly as if to take the sting out of her rejection before turning away.

Ellie saw the dejection on Mickey's face and sighed. Mum hadn't really changed that much, she realised. Poor Mickey. He'd been good company for Alicia, generous with his time and his gifts – a bright interval between the long episodes of struggle – and Alicia was shamelessly using him for her own amusement. Marriage to a man like Mickey Maughan was the last thing she'd contemplate.

Aurelia had finished lunch and she and Claire had decided to take a turn around the garden Ellie had planted when she first moved here. The flowers were bright and planted in a haphazard manner that made them look as if they'd always been here and had been allowed to flourish of their own accord. Creamy roses vied with scarlet poppies and purple banksia, long slender succulents drifted amongst ferns and the tiny blue flowers that reminded her of periwinkles. The scent of the roses drifted up to them as the first drops of rain began to fall, and Aurelia shivered. The memory of Jack was overwhelming.

'The drought during those war years nearly killed us,' she said as they crossed home yard and headed back to the verandah. 'What we would have done for just a drop of rain – just one measly shower.'

'I know how bad it is, Aurelia,' murmured Claire. 'I've lived through several droughts, remember?'

Aurelia looked at Claire and was reminded sharply of Alicia. The two women shared the same height, the same colouring, even the same elegance in the way they carried themselves, and yet the likeness stopped there. For in Claire she could see Ellie's warm spirit, and her eagerness to learn, to adapt and make the best of things. 'You must find all this talk of the past very

257

confusing,' she said as she climbed the steps to the verandah. 'And I know some of the things you'll hear will make little sense because of course you know how things worked out for me and your mother eventually.' She saw the frown and hurried on, afraid of having said too much. 'But it's best you know it all so there won't be any misunderstandings.'

Claire opened the screen door for her and they went into the house. The kitchen was warm and cluttered but welcome after the chill breeze that had come with the rain. 'I must admit I can't see where all this is leading,' she said as she made tea and cut two slices from Ellie's chocolate cake to go with it.

Aurelia pulled off her jacket and with much huffing and puffing untied the laces of her brogues. 'Indulge an old woman for a while longer, my dear. It'll soon become clear.'

Claire pulled out a chair and poured the tea. Her voice was low, almost hesitant as she spoke. 'Go on then,' she prompted. 'Tell me more about you and Jack.'

Aurelia sipped her tea, at ease in the chair, the warmth from the new range belting out enough heat to make her damp trousers steam. 'It was Christmas 1941 and Jack and Mickey Maughan had flown in to celebrate with us.' She fell silent for a moment. 'Not that there was a lot to celebrate. Pearl Harbor had been bombed and Singapore was about to fall to the Japs.'

She drew her pipe from her pocket and fiddled with the tobacco and matches. It gave her a moment's pause – time to gather her thoughts, time to remember the joy and the sadness that had overwhelmed her that day.

Christmas was over too soon, and as Boxing Day dawned Aurelia had walked with Jack to his plane, her arm linked with his, reluctant to let him go. 'You'll write?' she said.

'Of course,' he replied. Then he stopped and put his arms around her. 'Don't let's waste time talking mundane nonsense, Aurelia,' he said firmly. 'I want you to know I love you and I'll come back even if I have to crawl all the way from Broome.' He put a finger against her lips to still any argument. 'And I want you to marry me the minute this is all over.'

Aurelia could only nod, she was so full of emotion she had no words for him – nothing she could say that would change his mind about leaving – nothing that would keep him here, safe and in one piece.

Jack kissed her thoroughly, crushing her to his chest as if he was a drowning man. Then he was gone, into his plane, the engine roaring as the propellers spun and the wheels turned on the red earth taking him away from her.

Aurelia stood at the end of the dirt runway, her vision blurred as the plane lifted off and all too soon became a speck in the sky. 'God speed,' she whispered. Then she shook her fist at the sky. 'And you'd better come back, Jack Withers,' she yelled. 'Because we've got unfinished business.'

She came back from the past and realised Claire was still waiting for her to speak. 'Jack asked me

259

to wait for him,' she said as she puffed her pipe. 'I promised I would. I suppose you could say we were engaged.'

Claire had her elbows on the table, her chin cupped in her hands. Her hair drifted over her shoulders and down her back, catching the last of the light as the rain became more determined. 'Good on you,' she said with a smile. 'But what about Mum? How was she coping?'

Aurelia chewed the stem of her pipe. 'At first she was good. Letters were sporadic to say the least. And when they did come they were usually hopelessly out of date and almost illegible after the censor chopped them about.'

'Did he write to her as he promised?'

Aurelia nodded. 'Stacks of letters would arrive every month from Joe. Seamus wrote fairly often and his letters were always amusing. Filled with anecdotes and wickedly accurate cartoons of the world's leading politicians, but it was Joe's letters she waited for.'

They both fell silent, each with their own thoughts until Aurelia began to speak again. 'My parents were holding out reasonably well, but I suspected they were both weary of war and rationing. The estate had been taken over by the military and turned into a hospital. Pa was not impressed and used to write short, acerbic post scripts to Mother's letters to vent his spleen. He was concerned with the damage hobnailed boots were doing to the parquet flooring.'

Claire grinned. 'His priorities were obviously different from yours.'

'Hmm.' Aurelia laughed. 'Mother was far more

practical,' she spluttered. 'I remember she got the gardener to help her pack all the antiques and paintings and store them in the cellars with the vintage wine.' She shook her head, still smiling. 'She had a bolt and padlock put on the door and kept the key under her pillow at night, and down her corsets during the day.'

Claire laughed. 'I remember that picture of her on your cabinet. Reckon that key was in the safest place.'

Aurelia nodded as she remembered her rather fierce looking mother. It wasn't hard. She looked at the same face in the mirror each morning. 'Mother was rather a stern looking woman – but she had a wonderful sense of the ridiculous.'

'You said Mum was good to begin with,' Claire said with quiet firmness. 'What happened to change that?'

'Two things,' replied Aurelia. 'One rather more serious than the other.'

Claire looked back at her, the blue gaze steady and unflinching.

Aurelia cleared her throat. 'She got a letter from Charlie.'

'Charlie?' The eyes widened and there was an alertness in her expression that hadn't been there before.

Aurelia nodded. 'He wanted Joe to know he was sorry for what he'd done. He said he thought of him often and wished they could be together again. The war had made him realise life was too precarious to carry on a feud and he wanted Joe to write to him. The censor had cut the letter to bits, but we guessed he was somewhere in Africa because Seamus had mentioned that they were in the same regiment.' Aurelia bit her lip. 'Ellie sent the letter in with one of hers. She knew Joe would want to hear from him again, and hoped the letter would heal the breach. It was an old wound – it was time it healed.'

'You said two things changed Mum during that time. What was the second?'

Aurelia thought of Ellie and how she'd been all those years ago. 'The spirit of Warratah was dying along with the grass. Your mother became rootless and restless, unable to find the inner peace she needed to see her through. She kept up a facade of course, a sunny disposition, to hide the almost driven need to work and spend long hours in the saddle. But I could see her nerve was wearing thin and I wished I could have done something.'

She looked at Ellie's daughter and sighed. 'But what could I have said that wasn't a cliché, a false hope that could be dashed at any moment?' She paused. 'Prime Ministers Curtin and Churchill agreed that the Sixth and Seventh Divisions should be transferred from Africa to the Dutch East Indies as Australia was now being seriously threatened, but the sheer pace of the enemy advance ruled this out.'

Aurelia closed her eyes. The agony of those days were returning with such force it almost took her breath away. When she felt calmer she looked back at Claire. Her voice was almost a whisper. 'Singapore fell on the 15th of February, 1942. Ellie didn't hear from Joe after that.'

With her mind occupied by memories and the worry for Claire and Leanne, Ellie almost turned the ute over in a deep rut. Struggling to keep control, she finally managed to get the utility off the track and on to a sweep of shale that lay beneath a stony outcrop. She needed a rest. It was impossible to think clearly when driving through the bush. There were just too many hazards.

She climbed out and pulled on a jacket. The day was overcast and cool and as she looked up at the outcrop she shivered. It looked forbidding in the half-light – not the magical haven of ancient caves she and Joe and Seamus had explored as kids. Lighting a cigarette she tramped over the shale and stood beneath an overhang. There was a cave up there, she remembered, that had drawings on the walls which had survived for centuries. Crude sketches of kangaroos and wombats, of warriors with spears and nulla-nullas and totem spirits from the Dreamtime.

After thinking for a moment she stamped out her smoke and began to climb. It was years since she'd done this, and until she tried, she wouldn't know if she was capable of doing it again. Yet the view would be worth it, for she had once spent long hours up on that overhang just gazing out over the land, and it had become a place of sanctuary – a place where she could cry – a place where she found the inner peace to pray. Perhaps it could still work its magic.

The rock was slippery after the rain, but her thick-soled boots gripped firmly as she picked her way over the boulders and scrub. The clouds drifted away and the sun beat down as she climbed higher and higher. She tied her coat around her waist as she paused to catch her breath. I should really give up smoking, she thought. I never used to get this out of breath. 'Probably something to do with your age,' she muttered as she finally reached the overhang and collapsed in a heap.

Once her pulse had returned to normal she used her coat as a cushion and sat with her arms around her knees. Memory hadn't tricked her, she realised, as she stared out over the pastures that divided Warratah and Jarrah – the view was magnificent.

Humidity rose as the sun scorched damp earth, and made the cattle in the pastures look as if they were wading shoulder deep in water. Eagles drifted high on the warm thermals and she could hear the caw of crows and the laughter of a solitary kookaburra somewhere far in the distance. The scent of eucalyptus drifted up and she closed her eyes. It was as if the intervening years had never been and she was nineteen again.

The old grey horse had died that New Year's eve of 1941 and Jacky Jack had helped her to bury him beneath one of the pepper trees that shaded the horse paddock. He'd been the last real link to her father and the long trek they'd made to get here, and although she was nineteen and all grown up, she'd still felt the keenness of her loss and had come out here so no one could see her cry. She'd spent the night here, she remembered. Curled up in a blanket within the shelter of the cave behind her. It was to be the first of many nights following the fall of Singapore.

She glanced over her shoulder and felt a cold tremble run through her spine. The mouth of the cave yawned darkly, beckoning her to enter and discover its secrets. She looked away. Age and experience had taught her caves could be dangerous. You never knew what lurked in them, and she still remembered the time she and the boys had stumbled on the charred remains of the aboriginal clay mourning caps and had thought they were skulls.

Smiling at the memory, she looked out over the miles of shimmering grass. It rippled like water in an effortless flow as the breeze made it dance and catch the sunlight. And there, on the far horizon was the dust cloud that marked the bullock muster at Jarrah. It was time for her to finish her journey.

Yet she was reluctant to return to the noise and the bustle of the stockyards. It was peaceful out here – almost silent – and as that silence instilled itself into her thoughts they drifted back to the dust cloud she'd seen all those years ago. The dust cloud that had heralded a home-coming.

Ellie was in the vegetable patch a few days into the new year of 1942. She was fighting the weeds that seemed to grow when everything else wilted and died. The potatoes were ready to be dug, the beetroot too, but the beans were shrivelled and the slugs had eaten most of the cabbage. She leaned on the spade as she took a breather and wiped the sweat from her forehead. The flies swarmed around her and the heat was intolerable even here in the shade of the wilgas.

A movement at the end of the long approach to Warratah made her straighten and shield her eyes from the glare. Someone was walking down the dirt road, but they were too far away for her to see who it was. Dropping the spade, she reached for the rifle she always had close to hand. She was alone on the homestead, for Aurelia and the stock boys were busy in the branding yard with the clean-skins, and Mum was off somewhere with Mickey.

Ellie waited, poised and alert. There were too many suspicious characters roaming the outback these days. Rootless individuals who'd come out of the cities to escape the factories and enlistment, with little regard for other people's property. To avoid any trouble she and Aurelia usually provided tucker and water and saw them off the station, but sometimes these itinerant travellers would become belligerent and then Jacky Jack would have to be called to forcibly eject them.

The figure waded through the watery mirage of heat as it slowly approached and Ellie finally realised it was not just a man, but a man leading a horse with a small dog running along beside him. She squinted into the glare as the figure waved, then realisation hit and she began to run.

The horse was laden with bags, his neck drooping, the sweat drying in salty patches on his dusty coat as he plodded wearily down the dirt track. The terrier barked and ran in circles around the rotund little man with the beaming smile who waddled towards her.

'Wang Lee,' Ellie shrieked in delight as she threw herself into his arms and almost knocked him over. 'I can't believe it's you.'

The dog yapped and danced on his back legs. The horse came to a sagging halt and Wang Lee burst into tears. 'Is me, Miss Ellie. Wang Lee so glad he fin' you.'

Ellie held him tightly as they stood there in the middle of the track, aware that it was now her turn to offer comfort and refuge. Wang Lee seemed smaller somehow, less rotund and rather frail beneath that grubby tunic and baggy trousers. There were streaks of grey in the long pig-tail, and his shoes were held together with string.

When the storm of tears had subsided, Wang Lee gently extricated himself. He folded his arms in the voluminous sleeves of his tunic and bowed low. 'Wang Lee sorry for tears, Miss Ellie. But I have come very fa' to fin' you.'

Ellie smiled, so delighted to hear that musical voice again. 'We'll talk later,' she said. 'Let's get you up to the homestead. Looks like you and the horse could do with a long drink and a good rest.' She eyed the bulging pack saddles and pile of bags and pots. 'I see you've brought everything including the kitchen sink,' she gently teased.

'Wang Lee have many things,' he said with a touch of his old spark. 'Not leave behind.'

The little dog raced ahead of them before turning back and barking encouragement as they walked slowly down the track, their pace measured by the weary plod of the horse. Having reached the homestead paddock, Ellie helped to unload the poor beast before giving him a good rub down with the saddle blanket and setting him free.

She and Wang Lee leaned on the fence railings and watched as he dipped his greying muzzle into the water and drank thirstily. The little dog jumped into the trough and lapped voraciously before splashing his way out and shaking himself dry. He then turned avid attention to his fleas and began to scratch luxuriously.

Clipper, who was pining for the old grey's company, approached the other horse and nuzzled his neck, as if recognising a weary traveller and welcoming him home. The tired old horse gave a whicker of acknowledgement and together they wandered off and began to crop at the manger of hay and oats Ellie had put out that morning.

'Fu Man Chu happy now,' said Wang Lee with a tired smile. 'Animal walk too fa'.'

Ellie laughed. 'You've called your horse Fu Man Chu?'

He shook his head, the weary smile not quite reaching his eyes. 'Horse call' Chinaman. Dog is Fu Man Chu.'

'It's unusual, I'll give you that,' she replied, trying not to smile as she watched the brown and white terrier with the piratical tan patch over one eye roll in the dirt.

'Ah, Miss Ellie,' he said softly. 'Betta call Chinaman then people know Wang Lee not *Japanese*.'

Ellie noticed the emphasis and realised life must have become very difficult for him during these last few months. With the Japanese invading Malaya and bombing Pearl Harbor ignorant people would see only the almond eyes and pigtail to come to the wrong conclusion. 'Come on, Wang Lee. I'll get you some tucker and make you up a bed. You look as if you need a very long rest. We can talk later.'

Ellie had seen the two women approach and as she waited for Wang Lee to awake from his afternoon sleep she watched from the shadows of the hall. She could tell Aurelia was hot, filthy and in dire need of a large glass of something alcoholic after her heavy workload. For this had been the last day of branding and despite the lack of rain the herd had increased. Now all they could do was pray they could keep them alive long enough to get them over to the meat market in Brisbane.

'Repel boarders,' yelled Kelly. 'Bombs away. Flak, flak, flak.'

'Shut up, Kelly,' mumbled Aurelia. 'You're becoming tedious.'

'Urrgh?' He picked at one delicate claw, his yellow eye beady. 'Chin, chin,' he said brightly. 'Bottoms up.'

'That's more like it,' said Alicia as she took the verandah steps two at a time and threw her hat on the table. 'What I wouldn't do for a large glass of gin with lots of ice. Mickey insisted I tramp over half his damn property this afternoon, and I'm gasping.'

'Gin's finished. There's a tiny drop of whisky though.'

Aurelia poured the two fingers of whisky into the glasses and handed one over. 'No Mickey?' she enquired.

'I sent him back home. One afternoon with him is enough,' Alicia said firmly before knocking back half her drink.

Ellie was so keyed up she couldn't wait any longer to break the news. She slammed through the screen doors.

'What's happened?' Aurelia asked, her eyes wide with fear.

'We've got a visitor, Aunt Aurelia,' she replied breathless with excitement. Ellie stepped aside and Aurelia's monocle popped from her eye socket when she saw the tiny oriental standing in the shadow of her doorway.

'What's that Jap doing here?' Alicia demanded before Aurelia had time to speak. She slammed her glass on the table and stood up. 'We ought to call the police or the army or something. He should have been interned with the others.'

'He's not a Jap,' hissed Ellie. 'This is Wang Lee and he's *Chinese.*'

Alicia sneered as she looked him up and down. 'They all look the same to me,' she said rudely. 'And I won't feel safe in my bed knowing he's here.' She approached the door and found herself barred from the house by her daughter. 'Let me pass, Elspeth,' she ordered. 'It's our duty to inform the authorities and have him removed.'

Ellie looked to Aurelia for help. She hadn't expected her mother to react like this and was horrified.

Aurelia fixed her monocle and took charge.

270

'Alicia sit down and stop making a fool of yourself,' she commanded. 'Ellie, bring Wang Lee out here so he can sit down. The poor man looks exhausted.'

The little man came shuffling out to the verandah, his arms hidden in the folds of his tunic sleeves, his pigtail drooping down his back. He bowed low to Aurelia. 'Much honour meet aunt of Miss Ellie,' he said softly. Then he bowed to Alicia who was sitting very erect in her chair as if poised for flight. 'Very sorry cause trouble Missy. Wang Lee no stay if you no like.'

'Ellie's mother doesn't know what you did for her when she was on the tracks,' Aurelia explained. 'You'll have to forgive her rudeness.' Ignoring Alicia's sharp interjection she helped him into a chair and gave him her whisky.

'We owed you far more than you could ever realise, Wang Lee,' she said studiously avoiding her sister's glare of outrage. 'And you are welcome to stay as long as you like.'

He struggled from the chair and bowed again. 'Wang Lee most honoured.'

Ellie pulled up a chair and as the little man sipped the drink, she told her mother how she'd come to meet Wang Lee, and how he'd helped keep her identity secret and had ultimately saved her life with his gift of the mirror.

'I worked as Wang Lee's helper on the drove and slept in a hammock slung beneath the cook wagon. Snowy had given me Clipper by then, and it was when we were only a couple of weeks outside Longreach that Clipper was caught in a small stampede and was gored by a bullock. I fell

271

and hit my head and wrenched my ankle. I didn't wake up for nearly two days.'

She looked across at Wang Lee whose dark eyes were watching her thoughtfully. 'Wang Lee took care of me. He made me up a bed in his wagon and used his potions and ointments to help me get better. He also realised I wasn't a boy, but kept my secret.' She smiled at him. 'I never did ask why you did that, Wang Lee. It could have been the end of your job if the others had found out.'

'I Chinaman,' he said with pride. 'Know how hard to live in this land when different. Not easy for man find work with girl. Not easy for Chinaman either to let girl be sent away. Wang Lee grow very fond of her.'

Ellie smiled. In hindsight she had realised the truth. She and Wang Lee had a lot in common, for being a little girl on the matilda was as lonely as being a Chinaman in an alien country. 'I hurt my foot in the fall as well, and Wang Lee carved me the walking stick I keep on the wall in my room. But it was his gift of the mirror that saved my life.'

She fell silent and let Aurelia pick up the threads of the story. For it still hurt to remember those last few hours she'd had with her father, and the ordeal she'd survived with the dingo.

Alicia looked barely mollified and her nod of thanks was stiff as Aurelia finished speaking.

'Wang Lee good cook,' he said into the ensuing silence. 'Make tucker, earn keep while stay.'

'Excellent,' said Aurelia. 'Anything would be an improvement after Sally's cooking.'

Wang Lee took over from Sally in the kitchen. He did all the cooking, turning out delicious meals from what could only be termed rather basic supplies and demoted Sally to the kitchen chores. He made sure she did things properly whilst keeping a wary eye on the precious sacks of flour and sugar and the cans of kerosine. They no longer disappeared into the native humpies.

His arrival meant the women were released from the homestead to attend the stock. He took on the time-consuming tasks of feeding the chooks and milking the cows, and could often be found digging in the vegetable plot. He seemed to have a magic touch; for everything began to thrive. His potions were used to full effect when one of the stock boys ripped his leg open on barbed wire, and again when Jacky Jack went down with a fever. His skills at shadow puppets and his obvious delight with the native children made him a firm favourite with their mothers who happily let him babysit while they went off to hunt or to gossip.

Ellie and Aurelia wondered how they'd ever coped before his arrival and Wang Lee soon became an integral part of Warratah as he shuffled around the homestead and nearby paddocks, his little dog chasing after him. Fu Man Chu proved to be an excellent ratter as well as a bunny-killer, and it was as if he knew he had to earn his keep. Yet he wisely kept away from the kennels and the blue heelers as his enthusiastic willingness to make friends had backfired – he'd been badly bitten by one of the dogs and had to have his ear stitched.

Unlike everyone else, Alicia was still wary of Wang Lee, but she maintained a polite coolness and kept her opinions to herself, for which they were all grateful. There was enough trouble in the world without having it in the home.

The women were sitting around the table on the night of 19 February waiting for the newscast to begin. Wang Lee was crashing pots, Sally was preparing vegetables for the next day and Fu Man Chu was lying in front of the cooking range. He'd finally been allowed in the house following a bath in disinfectant and was making the most of the comfort this afforded. For the little terrier was a stray, a swaggie who'd walked the lonely wallaby tracks and never known a real home before, and his adoration of Wang Lee was his way of showing his gratitude.

The cattle had been brought as close to the homestead as possible, for the endless droving across the thousands of acres of Warratah was proving too much for everyone. Several hundred of the fats had been drafted down to Longreach with a couple of the stock boys and Jacky Jack, and now there were only the breeders, the bulls and the yearlings left. If they were careful, they might just see the drought through.

All activity stopped in the kitchen as the newsreader's voice boomed into the room.

'It is my sad duty to inform you that Darwin has been attacked.'

'Oh my God,' shrieked Alicia.

'Shut up,' ordered Aurelia and Ellie in unison as they turned up the volume.

The newscaster was still talking. 'Japanese

274

carrier-based bombers attacked Darwin earlier today, sinking eight ships. Over two hundred seamen are feared dead as well as countless troops and civilians.'

'Darwin,' breathed Aurelia. 'It's too close. Thank God Jack's safe in Broome.'

As they listened, the true horror of Australia's predicament slowly dawned. Enemy bombers had almost eradicated the northern town that had once been thought invincible. The war had finally come to Australia.

Then the broadcaster's tone changed and the atmosphere in the kitchen lightened. 'There is some good news from the north, however,' he informed them. 'Thousands of cattle have escaped the enemy bomb attack and are safely out of reach due to the bravery of a handful of elderly men, women and boys. The cattlemen whose stations are in the far north of Western Australia united several days ago and have already begun one of the biggest cattle droves known in the history of this country. They have left Wyndham and are expected to cross the state line into the Northern Territory in about a month's time where they will be joined by cattlemen and women from that state's northern stations. It is vital we keep our cattle out of Japanese hands, and these brave men and women of the outback are doing their bit by ensuring the cattle are moved as swiftly as possible out of the danger zone.

'This epic drove will cross some of Australia's harshest country and be joined by others coming down from the northern stations. It's estimated

275

there will be over sixteen thousand head of cattle in the main body of the drove and it will take at least eight months to reach Brisbane. The drove boss asks that all station owners on the route give them access to as much water as they can spare. He is well aware of the drought, and knows this is a desperate gamble, but it's vital we get these cattle through.'

Aurelia turned off the radio when the broadcast was over and sat back in her chair. 'They'll be lucky to get more than a third through,' she said with a sigh. 'As for water to spare...' She fell silent.

'Good on 'em, I say,' said Ellie forcefully. 'I only wish we were a part of it. It sounds exciting, and we'd be making history.'

'We're better keeping our stock alive here without dragging them all the way to Brisbane. The calves wouldn't make it, and the breeders would dry up. Jacky Jack said the fats were difficult enough to handle on the last drove to Longreach, and he had to keep pushing them through the night so they could make the miles between the surviving water-holes. He was lucky to have had so few losses.'

'I could do with a bit of excitement,' Ellie said restlessly.

'There'll be excitement enough if the Japs attack again,' said Aurelia sharply. 'Darwin's not that far away if they take over the northern shore and set up an airfield.'

There was a protracted silence as they all digested the reality of their situation. Life was hard enough, but the thought of invasion was something they'd never contemplated before.

Yet they were not alone – for Prime Minister Curtin had become angry at Winston Churchill's refusal to allow Australian troops to protect their own country. He ignored Churchill's protest and ordered the returning troops from Africa to be diverted to Australia.

Australia's position was critical. Her fighting strength was below par because of their dispersal around Europe and Africa, all were poorly equipped and there were practically no tanks or aircraft and very few fighting ships.

Curtin had to face the grim situation, and did it with a realism that won him many admirers. 'Without inhibitions of any kind,' he declared. 'I make it quite clear that from now on Australia looks to America, free of any pangs as to our traditional links or kinship with the United Kingdom.'

Ten days later a group of ten Japanese aircraft flew south from Timor to one of the main refuelling points in Australia. There were no defences except for a few .303 rifles of the Homeguard because intelligence believed this western port lay beyond the fuel range of Japanese aircraft.

The Japanese struck at nine thirty in the morning, jettisoning their long range fuel tanks on arrival, their tracer bullets setting fire to the group of sixteen flying boats that lay helpless in the water with their cargoes of women and children.

It was Broome's darkest day.

Chapter Eleven

Ellie came back to the present, shocked at how swiftly the day had changed. The sky was leaden, the sun masked by a blanket of cloud as the first heavy splashes of rain soaked her blouse and jeans. She hurriedly pulled on her jacket and zipped it to her chin. It wasn't the chill wind making her shiver, but the thought of climbing back down. For the rain had polished the rocks to gleaming ebony and she knew she wouldn't find the return journey quite so easy.

With a glance over her shoulder, she contemplated sitting the downpour out in the cave. But it could last for hours, right through the night, and the two-way radio was in the ute. There was no other choice. She had to go down. 'Bloody idiot,' she muttered as she eased her way from the overhang and found a tentative foothold. 'You knew it would rain again, yet you sat there dreaming the day away without an intelligent thought in your head.'

She gripped the slippery stone, edging ever downwards, her feet scuffling for purchase. One wrong move and she'd plunge to the ground. Although she'd never been fearful of heights – this was definitely too high, too wet and too bloody dangerous. The rain soaked her, the sweat chilled on her skin as the wind grew stronger. She was in deep trouble but determined not to panic.

She paused to catch her breath, clinging to the face of the outcrop, her fingers numb from gripping the narrow fissures in the rock. Edging her foot over she found a niche, but as she put her weight on it she felt it give. Her foot slid away with the loose stones, her fingers clawed as she desperately tried to maintain a hold and return her balance to the other foot. Swinging her free leg up, she rammed her boot into a shallow hollow and with every ounce of strength she possessed, hauled herself back into position.

Her breath was a sob, her heart banging against her ribs. Rain and sweat stung her eyes and her hair plastered wetly to her face as she clung to the outcrop. She had to get down. Had to get off this rock. But most of all she had to remain calm – one moment of panic could make her careless.

Ellie sniffed and blinked the rain and sweat from her eyes. If it had been sunny and warm she wouldn't have been such a baby, she thought scornfully. It was just a rock – one she'd climbed hundreds of times as a kid. She'd climbed up – she could get down. With cold determination she clawed a hold on a narrow ledge. Keeping her chest close to the rocks, she scraped the toe of her boot down until she found a fissure and dug in. Then she moved the other foot – the other hand.

She lost all sense of time as she slowly and painfully descended that steep rock-face, and was just congratulating herself on how well she was doing when a startled bird shot out of a hole and into her face.

With a cry of surprise she lost her balance. But

this time it was too late to find another hold. This time she had no chance to save herself.

'I thought your mother was coming over today?' said Angel as they watched the vast road train splash through the mud on its way to the main highway.

Leanne looked at her watch. The rain was dripping off her hat brim and down her neck, and although she wore a full-length waterproof coat over her moleskins and sweater, she could feel the chill of it seeping through. 'I expect she decided not to come because of the weather. No worries. I'll give Warratah a ring when we get back to the homestead.'

She trudged through the mud to where they'd tethered the horses. The animals looked miserable, their heads drooping as they reluctantly cropped the grass beneath the coolibahs. She knew how they felt. She too was cold and miserable and she regretted the hasty words she'd flung at Angel the night before. He'd tried to explain he hadn't meant for her to hand over half of Jarrah, but that he simply wanted to be a part of it. He felt isolated, and not a little miffed at her passion for the place, and she couldn't blame him. It was as if Jarrah had taken her over.

'Let's hope the road train makes it to the highway before the track gets impassable,' said Angel as he swung his leg over the saddle and caught the reins. 'Won't this weather hold up things?'

She glanced across at him and felt the familiar lurch of longing. He still looked handsome, even with the rain dripping from his bush hat and the dust of the day's work clinging to his face. 'It will if it keeps up,' she said. 'But the forecast is good and this should clear by tomorrow.'

Angel smiled back, his long lashes sparkling with raindrops. 'At least we can go home each night,' he said. 'Your poor father is stuck out on the plains. It can't be very pleasant.'

Leanne realised he was trying to make amends and although she was sick with curiosity as to what was happening over at Warratah with Claire, she felt her spirits lighten. 'He's probably spent more nights out in the rain than you've had hot dinners,' she said cheerfully. 'And after what he went through in the war, this is nothing.'

She saw him raise a dark brow, but she wasn't about to enlighten him. She had only a vague knowledge of what Dad had gone through for he rarely talked of it, but she knew it had been bad, because she could still remember the nightmares he'd suffered when she was a little girl.

They rode back to the homestead with the rest of the men. They were a bedraggled lot, with their sodden clothes and miserable horses. The rain hammered down as the horses' hoofs turned the earth to a red, sticky mud. Trees dripped dolefully and the smoke from the cookhouse fire struggled to find its way out of the chimney. Leanne grinned as she watched the ducks splash and revel on the billabong, then chuckled when she noticed the gallahs hanging upside-down to wash the ticks from their wings. 'Silly buggers,' she murmured into her coat collar. At least someone was enjoying the rain.

They passed through the final gate, across home yard and towards the stables. The horses were rubbed down and fed and watered as Leanne chatted to the drovers and joined in their banter. 'We're eating in the cookhouse tonight,' she told Angel as they prepared to leave the stables. 'I'm too tired to cook.'

Angel eyed her for a long moment as if to give her an argument, then obviously thought better of it and shrugged. 'I could eat anywhere,' he said. 'I'm starving.'

Leanne ducked her head and made a run for it to the cookhouse with Angel following closely behind. The heat was almost overwhelming as they pushed through the door and entered the dining room. It was a large room, with the kitchen at one end, and long tables laid out with benches down the middle. The windows were running with condensation and the noise of boot heels on the wooden floor was accompanied by many voices. Steam rose from the vast cooking pots on the industrial size stove and Cookie was, as usual, in a bad temper.

'Get into flamin' line,' he yelled as he waved a meat cleaver about. 'How am I supposed to feed you blokes if you don't wait yer bloody turn?'

'Come on mate,' yelled one of the ringers. 'Get a flamin' move on. Me stomach thinks me throat's been cut.'

'Might as well be,' yelled another of the men. 'When you taste it, you'd wish it bloody was.'

Leanne shoved Angel in front of her and joined the shuffling, raucous queue. She loved it in here, for there was no standing on ceremony, no prissy manners – just honest, hard-working men who spoke their mind and accepted her as one of them.

Angel looked back at her over his shoulder. 'You like eating here?' he asked, his eyes round with amazement.

Leanne grinned and nodded. 'Best restaurant in town,' she replied.

Cookie slammed the meat cleaver into the chopping block. There was immediate silence. Everyone knew from past experience that Cookie had had enough. He was a big man to argue with – a very big man – with a short fuse. 'One more word about my cooking and I'll knock yer flamin' blocks off,' he shouted. He glowered over the shuffling queue, arms folded across his vast chest. Satisfied he'd got them under control he nodded. 'That's more like it,' he grumbled as he turned and began to dish out the meat and potatoes and piles of vegetables.

The noise broke out again as the men carried their loaded plates to the table, but died as the scrape of cutlery took over. Leanne found a place for her and Angel and was soon in conversation with one of the old-timers who'd been on the place for as long as she could remember. She glanced across at Angel who was surreptitiously cleaning his knife and fork on his shirt-tail. 'I wouldn't let Cookie see you doing that,' she murmured. 'He takes great pride in the cleanliness of his kitchen.'

Angel looked down the length of the table. Cookie was a towering presence, his red, sweating face glowering as he stood like a monolith overseeing the meal. Angel ducked his head and winked at Leanne. 'Reckon I'd better do as I'm told,' he muttered. 'Matron's watching.'

Leanne grinned. His joke was endearing and it meant their row was forgotten. She would have to learn to keep her brain in gear with her mouth. They'd had too many arguments, and although the sex was usually terrific afterwards, it didn't bode well for their future.

'There's no reply at Jarrah,' said Claire as she returned to the sitting room. 'They must all still be out. But I'm surprised Mum hasn't called.'

'Probably busy,' muttered Aurelia as she tried to finish the crossword in the paper. 'It takes time to load the animals up, and with this rain I expect it'll be the devil's own job to get those road trains up the track.'

'How soon before Dad gets back?' Claire sat down, picked up a magazine and then put it aside. She didn't feel like reading. She was too restless.

Aurelia looked up from her paper. 'When he's finished.' She put down her pen and sighed. 'You know how long these things take, Claire. He could be another week or ten days. It depends on the number of stock and how far they had to go to round them up.'

Claire lit a cigarette and listened to the rain hammering on the roof. It was cosy in here, with a fire roaring up the chimney and the lamps lit, but it felt strange not having either of her parents here to share it with her. 'I'm surprised he went out on the muster,' she grumbled. 'He knew I

284

was coming home.'

Aurelia gave up on the crossword and folded her arms. 'The work doesn't stop just because you've come home,' she reminded her. 'You had the chance to see him at your graduation, but you didn't want him there – that hurt, you know. Your parents thought you were ashamed of them.'

Claire blushed. Her refusal to let them come to her graduation had nothing to do with shame – only on her part. She didn't think they'd want to be there. 'I'll try Mum again,' she said. 'They must be back by now.'

Aurelia grunted. 'She'll phone when she's ready. Do sit down, Claire, you're making me nervous.'

Claire hovered in the doorway, eyed the telephone in the hall and tried once more. There was no reply and she put the receiver back. 'I hope she's all right,' she muttered as she returned to her chair by the fire.

'She's got the two-way in the ute,' said Aurelia with a hint of sharpness. 'And Leanne knows she's on the way. If there was trouble we'd have heard by now.'

Claire stared out into the darkness then into the fire where the orange flames danced up the chimney and the wood settled into the ashes. The doubts were legion, the question burning to be asked. 'When Mum first came to Warratah,' she began.

'Yes?' Aurelia reached for her pipe.

'Jarrah was a separate station back then, wasn't it?'

Aurelia nodded, the pipe in her hand, the

matches still on the table beside her.

Claire noticed the whites of her knuckles as she held that pipe, the tense quality in her shoulders and the alert gleam in those grey eyes. 'How come we own it now? I thought the Maughans had farmed Jarrah for over a century? Why would they give it up?'

Aurelia concentrated on lighting her pipe, but Claire noticed how she'd paled, the way she'd avoided eye contact, and wondered why this innocent question should make her aunt look shifty.

'It's a long story,' she muttered finally. 'And very involved. I'll tell you another day.'

Claire sat forward, willing her aunt to look her in the eye. 'We've got plenty of time. It's still early, and I'm staying up until I can get hold of Mum.'

Aurelia gave an abrupt cough of laughter. 'It's all right for you young things,' she prevaricated. 'Late nights are all very well, but it'll soon be way past my bedtime.' She finally looked at Claire. 'Besides, shouldn't you be thinking about to-morrow? Don't you want to look your best for Matt?'

Claire waved her suggestions aside. 'You instigated my home-coming,' she said quietly. 'You said there were things that needed airing. Things about Jarrah and the row I'd had with Mum and Dad. You said I was adult enough to face the truth. So why are you reluctant to talk about Jarrah?' Her tone was calm but firm.

Aurelia heaved a sigh and stared into the fire. 'I do wish you weren't quite so like your mother,'

286

she murmured. 'Questions, questions, questions.' She looked back at Claire and realised she had no alternative but to reveal how Jarrah had become a part of Warratah. 'It all started during the war,' she began.

Claire leaned back into the chair, but couldn't relax. There was something odd going on – but how on earth could the ownership of Jarrah have anything to do with the suspicions that had driven her away? Then she remembered the solitary gravestone and a chill ran up her spine. Perhaps there was a link – a link that until this moment she hadn't considered.

Aurelia sat forward in her chair, her gaze fixed on the fire. Her pipe remained cold and forgotten in her hand. 'After Curtin told Churchill where to stuff his organisation, General MacArthur arrived in the Philippines. He brought the American fleet and thousands of troops, equipment, munitions and aircraft – all the things we were so short of. The enemy had now moved into New Guinea and the Solomon Islands. Invasion was imminent, and Australia went on full wartime footing. Civilian labour was directed to munitions factories, the docks, building airfields and a strategic north-south road through Australia's heartlands. Food, clothing, petrol and all luxuries were rationed and taxes were increased.'

Claire shifted in the chair. 'I asked about Jarrah,' she said with restless impatience. 'Not about the war.'

'The war had a bearing on everything we did,' retorted Aurelia as she gave Claire one of her withering glares. 'If you want to hear about

Jarrah, then you'll have to be patient.'

Claire reddened and kept silent. Aurelia still had the power to make her feel like a naughty child, and she knew she'd overstepped the mark.

'Mickey Maughan arrived at Warratah shortly after the attack on Broome. His usual jovial mood seemed muted, but there was a purpose in his long stride as he crossed the yard to the homestead verandah. Alicia and I were having a quick breakfast before joining your mother in the pasture where she was helping with the fence posting.'

Taking the steps two at a time, he flung his hat down and gratefully took a cup of tea from Wang Lee. 'I'm sorry to hear about Jack,' he said quietly to Aurelia. 'Still no news?'

'No.' She put down her cup and looked at him squarely. She couldn't talk about Jack. Couldn't bear to think he might never come home. 'What can we do for you, Mickey?'

He might have known Aurelia would come straight to the point, but he wished she'd given him a few moments' respite for what he had to tell them. He glanced across at Alicia, admiring the way her skin had tanned from exposure to the elements, and how neat she looked in the new moleskins and shirt he'd bought her in the Curry.

She was one hell of a woman – for she had learned to appear as at home here on this isolated station as in the smartest of hotels – and he could fully understand why she kept rejecting his proposals. He was a bushman, through and through, with few social graces despite his wealth, and nothing to offer her but his heart and a lifetime of hard work and devotion to Jarrah Downs.

He cleared his throat and fidgeted with his hat. Having rehearsed what he wanted to say on the flight here, he was suddenly reluctant to begin. His life's work was finished for now, his future uncertain; it was a great deal to absorb, let alone discuss with calm authority and he was almost afraid to voice his plans, for it made everything seem too permanent, too real. He became aware of the expectant silence and Aurelia's restlessness. 'I've sold off most of the mob,' he said quickly. 'Jarrah's closing down until the war's over.'

Alicia's surprise was clear. 'But you can't,' she said sharply. 'We have to keep the mobs going to provide meat for the country and for the troops.'

Mickey reddened and looked down at his large brown hands that were scarred from years of working his property. 'My Seamus is fighting somewhere in Africa,' he said quietly. 'The men I've worked with all my life are spread hell west and crooked over the world. I no longer have the heart to stay here looking after a mob of bloody cattle when I could be doing something useful.'

'Keeping the cattle alive *is* useful,' insisted Alicia. 'Besides, the army have already turned you down – you said so.'

'Things are different now,' he drawled. 'Australia needs every man she has – even old blokes like me.' He grinned, saw his attempt at humour cut no ice with either woman and carried on. 'I've been accepted into the RAAF as a senior pilot.'

Alicia paled, but remained silent as she calmly fixed a cigarette into an ivory holder.

'So you're leaving too,' said Aurelia with a sigh. 'I knew this would happen. One by one all our men are being swallowed up by this terrible, terrible war.' She seemed to draw herself up, as if dredging the remains of an almost bankrupt spirit to the fore. 'So what can we do for you, Mickey?' she asked again.

He pulled out the sheaf of papers from his jacket and smoothed them out on the table. 'These are the deeds to Jarrah,' he said solemnly. 'And this is my will. If anything should happen to me, then Jarrah is to pass to Seamus.' He looked away, staring off beyond the distant horizon as he thought of his twenty-three-year-old son – his only heir – with his mother's Irish blue eyes and dark hair. The homestead had been so silent without him. Sighing, he turned back to the women. 'If neither of us come back, then Jarrah is Alicia's.'

Alicia gasped. 'You can't do that,' she said sharply. 'I have no right. Besides, what do I know about running a cattle station?' She stubbed out the cigarette. 'There must be someone else?'

He bowed his head. He wasn't surprised by her refusal, but remained adamant. 'If me and Seamus don't make it, there's no one else. My wife died fifteen years ago, and my other son's buried on Jarrah.' Alicia remained silent as his steady brown eyes held her. 'You know how I feel about you,' he said gruffly. 'And I understand you probably think I'm trying to blackmail you into something you don't want. But there are other things to take into consideration – do this for me? Please?'

Alicia drew back, her blue eyes clouded with doubt, and Mickey could see she was desperately trying to find the right words to say that wouldn't cause him any more anguish or humiliation – he couldn't help but love her for that.

'You've made it very clear how you feel, Mickey, and I wish...' She paused for a long moment then seemed to come to a decision. 'Of course I'll do as you ask, but it really won't be necessary. You and your son will come back to Jarrah. I just know you will.' Her smile was brittle.

Mickey knew the odds were against him returning, but there was no point in making this harder than it already was. He watched Alicia's face as she lit another cigarette and wondered fleetingly if perhaps there was a chance for him after all. Yet common sense told him this was not the moment to declare himself again, not if he was leaving tonight. Another rejection would serve only to depress him further and he needed to keep his concentration on the task ahead.

Aurelia broke the awkward silence by clearing her throat. 'You said there were other things to be taken into consideration.'

He turned gratefully to her with a smile he knew was fooling no one. 'Remember after the last war how the government brought in a law about compulsory purchase? Parcels of our land were almost given away so they could be sold cheaply to the returning troops.'

Aurelia nodded. She'd lost thirteen thousand

acres herself. 'But I got it back when the young man went broke and returned to the city. A lot did, remember?'

'Some didn't,' he reminded her. 'My parents lost over twelve thousand acres – most of it good water – and it's still being farmed today.' He chewed his lip. 'It's my bet the government will do the same thing again when this is all over. But this time the stations are much bigger, far more widespread, and it's the more successful of us that will lose the most.'

Aurelia caught on quickly. 'So rather than put Jarrah and Warratah together by willing me the deeds, it's more sensible to keep them small and under separate ownership.' It was a statement, not a question.

He was relieved. He'd known she would understand his reasoning behind not leaving her Jarrah – even though he was fully aware she was far more capable than Alicia – and would probably make a better fist of things. Alicia might have made his pulse race, but when it came to Jarrah it was important his head ruled his heart and not the other way around.

'Warratah is a much bigger station that Jarrah, and you'll probably lose some of your land, but not as much as you would if the two properties are under one title,' he said quietly. He noticed Alicia seemed happier now things had been explained and it saddened him. He had hoped she would see his trust in her as the next step in their relationship.

'So this is just a business plan?' Alicia asked thoughtfully.

She gave him a sweet smile, and Mickey tamped down on the spark of hope that was all too easily lit within him. 'I would have liked it to be more than that,' he said evenly, pushing his feelings for her to the back of his mind. 'But as I can't have everything I want, this seemed the ideal way of conserving Jarrah for the future.'

He took a deep breath as he thought of the ninety square miles of pasture, the homestead and the tiny cemetery surrounded by native trees and shrubs. 'There are five generations of my family buried on Jarrah. I would hate it if strangers took over.' His gaze was steady on Alicia's face, willing her to understand how much this meant to him. 'If I don't get back, keep it safe – if not for Seamus, then for Ellie – I've set up a trust.'

Alicia felt a twinge of embarrassment for the way she'd treated him, yet it was tempered with more than a little irritation. Up until now, Mickey Maughan had been a means of breaking the monotony of the outback, providing reasonable company and a plane out of here when she needed to get to Cloncurry. He'd plied her with expensive gifts when she let him know she was depressed, and flattered her when she'd visited the hairdressers in the Curry to have the grey tended to. Dinners in a smart hotel, cocktails on the verandah – all little luxuries that had made life bearable out here. Now he was leaving, trusting her to take care of his precious Jarrah only to have to hand it over to Elspeth.

She lit another cigarette and blew smoke as she watched him and her sister go over the finer details of the documents. He was a good man, she admitted. But naive if he thought he could blackmail her into marrying him. Mickey Maughan had merely been someone she could rely on for a good time and it had been fun to keep him on a string. But that was as far as it went. Alicia shivered as she looked out beyond home yard and the outbuildings to the endless miles of nothing. His leaving would sentence her to months, maybe years of boredom and isolation – the last thing she needed was a blasted cattle station to watch over. If only this damn war would come to an end, she thought crossly. Then there'd be no need for any of this. I've had it with Australia.

Aurelia was tense. 'Wang Lee will see to those,' she said rather more sharply than she intended when Alicia let a cup and saucer crash to the wooden floor. She knew full well why her sister was fussing over the dishes – her conscience was bothering her and she was trying to ignore it. 'If you want something to do, then you'd better put these in the safe.' She handed over the deeds and the will.

There was a moment of silence after Alicia slammed through the screen door, and they listened to the sound of her staccato footsteps as she crossed the hall. 'When are you leaving?' Aurelia asked finally.

'Tonight.' He sat there with his hat crushed in his hand, his expression miserable. 'I reckon it's best I don't make a fool out of meself over Alicia again,' he said with a sigh. 'But I would've liked to say goodbye to her before I leave.'

Aurelia picked up her jacket and whip. 'I'm off to keep an eye on Ellie. She's been out too long on her own,' she said gruffly. She stood up, the monocle firmly fixed, the jacket buttoned tight. That's how it was for everyone these days, she thought wearily. Tense, buttoned up, all emotions under control, afraid to acknowledge the awful truths because if they allowed that to happen the dam would burst and they would all be lost.

'I'd better be going then,' Mickey said reluctantly, his gaze drifting to the screen door.

Aurelia shook his hand, felt the firmness and warmth in it that reminded her so forcefully of her darling Jack, and had to clear her throat before she could speak. 'Take care of yourself,' she rasped. 'And I'll see Jarrah comes to no harm.'

'Use the land as you see fit,' he said quietly. 'I still got good water on the southern pastures, bores are holding up and the river's still running so the grazing's fair. I've kept the three bulls and some of the breeders, but they won't need much looking after for a while.'

Aurelia nodded. She couldn't say more. She looked into his face, committing it to memory as she had done with so many others before she turned away. 'I suggest you walk Mickey to his plane, Alicia,' she threw over her shoulder to the shadow behind the screen door. 'Could be some time before we see him again.'

Alicia's aristocratic upbringing wouldn't allow her to appear rude or churlish, and although she knew she had to be careful not to give Mickey the wrong impression, she couldn't just let him go

295

without saying goodbye properly. She reached for her hat and together they stepped down from the verandah into the broiling heat. 'We can take the utility,' she offered stiffly.

'I'd rather walk,' he drawled. 'It'll give me a few minutes more of your company.'

Alicia dug her hands into her pockets, the brim of her hat deliberately low so he couldn't see her face. She suddenly felt awkward with him, tongue-tied and unusually lost for the right thing to say, so she walked beside him in silence. After a few steps she felt his hand on her arm and reluctantly came to a halt. Standing there in the middle of homestead yard she allowed him to tilt her chin with his fingers so he could look into her face. Trapped by his penetrating gaze, she had nowhere else to look and she was suddenly afraid he would read her thoughts.

'Don't spoil these last few moments by being afraid of saying the wrong thing, Alicia,' he said quietly. 'I want to remember your smile and the way you chatter in that funny pommy accent with all those long words that I have to pretend to understand. I couldn't bear it if the last memory I have of you was of a sad face and an awkward silence.'

She made an effort to relax. 'I don't want to spoil anything,' she replied. 'But it's not fair to either of us to expect too much of each other. Not when you're leaving so unexpectedly.'

He smiled, his height casting a long shadow over her. 'Will you miss me?'

'Of course,' she said truthfully. Then she saw the light of hope in his eyes and added, 'But as a friend. A very dear friend.'

He tucked her arm in his and they slowly walked across the yard and out towards the landing strip. 'I'll be satisfied with that,' he said softly. 'For now.'

In normal times Alicia would have put him straight. But these weren't normal times, and when he did return from the war she'd be long gone. Better to let him go thinking well of her and say nothing. 'Don't worry about Jarrah,' she said as they came to a halt beside the plane. 'I'll look after it for you until you and Seamus get back.'

He silently crushed her to him, kissed the top of her head then was gone. The propellers spun and the engine roared as the little craft sped along the runway and lifted into the sky.

Alicia watched the fragile craft disappear into the roiling blackness of the advancing thunder clouds and wondered if it was a portent for the future. For she had a sudden suspicion she might have made a fatal error of judgement.

Leanne was feeling pleasantly sated as she pushed through the screen door and shrugged off her coat. It had been another long day and she was knackered. Kicking off her boots, she left them where they'd fallen and headed down the hall. Angel had decided he liked it in the cookhouse and had stayed on to smoke and yarn with the rest of the men. It was nice to have a few moments to herself, she thought as she passed the small table. She could shower and prepare herself for Angel's return. Her glance fell on the telephone and she looked at her watch. 'Better ring Warratah and let Mum know we got that truck off okay,' she muttered. The phone was answered on the first ring. 'How y'goin' Claire?'

'Good. Is Mum there?'

Her sister sounded agitated and Leanne stiffened. 'I thought she'd decided not to come.'

'Oh, my God,' muttered Claire at the other end of the line. 'That means she's out there on her own.'

'When did she leave?' Leanne was doing her best to remain calm.

'Real early. Leanne, we've got to find her and quick. The temperature's dropped and she could die of hypothermia if she's had an accident.'

'Wait on a minute, Claire. She's got the two-way radio. If something had happened to the ute, she'd have called in.'

'But she hasn't, has she?' shouted Claire at the other end. 'That's why you're ringing me and we're wasting time. I'm coming over.' The line was abruptly disconnected.

Leanne grabbed her coat and impatiently pulled on her boots. If only she'd rung earlier. If only she'd not waited until after supper. The thought of her mother out in the black, wet night spurred her on and she raced out of the house and back across the yard. Yanking the screen door open she slammed into the cookhouse and was met by a dozen pairs of startled eyes. The silence was complete. 'Get the Land Rovers out and pack the medical kit. Mum's lost somewhere on the track from Warratah.'

They moved as one. Hats were rammed on

298

heads, coats shrugged into as they followed her out of the door and into the rain. They broke into groups of six and fired up the two Land Rovers. Cookie packed the medical kit and stretcher into the back of his truck and squeezed into the cab with an armful of blankets and pillows. Leanne raced to the utility, Angel not far behind her, and after a couple of coughs it started. Hearing the noise, heads poked from the bunkhouse and soon there were over twenty people heading out of Jarrah in Land Rovers, trucks, utilities and on horseback.

The night was black, the rain coming down like a curtain. Leanne and Angel drove in silence as the utility bounced and jolted and made the headlights dance over the muddy track, illuminating trees, startling grazing cattle and wallabies, sending a flock of emus into a shambling run. Leanne held grimly to the steering wheel as she smeared away the condensation and peered into the darkness. She'd never forgive herself if something happened to Mum.

As the convoy moved slowly towards Warratah and the hours ticked away she became frantic. There was no sign of the utility. Nothing to show Mum had even come down the track today. And yet she had to be here somewhere. Mum knew the rules and would never have just gone off without telling anyone. It was too dangerous.

'Did you see that?' she yelled above the drumming of the rain on the utility roof.

'It's a headlight,' shouted Angel. 'Someone's coming the other way.'

'Oh, God,' she sobbed. 'That's Claire. It means

she hasn't found her.'

'No. Wait. It isn't moving. Look, the interior light's on. Claire must have found something.'

Leanne put her foot hard down on the accelerator and the utility skidded in the mud, tilted and swayed alarmingly before it righted itself and shot forward. She was aware of Angel yelling at her to slow down. Aware she was driving recklessly. But she had to see what was up ahead. The utility came to a grinding halt as she slammed on the brake and tore out into the rain.

Claire was illuminated by the headlights. She was coatless and hatless and kneeling next to something on the ground. Something that was very still.

Leanne waded through the mud and stumbled over the shale. 'Mum? Mum?' She fell to her knees, mindless of the sharp stones, heedless of the drenching rain.

Ellie lay huddled beneath Claire's coat. She was very pale, and when Leanne touched her, she felt icy.

'She's banged her head and is unconscious,' shouted Claire above the drum of rain. 'I need help to get her into the ute. One of you get on the two-way and call the doctor. Tell him to meet us back at Jarrah.'

Leanne was roughly pushed aside as Angel took charge. 'We have to be careful,' he shouted into her furious face. 'She could have broken her neck, or her back. We must make sure she's stable before we lift her.'

'You're a bloody vet, not a doctor,' she yelled at him.

'I've had five years' medical tuition and five years of practice. What have you had?' he shouted back. 'Go and get the blankets and find me something to put around her neck.'

Leanne moved away as Claire and Angel worked on her mother. Cookie had taken the tarpaulin off the ute and he and three others held it over Ellie to protect her from the rain. Leanne grabbed the blankets and pillows from the truck and hurried back with them, then she stood aside feeling utterly helpless as her sister carefully wedged the pillow around her mother's neck and tied it there with a piece of string.

'Should be right to move her, but try not to jolt her at all,' said Claire as she finally stood up.

The men came with the stretcher and with much yelling from Angel and Claire, Ellie was lifted off the ground. Bundling her with blankets and shielding her from the rain with the tarpaulin they staggered through the mud and laid her gently in the back of one of the Land Rovers. Leanne and Claire climbed in next to her and the convoy set off for Jarrah.

'She looks so pale,' said Leanne through chattering teeth. 'Will she be right? Why won't she wake up?'

Claire shivered as she smeared back her sodden hair and checked Ellie's vital signs. 'Strong pulse, but slow. She's knocked herself out, but the cold and the wet couldn't have helped much. We have to keep her warm, Lee. Stop her temperature from falling any further.'

Leanne eyed her filthy, bedraggled coat – it was no use to her mother and she had nothing else.

'There's no more blankets,' she shivered. The shock had taken over and apart from being frozen to the bone, she was tearful – something she had never been before. But she was damned if she was going to let Claire see how scared she was.

'It's all right, Lee,' comforted Claire. 'Lie next to her, but try not to move her. We'll keep her warm with our own body heat.'

'What heat?' Leanne curled around her mother's still form. She was so cold she couldn't stop shivering and Claire's calm attitude to all this was making her angry. It was as if she didn't care.

'Anything's better than nothing,' said Claire.

The Landrover ploughed through the mud as the rain lashed the windows and the wind tried to tear open the rear tarpaulin flap. Ellie was still very pale, her skin like ice, her breathing erratic. Their father was over four days' drive away, and the flying doctor might not be able to land in such bad weather. They were in deep trouble.

Ellie was vaguely aware of voices, of being jolted and cold. There was a dull pain in her arm and another in her head, but she felt as if she was drifting. The darkness swirled around her and she floated there, contentedly. It was warm in the darkness. As warm as it had been all those years ago when she'd deliberately stayed away from the homestead and worked alongside Jacky Jack and the stock boys.

It had been the not knowing that tormented her and Aurelia. The lack of news from Broome and the army that had driven them into a desperate kind of silence. They had moved around one another as they completed their daily chores, barely able to meet one another's eye. Even Kelly had caught their mood and was unusually reticent.

But out here, in the warmth of the sun with the sound of the wind in the trees and the pipe of the bellbirds for company, she felt almost at peace. For she could hear his song, and knew Joe was with her.

The darkness faded and as the warmth disappeared, Ellie reluctantly accepted that her escape was over. She was being brought back from the past into the cold of the present, emerging into the darkness of a different kind – the darkness of half-told truths.

Yet, as she opened her eyes and stared around her she knew she was mistaken. For this was far worse. This was the place it had all begun. This was where the nightmare had started.

Chapter Twelve

The runway had been kept in good order for moments like these, and as the first grey streaks lightened the sky, the doctor's plane droned overhead and touched down. Claire was waiting in the ute. She'd changed into dry clothes once they'd made Ellie comfortable on the couch in the lounge, but her hair still clung damply to her neck making her shiver. The cold seemed to have got into her bones and no matter what she did she couldn't shake it off.

'Lucky I was out your way,' the doctor said cheerfully as he and the nurse climbed in. 'I was delivering a baby in the Isa when your call came through.' He smiled as Claire swiftly did a U-turn and headed at speed back to the homestead. 'You drive like all the women from Warratah, so I reckon you must be Leanne's sister,' he said. 'Phil Kominsky's the name. This is my nurse, Sandra. Pleased to meet you.'

'Claire. Glad you could come so quickly.' She glanced across at him. He was middle-aged and of sturdy build – a comforting presence at this troubled time. 'Mum's got a fever,' she said as she stamped on the brake and cut the engine. 'And I think she's broken her arm. But she took a nasty bang on her head and that's what's really worrying us. She doesn't want to wake up.'

They climbed out of the ute and ran up the

steps into the bluestone homestead. The lounge was warm and cosy, the fire roaring up the chimney. Ellie was lying on the couch, her neck still braced by the pillow, her face pale and sickly above the blankets.

'Perhaps someone could make a cuppa?' Phil said as he put down his medical bag and eyed the assembly. 'I'd like to examine Ellie in private.'

Claire followed the others reluctantly out of the room and shut the door. She was still shivering despite the warmth in the house. 'A hot drink seems like a good idea,' she said. 'Let's go in the kitchen.'

They huddled around the range, the mugs of tea cupped in their hands. 'Don't you think someone should tell your father what is happening?' said Angel into the silence.

Claire looked at the handsome, dark haired vet and knew exactly why Leanne had fallen for him. He was gorgeous. 'No point in telling him anything until the doctor's seen to her,' she said calmly. 'We'll decide once we know what's wrong with her.'

'What the hell was she doing coming over anyway?' stormed Leanne as she dragged out a chair and sat down. 'She knows I'm perfectly capable of dealing with the bullock transport.' She glared at her sister. 'This is all your fault,' she snapped.

Claire was taken aback. 'How the hell do you work that one out?' she demanded.

'If you hadn't come home and upset everyone, Mum would have kept her mind on what she was doing.' Leanne's gaze was accusing. 'Why don't you go back to Sydney?'

'I came because this is my home and Aurelia wisely knew it was time to clear the air. If you don't like it, then I'm sorry. But I have as much right as you to be here. She is my mother too.'

Leanne's mouth was a thin line and there was a dark glint of something malicious in her eyes. Yet she remained silent and Claire wondered what she'd been about to say.

Angel's gaze flickered over Claire as he put his arm around Leanne's waist. 'It is not the time to fight,' he said quietly. 'Ellie is very crook.'

Claire blushed, ashamed she could be goaded so easily. 'You're right,' she murmured. Yet her sister's outburst troubled her. She hadn't realised the animosity was so great, or so venomous.

Her thoughts were interrupted by Phil coming into the kitchen. He put down his bag on the table and accepted a cup of tea from Leanne. 'Ellie's lucky she didn't kill herself,' he said as he sipped the steaming tea. 'She's broken her arm which I've plastered and that should mend in about six weeks. The bang on her head could have been far more serious. But she's come round and as there's no vomiting and she knew where she was, I've given her an injection so she'll sleep.'

'What about the fever?' Claire asked. 'She was mumbling all sorts of strange things when we drove her home.'

'Being out in the rain for so long has caused that. Keep her on the couch by the fire, but don't pile too many blankets on. Give her plenty of fluids and make sure she takes one of these every four hours. The fever should break by mid-morning.'

306

'And if it doesn't?' Claire asked.

'It will. Trust me.'

Claire raised an eyebrow. That was the one phrase certain to have the opposite effect. 'But if it doesn't?' She persisted.

He sighed and put his cup down next to his medical bag. 'Call me,' he said wearily. 'You know the number.'

Leanne offered to take them to the plane, and as she left the room, Claire noticed Angel. He was leaning nonchalantly against the dresser, his gaze drifting over her as if she was a prize breeder at a stock show. She glared back and he had the cheek to shrug and smile. 'I look, but never touch,' he murmured. 'It is a compliment only.'

He might be highly qualified with eyelashes any woman would die for, but as he was unworthy of even a mild insult, she left the room.

Ellie had returned to the welcome allure of the soft, floating darkness. She had escaped the other place and was back at the old homestead on Warratah. Had turned back the clock to a time when she'd still been young. Yet as she drifted between past and present she realised there had been no real escape, for she could still feel the chill – could still hear the rain. The shadows returned and they brought a visitor.

He arrived at Warratah towards the end of April 1942 in the middle of a downpour. The drought had broken the night before and the women were preparing for the long trek down to Jarrah's southernmost pastures. The cattle had been moved there because the land was low-lying and the water fairly plentiful despite the drought. Now there was the danger of flash floods and the river running a banker, and it had become necessary to bring the mob back to higher pastures.

Ellie was emerging through the screen door laden with saddle bags when she saw the battered utility draw up in the yard. She dropped them with a thud as she realised who it was. Frozen, she watched him gather up his soutane and splash his way through the mud.

'G' day,' he said mournfully. ''Tis surely the weather fit only for ducks?' He shook out the long black robe and straightened his dog collar.

Ellie was trembling, her legs almost failing her. The arrival of the priest was more than just a surprise – they weren't even catholic – but a portent of doom. For she'd heard of his visits to other families. Families that were now in mourning.

He stood there, his doleful brown eyes shadowed by the burden of office, the grey in his hair more marked than when they'd seen him a year ago at a cattleman's meeting, ageing him beyond his thirty-five years. 'As you must have guessed, I have news,' he said in his weary, Irish brogue. 'Some good – some not so good. Is there anyone else at home?'

Ellie grabbed the arm of the verandah chair and sank into the cushions, her gaze fixed on this harbinger of doom. 'Aunt Aurelia,' she called hoarsely. 'Aunt Aurelia come quick.'

'What's the matter?' Aurelia came crashing through the screen door closely followed by Alicia. They stopped abruptly when they saw the

308

priest. 'Who is it?' Aurelia demanded, her face bereft of colour.

'Mrs Bligh-Hamilton?' he stammered.

'Yes, yes. Get on with it man,' snapped Aurelia. 'Can't you see we're on tenterhooks?'

Ellie followed his every move as the priest pulled an envelope from his pocket. 'Jack Withers asked me to hand this to you personally,' he said with a soft smile.

Aurelia sat down with a thud, the envelope in trembling fingers, her eyes wide as she read and re-read the scrawled address.

The overwhelming relief was replaced by rising panic. The priest said there was bad news. He hadn't come all this way just to deliver a letter from Jack. Ellie closed her eyes and tried to remain calm, forcing back the dark thoughts, tempering her dread with the certainty that Jack was alive. Steeling herself for what would surely come next. Ellie squared her shoulders, took a deep breath and opened her eyes.

Aurelia was still turning the envelope over and over as if she couldn't believe what she was seeing. 'He's safe? He's alive?'

'He is indeed,' said the priest with a smile. 'He had engine trouble on his way back from Java, but he managed to bring his flying boat down and hide it behind one of the many volcanic islands so he could do repairs. It took him almost a month of island hopping to avoid enemy planes and get home. He had over thirty women and children on board and not one of them was injured. By all accounts he's up for a medal.'

Ellie didn't want to take the shine from

309

Aurelia's happiness, but she could no longer bear the agony of waiting. 'You said there was good and bad news,' she said hoarsely.

Aurelia's laughter came to an abrupt halt. Alicia put a comforting hand on Ellie's shoulder and the priest took a deep breath before he sat down.

Time stood still for Ellie and she became aware of the ticking clock in the hall and the drip of a tap in the kitchen. Sounds she wouldn't normally hear out on the verandah – yet were so clear in the brittle silence. The world was in sharp focus, cruel in the grey light of this gloomy morning, and as raindrops trembled from the wrought iron trellis on the verandah railings she thought she could see the tiny prisms of light that emanated from each one – beautiful, but cold – ice cold.

Her gaze followed the priest's hands as he took another brown envelope from his pocket. She heard his voice through the roaring in her head, his words coming to her as if from a vast distance, slow in cadence, muffled and bleak.

'I've had communication from the army.' He paused as if weighing up the consequences of what he had to tell her – choosing which words would help to ease the anguish. 'Snowy is a prisoner of war in Burma,' he said finally.

Ellie found she'd been holding her breath, and it hissed in a long sigh of relief and sadness. 'Prisoner of war?' she repeated as her mind went blank and her thoughts froze.

The priest nodded. 'His name was on the list the Japanese released two weeks ago, but as yet we have no idea where the POW camp is, or what state of health he's in.' He leaned forward, his hand hovering above her tightly clasped fingers. 'He's alive – that's all I know, and I hope you can take heart at that.'

Ellie stared at him, seeing the false, bright hope he was offering and realised he was trying his best to soften the blow, yet what words could he say that would make his news easier to bear? Poor Snowy, she thought distractedly. Poor, funny, kind, sweet Snowy. She closed her eyes, her emotions in turmoil. She was overwhelmed with relief it wasn't Joe, but the thought of easy-going Snowy in the hands of the Japs was almost too awful to contemplate. For Snowy was a man born to freedom. An aboriginal who needed to go walkabout to refresh his links with his ancestors and pay homage to the land that was his mother and father. He would die behind the barbed wire. His spirit would be crushed.

The electric silence finally pervaded her inner turmoil. Her eyes snapped open. There was a third brown envelope. 'No,' she said through chattering teeth. 'No,' she repeated as she backed away and knocked the chair across the verandah. 'No,' she whispered as she warded off her mother and aunt and stood in trembling terror.

The priest looked at each woman in turn, but none of them were capable of helping him. He gave a sigh. 'There is no easy way for me to be tellin' you this, so I'll not beat about the bush,' he said quickly. 'Joe is listed as missing in action. He disappeared during the battle for Singapore.'

'Missing?' hissed Ellie as she gripped the veran-dah railings. 'What do you mean?' She watched as the priest brushed lint from his soutane. If

311

she'd been asked at that moment how she felt, she couldn't have described it. Her emotions were running helter-skelter at such a rate she was barely able to take it all in. She looked first at Aurelia and then at her mother, despair and hope ebbing and rising, making it impossible to contain coherent thought. Yet she noticed the priest's eyes were troubled, his gaze drifting as they waited for his reply.

'It means he's presumed dead,' he said quietly. 'The army have no record of him being killed, but he's not been seen or heard of for weeks.' He attempted a smile of encouragement and failed miserably. 'There's the remote possibility he's managed to hide amongst the natives. But it's unlikely. The army are rarely wrong in these matters.'

Ellie felt Aurelia's arms around her. Was aware of her mother clutching her hands. Yet all she could see was Joe riding the plains. Joe laughing with her at some joke they'd shared. Joe kissing her goodbye. He'd promised he'd come back for her. How could he be dead? Not her Joe. She could still hear the wind in the trees and the song of the bellbird.

She pulled away from them, certain there had been a mistake, intent upon the word 'presumed'. 'He might be missing, but he's not dead,' she said firmly. 'The army admitted it was only presumed, and...'

'Ellie,' interrupted Aurelia with a sharpness that made her wince. 'Ellie, you mustn't do this. False hope will only make it worse. You must accept the truth – then you can begin to mourn.'

312

Ellie knew that if she was to get through the next few hours she had to cling to the fragile hope this was just a terrible misunderstanding. For his spirit was with her, living and breathing in every corner of Warratah. She could feel it each time she rode the plains. Could sense his presence beside her throughout the long nights and endless days. Could hear their song in the sigh of the wind and the call of the bellbird. 'He's hiding somewhere, waiting for the allies to free Singapore,' she said stubbornly. 'I refuse to believe he's dead.'

'You must,' said her mother. 'The Japanese would have informed us if he was a prisoner of war – like they did about Snowy.'

'Not necessarily,' Ellie argued. 'There are thousands of prisoners in the camps, records must be in a mess.' She pulled away from her aunt and leaned against the verandah railings. Staring out over Warratah's home pastures, she tried to come to terms with yet another unknown as she clung to the belief he'd return. For it was all she had to keep her going.

The outback blossomed as the rains continued to refresh the parched earth. Wild flowers appeared in a blanket of riotous colour across the plains, grass waved in ripples and rivers and billabongs were invaded by duck and bush turkeys. The cattle grew sleek and fat and the number of calves born in the following years meant the account books for Warratah and Jarrah were in the black for the first time since the depression.

The Japanese aggression in the Pacific gradually waned in the face of Allied resistance, but in the western desert the position remained critical. Tobruk fell and the Australian Ninth was moved from Syria to reinforce the Allies. In October 1942 they played a vital part in General Montgomery's decisive breakthrough at El Alamein. The surrender of all Axis troops in North Africa came in May 1943.

Ellie put her energy into the daily round of work and gave herself little time to think – for it lowered her spirits – and as month followed month and a year passed since the priest's visit, she became ever more adept at keeping her darkest thoughts at bay. There had still been no news of Joe. Yet despite Aurelia's almost desperate attempts to make her see she was fooling herself, Ellie stubbornly remained hopeful.

Jack and Mickey wrote regularly, but there was no chance for visits home as they were fighting in the Malayan Peninsula. There were a few, scattered letters from Seamus and some from Charlie which Ellie included in the letters she still wrote to Joe. She had to believe he might get to read them for if she didn't, she would betray his memory – and deny the song she could still hear.

The news from England reassured them that the old people were alive and well and coming to terms with sharing their home with a hundred injured soldiers and airmen. Apart from the night bombing raids and the blackouts, it was rationing that was causing hardship for the elderly couple and the women of Warratah felt a pang of guilt. For it was easy to shoot duck and rabbit here.

Easy to fish for yellow bellies in the rivers or dig yabbies from the muddy creeks so they could be served up with Wang Lee's fresh vegetables.

The fences between Warratah and Jarrah had been taken down shortly after Mickey left and the grasslands became a sea of green that stretched beyond the horizon. Mickey's bulls strengthened Warratah's blood-stock and their yearly drove to the beef market at Longreach had netted handsome profits which Aurelia invested in new machinery and repairs to both homesteads.

Ellie learned how to keep the account books and found she had a natural flair for figures – perhaps something she'd inherited from her father – but she also had a keen eye for a good investment. Under Aurelia's guidance she had soon put together an impressive portfolio which encompassed holdings in the flourishing steel works, sugar refineries, mines and construction companies that had sprung up during the war years. 'We won't always have the rain,' she said to Aurelia that August morning of 1944. 'And I never want you to come so close to losing everything again. These investments should see us through and when the war's over we'll rearrange the portfolio to take advantage of the postwar boom that's bound to come.'

Ellie smiled brightly. It had become a habit lately, and where it had once been forced, it now seemed quite natural. 'The tide's turning,' she said as she closed the portfolio. 'Japanese resistance has collapsed in New Guinea and Mac-Arthur's moving his headquarters there. All they've got to do is flush the Japs out of the islands and the boys can come home.'

Aurelia remained silent as she stacked the account books and put them beside the pile of letters waiting for Wilf and his mail plane.

Ellie sighed as she stared out of the window. Aunt Aurelia had stopped voicing her opinions on the war and Joe's disappearance long ago and somehow her silence only served to enforce the truth. Joe had now been missing for two years and hope for his return had finally died. She no longer waited tensely for the mail plane – no longer believed in miracles.

Aurelia had remained awake through the night. Now, as she disconnected the two-way radio she began to pace. The doctor's visit, coupled with Leanne's assurance they could cope should have reassured her, but she was frustrated not to be there when she was needed. She had two choices. She could take her ute and drive over to Jarrah – or stay here and worry herself to death. Ramming her hands into her pockets she glared out at the rain. Dawn was struggling to surface on the far horizon and the day promised more bad weather.

The blasted weather was against her as well as her age, she thought crossly. There had been a time when she wouldn't have thought twice about driving in heavy rain. A time when she'd spent the night out in all weathers. Yet she knew that to rush across two hundred miles of dirt track at her age was stupid. She'd lived long enough to know she could break down, get caught in a flash-flood or overturn the ute – then what kind of help would she be? The last thing the girls needed was an old fool making a nuisance of herself.

She turned from the window and walked across the hall into the lounge. The fire was still burning brightly, but the heat didn't seem to touch her. The chill of winter was in her bones – the chill of acceptance that she was no longer the same woman. Age was cruel, she thought as she rested a gnarled hand on the mantelpiece and glared into the flames. What was the use of it? It made you weak and incapable of the things you'd once done without thinking – made you a burden. Perhaps humans should be put down like an old horse when it got too long in the tooth to work?

'Now you're just getting maudlin,' she snapped. She reached for her pipe, realised she was out of tobacco and swore. Kelly had taught her well, and when she'd vented her spleen she blushed and even looked furtively over her shoulder. 'Good grief,' she muttered. 'I hadn't realised I knew so many awful words.'

She stomped out of the room, crossed the hall and went into her bedroom. Rifling around in one of the drawers she found another pouch of tobacco and filled her pipe. Once a pleasant fug filled the room, she sat on the bed and was soon lost in thought. Here she was, bemoaning her inability to do anything but sit at home and wait by the telephone, while poor Ellie was fighting delirium on Jarrah and the girls were fretting. 'Selfish old bat,' she muttered around the pipe stem.

She looked around the room that was so different to the one at the old homestead. The paintwork was clean and fresh, the curtains crisp. Soft watercolours were hung on the pale green walls and the bed was covered with a cream satin spread. It was peaceful and welcoming, the furniture painted white and uncluttered by anything more than a vase of flowers or a piece of porcelain, the polished floor enhanced by the three apricot-coloured rugs. Ellie was a superb home-maker and so tidy.

Aurelia struggled off the bed and pulled the cover straight. She'd never really found housework appealing and had avoided it for most of her life – what was the point of it when it had to be done all over again the next day? She was turning towards the door when she caught sight of her reflection in the dressing-table mirror. Her mother stared back at her, grim-faced, white haired and sturdy.

Aurelia grunted and hurried out of the room. The night seemed full of ghosts, and like Scrooge she could see the past, the present and the future – and she didn't like it one bit. And yet, she thought as she returned to the fireside chair in the lounge, what was the alternative? There is a time to live and a time to die and I've had a good innings. Not like some.

As the rain thundered on the iron roof and rattled against the windows, Aurelia sank back into the chair and stared up at the ceiling. There would be no sleep for what was left of the night. The memories were coming back to haunt her. Memories of the long dead – memories of those who'd never had the chance to live a full life's span.

The homestead at Jarrah was a mellow bluestone building that sprawled beneath the shelter of wattle trees and blue gums. The outbuildings and the yard were silent in the sweltering heat as Alicia sat on the verandah in the shade. Mickey's last letter was on the table beside her. It had been read so many times the paper was frayed, the creases almost torn through.

With a sigh she tapped a cigarette on the table and lit it. His letters had been almost impersonal to begin with, and as the years passed it was as if he found it easier to discuss their common interests rather than touch on his deepest thoughts and hopes for the future – it was as if he was afraid to commit them to paper – and for that she had been relieved. Alicia had kept him up with news of the stations, the cattle, Aurelia and Ellie, and he in turn had tried to convey the excitement and fear that kept the adrenaline flowing each time his squadron went out on a raid.

It was an odd relationship, she thought as she sat there staring off into the distance where Aurelia and Ellie were waiting with the horse and cart. A relationship that blossomed despite their differences but one which could never have been more than friendship. For Mickey longed for the war to end so he could pick up the threads of his life again and Alicia knew she could never be a part of that life. Her threads were of a different hue and calibre, waiting for her back in England.

She brought her thoughts to order and eyed her

nails ruefully, remembering how they'd once been long and polished. Yet it no longer seemed to matter. The things she'd regarded as important before the war seemed so silly now, and she'd surprised herself as well as the others by the way she'd fallen so easily into the order of things on Warratah and Jarrah.

Ellie had shown her the way, of course, she admitted silently. That tough little girl who worked from dawn to dusk. The child who'd grown into a woman; a capable, intelligent woman who had learned so much more from Aurelia than she ever would have done from her.

She smoked her cigarette, deep in thought. She would be returning to England alone, she realised. For Ellie would never be happy away from this land she loved with such a passion. Would never leave the one place where she still felt the spirit of her Joe so keenly. If only I could have found a love like that, she thought sadly. An all-consuming love that never faded despite the time and distance that had been put between them. Ellie's first love was always with her and, although Joe was dead, their love would remain alive and real.

Yet the sadness of her daughter's situation hadn't escaped her. Alicia realised Ellie would never find another man to take Joe's place. Her daughter would remain barren on this great sprawl of land in the middle of nowhere. She would dry up and grow old like Aurelia and that wasn't the future she would have liked for Ellie. Perhaps such a deep, all invasive love should be avoided? The fleeting attraction more appealing than something that would overshadow one's life?

Alicia thought about the men she'd met and the lovers she'd discarded. Her life might have been. fractured and unfulfilling, but surely anything was better than the pain Ellie was going through? Her gaze drifted across to Ellie who sat so calmly at the reins of the big horse. The bridges had been built between them, and although Alicia realised she could never be the mother Ellie wanted or needed, they had become friends. Their friendship one that only women could understand. Women thrown together in adversity, the ties that bound them tighter and longer-lasting than any other.

She stretched, easing her back and shoulders. They'd all had little sleep since the telegram arrived a week before and she was tense as she waited for the sound of the plane's approach to Jarrah. For today would bring a different cargo in the mail, and once again the war raging in the outside world would make its mark on the people of the outback.

Ellie was sitting on the buckboard as she watched the skies. The rain had brought a freshness to the earth and the blue heavens looked cleanly washed with their fluffy white clouds. She could hear the cackle of a kookaburra in the distance and see a mob of roos foraging in the long grass beneath the stand of gidgee. This was all she needed now, she realised. With Joe gone, her life's path was set and she would never leave this wonderful place that echoed of the man she still loved. For it was home.

With a heavy heart she heard the drone of the plane and stilled the horse as it began to dance between the traces. The beauty of the day was marred by this home-coming, the darker clouds of war brought nearer as the plane hovered over the runway and finally touched down. The three women rode out to meet the plane. They remained silent, each with their own thoughts as the gentle plod of the horses and the creak of the wagon enhanced the sadness of this short journey.

Wilf climbed down, his expression solemn as he helped the priest alight. The women stood and waited. They could all see the coffin in the dimness of the cabin, the bright stars of the Southern Cross on the Australian flag gleaming dully in the half-light.

Then a figure emerged from the gloom into the doorway. A figure dressed in the khaki uniform of the Australian Army with the glint of medals on his breast. A man whose face was in shadow as he bent to pass through the low opening and missed his footing.

Wilf and the priest reached quickly to break his fall.

Ellie's heart drummed, her breath caught in her throat. Ignoring the murmurs of concern she tried to believe what she was seeing. 'Joe!' It was a shriek of pure joy, an outpouring of all the heartache and desperate hope she'd been storing away over the years. She dropped from the wagon. Pulled away from Aurelia's cautioning hand. Rushed towards him, pushing the priest aside in her desperation to hold him again.

He took off his hat. 'Sorry, Ellie,' he said quietly.

The disappointment was a dagger thrust. It took her breath. Brought her to a juddering halt. Froze all coherent thought. Then the truth washed over her. Miracles didn't happen. Not now. Not ever. 'Charlie?' she gasped. 'What are you doing here?'

He shouldered off the priest's hand and leaned against the side of the plane, his legs trembling, the breath coming in shallow gasps as sweat glistened on his ashen face. 'Caught a bit of trouble in North Africa,' he said through gritted teeth. 'Army sent me home with me mate here.'

Ellie tried to pull her emotions into some kind of order. She burned with shame as she looked from Charlie to the coffin. Trembled from the rush of joy that had so swiftly been dowsed by the cold reality that it wasn't Joe who had come home. 'I'm sorry, Charlie,' she began. 'I thought...'

He shook his head. 'No worries. I shouldn't have bothered you.' He winced as he struggled to remain standing. 'Wilf will take me back after the funeral,' he rasped.

Ellie's steely resolve took over. 'No he won't,' she said. 'Come on, Charlie. Let's get you in the wagon before you pass out on us.' The women took charge and as Ellie held his arm, she felt the tremor that ran through him and noticed the ghastly pallor of his face where the sweat rolled and splashed on his collar. His jacket was un-done, showing a glimmer of heavy strapping

323

around his midriff, and his left arm was in a sling. The war was over for Charlie, she realised, just as it was for the poor boy in the coffin – but what a terrible price they'd both had to pay.

'We have to get him up to the house,' she muttered as she helped lift him into the back of the wagon. 'The funeral can wait for a while.'

Charlie opened his eyes, his pallor ghastly. 'No,' he said forcefully. 'Got to see to me mate first. Me and Seamus have been together right from the start,' he muttered. 'Bought it in the same barrage. I promised I'd bring him home – see him right.' He leaned back and closed his eyes as if those few words had bankrupted him of strength. 'He's been waiting long enough.'

Ellie dragged a horse blanket from under the wagon seat and made it into a pillow, her anxious gaze trawling over his battered, wasted body. The emotional turmoil was churning again. Relief it wasn't Joe in such a pitiful state. Sharp grief that she would never have the chance to tend Joe's wounds – help to heal him, or take care of him.

Charlie slumped against the side of the wagon, eyes closed, breath ragged. His eyelids were pale and veined with blue, the fair lashes feathering his wan cheeks. She touched his face, shocked at how cold he was.

He caught her wrist and held it, his cheek nestled in the palm of her hand. 'You have no idea how good it is to feel a woman's touch again,' he whispered hoarsely. He opened his eyes and she found herself staring into dark blue depths of pain and bewilderment, but before she could speak he'd let her go, his eyes closing as if he was ashamed of what she'd see hidden there.

Tears were imminent as she turned to help load the coffin in beside Charlie. Her hands trembled as she rearranged the flag that was draped over the polished wooden box and carefully placed the hat with the jaunty cockade on top. This was all the hideous proof she needed of what was going on in the world outside Warratah and the grief for these two young men almost too much to bear. It suddenly became very important to keep Charlie alive.

Aurelia and her sister exchanged glances as they rode flank on either side of the wagon. They were still in shock from Charlie's unexpected appearance and Ellie's reaction. Yet Aurelia hoped the awful day would finally make her niece face reality. Hoped she could now begin to mourn and release the pain she'd so obviously been holding back. Yet darker possibilities had dawned as Ellie slapped the reins and they headed for the little cemetery at the back of Jarrah homestead. Charlie was Joe's twin – the other half of the man Ellie still loved with a passion – what effect would his home-coming have on her niece? What harm would it do?

Aurelia glanced across at the others. The priest sat alongside Ellie, his back straight, his head erect. Wilf slumped beside him, a shrivelled man who'd seen too much in his lifetime and must wonder at the justice of so many young ones dying while he still shambled into old age.

She turned her attention to the young man riding in the back of the wagon, trying to equate this haggard, war-weary veteran with the rather charming rogue she remembered. There was no cheeky grin or gleam of excitement in his eyes now despite the medals he'd earned, she realised sadly. War had taken the shine from him, killed the lust for life and adventure as surely as if it had killed the man himself. And as for Seamus... Aurelia looked sadly at the coffin. She'd had such plans for him and Ellie, and as they'd grown close she'd really thought it might have come to something. Yet her memories were of a boy, a young larrikin who rode his horses with skill and speed and who could round up a mob of clean-skins as well as any man twice his age. His blarney had charmed them and made them laugh, and she could still see the twinkle in his blue eyes as he laughed at one of his own jokes.

She sniffed back a tear. They would all remember him differently. Ellie would remember the boy she'd come to love as a brother. Charlie's memory of him would be of the man he fought beside. The man who'd joined up at the same time. The man who'd not been so lucky in that battle for El Alamein.

Charlie winced as the wagon shuddered over a stone and Aurelia watched as he put out a hand and rested it protectively on the coffin. Noticed how his fingers trembled over the flag, drifting across the cockade as his lips shaped words only he could hear. His fair hair was dark with sweat, his uniform stained by the patches that spread beneath his arms and down his chest, but he seemed oblivious. He was a pitiful sight and although she had strong misgivings about his return, her heart went out to him.

The cemetery was fenced off from the pastures by a white picket fence and hedged with fledgling shrubs and shady trees. Most of the headstones had been dulled by the elements, with lichen and moss obliterating the epitaphs of the older ones, the table stones coming adrift from their moorings. Willows drifted fronds, the grass rustled in the light breeze and the hum of insects made it seem a drowsy place – a peaceful place – a place where the weary soul could surely find eternal rest. Now you're getting maudlin as well as fanciful, she thought crossly as she hastily blew her nose. All this death and war was having a strange effect on her and she had realised quite early on that she was no longer the same woman she'd once been. Her bluff, hearty manner had been replaced by a calmer, less domineering way of doing things, and she no longer spoke before she thought, aware of what harm it could do in the tense atmosphere they all lived in. She was getting soft in her old age, she thought furiously. Lost her backbone.

She dismounted as they drew up at the cemetery gate. Wilf and the priest struggled to lift the coffin as Charlie dragged himself from the wagon. Aurelia stepped up to help, but as she reached for the coffin was gently pushed aside. 'I need to do this for him,' Charlie rasped as he took the weight on his frail shoulder. 'Can't leave Seamus to make this last journey on 'is own. Not after what we've been through.'

'So do I,' said Alicia, coming to stand beside him. 'I promised his father.'

The coffin was grasped in Alicia's strong hands, the corner placed on her narrow shoulder. Aurelia and Ellie followed them, the solemnity of the moment not quite disguising the fact that one upright priest, one shambling old man, a sick boy and a slender woman made an incongruous cortege.

Jacky Jack and the stock boys had dug the grave the night before, and they now stood, wide-eyed, hats in hand, watching the strange little procession approach. What on earth they made of all this, Aurelia didn't know. Their way was more simple. A last walkabout as the earth sang them to their final sleep. A return to the dust, out in the open where nature took its toll on the human shell – not buried in a wooden box, the spirit forever tied to darkness.

Aurelia thought fleetingly of Snowy and his imprisonment, then pulled her thoughts together and concentrated on the priest. It had been years since she'd been to church, and not having ever attended a catholic burial she was bemused by the stream of Latin and unable to follow the ceremony. Yet it was right Seamus hadn't been buried in a foreign field. This was a fitting place for Mickey's son. He'd come home to lie in the earth beside his mother and brother, at one with those who'd cleared this land and made it worth fighting for. Here, his spirit was free at last of war and the trials of life.

But what of Joe? She glanced across at Ellie. Was his spirit at peace? How could it be when he was so far from home? How could he be free when he was lying in some anonymous grave beneath an alien soil? Aurelia was dragged from her gloomy thoughts by the muttered 'amen', signalling the end of the service.

Charlie stood beside the grave, unsteady on his feet, the colour drained from his face as he saluted his dead friend. 'So long, mate,' he muttered. 'You can rest easy now.' He put his hat on and stepped back.

Aurelia grabbed him just before he fell. 'Better get him indoors,' she said gruffly. 'Otherwise this won't be the only funeral today.' She turned to the stock boys. 'One of you ride and get Wang Lee,' she ordered. 'And make it quick.'

They carried him up the steps and into the house, gently depositing him on the sagging couch in the lounge. Ellie stoked the fire to life whilst Aurelia began to ease off the jacket and sodden shirt. She turned to Ellie who was hovering. 'Make some tea, and bring me hot water and clean cloths. He's been bleeding.'

Aurelia clucked as she heard the soft moan come from the boy. 'It's all right, son,' she murmured. 'I just want to clean you up.' She gently removed the jacket, noticing the medals he'd won. Charlie had been a hero – but at what price, she thought sadly. She carefully unwound the bloody dressings and felt the onslaught of angry tears when she saw the terrible scar that started high under his arm and swept down over his ribs almost to his navel. He was just a boy, she thought furiously. Just a young man trying to do his bit for his country. God knows what he'd been through, or how permanent the damage would be – not only to his body, but to his mind.

She battled to keep her rage under control, and her hands steady. It would serve no earthly purpose to rant and rave, for who was there to blame? God? Hitler, Churchill, Stalin? As far as she could see one of them had given up on the human race, and the others were too busy warmongering to see the price being paid by ordinary country boys. 'Hurry up with that hot water,' she snapped. 'The boy's running a fever and I need to clean him up.'

It was dark by the time the blood was staunched and fresh bandages tightly bound the wound. Wilf had already taken the priest on to his next call and the silence of night had fallen over Jarrah as Aurelia checked Charlie's shattered arm. It was still heavily plastered, but hopefully it would mend. She took off his boots and trousers and cocooned him in blankets. He was terribly thin, she noticed, the ribs standing out, hip bones sharp beneath the army issue underwear. But the fire was roaring up the chimney now and there was a little more colour in his face as he opened his eyes and stared around him in bewilderment. 'Ellie?' he said weakly.

Aurelia moved away as her niece came to kneel by the couch. 'I'm here, Charlie,' she said softly. 'Don't talk. Get some rest.'

He shook his head, wincing as the pain shot through him. 'Where's Joe?' he mumbled. 'I gotta see Joe.'

Ellie bit her lip, glanced up at Aurelia then took his hand. 'He's in Singapore,' she said gruffly.

Charlie closed his eyes, he was obviously fretting. 'Did he get my letters?' he whispered.

Aurelia held her breath as Ellie hesitated. Perhaps this was the moment her niece would finally accept the truth.

'I don't know,' Ellie replied. 'I sent them with mine, but I've had no reply.'

Aurelia watched this little scene with growing unease. It was going to prove tough for Ellie now Joe's twin had turned up, perhaps it would be wiser to get the girl away for a while so she could let things take on a clearer perspective? 'I suggest Alicia stays here to look after Charlie, and you and I get back to Warratah for tomorrow's branding,' she said with authority. 'We'll be back in a couple of weeks and by then this young man should be up and about.'

Ellie shook her head. 'I'll stay with Charlie. It's what Joe would have wanted.' She looked up at her aunt, the agony clear in her brown eyes. 'It's as if part of Joe's come home – I can't leave him,' she said firmly. 'Not when he's just buried darling Seamus.'

Aurelia don't like what she heard. She could understand why Ellie should want to look after Joe's brother, but she didn't want the girl letting her emotions carry her off track and into something she might regret later on. 'I think it'd be better if Alicia looked after him, dear,' she said hastily. 'There will be things that need doing for him that aren't seemly for a young girl, and even Joe wouldn't expect that of you.'

Ellie looked down at the youth on the couch, her thoughts in obvious turmoil. Then, as if she'd come to a decision, she straightened and shook her head. 'It's better I stay,' she said firmly.

'Mum's useless around sickbeds and if I get into trouble there's always Wang Lee to help me.'

As if on cue the little Chinaman came into the room with a tray of bottles. 'Wang Lee make boy betta,' he said pompously. 'Women go look after cow.'

'I'm staying here,' repeated Ellie stubbornly.

Aurelia folded her arms as she glared down at her niece. 'You'll do as you're told,' she said sharply. 'Wang Lee can manage perfectly well on his own, and I need you to help with the branding.'

'You've got Jacky Jack and the stock boys,' she retorted. 'You don't need me at all.'

Aurelia looked at Alicia, who merely shrugged her shoulders and turned away. 'Leave her,' she said. 'Ellie's as stubborn as you when she puts her mind to it. Besides,' she added as she picked up the bags she'd packed the night before. 'All this argument is wasting time, and we need to get back to Warratah before the next lot of rain makes it impossible to finish the branding.'

Aurelia sighed. She knew Ellie well enough to realise she wouldn't budge her. Not with that expression on her face. 'Very well,' she said wearily. 'But you leave the more intimate side of the nursing to Wang Lee.' She was aware of Charlie watching her as she approached the girl and put her hand on her shoulder. 'And remember, Ellie,' she warned softly. 'This isn't Joe.'

Something sparked in Charlie's eyes, but it was fleeting and as the moment passed Aurelia wasn't even certain she'd seen it, yet the effect remained with her and she shivered. It was as if she'd had a glimpse of impending darkness – a darkness none of them would emerge from unscathed.

Ellie could still hear the rain. Could still feel the chill cast by those long shadows. She opened her eyes and saw only the flames leaping up the chimney. It had been the same that night, she remembered as she drifted once more into the welcoming darkness. The rain had hammered for a week on the roof in a never-ending torrent that rushed down the gutters and flooded the yard. She had been missing home despite her exhaustion, yet it was impossible to make the journey back to Warratah until Charlie was well enough to travel.

In the face of Wang Lee's objections she'd had Charlie transferred to the comfort of the biggest bed at Jarrah and set up a blanket roll and pillow on the floor so she could tend to him in the night. He was plagued by nightmares and often woke two or three times drenched in cold sweat, eyes staring with horror at things she could only imagine.

That was when she'd sit on the bed and hold him. Rocking him like a baby she tried to comfort him, to still his fears and calm him before Wang Lee's sleeping potion took effect. Once it had, she lay sleepless in her bedroll as the images of war thundered through her mind and tears for Joe soaked her pillow.

The restless nights were over too soon and she rose early each day to check on the few animals still left on Jarrah before she set about digging up the remains of Mickey's vegetable garden. The potatoes were rotting, the carrots mildewed, but some of it was still edible and with rationing in full force this was no time to get fussy. The rain flooded the yard and the water rose to meet the verandah steps. Day followed weary day, interspersed with sleepless nights. Yet despite her depleted energy she was aware of a strange feeling of elation. She might not have Joe, but Charlie was the nearest thing, and in a way it was as if Joe *had* come home – if not in body, then in spirit. And as he began to get stronger they got to know one another again and she found comfort in hearing stories about the two boys growing up together. Of their home back in the little town in the south, and of their struggle to make ends meet that had set them on the tramp.

Joe had told her some of it, but it was interesting to hear Charlie's side of things, and as she listened to him she found she could forgive this raw-boned young man for what he'd done to Joe. For as he talked she began to understand that Charlie mistakenly saw himself as inferior to his twin. He suspected Joe's quiet ways hid a deeper intelligence that would take him far. Charlie's own lust for adventure had been his way of counteracting that stillness in his twin, but it had left him searching for something that was as ethereal as smoke – left him empty and unfulfilled. The jealousy had begun long ago, and with it had come the need to prove himself better than his twin, now the guilt over what he'd done was eating away at him.

Ellie was in a quandary. She knew Charlie had to be told of Joe's disappearance. Yet the belief he would see his twin again was keeping him going. It would be cruel to tell him the truth, cruel to have to voice her own deepest fears. Yet how much more cruel would it be to keep lying to him and to herself? The days drifted on and the right opportunity never seemed to arise. Ellie knew her courage had failed her. She just couldn't do it. Just couldn't acknowledge Joe was never coming home.

It was night almost two weeks after the funeral. The rain was still falling, but lighter now. The fire roared in the hearth and Charlie was propped against pillows on the couch, a blanket around his shoulders. He stared into the flames, the dark shadows around his eyes proof of sleepless nights and continuing pain, yet there was more flesh on the bones and his colour was better. 'You were just a skinny kid the last time I saw you,' he murmured. 'It feels as if it was a lifetime ago,' he sighed.

Ellie was knitting socks, but she was so tired she kept dropping stitches. 'It was,' she said with a yawn. 'We were kids then, but we've had to grow up fast.' She gave up on the knitting and stuffed the needles into the ball of wool. 'I'm for bed. It's another long day tomorrow and Mum and Aurelia will be here by lunch-time.'

He turned to her then, his blue eyes gleaming in the firelight, the fair hair flopping over his brow just the way Joe's did. 'Stay and talk to me, Ellie,' he begged.

Ellie gently brushed the straying lock of hair back into place, the lurch of longing for Joe almost a physical pain. How alike the two men

335

were and yet how different. One dark, one fair. One calm and gentle, the other battling an inner turmoil that might one day break him.

Charlie caught her hand, trapping it against his cheek as he'd done the first day. 'Hold me, Ellie,' he said softly. 'Just for a moment. It's been so long since anyone cared.'

His actions mirrored Joe's on their last day together. The words making her tremble with pity. Yet she curbed her natural instinct to comfort him. For she was unsure of what he really wanted from her. Reluctant to make any move that could be misconstrued. For this was not Joe, however much she wished it.

She looked deep into his eyes and saw the loneliness there, and the dread of the dreams that would come in the night to haunt him. This damaged man was all she had of Joe, she realised; he'd been sent to her so he could be healed both in body and in spirit, how could she refuse him? The fire crackled and a log shifted as she put her arms around him. The awkwardness left her as they sat there in the flickering firelight, for it was as if Joe had returned. She could smell the manliness of him, feel the rasp of his chin against her cheek and the strong hand at her waist. Burying her face in the crook of his neck she closed her eyes and let the fantasy take over. Sleep soon began to claim her and as she drifted thankfully toward it, she thought she felt the butterfly touch of Joe's kiss on her mouth.

Chapter Thirteen

Matt Derwent had been up since dawn. The rain had stopped and the sun was struggling to climb above the horizon as magpies warbled and gallahs and parakeets squabbled in the trees. With growing anticipation for the day ahead, he hurried to the stables with the dogs in full flight around him, and let the horses into the paddocks. Returning to the homestead he slammed through the screen door and brewed some strong coffee. It was too early to begin his journey to Warratah, but he wanted to be sure everything was right before he set out.

He padded barefoot into his bedroom and eyed the usual chaos. Clothes were strewn over the bed and chair, drawers were leaking sweaters and socks and his shoes lay where he'd left them. His gaze drifted to the neatly folded moleskins and shirt and the clean underwear he'd laid out the night before. His boots had been polished to a gleam, the dangling button fixed more securely on his jacket. With a rueful grin he remembered how he'd stabbed himself with the needle. Fine vet he was, when he couldn't sew a button on without harming himself. Yet he knew the ham-fisted attempt was more to do with his excitement over the coming day, than his lack of prowess with a needle. 'I hope she thinks it was worth it,' he muttered as he finished his coffee.

He caught sight of his reflection in the mirror above the dresser and pulled a face. 'Matt Derwent, you're a fool.'

He walked out of his bedroom and into the tiny office he'd built on at the side of the house. The familiar clutter had given way to order, with files and records neatly lined on shelves and in cabinets, the medicines and tools of his trade carefully locked away. He pulled out the chair and sat down. There were bills to be made out and today's list of visits to be sorted. He had plenty of time. He wasn't expected at Warratah until eleven.

Some time later he looked at the moon-faced clock on the wall. Time moved so slowly when you least wanted it to, he realised. He pushed the chair away from the desk, his elation pricked by doubt. Was he about to make a complete bloody fool of himself? She hadn't replied to his call, and he had only Aurelia's word that he was welcome. Perhaps he should ring again and check?

Matt eyed the telephone, his hand already on the receiver when he changed his mind. If he arrived at Warratah Claire couldn't back out. He could take her with him on his rounds and they could get to know one another. But softly, softly, he told himself. Claire was young and beautiful with a fine career ahead of her. She might not want a grizzled widower for more than just friendship, and he didn't know if he could take a rejection.

Ellie opened her eyes, his name on her lips escaping before she realised it. She pushed back the blankets and lay there for a moment. Claire and Leanne were asleep in the chairs beside the cold ashes in the hearth, and thankfully hadn't heard her cry out. Light was streaming through the windows, making dust motes dance across the floor, and in the distance she could hear the bustle and clang of the men in the yard preparing to leave for the day. Yet, despite the hum of life and the sight of her daughters, the memories were still dark within her. As she tried to banish them, she lifted her hand to tuck her hair behind her ears and realised her arm was in plaster. She frowned, wondering how it could have got there. And why was she at Jarrah? She tried to sit up and gasped as a bolt of pain shot through her.

'Mum?' said the girls in unison as they snapped awake. 'Are you okay?'

She lay back into the pillows and smiled wanly. 'I don't know,' she muttered. 'What the hell happened?'

Claire and Leanne knelt by the couch, but it was Leanne who spoke. 'You had a fall, Mum. What on earth were you doing climbing Yorky's Pinnacle?'

Ellie closed her eyes. Now she remembered. It had been the ghosts of the past that had driven her up there, her own stupidity that had brought her back down with a thud. She had no idea of how long she'd lain there, but she could remember how cold it was – how wet – and the pain in her head where it had banged against a rock. And, although it had happened only a few hours ago, the dreams and memories had made it seem like years. She dredged up some energy to make light of it. 'Reckon I though I could still climb it,' she said with a touch of humour. 'I hadn't banked on the rain.'

'You've got to promise you'll never do such a daft thing again,' demanded Claire as she scraped back her tousled hair and caught it in an elastic band. 'You could have died out there if we hadn't found you.'

Ellie had a terrible thought. 'You haven't told your father, have you?'

Leanne shook her head. 'We wanted to wait to see how you were this morning. Phil said you'd be right so there was no point in worrying Dad.'

'Thank goodness,' Ellie sighed. 'He'd kill me if he thought I was dying.' She realised what she'd said and laughed along with the girls. 'Get me an aspirin,' she gasped as the headache returned. 'And a cuppa. My mouth's foul and my brain's turned to mush.' She frowned as the girls left the room. There was tension between them just like the old days. And she hoped it had nothing to do with Claire's home-coming.

The telephone rang and was swiftly answered. Then Claire came back with the tea and aspirins. 'That was Aurelia,' she explained. 'I told her you were on the mend and not to worry.' She sat down and grinned. 'I also told her that on no account was she to drive over here. She was all set to race over, but with her driving anything could happen.'

'Good on you.' Ellie sipped her tea and swallowed the aspirins. She was feeling foolish. 'I'm sorry I caused such a fuss,' she muttered. 'I just forgot the time.'

Claire bit her lip. There was obviously something on her mind. 'At least you're okay,' she said. 'I was dreading telling Dad.'

Ellie eyed her closely. Whatever it was, Claire had decided to keep it to herself. 'Where's Leanne?'

'She's organising the men for the day's work. Smoky will take on the overseeing in her place and Angel's already out there.' Claire smiled. 'And you were right about his roving eye.'

'He's Argentinian. He can't help it.' Ellie realised her daughters were quite capable of getting on with things without her help, and in a way it saddened her. They were grown-up, no longer little girls she could protect from the harsher side of life. 'What about Matt Derwent?' she asked. 'Weren't you supposed to be going out with him today?'

Claire finished her tea and lit a cigarette. 'I told Aurelia to put him off. I'd rather spend the day with you.'

Ellie heard the words, but could see a different message in her daughter's eyes. 'That's very flattering, darling,' she said as she purposefully tugged away the blankets. 'But I'm fine. Ring and tell her to send him over.'

Claire gaze shifted. 'Fair go, Mum. He's a busy man, and probably doesn't really want me hanging around. Besides,' she added. 'It's too late, he'll have been there by now.'

Ellie dipped her chin and hid her smile in the sweep of her hair. Claire might protest – but perhaps a little too much.

Matt came in low over Warratah. It was a beautiful place, especially after the rain. Everything looked newly laundered, the white blossom of the jarrah trees pristine against the rusting red of the corrugated roof, the green of the pepper trees and the citrus of the wattles almost startling against the cinnamon earth and verdant grass. His pulse began to race as he taxied to the end of the runway. The stockyards were empty, there was no sign of anyone in home yard or around the outbuildings. Warratah looked deserted.

He attempted to smooth back his springy hair, realised it was a waste of time, and climbed down from the plane. The scent of flowers drifted on the warm air and the silence was profound. With a sense of foreboding, he began to walk towards the homestead.

The screen door slammed back with such a crash it made him jump. 'There you are,' boomed Aurelia. 'You're late.'

Matt felt like a naughty schoolboy who'd been caught in the bike shed having a smoke. 'I got called to a difficult calving,' he said as he approached the sagging steps. He tried to pierce the darkness beyond the door way. 'Is Claire ready?' he asked hopefully.

'She's not here,' said Aurelia.

Matt swallowed. The disappointment was overwhelming and the sun seemed to have disappeared behind a black cloud. 'Oh,' was all he could say.

Aurelia gave a bark of laughter. 'No need to look so down in the mouth,' she said in her rich contralto. 'She's had to go to Jarrah. You're expected there.'

His spirits rose and he could have kissed her. But the stern old lady was glaring at him through her monocle and he wouldn't have dared. 'Thanks,' he stuttered.

'Off you go then,' she boomed. 'Time's wasting.' She yanked the screen door open and disappeared back into the homestead.

Matt had a spring in his step as he hurried to the plane. Things were looking up. It *was* going to be a lovely day after all.

Ellie had tied a plastic sack over the plaster on her arm and although she'd had some trouble shampooing her hair, had enjoyed the shower and felt much better. She was pottering about with a towel wrapped around her when she heard the approach of a small plane. Hurrying into the kitchen, she found Claire washing up the dishes. 'Leave that. You've got a visitor.'

Claire eyed her suspiciously. 'What have you and Aurelia cooked up?'

Ellie smiled. 'You didn't really expect your aunt to tell Matt to be on his way, did you? It's not her style.'

Claire dumped the dishcloth in the sink and turned her back on the plates. 'I look a mess,' she groaned. 'I've slept in my clothes and my hair's a bird's nest.'

'So go and do something about it while I get dressed. I'll keep him entertained until you're ready.' She smiled as Claire hurried from the room. 'So much for wanting to spend the day with me,' she muttered with delight.

343

The plane came to a halt as she hurried into the bedroom. Pulling on strides and shirt, she shivered. This was the room Charlie had slept in. The room where his nightmares had kept them awake. How distant those times were, yet how sharply etched in memory. With a sob of breath she left the room. The ghosts were closing in again.

Once the house was silent again she went out to the verandah. She leaned against the post and smiled. Such comings and goings, she thought. Who'd have thought that level-headed Leanne would suddenly marry a dashing, sexy Argentine she'd known for only two months? And Claire, so chirpy when Matt arrived that she almost danced out the door. She gave a soft laugh. She'd known Aurelia would send him over, nothing much missed the old girl despite her age.

Ellie hitched the sling more comfortably around her neck and stared out to the horizon. It was lovely to have both girls around again – she'd missed them terribly even though they fought like cats. Yet she knew this was merely a respite, for they were already immersed in their own lives and she would have to learn to take a back seat. The empty nest syndrome, she thought sadly as she stepped down into the yard. But at least I usually have plenty to occupy me.

Bored, she decided to reacquaint herself with Jarrah and wandered through the stables, breathing in the smell of fresh hay and watered cobbles. The tack room was redolent of leather and harness and expensive saddles. The bunk-house was freshly scrubbed with clean sheets and pillowcases on the iron bedsteads, but the ripe odour of feet and men meant she didn't linger.

Crossing the yard she entered the cookhouse. She stood in the centre of this vast room with the high, cathedral arched roof and realised its air was reminiscent of the thousands of meals that had been eaten here. Sunlight came through the windows, dust motes danced above the spotless stainless steel units and polished pots. It was all so different to the kitchen in her day, where the cook worked on a four ring butane stove, or, worse, a recalcitrant range with smoke and condensation all mixed with the aroma of roast mutton and boiled cabbage. Ellie shivered despite the heat. She couldn't stay on Jarrah. Her visits had been rare over the years, and when Leanne had begged to be given the chance to learn how to run a station, it had been granted with a sense of relief. For now she didn't have to be reminded of those early years, didn't have to sleep knowing that gravestone was near.

She turned and left the cookhouse and crossed the yard. There were only three or four horses in the paddock, and as much as she would have liked to, she knew she couldn't ride back to Warratah, or even take the ute. The headache was still lurking and her broken arm would make it impossible. With a sense of entrapment she turned away and headed for the fields behind the homestead.

With her back against the gnarled trunk of a coolibah, she closed her eyes and let the dappled sunlight filter over her eyelids. The hum of flies and the sibilant call of a myriad number of

345

insects made her drowsy. The scent of warm earth and dry grass combined with the perfume of roses and wattle and countless tiny wild flowers, and as the single, haunting flute of a bellbird drifted above her she was taken back to another time; a time when Jarrah had imprisoned Charlie – just as it was now entrapping her.

They returned to Warratah a month after Seamus's funeral. Charlie was sitting beside Wang Lee on the wagon seat, Ellie rode along-side. The long trek was exhausting him. Yet he was determined to appear strong for Ellie.

As they trundled over the lush pastures he breathed in the scent of eucalyptus, and the fresh, clean smell of damp earth and crushed grass that rose beneath the wagon wheels. The sepia dullness of drought was gone, drowned in a palette of colour that piqued the senses. Flower-ing red gum vied with the citrus yellow of wattle. The green, blue and red plumage of the rainbow lorikeets darted amongst the pale green foliage of the gums, and the stately perambulation of the orange and white cattle egrets amongst the vast herd of devons, shorthorns and herefords reminded them all that this wonderful country of theirs was one of vast contrasts and almost indescribable beauty.

His restlessness grew as he watched a wedge tailed eagle hover in the warm breeze, wing-tips rippling, gaze fixed on something far below. He held his breath, waiting for the moment of the kill – and when the bird swooped he sighed. Oh, to be free like that, he thought wistfully. To be able to soar above the earth and see everything in the blink of one glorious golden eye. He became aware of Ellie watching him, but he didn't mind. He was no longer the callow youth she'd once known, but a man who had learned to appreciate the beauty of his surroundings after witnessing the horrors of the world beyond the outback.

They crested the final hill just as the sun was dipping towards the horizon. Warratah valley was bathed in an amber glow, which caught fire to the white bark of the gums, softened the harsh edges of the buildings and threw long shadows across the landscape. The homestead nestled into the blood red earth of the yard, the outbuildings scattered like the forgotten bales that might have fallen from a cart and come to rest in the dappled half-light of the guardian gums.

Charlie looked down to where horses cropped beneath the trees and black swans glided amongst the squabbling ducks on the pewter billabong. The stock yards were full of cows with their calves and the ring of a hammer on anvil sang out a welcome.

'Beauty, ain't it?' said Ellie proudly as she reined in beside the wagon. 'No place on earth like Warratah.'

His gaze trawled the endless pastures, the vast mob of cattle and the finely bred horses in the paddocks. He'd forgotten how big this place was, how rich compared to some he'd worked on. His thoughts drifted. 'Your aunt owns *all* this?'

She laughed. 'Of course. Don't you remember, Charlie?'

He looked down at Warratah with renewed

347

interest, noticing how the setting sun cast a halo of gold around home pasture. 'What about Jarrah?' His tone was thoughtful, his expression studiously indifferent.

She frowned at the question. 'That belongs to Mickey,' she replied. 'We've just been looking after it until he comes home.'

Charlie sat deep in thought as the wagon trundled down the hill towards Warratah.

Three months after Charlie had arrived on Warratah, Aurelia stood in the shadow of the barn and watched as he struggled into the saddle and picked up the reins. His scars were healed, but the shoulder was frozen so he couldn't raise his arm higher than his chest. Yet he was looking so very different from the broken boy that had bravely withstood his pain so he could see his mate decently buried. She smoked her pipe as Charlie kicked the horse into a canter. Ellie was with him as usual. Watching over him as if by keeping him alive and well she could bring back a semblance of her lost Joe.

'You're not happy about that, are you?' said Alicia as she emerged from the barn.

'I'm glad he's in the saddle again,' replied Aurelia. 'We could do with another pair of working hands.'

Alicia dumped the saddles over the hitching post. 'You know I didn't mean that,' she said. 'It's Ellie's interest in him that worries you. Be honest, Aurelia, you never really liked Charlie, did you?'

Aurelia chewed her pipe stem. 'There's something about him that makes me uneasy,' she admitted. 'I admire his undoubted bravery, and his will to recover, but his reaction to Joe's death is worrying. It's as if he feels nothing. I can't help suspecting there's something going on in that flawed mind that he's not letting us see.'

Alicia eyed her sharply. 'You don't think he's been damaged mentally by what happened to him, do you?'

Aurelia looked over at Ellie who was climbing into the saddle, laughing up into Charlie's face, her brown, capable hand lightly touching his arm as if to assure him she would stay close. She noticed how Charlie possessively captured her hand and how intently he was looking at her. 'There's an intensity about him that worries me,' she said thoughtfully. 'And I don't like the way Ellie's been drawn to him.'

'I know what you mean,' said Alicia. 'She's getting far too close to him. Hardly ever leaves his side, and Wang Lee says they talk for hours after we've gone to bed.'

Aurelia knocked out the dottle, stamped on it firmly and put the pipe in her pocket. 'I've already tried talking to her, but she won't listen. Thinks I'm being overcautious.' She screwed her monocle in place and squared her shoulders. 'And maybe I am,' she said stoutly. 'I know I can be overbearing – but it's only because I care about her.'

Alicia frowned as she watched the youngsters. 'Joe's been dead for nearly three years,' she said quietly. 'She has no photographs of him, and only a few letters and poems that have been read so often they're almost illegible. I wonder some-times if she still remembers what he looked like. Do you really think she's seeing Charlie as a substitute?'

Aurelia sighed. 'She thinks she's still in love with Joe. Looking after Charlie is just her way of perpetuating the myth. Hopefully, she'll get over it.'

'You don't sound convinced,' said Alicia mildly. 'Ellie and Joe fell in love when they were kids. Even if by some miracle Joe is still alive, three years apart and a war to contend with will have made huge differences in both of them. I wonder if Ellie has grown so used to the idea of being in love with this missing hero that she hasn't realised it's now only in her mind.'

Aurelia watched them leave the homestead yard and head for the paddocks. They looked good together, she admitted silently. The har-mony obvious even from this distance. Yet one couldn't see the calculation in Charlie's eyes from here. Couldn't catch the occasional glint of something darkly disturbing when he'd thought he was unobserved. 'Absence makes the heart grow fonder,' she murmured.

'Precisely,' said Alicia. 'She still remembers Joe as the quiet, gentle boy who read poetry and books and loved the peace and solitude of the outback as much as she did. Her memory has kept their love alive through a false sense of romantic loyalty. His memory of her would have been of a skinny sixteen year old careering around on Clipper.' She dug her hands in her pockets and pulled out a squashed pack of cigarettes. 'Ellie's been so wrapped up in her romantic day-dream she hasn't realised she's falling for Charlie. Transferring all the love she had for Joe on to his twin.'

Aurelia watched the diminishing figures. 'I hope you're wrong.'

Ellie was unaware of their concern as she rubbed Clipper's nose and made a fuss of him. Poor old boy, she thought as she ran her hand over the sway back and bony hindquarters. Won't be around for much longer. She put a blanket over him and held out the carrots she always brought Chinaman and Clipper each morning. She stroked the grey muzzles as their whiskers tickled the palm of her hand, and laid her cheek on the warm, dusty necks. They were both so old she wasn't sure they'd still be here when she returned.

Ellie was looking forward to the bullock muster. She'd been cooped up for too long at the homestead, and now Charlie seemed to be finally on the mend, she didn't feel too guilty at having to leave him behind. She saddled her working horse and handed over the stock ponies to Jacky Jack. The horses were fresh, champing at the bit, propping and dancing in their eagerness to be on the move again after their long spell at grass. The mood in the yard was upbeat, for despite the long hours and arduous work it involved, the annual bullock muster was always a highlight of the year. It paid the wages.

Wang Lee was followed closely by Fu Man Chu as he shuffled across the verandah. He held tightly to the railings as he hobbled down the steps, his tunic and baggy trousers ill-fitting since he'd lost weight. There was no colour in his hair now and the long pigtail was a thin imitation of what it had once been. 'Wang Lee come say goodbye,' he puffed. 'Wish was going on musta like old time.'

Ellie reached down from the saddle and took his hand. She had no idea how old he was, but he was definitely too ancient to risk life and limb on a bullock muster. 'Take care of yourself, Wang Lee,' she ordered. 'And let Charlie do some of the chores. He's well enough now and you've earned a rest.'

The face that looked up at her was as shrivelled as a raisin, yet the eyes were still bright and he'd lost none of his asperity. 'Charlie no good in kitchen,' he snapped. 'Get in way.' Fu Man Chu danced on his back legs to get attention. 'Dog betta at cleaning plate.'

She smiled down at them both. 'See you in about a month,' she said. 'Hopefully, by then the war will be over.'

'Men come home,' he said with a beaming smile as he lifted Fu Man Chu into his arms and backed away from the prancing horse.

'Yes,' she said firmly. 'So you'd better get as much rest as you can, 'cos they'll need feeding up.' She smiled, the false brightness more for her own benefit than his as the memory of Joe darkened the early sun.

He scowled. 'Is good men come home, then Charlie leave,' he muttered.

Ellie frowned as she tried to control her horse

352

who seemed determined to fidget. 'Why should Charlie leave?'

Wang Lee shook his head as the little terrier licked his chin. 'Miss Ellie not see Charlie same as Wang Lee,' he said mysteriously.

Ellie turned away so he wouldn't see her smile. Wang Lee was getting fanciful in his old age and must be humoured. Yet a momentary thread of unease ran through her as she looked across and saw Charlie standing tense and watchful on the verandah. Wang Lee had always been astute. What was it he'd seen in Charlie that she'd missed?

She shrugged off the doubts, admitting silently that her emotions were taut, her judgement probably flawed when it came to Joe's twin. He was good company, and she liked being with him. She smiled and acknowledged his wave before turning back and joining the others who were preparing to leave.

The stock boys let the blue heelers out of their kennel yard and they came flying across to the riders, barking with the sheer joy of freedom. Aurelia cracked her stock whip and silence was immediate. 'Move 'em out,' she boomed.

The dust rose as the horses and dogs crossed the yard and out into the pastures where the long grass sent up the sweet smell of summer. The creak of saddle leather accompanied the stamping hooves, the yap of the dogs almost too sharp for such a soft daybreak. Ellie trailed at the back so she could watch the scene – it was one of which she would never tire. The stockboys were wiry and long-legged, riding easily in the saddle

353

as the laden pack horses strung behind them. Jacky Jack's face was almost hidden by the brim of his hat, the rooster tailfeathers in the plaited hatband riffling in the breeze as he rode the store wagon. The dray pulled the heavy wagon, his feathered fetlocks buried deep in the lush grass, the brasses on his harness jingling pleasantly.

She waved once more to Charlie and let her horse have his head. The sun was already shooting colour into the sky, the mist sparkling like gossamer where it was caught in the tops of the trees. An almost overwhelming sense of wellbeing flooded through her as she raced to catch the others. It was going to be a beautiful day and Joe's spirit was riding alongside her.

The country was mustered in sections over the next four weeks, the bullocks drafted out and yarded for the night. As the mob grew to over a thousand head they'd been watched rather than yarded, and this meant the women and the stockmen had to take turns to do night-watch. They were all exhausted. Ellie and her mother were taking their turn on this last night before the drover came to collect the mob and drive them to the meat market. It was a warm night, the sky clear and studded with thousands of stars, the moon a half sixpence of silver.

Ellie yawned. 'It's gunna be tough staying awake,' she muttered. 'I don't think I remember being this tired before.' She looked out over the thousands of cattle that shifted and cropped in the moonlight and heard one of the stockboys singing softly on the far flank. As long as the bullocks were lulled they wouldn't be frightened by their presence, for they were used to horses and riders after the long days of mustering.

Alicia walked her horse alongside Ellie's, her hands resting lightly on the pommel. 'What I wouldn't give for a feather bed and a large whisky,' she murmured. 'It feels as if I've been on the back of this horse for the better part of my life.'

Ellie was about to reply when the high-pitched howl of a dingo rent the silence. The cattle shifted, alert and uneasy. The howl was repeated, closer this time, accompanied by the pitter patter of scurrying paws through the undergrowth. The mob broke, heads lifted in alarm, eyes gleaming white in the moonlight as they balked and jostled.

'Get on the flanks,' hissed Ellie as she swiftly turned her horse. 'We have to stop them running.'

The leading dingo slithered out of the shadows, low on its haunches, muzzle sniffing the air. It showed no hesitation as it stalked a young bullock that was too intent on grazing to notice what was happening, and Ellie realised the dog had to be starving and beyond fear.

The bullock screamed in terror as the dingo snapped at his legs. The rest of the mob took flight, thundering across the earth, spreading hell west and crooked in their desperate attempt to escape the pack of dingoes that came flying out of the scrub.

Ellie and the others raced alongside the fleeing mob, twisting and turning their horses in an effort to gather in the breakaways and keep them

355

tightly bunched. The main body of the mob headed for the open plains where the ground was treacherous with broken timber, sharp stones and deep crevasses which could catch a hoof and break legs. About fifty bullocks took it into their heads to make for the gidgee scrub at full gallop. Jacky Jack, Ellie and one of the stock boys stayed with them, hurtling towards the dangers of scrub land at full tilt in the darkness.

Hoofs thundered over the ground, dust rose in a great cloud that blotted out the night sky and made it almost impossible to see. The racing, ghostly mob reached the scrub and tore through it like a tornado. Ellie lay flat against her horse's neck to avoid the whipping branches as they tore through the scrub. She was almost blind from the dust and debris being churned up by two hundred hoofs, but the adrenaline was high and she whooped and whistled with sheer elation.

Cold reality struck when the horse in front became impaled on the spear of a broken tree limb that stuck out several feet from the fork of a tree. The momentum of the stock boy's hectic race into the scrub sent him flying over the horse's head and he hit the dirt with a sickening thud. Then he was on his feet, racing for the safety of the nearest tree as the mob thundered down on him. He wasn't quick enough. Two of the bullocks knocked him back and trampled him as they thundered on.

Ellie managed to wheel her horse away from the stampeding bullocks, reined in and leaped down. The other horse had died instantly, pierced to the heart, still impaled on that wicked

356

tree limb. The stock boy was lying very still and there was blood on his shirt. Ellie carefully felt his limbs to see if they were broken, but she didn't like the way he moaned when she touched his midriff and ribs. With a saddle bag hastily put beneath his head for a pillow, she jumped back into the saddle. She would need help.

The main body of the mob had careered out into the open plains where they soon ran out of steam, and it hadn't taken long to round them up and settle them down again. Three dingoes lay dead, their skulls shattered by rifle bullets – the others were scattered back into the bush. Ellie arrived back at stock camp, filthy and badly shaken. 'Billy's been hurt,' she said breathlessly. 'I'm gunna need the wagon to get him back to the homestead.'

Aurelia ordered the wagon to be taken as far into the scrub as possible, and they gently carried the injured boy out of the bush and laid him on a pile of blankets in the flatbed of the wagon. Billy's saddlery was taken from the dead horse and laid next to him.

It was mid-morning when she reached home pasture. Their journey had been necessarily slow because of the bumpy terrain and Ellie was fretting. Billy lay moaning in the back, the blood a bright splash on the makeshift bandage. He was only young, about fifteen or so, yet he'd been working on Warratah ever since he'd learned to ride and was regarded like all the other Aborigines as an integral part of the station.

The sky was white with heat, touching the land with a stark glare that shot black shadows across

357

the yard. Ellie dropped the reins as Wang Lee came shuffling down the steps to greet her. 'Break rib,' he muttered as he ran expert hands over the limp body. 'Very sick boy. Bring into house.'

There was no sign of Charlie despite calling for him, so the two of them struggled to lay Billy on an old door and carry him into the homestead. Wang Lee bustled about and Ellie left him to fetch hot water, towels and bandages. She was hungry and thirsty and almost dead on her feet as she padded into the kitchen.

'You're back early,' said Charlie cheerfully as he looked up from the out of date newspaper. He poured her a cup of tea and resumed eating his lunch.

'Why didn't you come and help?' she demanded as she ignored the tea and set about collecting the things Wang Lee needed. 'You must have heard me calling.'

He sipped his tea. 'I could see you were managing,' he said. 'And I'm not strong enough to be lugging blacks about.'

Ellie glared. 'His name's Billy,' she said coldly. 'And he doesn't weigh very much.'

Charlie shrugged and munched his sandwich.

Ellie felt like throwing the tea in his face, but was too exhausted. She gathered up the towels and bowl and headed back to the other room. 'Mind you don't overdo it, Charlie,' she said with heavy sarcasm.

The sound of a utility coming up the drive stopped her. Turning, she looked out of the window. 'No,' she whispered as she clutched the

358

towels and slopped water on the floor. 'Please don't let it be who I think it is.'

'Who are you afraid of?'

Charlie was standing beside her, and Ellie moved away as his hand curled around her waist. She watched the utility grind to a halt. Watched as their visitor climbed out and dusted himself down. There was no escape. The chill of foreboding was overwhelming as she handed the water and towels to Wang Lee and moved like an automaton towards the door.

'I didn't want you receiving this through the mail,' the priest said hesitantly. 'If I can help in any way please don't be afraid to ask.' He handed her a large brown envelope.

Ellie looked at the military markings, the stamps, the unfamiliar writing. Her fingers trembled as she tore it open. Agony ripped through her as all her undelivered letters spilled to the verandah floor. She dropped to her knees, her hands drifting over those letters, gathering them up, crushing them to her. 'No!' The drawn out cry of despair and unfulfilled dreams echoed into the still morning only to leave a terrible void in its wake.

'The army thought highly of Joe,' the priest said softly as he knelt beside her. 'They've awarded him a posthumous medal for his bravery.' He held out a small box. 'The citation is in the envelope. I'm sorry, Ellie.'

She barely heard him. Was blind to everything around her as she clutched the letters and the medal and walked down the steps. Unaware of Charlie and Wang Lee watching, she crossed the yard and headed for the horse paddock. Clipper seemed to understand her need, for he shambled over and stood patiently as she clambered on to his back. Then, with no saddle, no blanket and no reins, they slowly moved out of the paddock and on to the plains.

Charlie stood in stunned silence as he watched Ellie stagger across the yard. The full force of the priest's news had left him numb, shattering the illusion of almost careless acceptance he'd manufactured when Aurelia had first told him of Joe's death. For he hadn't believed it. Couldn't believe his twin had died before they had the chance to make things right between them. Now here was the terrible proof and it hit him hard – far harder than he could ever have imagined.

He dropped into a chair and buried his face in his hands. Joe had been a part of him for ever. They had fought and played and vied for the attention of their parents. Tramped the roads, shared a bedroll and a prison cell. They had feasted and starved together, ridden the plains and survived the elements. It couldn't be the end. And yet it was. It was.

'Is there anything I can do?' murmured the priest.

Charlie shook his head, the tears seeping through his fingers.

'We could pray together,' the priest said hopefully. 'You'd be surprised how it can help in times like these.'

Charlie lifted his ravaged face. 'God's never been there for me before,' he rasped. 'Why should it be any different now?' He pulled himself out of the chair and swayed. 'Where was he when Joe bought it, eh? Where was he when Seamus got blown apart and I lost half me chest?' He pushed past the priest and headed for the verandah steps. 'Keep yer prayers and yer God,' he growled. 'Ain't done me no bloody favours.'

'You no go after Miss Ellie,' ordered Wang Lee sharply. 'She need time alone. Need find own way to say goodbye to Joe.'

'I'll do what I bloody want,' stormed Charlie. He was beyond reason, the anguish rising in him like a great tide that threatened to overwhelm him. He had to get away. Had to find Ellie. For she was the only one who could understand what he was going through.

'I'm thinking Wang Lee's right,' soothed the priest as he plucked at Charlie's sleeve.

Charlie swung his fist. It connected with the doleful chin and the priest fell spread-eagled on the verandah floor.

Wang Lee screamed a torrent of Chinese that rose and fell and reverberated in his head. Kelly screeched obscenities as he flapped his wings and danced on his perch. Charlie tensed. Ready to lash out. Then froze as he heard the sound of a rifle being cocked.

'I'm quite prepared to use this,' roared Aurelia. 'Step away from Wang Lee, and put your hands where I can see 'em.'

Charlie felt the colour drain from him as he turned to find he was within inches of a rifle barrel. 'I wasn't going to hit anyone,' he said quickly.

'Didn't look like that to me,' retorted a grim Aurelia. She glanced at the poleaxed priest. 'I

361

suppose he just decided to take forty winks on my verandah?' She waved the rifle in his face. 'Sit over there. And don't move. I'll deal with you in a minute.'

Charlie watched Aurelia as she checked on the priest and ordered Wang Lee to see him right. The rifle remained steady in her hand, its aim unwavering. He flinched as she turned her steely gaze on him. He'd never realised how chill her eyes could be – or how much she disliked him.

'I think you'd better explain what's been going on,' she said sternly.

Charlie told her. He didn't wrap it up in nice words, or give any thought for her feelings. He just let her have it.

'Dear God,' she breathed, the rifle wavering, the colour bleached from her face. 'Where's Ellie now?'

'Out there.' He waved his arm in the general direction of the open plains.

'Better Miss Ellie alone fo' a while,' said Wang Lee solemnly. He shot Charlie a scathing glare. 'She come home when ready.'

'Why hit the priest?' Aurelia demanded. 'It's not his fault.'

Charlie watched as Wang Lee helped the priest to his feet. There was already a dark swelling on his chin and Charlie felt a nub of satisfaction. 'Got in the way,' he mumbled. 'I was trying to go after Ellie and he stopped me.'

Aurelia eyed him coldly. 'Wang Lee's right,' she said finally. 'Ellie needs to have time to take it all in. I'm sorry about your twin, but fisticuffs is not the answer. I will not allow such behaviour on my

362

station.' She glared at him. 'Is that clear?'

Charlie nodded. The grief over Joe's death had suddenly been replaced by cold determination. One of these days he'd get his own back on this old battleaxe.

Ellie had no idea how long she'd been lying against Clipper's neck. They had plodded across the plains, drifting like the windflowers that came in the spring, the rhythm of the old pony's gait lulling her to an exhausted sleep. She dreamed of Joe, and how they'd ridden into the bush on their one and only night together. Dreamed of his kiss and the way the moonlight had turned his hair the colour of a raven's wing and his eyes into the deepest emerald.

Her thoughts meandered, dwelling momentarily on one snapshot of memory before moving to the next. She thought of her father and of the unmarked grave in the middle of nowhere. Thought of the months of tramping, the people she'd met and the places she'd seen. Thought of Joe and his beloved Satan and examined her burgeoning friendship with the complex and unsettling Charlie.

With deep sorrow she realised she'd known Joe's war was over. Yet there had always been a glimmer of hope to cling to – a chance he'd survived – until now. The tears came and she finally gave in to the grief she'd held back for so long.

Yet with the tears came solace. His spirit would ride with her always in the silence of the open plains. For this was their special place. Their grass kingdom.

Chapter Fourteen

Claire closed her eyes and let the last of the sun warm her face. With the darkness of Warratah's history and her sister's animosity far into the distance, she felt relaxed and happy for the first time since coming home. Matt's surprise picnic by the gorge was the perfect ending to a perfect day.

'Penny for 'em? Or should I say dollar?'

Claire smiled. She hadn't got used to the new currency either. 'I was just thinking you have the ideal life,' she murmured. 'You get to travel, to meet so many lovely people and to know all the best places for a picnic.' She glanced across at him. 'Thanks for a bonzer day.'

'It's not a bad life,' he said as he put kindling on the fire. 'But when you're called out in the middle of a lightning storm it isn't much fun. And some of the landing patches are mud slips when it rains.'

She watched him light the fire and set the billy. He moved with an economy of energy, swift and sure, just as he'd done throughout the day, and she found his presence not just reassuring but solid and dependable, and strangely arousing. There had been a horse with a nasty gash on its leg, a couple of cows with mastitis, a ewe with a difficult twin birth and a bull with an abscess at the root of its horn. She'd stood by and watched as he dealt efficiently with them all and, from the welcome he got, she knew he was well liked by the station owners. 'I almost wish I wasn't going back to Sydney,' she said drowsily.

Matt left the fire and came to sit on the blanket. They were shoulder to shoulder, their backs resting against a tree. 'There's always room here for another vet,' he said quietly. 'The area's so vast we're often racing against time to get to our patients. Vets come and go, and the youngsters only stay long enough to get their practical experience for their exams.'

Claire smiled. 'I have to plead guilty to that one,' she murmured. 'Did my practical experience in the Hunter Valley.' The sun was sinking fast, the heat diminishing. Her gaze drifted to him and she found herself looking into hazel eyes. He was too close for comfort – her sudden desire to kiss him too strong. She shifted away and set about grilling the fish for their supper.

'I was thinking of starting up a Flying Veterinary Service similar to the doctor's,' he said as he cupped his hand around a match and lit a cigarette. He brought his knees to his chest and rested his elbows on them. 'Would you be interested?'

She knelt by the fire, garnering warmth from the hot embers. 'I already have a job waiting for me in Sydney,' she reminded him gently. She hadn't missed the almost too nonchalant note in his voice. This was obviously something he'd thought deeply about and she didn't want to spike his enthusiasm.

'I'd base it at my place, because it's fairly

central. But I should be able to get some kind of government funding for the extra planes, and of course each vet would buy into the partnership and have equal share of the profits.'

Claire looked back at him as her imagination took flight. 'That's a brilliant idea,' she said. 'Each vet would have their own areas radiating from your place, and could cover for one another on days off or if they're crook.' She knelt back on her heels. 'Matt Derwent, you're a bloody genius.'

'So you might be interested after all?' His hazel eyes held her through the drift of cigarette smoke.

'It's a big decision, and I already have plans. I don't know...' She felt silent as she saw the crestfallen look in his eyes. She didn't want to rain on his parade, but her future was set in the city. She couldn't just veer off course. 'Tell me more,' she encouraged. 'How would you recruit other vets? You'd need at least four – and they'd all have to get pilot's licenses. Then there's the question of funding. You know how long it's taken the government to fork out for the flying doctors and it's still never enough.'

Matt laughed. 'I've drawn up a business plan already, and a friend of mine in local government reckons it shouldn't be too hard to get a grant. Most of the funding will come from the partners to begin with – it'll have to. But once we're up and running it should pay for itself.'

Claire looked away. She'd had a sudden, rather nasty thought. 'So you took me out today to sound me out about becoming a partner?' she said with a hint of sadness. 'Not because you wanted my company, but because you knew I'd have the backing to join such a venture.'

He sat bolt upright, his face pale with shock. 'How could you think that? Of course I didn't,' he stormed. Standing, he crushed his smoke beneath his boot. 'Bloody hell, Claire, are you always this suspicious? Why shouldn't I want to spend the day with you? I like your company, and you're the one person I've met in a long time that I thought I could...' He came to an abrupt halt, the colour returning furiously into his face. 'Sorry. I didn't meant to shout,' he muttered.

Claire stood up. 'Thought you could what?' she asked softly.

Matt ran his fingers through his already tousled hair. 'I don't know,' he mumbled. 'Maybe I thought you and I could become friends.'

She smiled at him, relaxed in the knowledge that Matt could never be devious and under-hand. He could never hope to win at poker, either, she thought as she saw the obvious message in his eyes. 'I was hoping it could be a bit more than that,' she teased.

His hazel eyes were startled as he looked into her face. 'So was I,' he breathed. 'But you're so young, so beautiful. I didn't think I stood a chance.'

'I like older men,' she said with a teasing twinkle in her eyes. 'Must be looking for a father figure.'

'You'll be the death of me,' he murmured as he cupped her face in his hands and looked into her eyes.

'I hope not,' she whispered as the electricity sparked between them.

Matt hesitated as if unsure of himself and of her reaction. Then his lips touched hers and as she coiled her arms around his neck and drew him close everything else was forgotten.

On 1 May, 1945 Russian troops entered the ruins of Berlin and six days later Germany surrendered unconditionally. The Japanese held out for another three months then surrendered on 15 August. The war was over.

Jack arrived home lean and silver-haired, the effects of his war etched deep in his face. He stepped out of the utility and into Aurelia's waiting arms. 'Will you marry me?' he asked after he'd kissed her.

'Absolutely, you old fool,' she replied. 'I've waited quite long enough.'

The little church in Burketown had been built almost a century before, and this September morning it looked as if it had woken from a long sleep and was surprised to find itself decorated with flowers and ribbons. The organist thumped enthusiastically on the keys, her feathered hat bobbing in time to the wedding march as Aurelia emerged from the sunlight into the dim coolness.

She clutched Mickey's arm, the spray of roses trembling droplets of dew as she tried to compose herself. 'I hope to goodness Jack knows what he's letting himself in for,' she muttered as she fidgeted with the unfamiliar trailing skirt and cream silk blouse.

Mickey's ravaged face creased into a smile as he

patted her hand with trembling fingers. The malaria had hit him hard and it had been touch and go as to whether he'd be strong enough to attend. 'He's a lucky man,' he murmured. 'And you are a beautiful bride.'

She raised her eyebrows and the monocle popped out and danced on its ribbon. 'Don't be ridiculous,' she snorted. 'I look like the dog's dinner.' Yet she was flattered. She'd taken an inordinate amount of time dressing this morning and knew she looked better than usual, for the mirror had told her so. The colour was high in her cheeks, the loss of weight had taken years off, and she rather liked the way the long silk skirt swished around her feet. It was good to feel feminine again after all the years of drab jackets and plus fours. Yet the shoes Alicia had made her wear were killing her. How on earth women were supposed to totter about in high heels was a mystery, and she couldn't wait to get back into her comfy old brogues.

'Ready?'

She nodded, the diamonds in her ears and at her throat catching the morning sun that streamed through the stained glass windows. 'About as ready as I'll ever be. Let's get on with it, then I can have that lovely man all to myself.' She took a deep breath as Mickey escorted her down the aisle to where Jack was waiting. He looked so handsome in his suit, so distinguished now his hair was silver and the ravages of war had softened in his face. She trembled as he turned to watch her, the smile warm and so full of love. I'm a lucky woman, she thought as she stood beside

369

him. I've been given a second chance.

The ceremony was over all too quickly. The register was signed, the congratulations received and when Aurelia stepped into Jack's embrace his kiss confirmed the vows they had just taken. When they finally drew apart the organist crashed the keys in fanfare and made them both giggle. 'How does it feel to be Mrs Withers?' he shouted above the racket.

'Mrs Bligh-Withers, if you don't mind,' she said with mock severity. She'd always been rather proud of her distant link to the legendary sea captain.

He grabbed her hand as he laughed. 'Don't ever change, Aurelia,' he stuttered. Then he sobered, his expression solemn. 'You're quite a woman, Aurelia, and I love you monocle, bull-whip, plus fours, bloody mindedness and all.' He kissed her again, softly this time, conveying so much in that delicate touch that Aurelia had to blink hard to stop her emotions running away with her. 'Come on then, Mrs Bligh-Withers. Let's show this lot how to have a real party.'

There was always a certain atmosphere at weddings, Alicia decided, that made people act out of character. The insular world of the wedding party seemed to heighten emotions, bringing a sense of romance to the fore, making for careless declarations and some unwise behaviour. She sipped her champagne and eyed the people around her, aware as always of feeling distanced from these almost naive, reckless men and women of the outback whose homespun clothes and philosophies were in sharp contrast to her Dior suit and worldly experience.

Neighbours had come hundreds of miles to witness Aurelia marrying her Jack. It had been the subject of speculation and gossip for years and this was an occasion not to be missed – especially now the war was over and it only needed the slightest excuse to throw a party. The bright dresses and frivolous hats of the women vied with the sombre suited men as the noise rose in the function room above the hotel bar. Faces were reddening and collars were undone as jackets and ties were slung over the backs of chairs and the serious business of drinking got underway.

Alicia watched as the men drifted towards the bar and leaned against the counter. Their talk was of cattle and sheep, of their experiences in the war and the comparisons between the different beers they'd tasted abroad. The married women sat at tables, huddled in gossip, eyes flitting back and forth beneath hat brims taking it all in. The younger women stood in giggling clusters at the far corners of the room, their flirtatious eyes dancing across the men at the bar as they waited for the band to strike up.

'Thought you might like another drink,' said Mickey as he carefully deposited a glass of champagne on the table. His hand still trembled from his latest bout of malaria and he tutted with annoyance as the champagne spilled on the pristine cloth.

She smiled up at him. 'Thanks,' she said with a studied degree of warmth.

371

He stood beside her, awkward and ill at ease in his suit and tight collar. Yet he seemed reluctant to leave her and Alicia felt a touch of irritation. She did so hate being followed about and Mickey had been like a soulful puppy ever since he'd returned from the war. She had hoped to be long gone by now – back to England – but Aurelia's wedding plans had put paid to that.

The band was warming up, making a discordant rasp and twang as they tuned their instruments. Alicia noticed the girls begin to edge from their corners. The younger men leaned on the counter, beers in hand, eyeing each one as if they were prize heifers to be cut from the mob. Alicia sighed and sipped the lukewarm champagne. She was almost glad she wasn't young any more.

'Do you want to dance?' Mickey asked. 'Might be a bit rusty, but I'll give it a go.'

'I'd rather not,' she shouted above the din. 'Far too much of a crush.'

He eyed her soulfully before walking away. She watched him join the other men and order a beer. The ravages of malaria were clearly marked in his face and the doctors had told him he would always carry the sickness and it would recur frequently. Poor Mickey, she thought vaguely.

She put down the glass and lit a cigarette as she watched the youngsters on the dance floor. Charlie and Ellie had joined in with the others in some newfangled dance called the jive that had been introduced by the Yanks, and as far as she could see it was asking for trouble. Petticoats and stocking tops were on show and the men were overexcited enough – they didn't need encouragement. There was an air of desperation about it all that wasn't quite decent. It was as if these kids had to make up for the lost years of their youth, as if by drinking hard and laughing loudly they could banish the sights and sounds of battle they had lived with for so long. It was the same for the girls as well as the boys, she realised. They'd been left behind to work the land and the stock, with no chance for parties and courting and all the trappings of youth. She despaired for the consequences.

'They're just having fun,' gasped Aurelia as she plumped down beside her. 'I shouldn't worry too much.' She fanned herself with a handkerchief and took a long drink of champagne.

Alicia grimaced. 'I wish he'd move on. Ellie's grown too close to him. And after what Wang Lee told us about his sneaking into the safe, I wouldn't trust him as far as I could throw him.' She looked at her sister. 'Wang Lee was genuinely frightened of him, you know. He knew that if Charlie found out he'd been seen he'd be in trouble.'

Aurelia wiped the sweat from her face, drank the last of the champagne and stood up. 'I've made certain changes to things now Mickey's back,' she said firmly. 'Tied everything up so it's safe.' She grinned, the monocle glinting in the bright light. 'Charlie's going to find he's made a big mistake thinking he can pull one over on me.' She strolled off, grabbed Jack from the bar and whirled him on to the dance floor.

Alicia noticed she'd kicked off her fancy shoes

and the disreputable old brogues were peeking out from beneath the silk skirts. She sighed in exasperation. Aurelia would never be chic.

The party lasted well into the afternoon. The fancy hats had been discarded, the ties and inhibitions along with them; three fights had already broken out but thankfully these altercations were swiftly dealt with and the protagonists ended up the best of mates as they downed even more beer and broke into raucous song. Aurelia and Jack emerged hurriedly from the depths of the mayhem, in an attempt to escape the hullabaloo. They weren't quick enough and Jack had to almost carry Aurelia out to the car as they were showered in confetti and rice.

She stood laughing on the running board, the wilting bouquet held aloft. The young girls surged forward, hands high as it performed a graceful arc through the air. Ellie caught it and to a roar of applause looked up into Charlie's face and laughed with delight as he swiftly kissed her cheek.

Aurelia's smile wavered as she caught Alicia's horrified gaze, then she turned and climbed into the car beside her new husband and hid her expression beneath the brim of her picture hat.

The noise was horrendous as the bride and groom left for their honeymoon, the trail of boots and billies and firecrackers kicking up the dirt behind the car. Alicia waved until they'd disappeared behind the dust cloud, then stood for a long moment in the ensuing silence as the rest of the guests trailed back into the party. It was cooler out here, and quieter too. She needed this moment to herself after such a hectic day. Needed to think about Ellie.

'Alicia?' Mickey's almost apologetic voice startled her some moments later. 'Can we talk?'

With a sigh, she turned to him. She had a fair idea what was coming and she'd been dreading it. 'Let's walk a little,' she suggested. 'Do you feel up to it?'

He nodded. 'Legs are still a bit crook, but I reckon I could make it over to those trees.' He took her hand and placed it protectively in the crook of his arm as they set off down the dusty road to the stand of coolibahs and willows that lined the river. They found a picnic bench and sat down.

'I want to say something to you, Alicia,' he began. 'And although you've probably guessed what it is, I'd like the chance to tell you what's been on my mind before you come to a decision.'

Alicia's throat was tight. This had to be stopped before it went any further. 'I don't think...' she began.

He put a trembling finger to her lips. 'Shhh. Let me speak first. Please?' He eyed her solemnly and cleared his throat. 'I know I'm not the healthiest bloke in the world, or the most educated. I'm gunna be stuck with this malaria for the rest of my life, but I have a good station in Jarrah, and because of you and Aurelia there's money in the bank and a healthy mob of cattle in the pastures.'

Alicia could feel his rather damp grip on her hands and wished he'd release her. Yet she realised he was determined to have his say, and because of the fragile friendship she'd shared with this man she couldn't quite bring herself to her usual cutting iciness.

'War taught me many things, Alicia, and one of them is that a man isn't meant to live out his life alone. I want you to marry me,' he said firmly. 'I want you to come and live at Jarrah as my wife.'

Alicia froze. She had known this was coming. Had prepared for it ever since his return from the military hospital. It was time she put him out of his misery. 'I...' she began.

'Don't give me your answer now, Alicia,' he said with a touch of desperation. 'Think about it. We've got all the time in the world now the war's over.'

Alicia looked into his face. His skin was dark from the sun, the streaks of grey more prolific in the jet of his hair. He was too thin, but still handsome. Yet she wasn't prepared to sacrifice her life for an invalid – not when she didn't love him. 'I can't marry you, Mickey,' she said firmly. 'I'm leaving for England soon.'

'But you'll be coming back. Won't you?' His eyes were fearful, his hand suddenly cold as he gripped her fingers.

She disentangled herself and moved away. 'I don't belong in the outback, and I have no special feeling for Australia. It's been an experience working with Aurelia and Ellie – an adventure of sorts – but not one I wish to prolong.'

Mickey slumped on the picnic bench, his hands drooping between his knees.

Alicia forced herself to ignore his obvious

376

misery and forged on. He had to be made to realise she was adamant. 'I can't spend the rest of my life here,' she said, tamping down on her impatience. 'The open spaces are closing in on me and I need the bright lights of the city and the noise and bustle of people who think as I do.'

He raised his head and looked at her. 'We could always go to England for long holidays,' he said hopefully. 'I have the money.'

Alicia stood and brushed the dust from her shantung suit. 'It wouldn't work,' she said brusquely. She was tiring of this and wanted to return to the party. She needed a drink.

'What if I sell Jarrah and we move to England?' His face was alight with hope as he stood and grasped her hands. 'Would you marry me then?'

Alicia pulled away from him. 'No,' she said sharply.

The colour was gone from his face and perspiration beaded his forehead. The fever was returning and he looked ghastly. 'So there's nothing I can do or say that will change your mind?' he said in defeat.

'Nothing,' she replied as she turned and headed back to the hotel. Alicia was aware of him standing there watching her go and felt a twinge of unease at the callous way she'd rejected him. Then she lifted her chin and climbed the verandah steps. Life for her was about to take a turn for the better and she could hardly wait to step on to English soil again – to be amongst people she understood – to pick up the threads of the life she'd abandoned. Mickey would get over it, she decided.

Aurelia had eaten well and was tired despite the nap she'd had that afternoon. Now she rested back into the pillows and stared out of the window at the moon as she thought of her wedding day. She could understand her sister's reluctance to marry Mickey, but as things turned out it would have been a brief marriage. For Mickey had died only weeks later. His heart, weakened by the sustained attacks of malaria, had finally given out.

She closed her eyes and her sigh trembled as the tears began to seep through her lashes. Mickey had been a close, dear friend and she still missed his bluff heartiness. Yet he could have had little idea of the devastation he'd wrought by his good intentions later on. And would have been mortified to know they were still reaping the whirlwind he'd sown in those last days of his life.

Ellie was waiting for Leanne and Angel's return from the stockyard and was deeply engrossed in a raunchy novel she'd found on the shelves. She was rather shocked at how explicit some of the scenes were, and wondered if life really was like that in America – or if it was merely an over-charged imagination on the part of the author. She turned another page, unable to resist. The slam of the screen door and hurrying footsteps brought her from steamy LA to warm Queensland. With a guilty start she shoved the book down the back of the cushions as Claire appeared in the doorway.

'I'm back,' she said unnecessarily as she came

into the room and flopped into a chair. 'I've had a wonderful day.' She smiled, her eyes very blue, her cheeks flushed.

'So I see,' said Ellie with studied mildness. 'What have you done with him? Or shouldn't I ask?'

'He's had to go home. Early start in the morning,' said Claire airily as she poured herself a drink. 'I said you wouldn't mind if he came over to Warratah tomorrow night for dinner.'

'You can cook it then,' she replied. 'Can't do much with this blasted arm.' She grinned at her daughter. 'I'm glad you and Matt are getting on well. He's a nice man and it's time he moved on after Laura.'

Claire handed her a glass and sank back into the couch beside her. 'He told me about her today. She was very young when she died, you know. Only in her twenties.'

Her expression was sad, but Ellie noticed she couldn't quite disguise the happiness in her eyes. 'You're up to something,' she said. 'I can always tell.'

Claire's gaze drifted from her mother to the flash of colour peeking out from behind the cushion. 'So are you,' she giggled as she pulled the paperback from its hiding place. 'I know this book and it's filthy. Really Mum. Whatever next?'

Ellie lifted her chin and tried to keep her expression stern. 'I like to keep up with what's popular, so I thought I'd scan through it.'

'Yeah, right.' Claire flicked through the pages to where Ellie had turned down a corner. 'I see you managed to scan at least two-thirds of it,' she

379

teased. 'Enjoying it, are you?'

Ellie felt the heat rising in her face and burst out laughing. 'I didn't know people did things like that,' she spluttered. 'Quite makes me feel inadequate. For goodness' sake don't lend it to your father.'

'Daddy never has time to read,' Claire said as she sipped her drink. 'He doesn't sit still long enough.' She put down the glass and after tucking her feet beneath her she turned to Ellie, her expression solemn. 'I've been offered another job.'

Ellie watched her daughter's face as she talked about Matt's plans. It was a splendid idea and she was amazed no one had thought of it sooner. 'I don't know what to do, mum. Matt's a really nice bloke and it's an exciting concept. But the post in Sydney is an opportunity I won't get again, and I was so lucky to get it.'

'Are you still set on returning to the city?'

Claire chewed her lip. 'I thought I was. But now...' She lit a cigarette and expelled the smoke in a long sigh. 'I have to admit I'm tempted. Coming home has made me realise how much I love this place. But I hardly know Matt. What if we end up hating one another? Then there are the practicalities. I'd need money to buy in to the partnership, the patience and guts to learn how to fly, and somewhere to have as a base to work from.'

Ellie smiled. 'You could run your practice from here,' she said without thinking. 'Jarrah's perfectly placed to reach the interior.'

Claire frowned. 'Why would I want to live here?' she asked. 'If I did decide to go through with this totally insane idea, I'd prefer to live on Warratah. Leanne and I are hardly the closest sisters in the world.'

Ellie bit her lip. She'd been careless. But before she could speak a voice from the doorway interrupted. 'What's all this about Claire living here?'

'Mum was just saying Jarrah was a perfect place to set up my practice.'

Leanne came in to the room followed by Angel. She poured them both a drink and remained standing by the fireplace. 'I don't know what the hell you're talking about, so you'd better explain.' Her tone was flat, her eyes cold.

Ellie fidgeted while Claire repeated Matt's plans for the flying veterinary service. She was aware of the tension rising in Leanne and knew that a furious row was about to erupt between her daughters. She picked up the glass, but her hand shook so much she spilled some on the table.

'I never said I was planning to live here,' Claire protested. 'It was Mum's idea.'

'Good,' said Leanne coldly. 'I've got plans for this place and now I'm married you'd be in the way.'

'Plans?' Ellie realised she'd spoken sharply and a little too loudly. She reddened as the girls eyed her. 'What plans, Leanne?' she said with more calm than she felt.

Leanne put one hand in her pocket as she rested the other on the mantelpiece. 'Once Jarrah's in my name I'll tell you,' she said mysteriously. 'But until then you'll have to wait.' She cast a sly glance at her sister. 'I can guarantee you'll be amazed.'

There was a lump in Ellie's throat that threatened to smother her. 'I wish you'd said something earlier, Leanne.'

'It would have spoiled the surprise,' said Leanne. 'Beside, it's taken me this long to get the plans right. We don't all have the benefit of a university education and friends in high places.'

'That's unfair,' exploded Claire. 'Don't be such a bitch, Leanne. What did I ever do to make you hate me so?'

'There aren't enough hours in the day to even begin on that one,' snarled Leanne.

Ellie was almost numb from the pain of seeing her girls so hateful, but she had to clear this up before it got out of hand. 'Me and your dad never made you any promises, Leanne.' Her voice sounded as if it no longer belonged to her.

Leanne froze, the stillness within her transmitting confusion and anger as she looked down at her mother. 'But you said you wanted me to learn how to run a station. You know how much I love it here, and although you might never have actually *said* Jarrah would be mine one day, you implied it.' Her tone was icy.

Ellie clasped her hands on her lap. She could hardly bear to look in her daughter's eyes – but Leanne demanded it. 'It's time we had a long talk,' she said finally. 'There are things me and your father should have explained to both of you a long time ago. Things Aurelia knew had to be revealed. It's the reason why Claire's here.'

'Do you know what she's talking about?' Leanne whirled to face her sister, the spite clear in her pallor.

Claire glared back. 'No,' she said firmly. 'I was merely told to come home and clear the air.' She saw the chill in Leanne's eyes and the startled confusion in the silent, watchful Angel. 'Mum? What's going on? You've been telling me the history of Warratah and Jarrah, but there's more, isn't there? What are you hiding?'

'I don't know where to start,' she replied lamely.

'Try the beginning,' spat Leanne.

Ellie couldn't sit still any longer. She shoved her way out of the chair and began to pace. 'I've wrestled with how I was going to tell you both, but now the time's come I hardly know what to say. It's been with me night and day ever since you got home.' She put up a hand to silence her daughter's protest. 'It's not your fault, Claire. It's mine. Mine and Charlie's, Joe's and Mickey's.' She took a deep, shuddering breath. 'If I could turn back the clock, I would. I'd give anything for the chance to change things. But I can't. And we must all live with the consequences.'

Leanne knocked back her drink and lit a cigarette. Her eyes were cold as she glared at her mother. 'With Claire back in the city there's no reason why Angel and I can't have Jarrah. We've made our life here, and I've got plans for the future.'

Ellie ran her tongue over her lips. Once spoken, the words could never be taken back. The flood-gates were open and now she was being swept into the maelstrom that was the past. 'Jarrah was never yours,' she whispered. 'It belongs to Claire.'

383

Chapter Fifteen

'You bitch.' Leanne was vibrating with shock and rage. It was a dangerous combination and she shrugged off Angel's warning hand as she rounded on her sister. 'So that's why you came home. You knew all about this didn't you?'

'No,' gasped Claire, her eyes wide with horror. 'I'd never do something like that.'

'Miss perfect,' she spat. 'Little miss goody-two-shoes. Butter wouldn't bloody melt would it? You waltz in here and take over just like you always do. You've got Mum and Dad wrapped around your little finger and you expect us all to dance to your bloody tune.' She poked Claire in the chest – hard. 'Well you've struck out. I'm not playing your game. Jarrah's mine and I'll kill you if you try and take it away.'

'It's not a game,' shouted Ellie. 'And it's nothing to do with Claire. Please, Leanne, can't we discuss this like adults?'

'That's it. Defend her as always.' She glared at Ellie, the rage so great she could barely focus. 'I've sweated and struggled to make a go of it here while Golden Girl's been drifting about on Dad's allowance in Sydney, and you've never given me a word of praise. I've had to work bloody hard to get what I want, but all *she* has to do is crook her little finger and you slobber all over her.'

'That's not true, and you know it,' protested a

white faced Ellie.

'Isn't it?' she hissed. 'Tell me, Mother – who left home under a cloud? Who caused so much trouble five years ago that you've hardly spoken to her since? Who has just been handed my Jarrah on a bloody plate?'

'It's not like that. Please, Leanne...'

Leanne was on a roll. All the years of bitterness rose to the surface and she wasn't about to let the moment pass. 'The prodigal returns! Hallelujah! Bring on the fatted calf as well as the rest of the mob. And here's Jarrah, just in case you felt left out.' Tears sparked in her eyes and she angrily dashed them away. 'I was the one who stayed here. The one who desperately needed you to notice me. I thought you would love me once she'd gone. But nothing's changed, has it?' She ignored her mother's gasp of horror as she caught her sister's glance at Angel. 'Why don't you take him as well?' she stormed. 'I've seen the way you look at him, no doubt you won't be satisfied until you have it all.'

'Leanne!' Angel stood helplessly between the girls, his dark eyes pleading with Leanne to calm down. 'Is bad these things you say. I want you. Only you.'

Leanne's cold gaze swept over her sister, noting the slender hips and flat stomach, the elegant neck and the long fair hair that fell to her waist. Even in times of trouble she still had the capacity to appear cool and composed. Bitch.

'Grow up, Leanne.' Claire's tone matched the coolness in her eyes. 'I don't want your husband or your bloody station. One's a pretty boy gigolo

385

and the other's a millstone.'

'Is not so!' Angel argued loudly. 'I love Leanne – only Leanne.'

Leanne struck out, her hand connecting with Claire's cheek so hard it left the imprint of her fingers. In the shocked silence that followed she stormed out of the room, her bootheels rapping loudly on the floor.

Slamming into her bedroom, she leaned against the door and closed her eyes. She couldn't believe her parents could have betrayed her like this. Couldn't believe that all she'd done here was for her sister's benefit. 'It's not fair,' she hissed through stormy tears. Claire had everything from looks to brains and the capacity to earn more than she ever could. Now she was being handed Jarrah. Her Jarrah.

Leanne pushed away from the door and found the roll of plans. She threw them on the bed, the tears hot on her face, the disappointment and hurt so great she thought she would die. All the hard work, the sleepless nights and harrowing days had been for nothing. Her future merely pieces of useless, flaming paper.

Moments later she gathered up the plans and strode back to the lounge. Tears wouldn't do her any good. She had to make a stand and fight for what she wanted. It was time to make Mum see sense. Time to sort this out once and for all.

Claire was isolated in her misery, her arms wrapped around her waist as she stared out of the window. A solitary tear trickled down her face, but she was almost unaware of it. How could

Leanne hate her so much? Why did she think Claire had deliberately stolen Jarrah from her when she'd had no idea of Mum's plans. What the hell were Mum and Dad thinking of to do this? She turned at the sound of her sister's voice.

'I want to show you something.' Leanne placed the plans on the sofa table.

'I don't want Jarrah,' Claire began. 'I never wanted Jarrah.'

'Doesn't alter the fact it's yours,' Leanne snapped. 'But then why should I be surprised? You always were Dad's golden girl.'

It was a snipe, guaranteed to force a reaction. 'That's not fair,' retorted Claire. 'Mum and Dad have always treated us the same. I'm as mystified as you by all this.' She approached Leanne, and hesitantly reached out in reconciliation. 'Please don't let's fight.'

Leanne slapped her hand away. 'I'm not going to stand by and let you take everything,' she said coldly. 'We might be sisters, but you know precious little about me if you think I'm going to let you get away with this.'

'Stop it. Both of you,' demanded Ellie. 'Claire didn't know anything, Leanne. And I'm ashamed of your outrageous behaviour.'

Leanne folded her arms. 'So what am I supposed to do, Mum?' she barked. 'Roll over and let her take Jarrah?' She breathed in sharply. 'It's mine by right. I demand you change whatever you've done and hand it over to me.'

'I can't.' Ellie's eyes were bleak.

'Why?' demanded Leanne. 'You own both stations.'

Ellie shook her head. 'We own Warratah, but Jarrah was put in trust for Claire before she was born,' she whispered.

Claire stared at her mother as she tried to come to terms with what she'd heard. 'I don't want Jarrah,' she said firmly into the shocked silence. 'I never wanted Jarrah. Have it, Leanne. Take it, do with it what you will, but please don't let's fight any more.'

Leanne looked from her sister to Angel then on to her mother. 'See how easily she can give it up?' she spat. 'She doesn't deserve Jarrah. If she did she'd fight for it.'

Ellie slumped on to the arm of the chair. 'It isn't as simple as that,' she said, her voice cracking with emotion.

Leanne slammed her fist on the table. 'Of course it is,' she exploded. 'Look at the plans I've made for Jarrah, then tell me I wasn't meant to be here.'

Claire and Ellie moved towards the table like sleepwalkers. 'What's all this?' Ellie turned the pages as Claire and Angel looked over her shoulder.

'Those are plans for building guest cottages,' Leanne said coldly. 'Jarrah will remain a working station, but will also be open for visitors. I am ... was ... planning to turn it into what the Americans call a dude ranch.'

'It's a brilliant idea,' breathed Claire. 'With the track leading out to the highway, Jarrah's perfectly placed. Good on you, Leanne.'

Leanne eyed her with a coldness that silenced her. 'Don't patronise me, you cow. You aren't the only one with brains in this family,' she said flatly.

Claire flinched at the barb and saw the momentary flash of satisfaction in her sister's eyes. She realised then that there were no rules in this battle, and Leanne wanted to inflict hurt – wanted them all to see how determined she was – and would go about it ruthlessly.

Leanne smoothed out the plans. 'Homestead stays are popular with city people. They want to live the romance and adventure of the outback, but they like to do it in comfort. These cottages will be fitted out with the latest luxuries, and the swimming pool and recreation room will offer entertainment if the weather lets us down.'

She looked up from the lovingly drawn plans, the tears glinting but unshed. 'People will come from the cities and play drover. They'll be able to ride the plains and help with the round-up. Or go with Jacky Jack's grandson into the Never-Never and learn about Dreamtime. They can have billy tea and damper around the camp-fire and listen to the aboriginal legends, then sleep under the stars. We can run trips up to the north coast, and jeep safaris into the Territory. There's fishing in the rivers and lakes, boating too. Then there's bush-walks and nature trails. They can get a glimpse of what life's like out here, and once I get it up and running, I'm positive the idea will grow.' She glared defiantly at her silent, stunned husband then back to her mother and sister as she paused for breath. 'The funding's already arranged. A travel company in Brisbane has said they'd be interested.'

Claire stared at the plans as her sister talked. It

was a wonderful idea, something she would never have thought of, but this shocking news of Jarrah's ownership was tearing them apart. She looked at her mother. Ellie was very pale, her eyes sunken and deeply shadowed in her little face. 'I don't want Jarrah,' she said again. 'Please, Mum. Give it to Leanne.'

Ellie drew away from the table, her arms tightly folded around her waist. 'I've already said I can't do that,' she said in a shaky voice. 'Jarrah was left to you in trust and then in turn to your children.'

Claire recoiled in horror. 'What on earth made you and Dad come up with that crazy idea?' Claire realised she was shouting and had to battle to contain her temper. 'You've not only made Leanne hate me even more than she already did, but you've chained me and my unborn children to this place. How did you know if any of us wanted it? Why let Leanne think it would be hers when you knew all along it never could be?'

Ellie sank on to the sofa and put her face in her hands. 'I agreed Leanne could run Jarrah, but never promised to give it to her. I thought she understood that once she'd learned the ropes we would help set her up in a place of her own,' she sobbed. 'How was I to know she was planning all this? She never said.'

'Seems this family is lacking in communication skills as well as common sense,' said Claire with a sigh. 'Can't you change this silly trust? Jarrah's not worth all this trouble.'

Leanne's intake of breath was sharp, but she was stilled by her mother's voice. 'It has nothing to do with me. Your dad and I didn't know what he'd done until you were three years old. By then it was out of our hands. We can do nothing to change it.'

Claire experienced a chill of premonition and had to sit down. Surely the rumours hadn't been true? Surely her mother hadn't lied to her the other day? 'He?' she breathed. 'Who's he?'

The silence in the room was electric.

'I see I've arrived just in time,' bellowed Aurelia from the doorway. 'Drinks all round, Angel. Looks as if you could all do with one.'

Ellie gazed up at her in disbelief. 'What...? How did you...?' she stammered.

'Couldn't sleep, so I rang the head-stockman and asked him to fly me over. I had a feeling things weren't right.' She bent down and kissed Ellie's cheek, then collapsed on the couch beside her.

Ellie took her hand. 'Thanks,' she said with simple sincerity. 'I've made a mess of things as usual, and I don't know how...' Her voice tailed off.

Claire and Leanne moved around one another in stony silence as they handed out the drinks. Angel tried to persuade Leanne to calm down and was ignored, and Ellie was obviously struggling to remain coherent and strong. Claire returned to her place by the window, unable to sit still. The thought that Ellie could see condemnation in her eyes was hard to bear. Yet they were all trapped and there was no escape.

Ellie looked at her daughters. She silently begged them for forgiveness and understanding, but knew she had no right. She'd lied for too many years – lied by omission. For she hadn't had the guts to tell the truth and had refused to let her husband take the burden from her and tell the girls. Now she was faced with her worst nightmare. 'I said earlier that this isn't a simple story,' she began. 'And for you to understand how Jarrah came to be entrusted to Claire and any children she might have, I'm going to have to take you back again to the war years.'

Aware her daughters were looking at her with suspicion and not a little coldness, she almost lost her nerve. For how could she tell them the truth – the unvarnished, naked truth that could ultimately destroy both of them? She ran her tongue over dry lips as Aurelia gripped her fingers in encouragement. It was a dilemma she'd hoped she'd never have to face once the principal players were dead and buried – but it was not to be. For Mickey Maughan had seen to that. 'You'll remember I told you, Claire, that Mickey had made provisions for Jarrah should he not return from the war?'

Claire nodded, the fair hair drifting around her face as she remained against the backcloth of the night beyond the window. 'He put the deeds in Alicia's name, trusting she would give them back if he or Seamus returned. If they didn't, Jarrah was to be yours.' Her gaze was bewildered. 'But you said you didn't own it. How could that be?'

Ellie realised Claire had missed the point. 'Mickey came back,' she said softly. 'The deeds were returned to him and remained with him until he died.'

'But Mickey died six months before I was born. I've seen his gravestone...' Claire moved away from the window. The darkness returned to her eyes as she looked into Ellie's face. 'You said I was three years old when you found out about this inheritance. Has it got something to do with the other man buried in that graveyard?' It was a whisper – yet there was a tensile quality in those few words that demanded the truth.

The silence in the room was ominous as Ellie met her stare and returned it. 'Yes.' It was as if a great burden had been lifted from her shoulders.

Claire swayed and had to sit down. 'You'd better explain, and no more stories. Just the plain, hard facts.'

Ellie wet her lips and reached for a cigarette. Leanne's shock was clear in her face, but at least she'd remained silent, and for that she was grateful. Angel obviously was having a calming effect as they sat entwined on the same chair. She looked back at Claire, her heart heavy. 'What I have to say is going to hurt you, Claire,' she said softly. 'Yet I want you to know that your father and I love you, and that whatever happens after tonight, we will still love you.'

The silence was profound, but the welcome pressure of Aurelia's hand spurred her on. 'Weddings have a strange effect on people,' she began. 'I was missing Joe terribly, and I knew Alicia wouldn't be staying on once Aurelia was back from her honeymoon. I was surprised how much that saddened me. We'd forged a good friendship over the war years, and I would miss her.'

Ellie chose her words carefully as she carried on

393

speaking. But the scenes gradually unfolding in her mind brought her so much pain she stumbled over her words. 'I suppose I was slightly tipsy and a little maudlin that day, and when Charlie suggested we leave the reception and find some peace by the lagoon, I was happy to go with him.'

She paused as the memories returned, the snapshot moments of that day so clear it was as if it had all happened a few hours ago. Charlie was a little unsteady on his feet from too much beer, and when she told him she'd been mourning Joe, she'd thought she'd seen a flicker of something dark in his eyes. Yet it had been so fleeting she hadn't had time to analyse it, and when he'd put his arm around her waist and held her, she'd known she'd been mistaken. Charlie was mourning his loss just as much as she was, and it was a comfort to them both that they had each other.

'Charlie went back into the hotel and fetched a bottle of champagne, then I drove us out to Five Mile lagoon. We didn't talk much, but then we didn't need to. We'd become very close over the past few years and I was grateful for his friendship and support.'

Ellie remembered how she'd parked up and reached into the back of the utility for a blanket before they headed for a grassy spot well away from the water. This was freshwater croc country and it was wiser to remain in the open than further down near the water where the prehistoric reptiles lurked. 'We shared the champagne and talked about the future, just as close friends do, there was nothing else between us.'

Claire rammed her hands in her pockets, turned her back on Ellie and stared into the fire. Her tone was sharp, the colour bleached from her face. 'What's this leading to?' she demanded.

Ellie stared at her, unable to reply. She'd said too much. Had given away the one thing that might have kept some semblance of dignity to the story.

Aurelia could tell Ellie was at her wits' end. Leanne was obviously confused and angry, and Claire was suspicious. She hadn't been a bit surprised when Ellie had fallen into silence – she couldn't blame her for wanting to avoid the truth. Yet things had progressed to a point where it had to be told and, because of Ellie's slip, she knew the consequences would be stark.

'I got back from my six week honeymoon to find Alicia very restless. She'd had enough of cows and horses – enough of the heat, the dust and the flies. She needed to go home to England.' Aurelia eyed the two girls, and despite their glares refused to be intimidated. She would tell this story her way – otherwise she'd get muddled and make a pig's ear of the whole thing.

'Poor Alicia. Fate seemed determined to keep her here and although she did her best to hide it, I knew immediately something was wrong.'

'What's the matter with the girl?' she demanded. Ellie had silently drifted into the kitchen, picked at her breakfast and drifted out again without a word to anyone.

'I have no idea,' Alicia replied. 'I've tried talking to her. Tried talking to Charlie, but I can't get any sense out of either of them.' She lit a cigarette – the third that morning Aurelia noticed, and it was still only seven o'clock. 'There's something going on between them, but they refuse to talk to me.'

Aurelia's scrutiny was sharp. 'What do you suspect?' she demanded.

Alicia looked away. 'Ellie came home from your wedding on her own and locked herself in her room. She wouldn't speak to me or Wang Lee for days. Then she emerged as if nothing had happened and refused to enlighten us.'

'And Charlie?' The tone of Aurelia's voice was ominous. There was something in Alicia's manner that made her uneasy.

'He came back a few days later, and I came across them having a heated exchange behind the barn. They stopped when they saw me and I still don't know what it was about. Charlie then went on muster for three weeks. He was home for about a week after that, then Mickey rang and asked him to go out to Jarrah. I have no idea why, and Mickey was keeping tight lipped about it. Ellie was clearly impatient to see Charlie again, and when he got back from Jarrah they rode off and were gone for nearly two days.'

'It's time I had a word with her,' Aurelia said firmly. 'But first, I'm going to talk to Charlie.'

Alicia's hand stilled her. 'Don't do anything rash, Aurelia,' she counselled.

Aurelia reached for her hat. 'Jack's not here, so it's up to me to sort things out. Just like a man,' she snorted. 'Never around when they're needed. But I will not have secrets in this house, and I'm determined to get to the bottom of this.'

Charlie was sorting out shoes for the horses, the forge lit only by the hot red glow of the fire as he hammered them into shape. His shirt was off revealing the cruel scar down his side, his broad chest slicked with sweat as he worked in the heat.

'Put that down,' Aurelia ordered. 'I want to talk to you.'

He eyed her from beneath his brows, dropped the hammer on the brick fire surround and stepped away from the flames. After smearing the sweat from his forehead he pulled off the leather gloves and tucked them into the pocket of his moleskins. 'What do you want?' he asked with a touch of belligerence.

Aurelia ignored his lack of manners. They had been scratchy with one another ever since he'd hit the priest. She eyed him thoughtfully. Something was different about him, just as it was with Ellie. It was as if the two of them were on edge – waiting for something to happen. She took a deep breath. 'I want to know why Ellie's behaving so strangely.'

'Why ask me?' he muttered. He picked up the wooden ladle and took a long drink from the bucket of water before wiping his mouth with the back of his hand.

Aurelia took two paces towards him, eyed the hammer and thought better of it. Charlie was tense, she could see it in his eyes and in the set of his shoulders. He was suddenly much more than a man with a secret – he was a man cornered.

'Because you seem to be the cause,' she said with her usual bluntness.

His insolent gaze flickered over her. 'As I said before. Talk to Ellie.'

Aurelia was fast losing what little patience she had. 'I'm asking you,' she snapped.

He eyed her from beneath the lock of hair that had drifted over his brow. 'Not my place to tell you,' he said with a secretive smile.

'Then I will ask Ellie,' she snapped. 'I'm determined to get to the bottom of this.'

'Ask me what?' said the voice from the doorway.

Aurelia whipped round as Ellie emerged from the sunlight into the dimness of the forge, her slight figure haloed by the sun's glare at her back. Her gaze softened, the concern for her niece rising in a great tide of affection. 'I was asking Charlie why there has been an atmosphere in the homestead,' she said quietly. 'Your mother and I are concerned.'

'I've had a lot on my mind,' replied Ellie. 'I'm sorry if I've troubled you.'

'Perhaps we should go back to the homestead and talk in private?' Aurelia said with a glance towards the silent, watchful Charlie.

Ellie shook her head and went to stand beside him. 'There's nothing that can't be said right here,' she said firmly. 'Charlie and I are getting married.'

The declaration took Aurelia's breath away. 'Don't be ridiculous,' she gasped.

'I'm old enough to make up my own mind,' said Ellie quietly. 'And as I'm over twenty-one, I don't need your permission.'

'But you don't love him,' declared Aurelia, hoping desperately she was right. 'How on earth could you come to this decision so quickly – and so secretively?'

'Charlie and I are getting married next week. It's all arranged.' Her stare was one of defiance as she waited for Aurelia's response.

'Next week?' Aurelia bellowed. Then she saw the glint of victory in Charlie's eyes, the possessive hand on Ellie's shoulder. There was something very wrong here. Aurelia shivered as the only possible reason dawned. 'Why?' she asked baldly.

Ellie dug her hands in her pockets. She dropped her defiant stare and fixed it on her boots. When she spoke, her voice was just above a whisper. 'Because I'm pregnant.'

Chapter Sixteen

The gasp was like a cold wind sifting through dead leaves. Claire was frozen where she stood. She couldn't look at her mother, couldn't bear to see confirmation in her eyes. For this was the darkest moment she'd known.

'You must put the time and place in context,' Ellie pleaded. 'We didn't have the pill in those days, an illegitimate baby was stained for life. There would have been no proper birth certificate, no rights to an inheritance, no proper registration for work or enlistment into the forces. We had to marry.

'But you didn't love him,' Claire muttered. 'You said so. So why did you do it with him?' She finally dredged up the courage to face her mother, and what she saw was shocking. For Ellie had seem to shrivel and grow old in the past few minutes and her stare was that of a frightened rabbit caught in headlights.

'I ... I...' Ellie stammered. She fell silent. It was obvious she didn't want to answer the question.

Claire looked at Aurelia who was grey with weariness and sorrow. Then to her sister. Leanne was white faced, her green eyes haunted as she sat on the edge of the chair and stared at their mother. Claire regarded Ellie for a long moment. It was as if she was seeing her for the first time, and she was unsure how she felt about that in the light of her revelations.

'I realise you all have many questions, but please, let me finish this before you ask them. It will all become clear very soon and although I know how hard this must be for you, Claire, try and understand how difficult it is for me.'

Claire was trembling. 'Difficult?' she breathed. 'You've lied to me for years and yet you expect me to understand how *difficult* it all is for you?' She sank back into the chair. 'So what else have you lied about?' she said coldly. 'There's obviously more.

It was evening and Ellie and Alicia were arguing as she finished her nightly chores. 'You don't have to do this,' pleaded Alicia. 'Please, Ellie, think about what you're letting yourself in for. Charlie's not the man for you.'

Ellie finished her chores. There was no way out of her predicament. A single girl with a baby would bring disgrace, but Aurelia would feel it the most and she couldn't betray her like that. 'I'm marrying Charlie, and that's an end to it,' she said firmly as she clanged the water buckets and filled them from the standpipe. 'The sooner we do it, the better for the baby.'

'You're marrying him for all the wrong reasons,' Alicia persisted as she followed her around the stableyard.

'He's the father of my child,' she replied.

'Charlie's only marrying you because he wants to get his hands on Warratah,' Alicia snapped. 'He's been poking and prying into Aurelia's safe, reading documents and wills and goodness knows what. If you don't believe me then ask Aurelia. Ask Wang Lee. He was the one who caught him at it.'

'I don't know what you're talking about,' Ellie replied. News of Charlie's snooping had come as a shock and she felt a lurch of uneasiness.

'Then I'll enlighten you,' rasped Alicia. 'We were all out the day Charlie decided to snoop, but Wang Lee knew he was up to something and followed him. He looked through the door and saw Charlie on his knees in Aurelia's room. The floorboards were up, the safe open. He was reading the papers we stored there. The deeds to Warratah and Jarrah, the wills, the trusts. He was almost sweating with excitement.'

Ellie knew she had to maintain a veneer of calm despite what her mother was telling her. 'Charlie loves me,' she insisted. 'And even if...'

Alicia had had enough. 'You don't sound terribly convinced,' she snapped. 'Charlie's greedy. He's seen Warratah, seen you and the way you've hankered after Joe. Now Joe's gone there's nothing standing in his way. Marry you and he's got it all. This baby was a deliberate act, Ellie. I wouldn't mind betting he's been planning it since the first time he set eyes on Warratah.'

Ellie's eyes filled with tears. 'That's a cruel thing to say,' she retorted. 'He wouldn't... He couldn't...' She fell silent as the suspicions crowded in and the truth began to dawn. She felt cold, used and dirty – not just by what had happened that day – but by how easily she'd been taken in. How naive she'd been. Charlie's resentment of his twin went far deeper than she could ever have imagined. His professed love for her merely a means to an end. He would see the consequences of that day as a final victory over his twin – one that could never be challenged. She looked back at her mother, the words she'd wanted to say were ashes in her mouth. 'It's too late,' she said flatly. 'The wedding's arranged, the baby's a fact of life. I have no choice.'

'I wish to goodness Jack would come home,' said Alicia crossly. 'There's far more to this than meets the eye.' She took a deep breath. 'Jack would soon get to the bottom of this if he had a chance to talk to Charlie man to man. I don't know what he's doing in Darwin, but he's way overdue and when he phones he tells Aurelia nothing.'

'This has nothing to do with you or Jack, or even Aurelia,' Ellie said firmly. 'Leave things alone, Mum,' she warned.

Alicia eyed her sharply and Ellie kept her expression bland. 'If you won't talk to me, then talk to Aurelia,' Alicia said with exasperation. 'You cannot go through with this.' She rammed her hands into the pockets of her moleskins and strode away, the frustration apparent in every stride.

'I watched her leave, wishing I had the guts to confide in her. I knew the marriage would be a sham.' Ellie looked down at her hands clasped in her lap. 'But the way things were back then meant my child's future was at stake. He or she would be victimised all through life, and I had no right to deny the child a name and with it a veneer of respectability.' She lifted her gaze to Claire's. 'I had to pay for breaking the rules.'

'But you said Charlie loved you,' said Claire. 'Surely, even...'

'You heard me tell you what he was like. Acquisitive, jealous, possessive,' she snapped without thinking. She bit her lip and made a tremendous effort to remain calm. 'We had once been close,' she said evenly. 'But I couldn't love him the way he wanted. Not after what he'd done.'

'So I was just a pawn in a game?' said Claire into the silence.

'No one really knew what was going on in Charlie's mind,' Aurelia said carefully. 'But you were never a pawn in your mother's eyes. She always wanted you – always loved you.'

'She's lied to me all my bloody life,' snarled Claire. 'My dad's not my dad. My sister's not my real sister, and my mother...' She glared at Ellie. 'My mother's a liar.'

'That's enough,' snapped Aurelia. 'You will not talk about your mother like that, regardless of how hurt you are. Listen to what we're telling you, Claire.'

'Why should I?' she retorted as she stood up. 'I'm surprised you've given me houseroom all these years. You obviously hated my father – but what did he do that was so wrong?' She looked from Aurelia to Ellie and back again. 'He and Mum got carried away after a wedding reception. She regretted it. But at least he was doing the honourable thing and sticking by her. Why should he take all the blame?'

Aurelia was about to reply when Ellie broke into a fit of sobbing. 'Because he was a bastard,' she gasped. 'I hated him for what he did. Hated him more than I've ever hated anyone.'

Claire slumped back into the chair. Her eyes were shadowed with pain, her face white with shock. 'Why?' It was a demand.

It was a troubling time for them all. Mickey Maughan had had a very bad attack of malaria and his weakened heart just couldn't take it. They buried him in his beloved Jarrah soil beside his sons and mourned his passing. He would be missed.

Two days after the funeral Aurelia was sitting at the table in the kitchen with her rifle to hand and Jacky Jack on the back porch with the stockboys in case she needed help. She had discussed this meeting with Alicia and had chosen a time when Ellie was out collecting firewood. Neither of them wanted her coming home in the middle of things.

She watched as Charlie opened the screen door and strolled down the hall into the kitchen. There was a cocksureness about him she didn't like, and his almost insolent expression made her want to spit in his eye. 'Sit down,' she ordered.

Charlie took his time to sit in the hard wooden chair on the other side of the table. He began to roll a cigarette. 'I know what this is about,' he muttered. 'But you're wasting your breath. Neither of us will change our minds.'

Ignoring him, Aurelia spread papers across the table. 'You've already seen most of these,' she said coldly. 'But certain things have been changed since the last time you sneaked into my safe.' She saw the glint of apprehension in his blue eyes and noticed how his hands stilled for an instant before he cupped them to light his cigarette. Despite his nonchalance, she knew she had his full attention. 'I have no rights over Ellie's decision to marry you,' she said. 'But I do have the power to protect her inheritance.'

'What do you mean?' His voice was icy, his arctic gaze fixed on her through the cigarette smoke.

Aurelia glared back at him. She had no intention of enlightening him just yet. He didn't frighten her, and she had the upper hand. 'I have a proposal for you,' she said coldly.

He took the cigarette out of his mouth. 'Let me guess,' he said with heavy sarcasm. 'You wanna buy me off.'

'Exactly. I knew you'd understand.' Aurelia showed him a cheque she'd made out earlier. 'I give you this once the wedding ceremony is over. In return I expect you to leave Warratah and never come back.' She saw his eyes widen as he read the figures on the cheque. Two thousand pounds was a great deal of money – enough to set him up for life. Yet there was something secretive in his eyes and she felt the first tremor of doubt.

'Give me a cheque every year for that amount and I might consider it,' he drawled.

Aurelia had known something like this would happen. 'This is a one-off payment – not a licence to blackmail,' she snapped. 'I've drawn up a legal document with the help of my solicitor. It's a binding contract whereby you receive the money and have no further claim on my estate or Ellie's inheritance. It's to be signed by you before you receive this cheque.'

He read the document slowly as the cigarette burned low between his fingers and ash fell on the floor. Then he shoved the paper back over the table. 'And if I refuse to sign? What makes you think I'd give up all this for a few lousy quid?'

Aurelia pursed her lips. She had known this would be difficult, but she was determined to see it through. 'Two thousand pounds might not seem much after your high hopes of getting your hands on "all this", as you put it. But it's better than the alternative.'

Charlie shifted in his chair, his expression grim, eyes uneasy. 'What are you talking about? What alternative?

'I've changed my will,' she said calmly.

His laugh was harsh, setting her teeth on edge. 'You silly old woman,' he sneered finally. 'Think I don't know you wouldn't see Ellie right? What you gunna do, leave Warratah to a charity, see Ellie on the tramp again?' He shook his head and leaned towards her. 'You don't fool me,' he said quietly. 'Ellie and I will get married and we'll live here with our kid, and there's nothing you can do about it.'

Aurelia found the appropriate page in her will. 'I leave Warratah to my husband, Jack Withers,' she read. 'On his death it is to be passed to my sister Alicia.' She looked up from the document. She didn't need to read it, she knew the words by heart. 'On Alicia's death Warratah is to be held in trust by my solicitors for Ellie's children.'

There was a long silence between them. Charlie smoked his way through another cigarette and Aurelia lit her pipe. They'd reached stalemate, but Aurelia had no intentions of losing this particular game of chess and was willing to wait it out. There was nothing like silence to focus the mind.

'I'll tell Ellie what you've just told me,' he said eventually. 'She won't admire you for it.'

'Please yourself,' she replied stoutly. 'Ellie is a sensible girl, she'll know I have only her best interests at heart.' She leaned across the table, her gaze steady and cold as she looked into his eyes. 'I know she doesn't want to go through with this marriage despite her denials to the contrary. She's doing it to protect the child she's carrying. And don't insult my intelligence by telling me you love her. I know better – and your pathetic attempts to blackmail me have only underlined that fact.'

Charlie's gaze followed her hand as she picked up the cheque and Aurelia saw he was trapped between greed and the disbelief she would disinherit her darling niece. Yet she was prepared to make any sacrifice to protect Ellie, and if things went the way she'd planned, then the new will could be torn up. 'Do we have a deal? she murmured.

The drone of a light plane interrupted the moment and Aurelia took a sharp breath of annoyance. She'd been so close to getting what she wanted. Now the moment was gone and she would have to go through all this again – time was precious – the wedding only days away.

Charlie stood up. 'I'll think about it,' he said as he grabbed his hat. He looked down at her. 'You've got me all wrong, you know,' he said forcefully. 'I do love Ellie. Warratah was just a bonus.'

'One you'll never have,' she replied. 'I don't trust you, Charlie. Never have and never will.'

He laughed then, the secret glint coming once more into his eyes as he smoothed his hair and put on his hat. 'You'll regret that,' he said with the soft sibilance of a snake. 'One day very soon you'll find out just how much I hate you, and you won't be able to do a thing about it.' He chuckled as he turned away, his boot heels rapping on the wooden floor as he slammed out of the house and made his way across the verandah and down the steps.

Aurelia was trembling. There had been a coldness in Charlie that had frightened her. An almost evil glint of malice in his threats. She gathered up the papers and wondered what secrets he was keeping. Then she squared her shoulders and decided it had been an empty threat, for what could Charlie do that could harm her more than marrying her beloved niece? She fixed her monocle and with a grunt of frustration stomped out to meet Jack.

Aurelia waited for him to climb down from the plane. 'Where the hell have you been?' she demanded.

He gathered her into his arms and kissed her. When they came up for breath he held her at arm's length and grinned. 'Nice to know I've been missed,' he drawled. 'But bloody hell,

Aurelia, you should hear the news I've got.'

'Can't be half as bad as the news I've got for you,' Aurelia said stonily. She gave him a short, sharp version of events on Warratah. 'Now you've decided to come home at last, perhaps you can get to the bottom of it all. I've tried, and got nowhere.'

'Can I catch me breath first?' he asked with a twinkle of humour in his eyes. 'I just got back from one of the most hectic visits to Darwin I've ever had, and what I've discovered will make all this nonsense of Charlie and Ellie seem like a storm in a teacup.'

Aurelia snorted. 'Have to be pretty important to do that,' she rasped. 'What exactly are you taking about?'

He gathered up his bags. 'I'll tell you once I've had a cuppa and bit of tucker. I've been traipsing over half Australia the past couple of weeks and I could do with a few home comforts.'

Aurelia frowned. 'Half Australia?' she said. 'Why? I thought you were going to Darwin to see if you could get your old job back?'

'Decided I'd had enough of doing the mail run,' he said excitedly as they headed for the homestead. 'Got in touch with a few mates from the air force and we're starting up our own airline. Qantas have had it their own way for too long. People are always gunna want to get around in a hurry, and the distances here make it almost impossible. We've been thrashing out ideas and are planning to meet up again in about a month's time to sort out the finances. We've all earned a packet during the war and an airline will make good use of the money.'

'So that's the big mystery,' she murmured as she linked her arm through his. 'Thought it was something earth-shattering.'

He looked down at her and smiled. 'Sounds like you're not surprised by my news, darlin'.'

Aurelia laughed. 'I knew you wouldn't be satisfied with running the mail – not after the excitement of war. I've had a suspicion you'd do something like this.' She kissed his cheek. 'Good on you, Jack Withers.'

He looked thoughtful as he glanced across the homestead yard at Charlie and Ellie who were deep in conversation. 'That's not the real news, Aurelia,' he said softly. 'The real news is so astonishing that it will blow you outta the water.' He pulled her close as she looked up and frowned. 'I learned something in Darwin that I'm gunna need you to help sort out,' he said grimly. 'It ain't something I can deal with alone, and we have to move fast.'

'Sounds serious,' she said quietly as Jack made a fuss of a fawning, subservient Kelly. 'How come that blasted bird never bites you?' she said sharply. 'He's been a positive terror lately.'

'Knows who's boss,' Jack drawled as he tickled Kelly under the chin. 'Don't you, mate?'

'Urrgh,' purred Kelly as he offered his neck for more attention.

'Enough with the bird,' Aurelia snapped. 'You can't come home with mysterious news and leave me on tenterhooks. What exactly did you find out in Darwin? And how could it possibly affect us?'

'Patience,' he drawled. 'I need a cuppa to get

411

the dust out of me throat, then I'll tell you everything.'

Aurelia crashed through the screen door. 'Wang Lee,' she yelled. 'Get the tucker on, and bring Jack a cuppa.'

The little Chinaman came shuffling out of the kitchen, the dog at his feet as usual. 'Good see boss home,' he said softly as he bowed a welcome. 'Miss Ellie have bad trouble.'

Jack threw his hat on the table and sat down with a sigh. 'Am I ever gunna get this bloody tea?'

The tea was duly brought along with a pile of sandwiches and a slab of cake. Aurelia sat watching him, her impatience growing until she thought she'd burst. 'Will you please tell me what this is all about?' she demanded as Jack drained his cup and reached for yet another sandwich.

He grinned and took his time to chew through the bread and mutton. 'Wondered how long it would take for that temper to boil over,' he said finally.

'You seem horribly pleased with yourself,' she said through gritted teeth. 'This better be good, Jack Withers, or I'll personally take my bull-whip to your backside.'

He raised an eyebrow, his cheerful grin almost daring her to carry out the threat. Then his expression grew serious. 'Good enough,' he said quietly. 'Or bad enough,' he added mysteriously as he pulled a sheaf of papers from an inside pocket. 'Depends on how you see it – and who it will affect the most.'

She snatched the papers from him and began to read. 'Snowy's alive,' she gasped. 'Thank God. So

412

many of those men never made it further than that awful railway. How is he? Did you get to see him?'

Jack nodded. 'Spirit's up as always, but the bloke's skin and bone. It'll be a while before he's right. Being tied to one place has almost killed his spirit. He's desperate to return home to his tribe.' He leaned back in his chair. 'Snowy's an amazing bloke, Aurelia. He's already making plans to write about his experiences and a publisher in Sydney's offered him a fair amount of money to do it. Reckon he's set up for life.'

Aurelia sighed with satisfaction. 'Good to know some good's come out of the war – I'm glad his missionary education has given him the ability to do something for himself.'

'Read the rest of the documents, Aurelia,' said Jack grimly. 'There's more.'

Aurelia frowned as she returned to the tightly written pages. Then her frown deepened as she scanned the letter that was with them. 'Oh my God,' she gasped. 'It can't be true.'

'I can assure you it is,' he said as he reached for her hand. 'Reckon we got some serious talking to do. The way I see it, things are about to come to a head, and we need to have a clear idea of what to do when it does. Reckon we have a couple of days at most before this busts wide open.'

Aurelia looked out of the window, caught a glimpse of something on the horizon and knew instinctively what it was. 'You've been too optimistic,' she said with despair. 'Looks like we've just run out of time.'

Ellie pulled away from Aurelia and blew her nose. She was ashamed at having broken down like that, but her nerves were frayed and she'd realised some time ago that she'd been unfair to Claire. She deserved to know all of it, regardless of how painful it was, for until she did she wouldn't be able to move on with her life. None of them would.

She pulled herself out of the chair and crossed the room. Taking Claire's cold hand she sat on the arm of her chair and stroked her hair. 'Remember how we joked about the strong Warratah women?' she asked with great gentleness.

Claire nodded, her beautiful blue eyes swimming with tears as she looked up at her mother. Her heart was breaking, and so was Ellie's.

'Then this is the time for both of us to show what we're made of,' she said softly. 'Because the next few minutes will be the hardest either of us will have to survive.'

'Don't,' whispered Claire. 'Please don't say what I think you're about to.'

Ellie took a shuddering breath and closed her eyes. 'I must,' she whispered. 'Then it will be done.'

'Sounds like a good deal to me,' said Ellie as she hoisted logs. 'I get a marriage certificate, the baby gets a name and you get what you wanted. I should take the cheque if I were you.'

This wasn't what he'd expected to hear, and after the humiliation Aurelia had meted out, his temper was rising. 'Why won't you believe I love you?' he said heatedly. 'Why won't you understand that it isn't only Warratah or the money that matter?' He stilled her hands. 'Stop that, and listen,' he ordered.

She pulled away. 'Don't touch me,' she hissed. 'I don't ever want you to touch me again.'

Rage tore through him. 'I bet you wouldn't say that to Joe if he was here,' he stormed.

'You're damn right,' she yelled back. 'Joe was twice the man you'll ever be and he would never have done what you did.'

He almost hit her then, the rage so great he was barely able to keep his hands to himself. 'Joe's dead,' he roared.

Ellie squared her shoulders and looked up at him stonily. 'I know,' she said coldly.

The frustration and years of torment finally boiled over. 'No you don't,' he yelled. 'He's still alive as far as you're concerned. He haunts you, just as much as he haunts me. I had to get rid of him. Had to make you see *me*.' He grabbed her arms, shaking her as if by doing so he could force her to understand. 'Me,' he shouted. 'Me. Charlie.'

Through the red haze of rage Charlie became vaguely aware of the utility coming at speed into the yard. Aware of dark eyes watching from the native humpies and the presence of Aurelia and the others on the verandah. Yet he was beyond reason. His grip on her arms increased and he shouted down into her face. 'Joe, Joe, Joe. I'm sick of playing second fiddle to my blasted twin. It's always been Joe who got the attention. Always Joe who got the good toys when we were kids. Joe who won the school prizes and the teacher's praise. Mum loved him the best and Dad gave him the rifle. Joe got the best horse. Joe got you. And if he hadn't died he'd have had flamin' Warratah as well.'

Ellie was stiff in his grip, her face pale and set. 'It doesn't excuse you for what you did,' she snapped.

He shook her again. 'Joe's shadow's always been between us. I see it every time I look in your eyes. I had to get rid of him. Had to wipe him out of our lives once and for all. He's dead meat, Ellie. Bones buried six foot under. I'm here, warm and alive – I had to make you see *me*.'

Ellie stood pinned against the side of the utility, her eyes sharp with disgust. 'You didn't have to *rape* me to do that,' she yelled. Her voice rose higher and higher until it echoed around the yard. 'Yes, Charlie. You raped me. Had your way with me – took me by force. There's a lot of ways of describing it, but you can't dress it up nicely. It's a dirty word for a dirty act and it's the last time you touch me.'

'Shut up,' he hissed. 'Shut up or I'll...'

He fell silent as Ellie's expression suddenly changed. Her eyes were wide, her mouth gaping. The colour had bleached from her face and there was a blue tinge to her lips. 'Ellie?' he shouted, frantic that somehow he'd really hurt her this time.

Ellie's eyes rolled back and she fell limp in his embrace.

Charlie was turning to look behind him when the fist came from nowhere, smashing into his face, cracking his nose, showering his lips with

416

the warmth of his own blood.

Ellie slid from his arms and crumpled to the ground as strong hands flung him away from her.

Stunned and bloody he looked up and met another punch that jarred his jaw and loosened his teeth. He staggered, the sight before him so bizarre he thought he must be hallucinating. As he blinked he caught another punch on the cheekbone that resounded right through him. The fear was acid in his throat, the spectre too awful to contemplate as another punch sent him reeling. He lost his balance and fell into the dirt. 'No,' he gasped. 'No. You're not real.'

'I'm real enough. Get up and fight you mongrel.' Joe stood before him, his dark hair raven in the sun, his green eyes arctic.

Charlie put up his hands to shield his damaged face as he crawled away from his nemesis. 'You're dead. You're dead,' he moaned in endless repetition as something clicked and slid sideways in his mind.

Rough hands dragged him to his feet, fingers tight on his collar, almost choking him. 'Believe it you bastard. Wanna pick on someone your own size for a change? Show us what a real man you are?' Joe hissed. 'Come on Charlie. Let's see what you're made of when it ain't a girl yer bullying.' He let go of the collar and pushed Charlie away.

Charlie wiped the snot and the blood from his face. His vision was blurred, the fear of seeing his dead twin still clouding his judgement – but the rage was so great he didn't give himself time to think. He brought up his fists as he rocked on his feet and took another two deft punches in the gut as his upper-cut scythed fruitlessly through the air. Winded, he fell back against the utility. There had to be something he could do to beat the bastard – to get rid of him once and for all – but how to stop a ghost? How to fight the demon that had always shadowed him?

He caught sight of the wood Ellie had been chopping and snatched up a tree branch. It was about the length of a club and weighed heavy in his hand. He bent double, feigning a pain in his gut so he could catch his breath, then as the toe of Joe's boot came into sight he used the last of his strength to whip the heavy wooden club in a vicious upward arc. It connected with the side of Joe's head with a satisfying thud, and Charlie thought he heard the crack of bone. He shook the sweat from his eyes and leaned against the utility, his chest heaving from the effort it had taken and the pain it had caused. 'That good enough for ya?' he yelled as Joe went sprawling in the dirt.

Ellie must have come to during the fight, for her screams pierced right through his throbbing head. 'You've killed him,' she screamed. 'You've killed Joe.'

'Nnno,' he stammered as he tried to focus on his brother's still figure. 'Just knocked him out.' He fell to his knees and tried to reach him, but there were people swarming from the native humpies, running from the verandah and barns who shoved him out of the way, blocking off his view of Joe – leaving him isolated and more afraid than he'd ever been.

The fear grew. It was copper on his tongue,

hammering in his ribs as the sweat turned cold and blood congealed on his face. Thoughts and emotions whirled, darkness tore through him as incoherent flashes of something twisted ran through the canyons of his mind. He reached out and tried to touch his twin. 'Joe?' he sobbed. 'Joe. Wake up. I didn't mean it.'

Ellie flew at him, nails clawed as she went for his face. 'You've killed my Joe,' she shrieked. 'You've killed your own brother.' She pounded his chest as he tried to shield himself from her attack.

'I didn't mean to,' he stammered. 'It was an accident. He's not real. He can't be real.'

'Get out,' Ellie screamed. 'Get out and don't ever come back.'

Charlie cowered from the ferocity of her attack as Alicia and Aurelia struggled to get her away from him. He saw how the rest of the people of Warratah eyed him with loathing and knew he had to leave this place he'd once dreamed of owning. He shivered as he thought of a lifetime in prison. Trembled in the coldness of their glares. He had never felt so alone.

'Go,' yelled Ellie. 'I hope you rot in hell for what you've done. You'll never see your baby. Never know it. I'll make sure of that.'

Charlie got to his feet and tried to clear his head of the darkness whirling there. He became aware of the man standing beside him and flinched as his hand touched his shoulder.

'There's nothing here for you. Charlie,' said Jack as Wang Lee dropped down next to Joe and ran expert hands over him. 'But because of what

419

you did for Mickey's son I'm giving you ten minutes to pack up and leave before I call the police.'

Chapter Seventeen

The sun was setting as horse and rider reached the plateau of the guardian hills that surrounded Warratah and Charlie couldn't resist one last look at the land that had so nearly been his. His head throbbed and one eye was almost closed, but he ignored the searing pain in his side and trawled the sprawling acres that seemed to stretch to infinity. The homestead looked so small from here, the scurrying figures like ants. It was as if Warratah was diminishing as he watched – growing distant and ethereal in the orange glow of sunset like a beautiful dream he'd once had.

Ellie was down there. The girl he'd loved and wanted with as much passion as the need for somewhere to call home. The tears rolled down his battered face as he remembered her final, brutal words. Remembered the hatred in her brown eyes that he'd thought had once looked upon him with affection. 'I really did love you,' he whispered. 'I didn't mean to hurt you.' Yet a part of him knew that Warratah had meant more to him, for it had become a symbol of victory over his brother – a victory that now rang as hollow as a death knell.

Charlie sat there until darkness threw a veil over the lush pastures. The raucous laughter of a pair of territorial kookaburras seemed to mock him as he turned his horse towards the northern boundaries of Warratah for the last time. He had no plans – no idea of where he was going.

The only awareness he had was the haunting whisper that sifted through his mind. 'You're the bad seed. You killed your brother. You killed a part of yourself.'

Charlie slumped in the saddle, turning within himself as the darkness filtered into his mind and echoed its torment. The image of his twin was bright flashes in that darkness, the spectral shadow of him following just out of reach and out of sight – yet he knew he was there. Knew he would haunt him for the rest of his days.

The sandstorm had blown up with little warning. It swept across the empty miles of deep red earth in the Northern Territory hunting down anything in its path.

Charlie had spent several months riding aimlessly across the state lines of Western Australia, through the Northern Territory into Queensland and back again. He'd found work on some of the isolated stations, but somehow could never settle – could never find a point of contact with the other men. He knew they thought him strange. Knew they regarded him as something of an enigma. Yet he'd had to keep himself isolated, for no one must know he was a wanted man.

He spent his days looking over his shoulder and his nights dreaming of gunfire and sniper bullets that were interspersed with ghostly images of his twin and Ellie. He found these dreams confusing and very frightening and had become aware of a strangeness within himself as reality seemed to slip from his grasp and leave him in a void of great darkness that was growing increasingly difficult to escape from each time it happened.

He was aware of the darkening sky. Aware of the sudden drop in the wind and the stillness that heralded the approaching storm. Yet the dull pain in his head was all-encompassing and he rode on heedless of the danger. The doctors at the army hospital had warned him this might happen. The bullet fragment was moving – he could feel it – time was running out and he welcomed death.

He finally looked up at the yellow sky and the dark red bruise of the storm's approach. Swinging down from the saddle he slapped the animal's hindquarters and sent it galloping back the way they had come. Then he stood and faced the maelstrom, arms outstretched, daring it to take him.

'Look at me, Joe,' he shouted into the gathering darkness. 'Watch me ride the wind!'

The dust came first. Choking, blinding, swirling and buffeting him until he could barely stand. He closed his eyes, palms open to the sky as the wind tore down on him and whirled him into the vortex of its fury. He was finally free. Flying like the great eagles that soared above this land he loved – and in the blink of one glorious golden eye he knew he would never be tied to the earth again.

Chapter Eighteen

Claire took a long, shuddering sigh and stood up. 'I need to be alone,' she muttered. She walked into the hall and, pushing through the screen door, stepped on to the verandah. Dawn was chasing away the shadows on home yard, bringing light and warmth to Jarrah. Yet the shadows that remained within her were remorseless and chilling. The perfume of flowers and dewed grass a mockery.

Her emotions were in turmoil as she stepped into the yard, yet her feet seemed to know where she had to go. Unaware she'd left her shoes behind, Claire stumbled around the homestead and waded through the long grass. The picket fence still needed mending. The wild flowers and ivy still covered that lonely grave in the corner.

CHARLIE PEARSON
1918–1946
YEA, HE DID FLY UPON
THE WINGS OF THE WIND

Psalm 18

She knelt beside the headstone and wondered if she was like her father, and what she'd have thought of him if they'd met. Yet in her heart she could only despise him. For he had brought a curse on Jarrah and Warratah – a curse that had almost destroyed her mother and everything Claire had known. No wonder he'd been banished to this distant corner.

Turning her back on his last resting place she looked out at Jarrah as the sun brought colour and light to the bluestone homestead. The birds were singing, the crickets rustling, even a few flies hummed in the grass. The outbuildings were coming alive with the sound of men rising from their beds for a new day, and smoke was drifting from the cookhouse chimney. Horses dozed beneath the trees and the remaining blue heelers were stretching and yawning in the kennels. She had once loved this place almost as much as Warratah. But now she hated it. There were too many shadows lurking here – shadows that would always come from that silent gravestone – shadows that perhaps reflected flaws within herself. For his legacy to her was unknown.

As she pushed through the gate she was suddenly filled with a sense of purpose. Crossing the yard she checked the fuel and climbed into the utility. Within moments she had left Jarrah behind her and was heading across the plains. She was in search of peace of mind, freedom, and the strength to forgive. For until she'd found all three, she couldn't return to Jarrah. Couldn't hear the rest of the story. And there was more – she knew it as surely as night would follow day. For there was still the question of her ownership of Jarrah.

Leanne kissed Angel's cheek before she stood and stretched. She was still in shock, yet she burned to know why Mickey Maughan had willed Jarrah to Claire. Eyeing the crumpled Ellie she realised this was not the time. They were all exhausted.

She ran her fingers through her hair and tried to bring some sense to her jumbled thoughts. Claire had to be devastated, and she wondered how it must feel to suddenly learn you weren't who you thought you were. That you were the consequence of rape. Her animosity suddenly felt petty, the words she'd spat with such venom shameful. She'd hurt the people who mattered most, and she wished she could take back those awful words. She lit a cigarette and put it out. It tasted foul and she had a headache lurking. Staring out of the window at the early morning she once again saw how beautiful it was. But that was the magic of Jarrah.

Leanne's thoughts were jumbled as she tried to make sense of everything she'd heard tonight. 'I suspected something was wrong years ago,' she said into the silence. 'And that photograph Aunt Aurelia took. It wasn't all it seemed.' She glanced over her shoulder at Ellie who was wiping away tears. 'When I looked at it closely I realised why Claire asked questions.'

Ellie pulled a rug over Aurelia who had fallen into an exhausted sleep on the couch. 'What did you see?' she whispered.

'I suddenly realised Claire didn't look like any of us,' she said bluntly. 'She's tall like Dad, and in some lights you can see a certain expression that's vaguely familiar. But no one has her eyes, or her colouring – and although you often used to say how she reminded you of Alicia, I could see very little evidence of it from her photographs.'

Leanne's thoughts were slow and tangled. 'I suspect Claire thought she was adopted,' she said finally. 'And after examining that photograph I thought the same. But the truth is much uglier, isn't it?'

Ellie's expression was sad as she led the way into the kitchen and began to make a pot of hot strong coffee. 'I might have known you two girls couldn't be fooled for long,' she murmured. 'You're both far too intelligent.' She took her hand and looked into her eyes. 'I'm sorry about Jarrah,' she said softly. 'But don't make things worse for Claire by blaming her. None of this is her fault.'

'I realise that now,' replied Leanne as the shaming heat rose in her face. 'And I wish I hadn't said all those terrible things to her – or to you. It was unfair and unkind.'

'Yes,' retorted Ellie. 'It was. She's your sister and she's worth more to you than Jarrah. Try to learn to love her without question – the way she's tried to love you.'

The guilt was enormous and Leanne bit her lip, for she knew her mother spoke the truth. She eyed her curiously as she made the coffee. Ellie had always appeared so straightforward, so honest about everything. Yet after last night she was seeing her in a different light. Mum had secrets they wouldn't ever have guessed. A past she'd buried for years that must have tormented her. She couldn't have carried the burden alone. 'Does Dad know the full story?'

427

Ellie glanced at her before looking away. 'He found out eventually,' she whispered.

Aurelia was exhausted by the trauma of the past few hours. She lay snuggled beneath the blanket on the couch, her head pillowed by cushions, dreaming of Jack. Darling Jack, how she'd loved him. Yet he'd broken her heart despite his promises.

The years together had been good for both of them. Jack had started up his airline, and as its popularity grew he'd had to stay away from Warratah more frequently. That was when Aurelia had asked Ellie to take over the station. Warratah had survived the war and the drought and Ellie's trucking business and portfolio of shares would ensure their continued growth. Ellie had turned out to be more than a daughter, but the dearest, closest friend she would ever have and she blessed the day she'd arrived on Warratah.

Sadness crept over her as she realised she was no longer on Warratah. The old homestead would echo with silence, the yards and outbuildings giving off a sense of abandonment beneath the sheltering gums. She wondered how the jarrah blossom had fared against the wind and the rain. Would the white petals drift like confetti over the red earth of home yard as they always did this time of year? Would the roses and bougainvillea wilt? She breathed deeply. The scent of roses was returning, so strongly it was as if they were here in the room.

With a dull ache in her heart she remembered the day Jack had left her. He'd promised to always be there. Had promised they would stay together for ever. Yet the day before his seventy-fifth birthday he wouldn't wake up. He'd slipped away from her during the night and she hadn't even noticed. She had been inconsolable. Had wept bitter tears. Tears of remorse. Tears of pain. Then the anguish had turned to anger. How dared he leave her when he knew how much she loved him? What right did he have to his endless sleep while she still battled on into precarious old age? Then finally had come acceptance, and the certain knowledge that one day they would be together again.

Aurelia was vaguely aware of voices nearby. The voices of people she loved. And she wanted to tell them so. Yet something was drawing her away from Jarrah – away from the voices and the heartache of what had happened tonight, and as she fell deeper into the warm darkness of sleep she smiled. For there was Jack.

Tall and lean with silver hair, his brown eyes were laughing at some private joke as he looked down at her. And there, perched on his shoulder, was Kelly.

'Avast behind,' the cockatoo shrieked. 'Up yer gunnels.'

'That ain't right in front of a lady,' murmured Jack as he stroked the white feathers.

'Urrgh,' muttered Kelly as his yellow coxcomb fanned with mischief.

Jack laughed. 'He's still the same old Kelly,' he said with affection. Then he drifted closer and Aurelia thought she could smell his favourite cologne.

'Jack?' she murmured. 'Where have you been? I've missed you.' The words were a sigh.

Jack smiled as he held out his hand. 'I've been waiting for you my darlin',' he whispered. 'Come, Aurelia. Let's take a walk.'

Aurelia felt the rough warmth and strength in his hand that was so gloriously familiar. She didn't look back. For this was what she'd been waiting for.

He smiled down at her and tucked her hand in the crook of his arm. 'Did I ever tell you how much I love you, darlin'?'

She nodded, and together they walked joyfully into the bright, warm light.

Leanne had gone out to supervise the day's work, leaving Ellie alone in the kitchen. She sipped her coffee. It was strong and black, but did little to invigorate her or lift her spirits. For the sleepless night compounded by the retelling of the story had bankrupted her of strength and all she really wanted to do now was get into bed and curl up like a child and go to sleep. It was a way of escaping. A way of blocking out the harsh reality of life and the damage she and Charlie had caused. Yet how much more difficult must it be for Claire? The girl would have to come to terms with so many things – few of them pleasant.

With a sigh she put down her coffee and smeared away the tears. She had to remain strong. Had to live up to the reputation of the Warratah women. For she was a mother – a wife – the one person they would look to for strength and comfort. She couldn't let them down. Not when they needed her the most.

As Ellie sat there in the early morning beam of light she suddenly realised Charlie no longer had the power to hurt her. No longer had the strength to overshadow her life. Their secret was out – the consequences the next hurdle to face. She was ready to do battle for those she loved. Ready to vanquish the past and come out of this mess untarnished and unbowed. The women of Warratah would not be defeated.

Hunger pangs gnawed and she realised none of them had eaten for hours. The girls would be starving when they got back. As she busied herself at the stove, she cocked her head and grinned. Aurelia was making the most dreadful racket. Her snoring was reminiscent of a sty full of pigs and she was amazed she hadn't woken herself up.

Minutes later she stilled. The stentorian snores had come to an abrupt halt. Ellie took the frying pan off the hob and listened. The silence was ominous. She raced into the sitting room and fell to her knees beside the couch. 'Aurelia?' Her tone was sharp, filled with anxiety.

Aurelia lay still beneath the rug, her hand lying at her side, the palm open as if she was reaching for something. There was a smile on her face of such sweet contentment Ellie knew she'd gone. Aurelia had seen her through the worst of it. Had stayed long enough to give the support and love she'd always given. Now she'd had enough. Jack had called her to him and she must have gone willingly.

Ellie's tears coursed unheeded down her face as

she took the hand and kissed it before tucking it beneath the rug. She rested her head on the still shoulder and closed her eyes. Aurelia had been mother and father to her, had loved her without question and guided her into maturity. There would never be anyone like her again and after the trauma of the night this was all too much. 'You don't need me to tell you how much we all love you,' she sobbed. 'But I want to thank you. Thank you for always being there. Thank you for loving me and my family. Thank you for just being you.'

Ellie knelt by the couch as the tears flowed. The old homestead at Warratah would seem so empty and lifeless now she'd gone, for Aurelia and Jack had figured large in everything that had happened there. They had been her rock – her protection against all ills – her solace and her haven when times had become almost too hard to bear.

Ellie sat on the floor of Jack's plane, her whole being fixed on the man who lay next to her as they touched down and came to a halt beside the waiting ambulance. He was so still, so pale, so thin. Yet a meagre throb of life pulsed at his throat and she willed it to remain. Joe had come back to her. Joe had kept his promise. Surely fate wouldn't be so cruel as to snatch him away again?

Jack clambered over the stretcher and unfastened the door. The furnace blast of Darwin's humidity was almost suffocating after the dry heat of the cabin and as she helped Snowy lift out the stretcher her clothes clung damply to her skin, the sweat stinging her tear-swollen eyes.

'You gotta let him go, luv,' said Jack softly as the doors were slammed and the ambulance raced down the dirt road to the hospital. 'They'll know what to do, and we'll only get in the way.'

She nodded, knowing he was right, yet wishing she was at Joe's side as the cloud of dust trailed the racing ambulance. They would already be working on him, fighting for his life – their knowledge and skill so very much more important to Joe than her anxious, tearful presence.

The heat battered them as they walked down that long road to the white bungalow nestled in an oasis of palm trees and lush ferns. The sweat rolled down her back, plastering her shirt to her skin as she focused on the hectic activity following the ambulance's arrival.

'He'll be right,' muttered Snowy as he loped alongside her. 'They know what they're doing here and I should know – been here long enough, me and Joe.'

Ellie stared up at him. 'You were here? And you didn't let me know?'

Snowy glanced across to Jack then down at his feet as they climbed the verandah steps and pushed through the screen door. 'It was touch and go,' he murmured. 'I didn't want to raise your hopes. Joe was fair crook.'

'He was well enough for you to drive him all the way to Warratah,' she snapped. 'Why didn't you warn me?' Her face crumpled as shock took hold. 'I thought he was dead. I finally believed he was never coming home.' She lifted her tear-stained face to him. 'Can you imagine how I felt when he

433

just appeared like that?'

Jack's arm went round her shoulders as she collapsed against his chest. 'It was my fault,' he murmured. 'I knew Joe was coming home, but I had no idea of what had been going on back at Warratah and thought I had time to prepare you.' He fell silent for a long moment. 'Joe wanted me to tell you face to face – not over the two-way radio or by letter. He knew what a jolt it would be.'

'G'day, Jack.' The voice drew Ellie from his embrace and she smeared away the tears. She had to be strong. Had to be prepared for yet another devastating blow. Yet she was almost bankrupt of spirit – at her lowest ebb.

The doctor was elderly, with a shock of white hair and steel glasses perched on the end of his nose. 'He's in poor shape, Jack. What the hell happened?'

'Got in a fight,' said Jack quickly before Ellie could speak. 'What's the damage?'

His mouth formed a tight line of disgust. 'Had no bloody business getting into fights. Ended up with a fractured skull,' he replied flatly. 'There's the possibility of an internal bleed so I'm taking him straight into theatre.'

'But he'll be right, won't he?' asked Ellie fearfully.

Grey eyes regarded her solemnly, the face creased with concern. 'He's been through worse,' he said softly. 'But coming on top of everything else, this isn't good news. Don't expect too much. We do our best here, but miracles don't come easy.' He turned on his heel, slammed through the swing doors and was gone.

Ellie followed Snowy and Jack to the verandah. A mistral breeze wafted along the dusty floorboards, the cool green shadows of the surrounding bush and the cries of the colourful birds making it a pleasant place to sit after the searing heat. Yet Ellie was restless, unable to put her mind to anything but what was happening in the operating room. She paced the verandah, stared out at the broad dirt road that led into town, watched the bright birds flit amongst the ferns and tried not to think about what she would do if the worst happened and she lost him again.

'Aurelia and yer mum will be here soon,' said Jack from the depths of the cane chair he was sprawled in. 'Head stockman's bringing them up.'

Ellie nodded and resumed her pacing, arms tightly folded around her waist, boots tapping out a rhythm on the bare boards. She didn't care if the whole of Queensland turned up. She was an island. Nothing could touch her – nothing could thaw the ice around her heart – or wipe away the images of what had happened today.

She finally stopped pacing, her hands deep in her moleskin trousers, her thoughts clear. There were questions she needed answering. She crossed the verandah and stood squarely before Jack. 'How long have you known Joe was alive?'

'About a week,' he replied as he dry scrubbed his face with his hands. 'I bumped into Snowy here in Darwin and he told me. I meant to get back sooner, but I needed a spare part for the

435

plane and had to wait around for it to be trained up from Sydney.'

She turned to the Aborigine who was leaning against the verandah rail post. 'You could have written,' she said flatly. 'Could even have sent the priest. Why didn't you?'

His amber eyes looked down at her, the caramel coloured face lined with defeat and weariness. 'Remember me telling you the Dreamtime story about the sick spirit and how it has to travel like a pilgrim until it finds peace?' He acknowledged her nod with one of his own. 'Joe's spirit was dying, his pilgrim soul was floating in the darkness between life and death, waiting for someone from the Land of Perfection to come and rescue him. The spirits were singing him, Ellie. Calling him to rest. He had to choose which path to take. Had to decide if he was ready to listen to their song.'

'Don't give me that bullshit,' she snapped. 'Dreamtime fairy tales are all very well, but Joe needed me and I needed him. You had no right to keep this from me.'

Snowy's amber eyes closed and his nostrils quivered as he took a trembling breath. 'The song he heard was from you, Ellie. Your belief that he would keep his promise to return home was all that kept him going in the camp. He didn't want you to see him as he was when he came back – he wanted to be whole again.' His gaze rested on her, stilling her, holding her there on the verandah. 'He didn't know he'd been classed as missing presumed dead until long after we'd been liberated. He understood what it would mean to you if he suddenly just appeared out of the blue. It was his decision to keep the news from you until he was well enough to find a way of telling you.'

He spent a moment rolling a smoke, and when he'd lit it he inhaled deeply. The shadows of his experience on the Burma railway darkened his eyes and etched deep lines either side of the broad nose and mouth. 'Me and Joe came out of that hell-hole barely alive. We were skeletons, our flesh eaten away by starvation, dysentery and malaria. We were ghosts of men. Naked and stripped of all humanity, we had become nothing. Yet the need to survive is the most powerful weapon a man can have. Even if he's become less than the crawling ant, that will to survive remains his strength. That pulled us through.'

Snowy moved away from the verandah post and took her hands. The skin was calloused and rough on his fingers and palms, the scars tracing white lightning strikes deep into the brown flesh. 'You thought he was dead – and to all intents and purposes he was,' he said softly. 'Joe didn't want you to see him like that. Didn't want to raise your hopes to have them dashed again in a second mourning. He loves you too much.'

Ellie sank into a chair and with a tremor of something akin to horror she realised Joe's wisdom in keeping his return secret. Yet fate had decided to twist the knife – to punish them both once more before she decided which way things would turn out. And Ellie could do nothing about it but keep singing the song of hope – the song Joe had heard against the backdrop of a distant jungle – the song that had brought him home.

She regarded Snowy for a long moment, trying to imagine what they had gone through and the strength and courage it must have taken to survive such brutality. She noticed how thin he still was, how grey the halo of brown, tangled hair had become – and how aged his eyes were. They were the eyes of a man who had seen things no man should see. Eyes of a man who had witnessed what hell was like and who would carry that image with him until the earth sung him to his final sleep.

The others arrived in the cold, clear darkness of the outback winter night and they gathered in the tiny waiting room that had been built as an extension to the hospital bungalow. Joe had been in theatre for over five hours, and there was still no word. Aurelia had brought a hamper of food and four thermos flasks of hot, sweet tea to keep up their spirits. The cold chicken and mutton was passed round with chunks of damper bread liberally spread with thick chutney and they ate in silence.

'You must eat,' she said softly to Ellie. 'It's not good for you or the baby if you starve yourself and you need something inside you to ward off the shock of everything that's happened today.'

Ellie came out of her trance-like state, her eyes wide in horror as she looked at her aunt. She'd forgotten about the baby. Forgotten what it would mean to any future she might have with Joe once he discovered the consequences of Charlie's rape. Charlie's name reverberated in her head, bringing back the awful clarity of her situation. Then she became aware of four pairs of eyes regarding her with concern and felt the blood drain from her face as she realised she could never expect Joe to take on his own twin's bastard.

What an ugly name for an innocent child that had yet to be born. What a legacy Charlie had left in the guise of the helpless infant that had come from a bad seed – a seed of sorrow that could only be harvested in tears. For the child's presence would always be a reminder of rape. A reminder of murder if Joe didn't survive.

'Why did you let Charlie go?' she asked Jack coldly. 'Why did you leave him free when he deserved to be punished for what he's done?'

Jack glanced across at Aurelia who took his hand and clasped it tightly in her lap. 'The boy was sick, Ellie, and I gave him only a few minutes' head start before I called the coppers,' he began hesitantly. 'It was probably the wrong decision but it was the least I could do under the circumstances.'

Ellie got to her feet and stood over him, fists at her sides, the rage making her tremble. 'What circumstances, Jack? The rape, or the attempted murder? Which one of the two was unimportant enough for him to escape justice?'

'Neither,' he admitted. 'But Charlie had little idea of what he'd done – has no sense of right and wrong any more. He was damaged by what he'd been through in the war and police and prison cells, courtrooms and a trial wouldn't change that.' His eyes were tortured as he looked

439

up at her. 'What he's done to you and Joe is unforgivable and you will both have to learn to live with that for the rest of your lives. But so does Charlie. He's been on the road to self-destruction ever since he came back to Jarrah with Seamus. And because of what he did for Seamus, I felt I owed him at least ten minutes more freedom.'

'My heart bleeds,' hissed Ellie with cold sarcasm.

'He won't get far,' Jack said wearily. 'He's a broken man with nowhere to turn and no one to care what happens to him. The ten minutes I gave him were illusory – he won't escape justice. It might not be the justice you're thinking of, but it will be justice enough.'

Ellie glared at him and began to pace. 'I hope they catch him,' she snarled. 'I hope they lock him away for ever.' The silence that greeted this pronouncement made her stop pacing and she eyed each of them in turn. 'What is it you're not telling me?' she demanded. 'What could possibly excuse him?'

Ramming his hands into the pockets of his moleskins Jack stood up and gazed into the night. The moon was bright, veiled sporadically by drifts of grey white cloud and the fronds of the giant ferns that grew in the hospital garden. 'Charlie came home to Warratah to die,' he said quietly.

Ellie slumped into a chair, her eyes wide in disbelief, her tone coldly dispassionate. 'His injuries were bad, but not life-threatening. He was riding again within months and working in

440

the forge soon after that.'

Jack remained staring out of the window into the darkness as his soft drawl filled the silent room. 'Charlie and Seamus were caught in the barrage at El Alamein. Seamus was badly injured and Charlie put his own life in danger by trying to get him to the field hospital.' He sighed. 'Charlie was a hero that night. Not only did he carry Seamus on his back across the battlefield, he'd also tried to save his sergeant. That poor man was torn in two, but Charlie thought he had a real chance of getting Seamus to the medics' tent. They were within sight of the dark green canvas when a sniper's bullet caught Charlie in the side. Another glanced across his temple. Charlie felt no pain. He hardly realised he'd been hit in his determination to get Seamus to safety.'

Jack fell silent for a long moment. 'Seamus was dead. The sniper's bullet had found its mark, torn through his head and glanced off Charlie's. Charlie's physical wounds would heal eventually, but the doctors couldn't remove the tiny piece of bullet that had embedded itself deeply into his brain. It was a time bomb. One that could shift and trigger death at any moment.'

'The damage was two-fold,' he said softly. 'For it had taken away the essence of the real Charlie. Had warped his sense of right and wrong and enhanced the dark side of his nature.' Jack took a deep breath as he finally turned to face her. 'I don't expect you to forgive him,' he said quietly. 'But try and understand why he did what he did.'

Ellie folded her arms around her waist and rocked back and forth, her eyes closed, her

441

thoughts in turmoil. Fate had decreed they should meet all those years ago on that long, lonely road to Cloncurry – but what a terrible price they'd all had to pay.

The operation had been successful in so far as the haemorrhage in the brain had been stopped and the crack in his skull was beginning to knit. Yet Joe remained pale and still against the pristine hospital pillows, the snowy bandages emphasising the shadows beneath his eyes and the frailty of those lightly veined eyelids.

'You must come home and rest,' urged Aurelia. 'It's been almost three months now and you're making yourself ill.'

Ellie yawned and put down the magazine she must have read at least a dozen times. 'I'm not leaving until he wakes up,' she said firmly. 'I want to be the first person he sees.'

'And what about the baby?' Aurelia crossed her arms beneath her bosom and eyed her sternly through the monocle. 'It can't be good for the poor little thing with you moping about indoors. You aren't eating properly and not getting enough fresh air and exercise. You'll have a hard time when it comes to giving birth.'

Ellie flicked a glance to Joe. The doctor had said he might be able to hear what they were saying, and had encouraged her to talk to him. Yet there had been no response when she'd read his favourite books or pieces of poetry. No recognition or reaction when she kissed his cheek and whispered that she loved him. Yet despite all this, she couldn't chance him overhearing this conversation – didn't want anything to hamper his recovery. 'Let's go outside,' she said quietly. 'We can talk there.'

Minutes later Aurelia sank into the verandah chair. 'What's the matter?' Her grey eyes were concerned, her tone no-nonsense.

Ellie laced her fingers over the burgeoning mound of her stomach and watched the passing traffic. She didn't want to voice her fears that Joe might not want her now she carried another man's child. 'Dr O'Neil says I'm doing fine. I could probably do with putting on some weight and he's given me a course of iron tablets.' She sighed as she squinted into the sun. 'I could certainly do with some fresh air and exercise, I hate being cooped up here. But until Joe wakes up I must stay.'

'And if he doesn't? What then?'

'He will,' she said defiantly. 'He promised to come home and he did. He'll wake up when he's ready.'

'Some patients never come out of their coma,' Aurelia warned. 'He could stay like this for years until his organs pack up and his heart gives out. You must face reality, Ellie. You can't go on like this.'

Ellie wriggled out of the chair and stood up. Her back was beginning to ache from all the sitting around and she didn't want to hear the gruesome details. 'I won't have defeatist talk from you or anyone else,' she said flatly. 'I know the reality of the situation all too well, but as long as there's hope I'm staying.'

'What about when it's time for the baby to

arrive? Are you going to stay here in Darwin in that hotel and struggle on alone? Or are you coming home where we can look after you both?'

'I'll cross that bridge when I come to it,' she replied stubbornly.

They talked for another half an hour and Ellie finally had had enough. She had left Joe for too long and this conversation was going nowhere. As she was pushing through the screen doors she bumped into a hurrying Dr O'Neil. 'There you are.' His lined face creased into a warm smile. 'Come on. He's awake.'

Ellie stared at him in disbelief. She'd waited so long to her those words – now it was as if she was rooted to the floor. Then joy released her and she was pushing through the doors and almost running down the corridor to Joe's room.

He was propped up on pillows, his eyes still bleary with sleep. The turban of bandage had been replaced by a pad of cotton and plaster strips and the colour was returning to his face. His dark lashes fluttered and his green eyes sought her out. 'Ellie?' he rasped. 'Is that really you?'

'His throat will be sore for a while, and he'll tire very easily,' murmured the doctor. 'So make this a short visit and give him time to recover more fully.'

Ellie nodded, but her whole being was centred on the man in the bed. Her Joe was alive again. Alive and breathing and within reach. She stepped into the room and approached the bed, hands reaching out for him, aching for him to hold her again.

The green gaze drifted to the swollen belly, stilling her as it travelled back to her face. There was confusion and hurt there – a pain that transmitted itself into her very core. 'Ellie?' he whispered. 'Tell me it's not true.'

It took all her strength to remain calm. 'I'm expecting a baby. But it's not what you think,' she said softly. 'And when you're better I'll explain.' She took his hand, willing him to try and understand.

There was no response – merely the cold green gaze of hurt bewilderment.

Ellie was in despair. She needed to say so many things, but the pain in his eyes told her he wouldn't listen. He had condemned her without trial or fair hearing. This was not the Joe she loved. Not the Joe she remembered. Yet how could she blame him? She was used goods – carrying his own brother's child. 'Don't you remember coming back to Warratah?' she asked hesitantly. 'Don't you remember the fight with Charlie and what it was about?'

Joe remained unresponsive, his eyes cold and accusing.

'Snowy brought you home,' she persisted. 'You both turned up when Charlie and I were having a row. You must remember what that was about. Please,' she said desperately. 'You've got to remember.'

He frowned, his gaze once more travelling to the swell beneath her shirt. 'You said you'd wait for me,' he whispered. 'You promised.'

Ellie flinched as he drew his hand from her grasp and turned on his side. 'Joe,' she begged.

'Please Joe. I can explain.'

There was no response.

The hand on her shoulder was warm, but firm. 'I think we'll leave him to sleep for a while, Ellie,' said Dr O'Neil. 'He's obviously confused and there appears to be some memory loss. Don't torture yourself by staying here. Go home and rest. Look after that baby and we'll look after Joe.'

'But he has to remember what happened,' she insisted. 'He must have heard what I said to Charlie or he wouldn't have come piling in like that. Surely he can't have forgotten what the fight was about?'

Dr O'Neil sighed. He knew the story from Aurelia. 'He's been very ill and there was some damage to the brain. Hopefully this amnesia will only be temporary, but I have to warn you that sometimes in cases like these the patient blocks off any incidents that are too painful and never regains full memory.'

'So what do I do?' She had never felt so helpless.

'Go home with your aunt. Leave Joe to recover in his own time and I will do my best to help him restore his memory. I'll keep in touch and let you know how we progress, but your presence here will only hinder his recovery.'

Hinder his recovery. The words rang in her head. This was not what she'd expected. Not the awakening she'd longed for over the past three months. She moved in a trance towards the door, and as she stepped over the threshold she turned back. 'Goodbye, Joe,' she said through her tears.

'Keep listening to our song and hold on to the thought that I love you, and that I did wait – despite appearances to the contrary.'

Chapter Nineteen

Claire hadn't noticed where she was heading. Her mind was on what she'd learned through the long, bitter night, and the consequences they would have on her family. Yet, as she'd caught sight of Warratah's outbuildings she wasn't really surprised. It was home – the one place she felt she could find solace – the one natural sanctuary.

Now, as she roamed through the little wooden house, she caught the spirit of the people who lived there – heard the voices – and remembered the love and security. She traced her fingers over well worn furniture, picked up photographs and letters, favourite books and ornaments, and all the while she felt she was taking repossession of her place within this family – this home. For her deepest dread had been that she didn't belong. That she wasn't one of them. A waif taken in by strangers, given a name and an identity that she had no right to.

Curling her feet beneath her, she snuggled into the corner of the couch, a fat cushion clasped in her arms, her hair drifting over her face as if to shut out the world and the sunlight. The truth had been harsher than she ever could have guessed. And yet how much more traumatic it had to be for Mum in the retelling of such a terrible tale? She took a deep, trembling breath and closed her eyes. The dream she'd had the other night had come true. This was her battle after the calm, her barrier of thorns which she had to vanquish before she could find the courage to forgive and step back into the light.

A deep calm came over her as she sat there in the silence. A calm that brought peace and the knowledge that she was strong enough to accept what fate had dished out. Her life had been happy until now. She was loved and wanted, the skeletons all in the open. There were no ghosts any more, nothing to shadow her footsteps and make her look over her shoulder.

The soft tap on the screen door didn't startle her, and when she saw who was standing there she realised she was glad to see him. 'G'day, Matt. What are you doing here?'

He ran his hand through his hair making it stand on end. 'You asked me for dinner,' he said as he shifted from one foot to the other. 'But I reckon you must have forgotten.' His hazel eyes had lost their spark, and he reddened as he twisted his hat.

Claire pulled him into the room. 'I'm sorry, Matt. You caught me on the hop. I don't even know what there is in the fridge.'

He eyed her with concern. 'What's the matter, Claire? You look crook.'

She tried to laugh her worries away, but knew he hadn't been convinced. 'Bit of a family upset,' she said with forced lightness. 'No worries.'

He put a finger beneath her chin and despite her reluctance, made her look at him. 'I thought you trusted me?' he said with a sweet softness. 'Has someone upset you? Talk to me, darlin'. Tell me what's made you look so sad.'

Claire sank into the soft couch and drew her knees to her chest. She began to speak as he sat beside her, and as the words began to flow she felt the tensions of the previous night lift, and knew the ghosts of the past were fading fast.

Matt remained silent until she'd finished speaking. Then without a word he enfolded her in his arms and held her close. Claire could hear the beat of his heart. Could feel the warmth and strength emanating from him and knew he understood. Knew it didn't matter where she'd come from or what she was. For this wonderful man loved her.

The sun was waning when they finally drew apart. 'I have to get back to Jarrah. Mum and the others will worry, and I need to tell them I'm okay.'

'Phone them,' he suggested. 'It's too far to drive, and I know it's selfish, but I'd like to be with you for a while longer.'

Claire shook her head. 'I want to see them. Talk to them. The phone is too impersonal.'

'Then I'll fly you over there,' he said firmly. 'I'm not risking you driving all that way in the state you're in.'

She looked up at him, the humour in her eyes and at the corners of her mouth. 'I hardly know you,' she murmured. 'We met less than a week ago – but somehow it's as if...'

He kissed her with a delicious softness that made her pulse race. 'As if we've always known one another,' he murmured. 'Yes. I feel it too.'

They arrived on Jarrah an hour later, and knew immediately something was wrong. The strange stillness of home yard was mirrored in the Aborigine women who were sitting around the fire, their faces and hair covered with white clay. Someone had died.

They quickly scrambled down from the plane and ran to the homestead. All the curtains were closed. Claire's mouth was dry, the fear beginning to rise. 'Mum?' she called as she pushed through the screen door.

Leanne met them in the hall. 'It's Aunt Aurelia,' she said as she glanced at Matt and put her arm around her sister. 'She's gone, Claire.'

'But she can't...' She fell into silence. Aurelia was old, and despite her appearance, had been plagued with arthritis and a dodgy heart condition – her time had come as it would for all of them. Yet the news of her death coming so swiftly on top of everything else left her weak. Aurelia had always been a tower of strength, not only to her but to all of them. It seemed impossible to imagine life on Warratah without her. 'How's Mum taking it?' She finally eased from her sister's embrace.

'On the chin as always,' replied Leanne. 'Yet she must be feeling crook. Aurelia was everything to her.'

'Are you going to be all right, Claire?' Matt stood in the gloom of the hall, his eyes troubled.

She nodded. 'You'd better get back,' she murmured. 'I'll be fine.' Her smile was wan as she kissed his cheek. 'And thanks for today.'

Matt hugged her then left. Claire took off her

hat and wiped the sweat from her face. It was hot outside, but the heat was rising in the house and the almost sweet smell of death was already present. 'Has someone gone to fetch Dad?' she asked.

Leanne nodded. 'I sent one of the boys. He'll meet us back at Warratah.' She hesitated, her green eyes troubled. 'I don't care if we have different fathers,' she blurted out. 'You're my sister, and I'm sorry I've been such a bitch.'

Claire's breath was a sob as they hugged. 'I love you too,' she said. 'And don't worry about Jarrah. I've thought of a way you can keep it.' They looked at one another and smiled. The ties were strong and invincible despite their stormy history – nothing would change that.

The sitting room was almost in darkness, the light coming only from the candles on the fire mantel. Shadows danced on the walls and ceiling, glinted in glass and copper and on Ellie's tears. She looked up as the girls came into the room and they saw the pain in her eyes. 'I was waiting until you came back, Claire,' she murmured. 'I'm so glad you have.'

Claire kissed her mother's tear-stained cheek. 'Let's go home,' she breathed.

Angel landed the plane as long shadows crept over Warratah. Birds were gathering, swooping in clouds of colour as they came home to roost in the trees and the tiny bush wallabies were loping out of the shrub to drink at the waterhole. Warratah was somnolent at the end of another scorching day. Its buildings settled and golden in the last of the light, the red earth of the yard

452

softened by the creeping shadows.

As the women stepped down they were met by Warratah's Aborigines and the three men who'd been left to look after things during the bullock muster. With solemn care they lifted out the roughly hewn wooden coffin and carried it into the old homestead. Death had come so swiftly there hadn't been time to do much but have Jarrah's carpenter knock the coffin together, but they all knew it didn't matter for Aurelia had never been one to stand on ceremony.

The old homestead already looked abandoned. The steps were off true, the corrugated roof drooping like sleepy eyelids over the deeply shadowed verandah. The windows were dusty, the paintwork peeling on the wooden walls. Yet the roses and the trailing flowers gave it an air of comfort, of restorative energy, and their scent was almost overpowering. Jessie stood in the doorway, her face white with clay, the traces of her tears on her cheeks.

She stood back as the men carried the coffin into the lounge and laid it gently on the board that had been placed between two chairs. 'Earth sing her, missus,' she said sorrowfully to Ellie. 'Jessie knowed. Sing alonga me in night. Missus boss sing 'im to sky.'

Ellie patted her arm, too exhausted to speak. She eased the sling and struggled to light the candles. Now she had to find the strength to keep the long vigil through the night, for Aurelia would be buried early tomorrow. The outback heat didn't allow for a long period of mourning – the vast distances involved meant there would be few visitors.

She became aware of Leanne and Claire taking charge. Jessie was sent to make something to eat, and the endless ringing telephone was answered swiftly. News travelled fast here in this great Never-Never and Aurelia was well-known and admired. Ellie cradled her broken arm, leaned back in her chair and closed her eyes. Bringing Aurelia home was the last thing she could ever do for her beloved aunt and she knew it was the only place her spirit would rest.

The homestead was shrouded in darkness, the flickering candles sending dancing shadows across the still, waxen face. Ancient timbers creaked and settled, the scurry of a possum on the roof and the soft swish of foliage from the trees against the windows were the only evidence of the outside world as the three women waited for the morning. Yet Aurelia's spirit remained strong within those wooden walls. Her presence felt in every shadow and corner.

The girls talked about their childhood and Aurelia's influence. Ellie recounted her kindnesses, her energy and resilience. They talked of Jack and even Kelly, for the cockatoo was as much a part of Aurelia as the monocle and brogues. The tears were abating as the fond memories took over. For they knew she would always be with them.

'I hope Dad makes it in time,' said Leanne as the clock on the mantelpiece struck three.

'He'll do his best,' replied Ellie. 'It just depends on how far out of Jarrah he was when he got the message. But I sent the plane back for him, so he

454

should be here soon.'

Leanne poured more coffee from the pot Jessie had left on the dresser and handed round the mugs. 'Matt phoned,' she said with studied nonchalance. 'Sorry, I forgot to tell you. He's flying in tomorrow to pay his respects.'

Ellie noticed how her daughter blushed. Despite all the terrible things she'd learned in the past twenty-four hours Claire still had the strength to overcome – to keep hold of the things that mattered. 'I suppose I should tell you how and why Jarrah was left to Claire,' she said as the coffee began to chase away the weariness.

'Only if you feel up to it,' said Leanne as she looked across to her sister and smiled. 'Claire and I will sort things out between us eventually.'

Ellie looked at both her lovely daughters. She was proud of them for their stoicism and resilience. 'I'm glad there's no more ill-feeling between you,' she murmured. 'Charlie would have won otherwise.'

She saw them frown and knew she had to explain. 'Mickey was devastated when my mother turned down his proposal. He knew he only had a short time to live, but he hadn't wanted to put my mother into the position of accepting him through pity, so kept quiet. With Seamus gone there was no one to pass Jarrah to. He'd considered Aurelia, but knew she and Jack had other plans, so when he heard Charlie and I were getting married he decided to repay Charlie for what he'd tried to do for Seamus.' She sighed. 'Poor Mickey. He thought he'd found the perfect solution.'

'He left Jarrah to Charlie?' Leanne paled as her gaze sought her sister. 'But they both died before Claire was born. How come you didn't inherit?'

Ellie stared beyond the coffin into the flickering shadows. 'Owning Jarrah gave him the opportunity to get back at me for not loving him, and at Aurelia for distrusting him. He knew our marriage would be a sham. Knew he was dying from his war wound. It would be his final revenge for all the imagined slights and hurts.' She looked at the girls and realised she hadn't told them what Jack had revealed that day at the hospital.

Claire paled as Ellie finished recounting Charlie's war history. 'So he wasn't really bad?' she said with hopeful softness.

Ellie smiled back at her, masking her true thoughts. 'No, darling. No one is all bad. He was just confused and bitter, and hit out without really understanding the damage his bequest could do.' She watched her daughter, knowing the white lie would bring her some comfort.

'Did he go to prison?' Claire bit her lip, her eyes fearful.

Ellie shook her head. 'He died in a dust storm somewhere out in the Territories. His body was found eventually and identified by the Victoria Cross they found in his pocket. He had no one else, so we agreed to bury him on Jarrah.' She fell silent for a moment, remembering that simple ceremony in the quiet graveyard. It had been an emotional home-coming – one that had been unwelcome.

'Charlie wrote a will shortly after Mickey died, and once his body had been identified, the

456

solicitor was free to reveal the full impact of it. We already knew Mickey had willed Jarrah to Charlie, but the solicitor informed us Charlie had left the station in trust for his unborn child – you, Claire – on your twenty-fourth birthday. And must be handed down to your children on your death. I was to have no part of Jarrah, and neither was Aurelia. It was his final defiance.'

Claire emitted a deep sigh. 'It doesn't matter any more,' she said. She turned to Leanne and took her hand. 'I'm going to get a solicitor to try to revoke the trust. If I can't, then I'll make one of my own and put the whole thing in trust for Leanne's children as well as mine. Leanne will have a life interest in Jarrah which will pass on to the next generation.' She gave a weary smile. 'That's if there is one – and if they want to be tied to Jarrah: I'll make sure it's open enough to give them a choice.'

'You'd do this for me despite everything I've said?'

'Of course. You're my sister.'

'But can such a thing be done?' There was a spark of hope in Leanne's eyes. 'I thought trusts were set in stone.'

'Laws are changing all the time, and if this trust is revocable, then there's no reason why we can't change it.' She put her arm around Leanne's shoulder and hugged her. 'Either way, we aren't going to fight any more.'

The ornate clock struck five and the first fingers of light were creeping between the curtain folds. The long vigil was almost over.

'Dad must have been further out than we

thought,' muttered Leanne. 'He should have been here by now.'

Ellie looked at the clock, surprised how time had moved on so swiftly during those still, almost silent hours of the night. 'He'll be here,' she said firmly. 'He's never let me down yet.'

Claire rubbed her eyes and yawned. 'I don't know how you can be so sure,' she said. 'Dad could have decided to go on one of the road-trains. He's done it before.'

'Not without letting me know first,' replied Ellie as she pinched out the guttering candles and let a little light into the room.

'You and Dad have a good marriage, don't you?' said Leanne as she cleared away the dirty cups and overflowing ashtray. 'You're never apart for very long, and yet I've never heard you fighting – not seriously, anyway.'

Ellie smiled and a warmth spread through her as she thought of the years they'd been together and the life they'd carved for themselves out here on Warratah. 'We've had our disagreements,' she said with a gentle laugh. 'When you girls were little we'd have furious rows, but they were conducted in whispers in the privacy of our room and were always patched up afterwards.' She smiled at the memory. 'We both have the same daft sense of humour and sooner or later one of us would say something stupid and we'd get the giggles. Once that happened it was all over and we made up.' She knew she was blushing as she caught the girls passing a knowing look, but was unashamed of letting them know she was still in love.

458

'You never told us how you and Dad got together,' said Claire, her eyes bright with curiosity. 'Or why you chose that particular day to get married.'

'We didn't really choose it,' began Ellie. 'It just sort of happened.'

The dry storm had come from the west and had been swiftly followed by rain. It lashed the yard and paddocks, drummed on the corrugated roof and swelled the creeks. Trees bent against the ferocity of its power. Cattle huddled miserably and the dogs howled in their kennels. Ellie and Aurelia knew trouble would soon follow.

'Typical of Jack to be off playing with his planes when there's work to be done here,' shouted Aurelia above the drumming of the rain on the iron roof. 'And I wish your mother hadn't taken it into her head to leave just when we need every pair of hands we can get.'

'Fair go. Jack's busy making enough money to set you both up for life – he was never going to settle down here twiddling his thumbs,' Ellie shouted back. 'As for Mum... She's been wanting to go for months. Me getting pregnant was the last straw, I reckon. And what with Joe and everything I think she's had enough. You can't blame her.'

'You'd have thought she'd at least have waited until the baby was born,' grumbled Aurelia.

Ellie put the hurt aside and smiled sadly as she thought of their last parting. It had all been done so swiftly, coming without warning a few days after Joe's hospitalisation. Alicia had packed her bags, said goodbye and left on the next ship out of Darwin. She would be in England now, and probably much happier. 'Mum wasn't particularly fond of her own child. I shouldn't think being a grandmother will change her much.'

Aurelia seemed to understand the underlying hurt of Ellie's declaration despite the spirited manner in which it had been delivered. She put her hand on Ellie's shoulder. 'How are you keeping? You look as if you're about to pop.' She stared out at the rain and the dismal sky that promised more to come. 'I hope you can hold on long enough to get the doctor out here. Though if this rain doesn't let up there's no way a plane will be able to land.'

Ellie fidgeted in the chair and tried to ease the ache in her back. She had tried not to think about the coming baby and the mysteries of giving birth. But it was difficult to ignore something that kicked and moved about and made even the simplest task difficult to perform. Her hand caressed the mound beneath the overalls protectively. 'We're doing fine,' she murmured.

She stared through the window at the drenched paddocks and dripping roofs. She hadn't thought she could feel so much love for this tiny being growing inside her. For it hadn't been wanted, hadn't even been made out of affection. Yet as the months progressed and the forthcoming birth drew ever nearer she found herself singing to it, caressing it to still it when it became restless. As long as they had each other they would survive the gossips. Life on Warratah would be sweet for this tiny scrap – she'd see to that. If only Joe was here, she thought sadly. If only he could remember why things had come to such an impasse. There had been no word from him, no letter or even a telephone call since that awful day at the hospital, and although Dr O'Neil kept her up to date with his progress it wasn't the same as being able to talk to him. To see his beloved face and hear his voice. To be able to explain that despite all that had happened she loved him – had always loved him.

The despair was almost overwhelming. Did Joe hate her that much? Did he really despise her enough to turn his back on her for ever? She sighed. Life could be so bloody unfair, she thought. So damned complicated.

It was as if Aurelia could read her mind. 'He's being released soon,' she said grimly. 'What will you do if he turns up here?'

'Welcome him,' Ellie replied with spirit. 'And hope we can at least be friends – there's nothing worse than being strangers. I hate being shut out of his life. Hate this silence between us.'

Jacky Jack came splashing through the puddles, the rooster feather in his hat drooping wetly over his eyes as he stomped into the lounge. 'River's running a banker, missus,' he shouted over the thunder of the rain. 'Gotta get them cows out of the top paddock before they gets drownded.'

Aurelia grabbed her hat and long waxed riding coat. Ellie grabbed her own wet weather gear and struggled to do up the buttons over her swollen belly. 'You're staying here,' ordered Aurelia. 'You're too far gone to be riding out in this lot – especially if the river's broken its banks.'

Ellie carried on struggling with the buttons. 'You need every hand you can get, remember? The baby isn't due for another two weeks. I'll be fine.'

Wang Lee appeared in the doorway, Fu Man Chu at his heels as always. 'Stay in house Miss Ellie. Baby come when on horse you in big trouble.'

'You should learn to stop listening at doors,' Ellie said more sharply than intended.

'You still very rude,' snapped the ancient little man. He stuffed his hands up the voluminous sleeves of his tunic. 'Wang Lee not like you today.'

Ellie gave him a swift hug of contrition. He was thin and shrivelled and as old as the hills, but she knew that when he was gone there would be an enormous void left behind that no one else could fill. She put a stop to further argument by ramming on her hat and pushing through the front door. Plodding down the verandah steps, she splashed through the puddles aware she was waddling and probably looked ridiculous. But it felt good to be doing something useful again. Good to be on the move and occupied so she didn't have time to think.

There were fifteen of them in all including the stock boys. Some of the men had returned from the war and had come straight to Warratah to get their old jobs back, but others had never returned and each time the men and women rode out their absence was a sharp reminder of the toll the war demanded. The top paddock was two thousand square acres that sprawled on either side of the steep-sided Six Mile Creek. The grazing was usually good and because they'd had a prolonged dry spell recently, the bullocks had been mustered up there to encourage them to grow fat. Now they were up to their hocks in mud, trampling the earth into a quagmire as they tried to shelter behind one another. Visibility was down to a few feet, the rain falling in an unremitting grey curtain.

The river was running high and fast, tearing down the deep gully that wound through the pastures, roaring over the low dams that had been built to keep the water in during the droughts and finally tumbled into Six Mile lake further down where it would spread across the plains forming islands of sodden grass.

'Round 'em up on this side and get them over the river before these banks go,' yelled Aurelia. 'Then we'll head them back up to high ground on Blackman's ridge.' She cracked the stock whip and the blue heelers raced to begin work.

Ellie cracked her whip and dug in her spurs. The movement of the galloping horse beneath her was excruciatingly uncomfortable and she had to stand in the stirrups. Aurelia was right, she admitted silently – she was too far gone to be messing about like this – but it was too late now.

The bullocks complained and tried to escape the hustling dogs and the determined riders. When they realised there was no alternative they grudgingly complied and with a great deal of persuasion finally began to wade across the narrowest part of the river.

Ellie remained on the far bank chivvying the

463

more reluctant of the animals as the rain dripped from her hat and down her collar and her hands became slick on the reins. The baby was squirming restlessly inside her, kicking hard as if to complain that this was no way to treat an unborn infant. She did her best to ignore the deep pain in her back that had begun to snake across her lower abdomen. Her legs ached from standing in the stirrups, and she was fast losing her strength. The unaccustomed, bruising ride was beginning to take its toll after so many weeks of enforced idleness, but she was determined to see the job through.

She followed the stragglers across the torrent. The water was almost belly high on her horse as it snorted and whinnied and rolled its eyes. 'Come on you bugger, move yourself,' Ellie shouted. 'It's only bloody water.' She urged him on, standing high in the stirrups as the water reached above her boots and swirled around her aching thighs. The rain was coming down so heavily she could barely see the complaining bullocks that swam beside her, the dogs riding their backs, nipping at their ears to keep them on the move.

Ellie dug in her heels as her horse finally reached the other side. She urged him up the steep slope, yelling encouragement, shifting her weight from his back in an effort to get him up. The animal slid and propped and tossed his head. Ellie clung to his back, her muscles quivering from the effort of staying on board. She was wet through and shivering so badly she could barely hold the reins as the horse beneath her struggled to fight its way out of the water and up the mud. Then with a mighty surge, the animal stretched his neck and his weary legs and reached the relative safety of the grass bank.

Ellie sat there for a moment to get her breath as the horse's great lungs heaved. The ring of pain had ebbed and the baby had finally stopped squirming, but now she was sweating despite the chill of the rain and her sodden clothes. This probably wasn't doing either of them any good, she thought crossly, but at least it was better than sitting about the homestead getting fat and lazy.

'Are you all right?' demanded Aurelia, emerging from the gloom.

'Fine,' she replied. 'Let's get this lot out of here.'

The bullocks strung out before them as they were herded towards the higher pastures and as the gloom of the day finally surrendered to night the wet and weary men and women headed for home. The bullocks were safe, but if this rain carried on there would have to be another muster to take the cows and calves further north to the hill pastures.

Ellie was exhausted, but she did her best to hide it from Aurelia. Stripping off her wet clothes and muddy boots, she was soon wrapped in a warm towel and old sweater, her feet immersed in a basin of hot water Wang Lee had brought from the kitchen. A cup of strong, sweet tea with a dash of whisky soon put them both to rights and they sat cocooned in the broken down old couch watching the rain outside the window.

The sound of a straining engine broke through

465

the drum of the rain and they went out to the verandah and peered into the darkness. 'Who the hell's that?' snapped Aurelia as she quickly grabbed a coat. 'What a bloody silly time to come visiting.'

The utility ground to a halt in a damp slosh of mud encrusted tyres. The wipers were making hard work of clearing the torrent that ran down the windscreen and the tarpaulin stretched across the utility's flat-bed was bulging from the miniature lake that had gathered there. The driver's door creaked open on complaining hinges and their visitor climbed out.

'Father Reilly?' Ellie drew the old blanket closely around her as the chill of foreboding made her tremble. The priest only came when there was bad news. 'What's the matter?' she asked sharply.

He climbed the steps, his mud-splattered soutane clinging damply to his ankles. 'I'm thinking the rain waits for me to come to Warratah,' he said in his Irish lilt. ''Tis the very devil on the old arthritis.'

Ellie shook his hand numbly. If there was bad news then she wanted to hear it, not go through the rigmarole of polite talk. Then she became aware of the slam of another utility door. Of the splash of someone running through the mud and rain to the verandah. Of footsteps thudding on the steps.

'Reckon that's where I came in.' The deep voice from the doorway made them turn.

'Dad,' said the girls in unison as they rushed to

greet him.

'G'day darlin',' said Ellie as he finally left the girls and came to her side. 'I knew you'd make it in time.'

He kissed her cheek and perched on the arm of the chair.

'I was real sorry to hear about Aurelia,' he said softly. 'She was a bonzer lady.'

'Mum was just telling us about how you two got together,' said Claire with a shyness that Ellie found touching and unusual.

Ellie looked up at him. There was grey in the dark hair now, and deeply etched lines cobwebbing the corners of his eyes and mouth, but he was still the most handsome man she'd ever known. 'They know the full story,' she said softly as she saw the question in his eyes. 'I was just about to tell them how you swept me off my feet that dark rainy night.'

He sank into the chair, squashing her to him. 'Better finish it then. Aurelia always did love happy endings.'

Ellie smiled back at him. 'I can remember so well how you looked that night,' she said. 'You were bareheaded, your hair plastered down by the rain.' She ran a finger along his stubbled jaw. 'You even had the same six o'clock shadow, but then it emphasised how pale you were, how ill you'd been.'

'I asked you if you could forgive such a bloody idiot,' Joe said softly. 'You came to me as if in a trance and looked into my face. You must have seen how much I loved you, because you said you would.'

They were silent as they looked into one another's eyes and remembered. His lips had sought hers and they had kissed. Tasting the sweetness of each other that neither of them had forgotten over the years, they felt the power of their love through the electricity of their touch. Ellie had thought she could hear the siren song of hope that had kept him alive so he could return to her. She had waited so long for this moment that now it had arrived she wanted it to go on for ever.

The giggles drew them from their silent memories, and they both blushed as they realised their daughters were finding it all rather funny. 'Everything went hell west and crooked after that,' said Ellie as she smoothed her hand over her crumpled skirt and looked back into the past. 'The pain came without warning. Hot, fast and as sharp as the lash of a stock whip.'

Ellie gasped and drew away from him, bending towards the pain, holding the swell of her belly protectively in her hands. The pain was unremitting. It encircled her, held on, and squeezed with remorseless determination.

'Ellie? Ellie, what's wrong?' Joe shouted. He was on his knees before her, looking up into her face as he grabbed her arms.

'Baby's coming,' she said through gritted teeth. Another pain, stronger than the last, tore through her and she leaned against the verandah railings and groaned as sweat rolled down her face. 'Get Aurelia,' she gasped.

'Not until you say you'll marry me,' he said urgently.

The pain ebbed and Ellie panted. 'This isn't quite what I had in mind for a proposal,' she said on the edge of hysteria. 'Are you sure about this? I thought you didn't want anything to do with me? Let alone the baby.'

'Jack and the doctor explained everything, and once I'd got my blasted memory back I realised what a complete drongo I'd been. I knew you couldn't have betrayed me, and I love you too much to let you go through this alone. It doesn't matter what happened before. We have the rest of our lives to live – together – I have no future without you.' He gripped her hands as he knelt before her. 'Ellie, will you marry me? Will you please spend the rest of your life with this idiot man who loves you more than he'd ever thought possible?'

Another pain, stronger than the last, began to encircle her. She was elated and excited but above all in agony. 'Yes,' she gasped through the tears of joy and pain. 'Yes, yes, yes. Now bugger off and get Aurelia.'

He kissed her cheek before slamming through the screen doors calling for her aunt. Within moments she found herself being led slowly to the bedroom and the soft comfort of pillows and a feather mattress. Joe held her hand and she clung to him, driving her nails into him as the pain clenched and rolled remorselessly to its climax. 'I brought the priest with me so we could do this now,' he said urgently. 'We must give our child a name.'

Ellie looked at him through bleary eyes as the pain began to ebb. *'Now?'* she gasped. 'I'm in the middle of giving birth and you want us to get married *now?*'

His hand gripped hers. 'This baby will be ours,' he said firmly. 'If I'm to be a father today then I want to be married to the mother of our child.' He stroked the damp hair from her forehead as another pain rose and ebbed. 'Do you love me, Ellie? Do you trust me to take care of you and the little one and to love our baby with no reservations?'

'Of course I do,' she whispered in the lull of her labour pains. Then the ridiculous situation made her giggle. 'But this isn't exactly the wedding I've been planning all these years. I wanted a white dress and flowers, a church and a beautiful veil – not a smelly old horse blanket, an ancient sweater and so much pain I'm going to start screeching any minute.'

The priest hovered into view as Aurelia shoved him into the room. The bible was open in his hands. 'I'm thinking this will have to be kept short,' he said blushing profusely. 'Seems the new arrival's in a bit of a hurry.'

'Get on with it then,' grunted Ellie as she puffed and panted and tried to find a comfortable spot on the bed to ease the fresh onslaught of pain.

It was the strangest wedding ceremony any of them had attended. Aurelia and Wang Lee watched on one side of the bed, Joe held Ellie's hand on the other as she struggled to give birth. Father Reilly kept his eyes firmly on his bible as Joe slipped the gold ring on her finger and she yelled in agony and began to bear down.

'I pronounce you man and wife,' Father Reilly declared hurriedly. He was obviously desperate to leave the room and was already halfway out of the door as he said, 'You may kiss the bride.'

Ellie grabbed Joe's hand. 'That'll have to wait,' she grunted. ''Cos the baby won't. It's coming. Now.'

Aurelia and Wang Lee took charge. Joe was shooed from the room and Aurelia swiftly dealt with the new arrival. Within minutes she had the squalling infant wrapped tightly in a white blanket and nestled in her arms. She looked at Ellie with a broad grin as if she'd done all the hard work herself. 'Good thing I had plenty of practice with the calves,' she declared.

Ellie took the tiny bundle in her arms as Joe came tearing back into the room. Tears pricked as she looked down at the tiny scrap whose hair was as soft and golden as an angel's wing, and whose lust for life could probably be heard as far as the Territory. She felt Joe's arm around her shoulders, his butterfly kiss on her cheek and when she looked up into the emerald eyes she saw the love and wonderment there she'd waited for over so many harrowing years. 'We have a daughter,' she whispered.

Epilogue

Despite the distances involved there was a good turnout for Aurelia's funeral. People arrived from their isolated stations to pay their final respects to a woman who had become a legend in the outback. A woman who'd shown great courage and fortitude, a woman who had survived some of the harshest years, but who had never lost her sense of fair play or her sense of humour.

The small cemetery was shimmering in the heat as the coffin was lowered into the rich red soil of Warratah. Aurelia would lie beside her beloved Jack, but Ellie had the strongest sense that they were already together. A warm breeze tinkled the little bells that marked Wang Lee's final resting place, reminding them that the spirit of those they loved still lived on in this far northern reach of Queensland.

Ellie stood beside Joe, her arm linked with his, garnering strength from him as she always did. She looked across at her daughters and felt the warmth of promise. Claire had shown great strength of character in the past few hours, and she knew her first-born would not let the shadow of her beginnings darken her future. For standing beside her was Matt Derwent, tousle haired, strong and purposeful – a man of the outback – a man like Joe. They would see their plans for a flying veterinary service come to fruition, for

Claire had finally realised this was where she belonged. Leanne stood within the circle of Angel's arm, obviously in love and content now she and her fiery husband had ironed out their differences. She would be busy with her plans for Jarrah – Angel kept occupied by his exhausting round. Yet, Ellie had a feeling Angel was made of sterner stuff than they'd once thought. He might appreciate an attractive woman, but he'd assured Leanne that was as far as it went and he would do nothing to harm their relationship. She smiled to herself despite the solemn occasion. Aurelia would approve of both matches. At heart she was as romantic as poor Lila down at Threeways.

She looked up at Joe and their eyes met. The shadows were receding, and like the outback after the rain, life would pick up again. Summer was here and the wild flowers were already carpeting the pastures with their bright colours. The seasons would come and go and Warratah and Jarrah would blossom. All was right with her world, for Aurelia would always be with her – her guiding hand for ever there.

The ceremony was finally over and as everyone left to return to the homestead for breakfast, Ellie urged Joe to go with them. 'I just need a few moments to myself, darlin',' she said.

He understood as always and with an arm around each of his daughters he headed back to the homestead.

Ellie looked out over Warratah as she remembered Aurelia's strength and courage. Then she sat on the rickety seat that was almost buried in the grass and the encroaching shrubs, and thought of that grave on Jarrah. Joe had decided on the epitaph, and although it might be enigmatic to those who didn't know the story, it was the only one fit for a man who'd always been at odds with the world.

It was hot and silent but for the crickets in the long grass, and she realised it was just the same kind of day as the one when Joe had surprised her with his plans for their new home. He had been away on one of his mysterious trips, but she'd expected him home soon. She knew he'd drawn up plans for their own little house on Warratah land, but had refused to tell her where it was to be built, or even what it would look like. Yet she'd suspected the only place that would be perfect for them would be the spot by the billabong where they'd spent their last night together before he'd left for war.

She'd turned as she heard the steady plod of a heavy horse approaching the verandah.

Joe was astride the old dray Aurelia kept for pulling the plough. The great horse plodded across the yard, his feathered fetlocks snowy against the red of the earth. His white mane and tail had been brushed to a gleam and his liver and white markings were clear in the soft light of the late afternoon sun. There was no saddle and no blanket – just a worn strip of leather for reins. He brought the gentle giant to a halt beside the top step of the verandah, and looked down at her, holding her there on the verandah with his wonderful eyes. Then he reached out for their daughter.

Ellie handed him the baby, then grasped his

outstretched hand. There was no need for words – their thoughts were clear in their eyes. In silent orchestration she rested her bare foot on his boot and was swung effortlessly up behind him on to the dray's broad back.

Joe handed her the baby and tucked her free arm around his waist. 'Let's go home,' he'd said softly.

Ellie had rested her cheek against his shoulder and they had ridden slowly away from the homestead towards the rainbow that arched high above the great sweep of land that was Warratah.

Ellie smiled as she left the cemetery. The rainbow was still there.

The publishers hope that this book has given you enjoyable reading. Large Print Books are especially designed to be as easy to see and hold as possible. If you wish a complete list of our books please ask at your local library or write directly to:

Magna Large Print Books
Magna House, Long Preston,
Skipton, North Yorkshire.
BD23 4ND

This Large Print Book for the partially sighted, who cannot read normal print, is published under the auspices of

THE ULVERSCROFT FOUNDATION